Praise for The Soldier's Bride

Book #1 in the Music Box Romance Series
Kindle Scout Winner & Whitney Award Finalist

"Romantic and full of tough decisions, life's twists and turns, and above all the rest—hope. Like the magical music box, Rachelle Christensen weaves a melody into the pages that stays with you long after the last page."

—Lucy McConnell, author of the Billionaire Marriage Brokers Series

"The stories of the lives that the music box touches are vividly and beautifully written. This book has an epic quality to it due to the lifelong stories that are told about the characters.

Each family that the music box touches shares a piece of themselves with the next owner.

This was a powerful story, and I loved every bit of it. It was honest and emotional. Rachelle J. Christensen brought this story to life in a wonderful way. I hurt when they hurt and I rejoiced when they rejoiced."

—Vicki Goodwin, Reviewer

"The Soldier's Bride is a touching romance that captures the imagination—from the first hint on the breeze to the final twist at the end. The story will fill your heart with warmth and remind you of the first love in your life . . . and the last. Kudos to Rachelle Christensen for weaving a romantic tale that could only be carried on the wind."

—C. L. Beck, author of numerous stories in the Cup of Comfort series.

“This story was exquisitely lovely! It was written so descriptively it felt like poetry without the rhymes.”

—Louise Pledge, Reviewer

“Once each person gives the music box to someone else, a piece of their heart has healed in a way that they will never return to the person they once were.”

—Karrie Glazner, Amazon reviewer

“This is one of those books that touch your heart and leave you mesmerized long after you have finished reading it. I laughed, cried and then prayed fervently for a happily-ever-after for the characters who soon became my friends and had me completely invested in their daily struggles.”

—Njkinny's World of Books & Stuff

“This book was simply well-done all around. Well-written, the characters well-drawn, and the way each character's story interacted and affected the others was really an intricate work of art. This isn't your simple romance or average woman's fiction but truly a cut above.... There is depth to the story, which was a refreshing change. This book will not let you down.”

—Love to Read! Reviews

“I really enjoyed this book. Reading it was like floating down a river on a warm summer's day. I felt compelled to finish yet never hurried or rushed. Each scene was well developed and complete. The romance was intriguing and I often found myself wondering what I would do in the same situation. This is one I'll be reading again and again.” —

—Write On Mom Reviews

A Music Box Romance

CARVE ME A *Melody*

Also by Rachelle J. Christensen

The Soldier's Bride (A Music Box Romance #1)
Diamond Rings Are Deadly Things (Wedding Planner Mysteries #1)
Veils and Vengeance (#2)
Proposals and Poison (#3)
Hawaiian Masquerade (Destination Billionaire Romance)
Wrong Number
Caller ID

Novellas:

Hope for Christmas: An Echo Ridge Romance
The Kiss Thief: An Echo Ridge Romance
The Princess Bride of Riodan: An Echo Ridge Romance
Silver Cascade Secrets
Double Take

Nonfiction:

What Every 6th Grader Needs to Know: 10 Secrets to Connect Moms & Daughters

Lost Children: Coping with Miscarriage
Ultimate Life: Create a Life Worth Living in 9 Simple Steps

Rachelle J. Christensen

Publisher's Note

This is a work of fiction. Names, characters, places, and incidents either are the product of the author's imagination or are used fictitiously, and any resemblance to actual persons, living or dead, business establishments, events, or locales is entirely coincidental.

Original Cover Design Image: Kelli Ann Morgan
Jacket Design: Kelli Ann Morgan
Cover Design © Peachwood Press
Formatting by Heather Justesen

ISBN 978-0-996876-4-8

Thrills for the Heart

FOR A LIMITED TIME

Sign up for Rachelle's
VIP Mailing List
to get your *FREE* book.

Get started here:

www.rachellechristensen.com

Dedication

To my friend, Frankie Williams Dick. Even at 98, you are still young at heart and your smile and cheerful attitude are a wonderful example to me. Thank you for what you've taught me about living and stopping to smell the roses.

Chapter 1 — Sophie's Secret

December 1945

The late afternoon sun hung low in the sky, casting its weak light against the field of snow outside Sophie Wright's window. A golden shaft of reflected light bounced off the kitchen wall. Sophie turned, startled to see the bronze medal sitting on the shelf, somehow catching the sunlight. Walking toward the shelf, she shielded her eyes from the light that seemed to grow brighter as she approached. She picked up the medal from the patch of green felt on the wooden shelf, turning slowly back toward the kitchen window. The medal was the Navy Cross, one of the highest medals a sailor could receive. It had a smoothness to it that reminded her of Cal. A signalman in the Navy, he'd always been larger than life, full of fire and grit.

"I'm headed to an island in the middle of nowhere. Ain't nothin' gonna happen to me in Hawaii," he'd said. It was October of 1940 and he was shipping out to Pearl Harbor. That was the last time she'd seen her husband, and it was only a few short months prior to Maggie's birth.

More than five years had passed since Cal left and Christmas 1945 would be full of celebrations that the war really was over. Sophie clenched the medal tightly and walked back to the shelf. Cal had earned the medal by saving many lives during the bombing of Pearl Harbor. His actions had been heroic, and many called him a hero. Holding her breath, Sophie dropped the Navy Cross onto the green felt piece. The fabric was crumpled from her grasp, but she didn't smooth it out. Her throat clenched with the familiar ache of the secret that she couldn't share. Blinking rapidly to clear the moisture that always came with remembering Cal, Sophie straightened and headed back to the stove. It was time to put the potato casserole in the oven.

She'd barely slid the pan in the oven when someone knocked on the door. She opened it and smiled at her older brother, Keith. "Hey, Sis, want me to plug these in?" He held the end of the extension cord that reached up to the brightly colored Christmas lights.

"Yes, thanks," Sophie replied, not letting Keith see the tiny shake of her head since he was the one who insisted on putting lights up on the little red brick home she rented. She was grateful for his Christmas spirit and his enthusiasm to back it up.

He plugged them in and nodded toward the man who must have driven the blue pickup parked in her driveway. "I brought a friend to help move that furniture. This is Leland Halverson." Keith smiled up at Sophie. "This is my sister, Sophie Wright."

Sophie's breath hitched when the man with reddish brown hair met her gaze. Her skin prickled with a pleasant current, as if some power arced between them.

"Leland Halverson. Pleased to meet you." He'd just repeated the introduction Keith had given him, and Sophie saw his cheeks redden. He inhaled and fumbled with the keys in his hand as he reached for hers.

"Nice to meet you." She shook his hand, the current of energy pulsing along the tips of her fingers. "Please, come inside."

Leland smiled and walked into her house behind Keith.

"Mom came over earlier and picked up the kids," Sophie spoke directly to Keith, "Maggie will be so surprised when she sees her bed." She looked at Leland. "Maggie is four. She's been sharing a bed with Garth. He's six, and he doesn't want to sleep with a baby and her dolls–in his words."

Leland laughed. "Sounds like it will be a great Christmas then."

Sophie smiled. Something about the way he spoke, soft tones with a rugged edge, set her heart to humming along with that unseen electricity in the air. She took in a breath and continued walking down the hall.

"Here it is." Sophie pointed to a pile of boards.

"Let's get started." Keith crouched down and began arranging the boards.

Leland crouched beside Keith and pulled out a length of board. "It looks like you've been busy."

"I have. I'm tired of painting though." The bedroom still smelled like fresh paint, and the wall's soft pink color glowed in the setting sunlight. "But it was worth it for Maggie. She's such a sweetheart and all girl."

Leland nodded and smiled at Sophie. "She's lucky to have a mother like you."

Sophie looked down and then back at him. "I'm the one who's lucky."

He hesitated only half a second before lowering his head and lining up his board with Keith's. There was something there, behind his eyes, in his soul. Something that seemed familiar to Sophie. She didn't know Leland, but she recognized that haunted look in his eyes. He had lost someone. He had weathered the storm and still manned his ship, sailing forward through life.

The image made Sophie pause. Was she manning her own ship? Or was she holding onto a lifeline, barely keeping her head above water as the ship plowed through the waves of her life? She averted her eyes from Leland, but not before she noticed his forearms corded with muscles that flexed as he helped Keith put the bed together.

It only took them about twenty minutes to finish. Sophie made eye contact with Leland several times, and she noticed Keith grinning and elbowing him. When they finished with the bed, they hauled in a dresser from under the carport. The dresser was freshly painted white with pink trim. Sophie busied herself by making up the bed with a patchwork quilt. She tucked a baby doll by the pillow.

"Maggie will love this. Thank you so much, Keith." She turned to Leland, and her smile widened. "And Leland. I appreciate the help."

Leland nodded and looked like he was about to say something before ducking his head.

"Leland doesn't mind," Keith replied. "He's happy for an excuse to get out. He's single, so he needs a few more excuses, I think. Sophie, why don't you invite him over for the Christmas party?"

"Oh. I–uh, didn't know if he'd be available." Sophie's cheeks felt warm.

Leland pushed Keith off balance. "Your brother is kind of a pest, you know."

Sophie chuckled. "I actually do know that very well."

"It's been a long time since I've–um, dated, so Keith here is trying to help me, I guess," Leland stuttered.

"Well, it's a small gathering with a big turkey, so if you'd like to come, maybe we could beat Keith at poker?"

"I'd love to." Leland glanced down at his boots, swallowed and looked back at Sophie.

She put her hand to the side of her mouth. "We play with pennies, but Keith still owes me from last year."

They all laughed. As they walked toward the door, Leland trailed behind with Sophie. "Thanks again for the invitation."

Sophie smiled. "Merry Christmas."

Leland nodded. "It will be, I think."

Keith opened the front door and unlatched the screen. He stepped out onto the porch. Leland hesitated, opening his mouth to speak at the same time the wind grabbed the screen door and slammed it shut behind him. Sophie jumped back and tripped over the toolbox she'd set out earlier. In what seemed like slow motion, she threw her arms out trying to regain her balance, but the movement didn't slow her fall. Leland did. His arms slipped around her back and he pulled her to a standing position. At his touch, the electricity that had been humming under the surface ignited, and Sophie looked up into Leland's hazel eyes. "Thank you."

His breath came in short bursts. "Are you okay?"

"I am now." His hand remained on the small of her back, his fingers burning an impression into her skin. "I'd better put that tool box away."

Leland pulled his hand back, leaned over and hefted the toolbox. "Would you like me to put this in the shed?"

"Sure, that would be nice." She missed his touch already, and the magnetism between them cried out as Keith opened the door.

"The wind is really picking up out here. I hope we don't get buried in snow." Keith stuffed his hands in his pockets. Sophie bit her lip to keep from laughing. She could see the question in his eyes asking "*What have you two been doing in here?*"

"I tripped over the toolbox, but Leland caught me." Sophie touched the sleeve of Leland's jacket. "Thanks again."

"Happy to help, and uh—well, it was really nice meeting you." Leland seemed a bit flustered, but his soft smile said more than his words.

After locking the front door, Sophie leaned against it, her eyes straying to Cal's medal on the shelf. She narrowed her eyes and pushed off from the door, focusing her energy on finishing up dinner. The casserole was almost done and the kids would be back any minute. Keith's friend intrigued her, and she found her thoughts dwelling on Leland's gentle smile. Only one glance at Cal's medal reminded her that it was safer not to think of a future for her heart. She concentrated on tidying up her house and thinking only of Garth and Maggie. Staying busy was the best medicine for what ailed her heart.

Chapter 2 — Leland's Christmas Orange

Even though Keith razzed him on the drive back to his shop, Leland couldn't stop smiling. He kept picturing the way Sophie's dark curls trailed down her back and how the dimple in her right cheek deepened when she smiled. He thought of his sweet angel daughter, Jessie, and felt a lightness in his heart with the knowledge that it was time to continue on to the next chapter of his life. Still, his soul had been tinged with sorrow for so long, he worried if he'd be able to hold onto happiness.

"Are you really going to come to the Christmas party?" Keith asked. "It's at my parent's house so you'll know everyone there."

Leland nodded. "I won't bail on you. Just let me know when your family is going to be there. I don't want to arrive before you."

"Well, I'll be. All this time I've been working on you and it only took one look at Sophie to do the trick." Keith grinned as if he'd already won a round of poker. "I'm glad my parents and I convinced her to move here. She wasn't too sure about returning to Aspen Falls from Kentucky, but she needed the help."

Leland listened intently. He wanted to know more about Sophie, but he didn't want to appear too eager. He wasn't sure why she wouldn't jump at the chance to be near family, but maybe she liked Kentucky. "Do you reckon she'll stick around?"

Keith brushed a lock of dark hair from his forehead. "I imagine so. Course, it'll be a lot easier for her if she *finds* a reason to stick around."

Leland gave him a pointed look and decided it was time to change the subject. "I might need you to help me deliver another desk similar to the one we took to the Tanaka's tonight. Maybe next week some time. Could you do that?"

"Sure, just give me a holler."

Keith's green and brown Oldsmobile was parked near Leland's shop, a light dusting of snow covering the hood.

"I wonder if they'll have a snow day tomorrow," Keith said. "Only a couple more days until Christmas break."

"I'm sure Debbie hopes so," Leland replied. Keith chuckled and waved goodbye as he got into his car. Leland tried not to focus on the emptiness surrounding Keith's departure. Keith's life was full with three kids, his wife Debbie, and a dog. Leland didn't even think of things like snow days during the school year, but if Jessie were still here, he would have. She would have been in first grade this year. He wondered briefly if Rhonda would be able to have more children. He held no animosity for his ex-wife, just an aching sadness for all that could have been. Hopefully God would smile on her wherever she was.

The door to the shop squeaked as Leland pushed it open and flicked on the light. He inhaled, loving the sharp scent of fresh cut maple and smoothly sanded cedar planks. Leland spent most of his days in the old garage that he'd converted into a shop almost eight years ago. He was nearly thirty-one and although his life hadn't turned out like he'd hoped, he wouldn't ignore the second chance he'd been given. With a roll of his shoulders, Leland grabbed his measuring tape and a pencil. Too much reminiscing was dangerous for any man's heart, but especially for Leland. Stepping back into the minefield of his memory always made him thirsty, so he flipped through his orders, ignored the hunger, and worked until the snow started sticking to the windows.

Keith stopped by on Christmas Eve holding a paper sack with three oranges. Leland invited him inside, certain that the visit was about more than a few oranges for the holiday. Almost as soon as Keith walked in, Leland could smell the citrus fruit and his mouth watered for the juicy treat. Everyone held their breath at Christmas time hoping that their ration coupons could buy the treasured holiday fruit.

"Clyde let Debbie buy a few extra oranges this year." Keith handed the oranges over. The grocer at the Safeway had more leeway since the war ended, but the ration coupons from the war still ruled the families in Aspen Falls.

"Tell Debbie thanks for these." Leland set the oranges on his kitchen counter.

Keith nodded and pulled out a chair by the kitchen table, stretching his long legs out in front of him. "You ever think about making more dining sets like this one?"

Leland flinched, gripping the back of the chair tightly. "It probably would be a good idea." It would be another bridge to cross as he walked from the past into the future. He'd built the table for Rhonda, for their family and the future children they'd hoped would fill the chairs, but that dream had died with so many others. If he were to build another dining set to fulfill someone else's dreams of happiness, perhaps it would help him face his own empty table.

Keith rubbed his hand along the dark mahogany table. The satin finish gleamed under the kitchen light, the grain of the wood so fine that the shades of dark wood blended seamlessly. "I know Debbie would give a lot to have a set as nice as this. Ours is pretty worn out."

"Maybe I could start with hers, then." Leland swallowed against the memories creeping up the back of his throat. It didn't help. He could still see Rhonda with her rounded belly applauding the fine craftsmanship of the family table Leland had built. He cleared his throat. "Seems every piece holds so many memories."

"Not all bad, right?" Keith studied Leland, waiting for his response.

Leland thought of the time he'd spent sitting at the table alone since Jessie had died and Rhonda had left. "Not all good either," was all Leland could say.

"About the Christmas party," Keith rapped his knuckles on the table. His hands were broad and calloused—the hands of a farmer who knew the meaning of hard work. "We'll be there by one o'clock. My dad always makes a batch of homebrew for Christmas. He squirrels away the sugar for months so that he has enough. Some of the neighbors pitch in too, 'cause Dad makes the best. Anyway, I'm sorry, Leland, I didn't think of it until Debbie brought it up. Will you be okay?"

Leland grimaced. He hated being the topic of other people's conversations, but at the same time, he couldn't ignore the kindness that Keith and Debbie had shown him during the hardest years of his life. He glanced at the bag of oranges, understanding the real reason for Keith's visit. "Tell Debbie I appreciate her looking out for me. I'll be all right, and if I'm not, you'll be there to help me out."

Keith looked down and shook his head. "Glad that's out of the way. Do you want me to say anything to Sophie about..."

Leland held back a chuckle at Keith's reticence on touchy subjects. He hated it when Debbie put him up to things like talking to his best friend—the former alcoholic—about beer at the party. "Actually I'm looking forward to a clean slate." Leland paced in front of the kitchen sink. "It's something else to think of spending time with someone who doesn't know every detail of my history."

"Right." Keith sounded hesitant, as if maybe he thought Leland should tell Sophie everything up front, but he didn't press Leland. "I'll see you tomorrow."

"Should I bring something?"

"If you still have some of those winter pears, that'd be great," Keith said. "But I don't want you worrying. Bringing yourself is the most important thing."

After Keith left, Leland took an orange from the sack, rinsed it in the sink and rolled it between his hands. He sat at the kitchen table and removed the peel in chunks with his calloused fingers. He inhaled the fresh scent of citrus and popped a slice into his mouth. Concentrating on the flavor of the orange covered the memories of sipping an ice cold beer over dinner and afterwards, sharing a glass of wine with Rhonda because it was Christmas Eve. Leland chomped on another slice of orange. Fifteen months. It seemed like forever to Leland, but was barely a blink of an eye compared to the rest of his days and the years he'd spent in a drunken haze after Jessie died. Most people still didn't trust that he wouldn't fall back down that hole again, especially after Rhonda left him—divorced him. But Leland knew, somewhere beyond the weakness that he was a different man.

Memories of the music box and its ethereal melody helped Leland remember the day that his life had changed. A note, a music box, and the whispers of the wind had opened a door to a different life—a chance for him to live again.

Chapter 3 – Christmas Day 1945

Sophie fingered the chip on the edge of her favorite light blue bowl. Garth had dropped a cup in the sink and it had hit the bowl just right. Sophie had reprimanded him, showing him the broken piece of china and Garth had apologized. At six years old, Garth's energy hadn't abated and he continued to spin through the house like a tornado. Sophie had already put away several keepsakes that she didn't want destroyed. She swallowed. It was just a bowl, but it felt more than that. Calvin's mother had given it to her for Mother's Day in 1941, understanding the difficulty Sophie faced with a brand new baby and a husband overseas. Cal was stationed at Pearl Harbor and sent postcards describing the beautiful Hawaiian weather. No one thought that Hawaii was anywhere near the war–but they were wrong. Sophie had given birth to Maggie a few months after Cal left and then when he died, she remembered thinking that her sweet daughter would never know her father. Despite everything, that injustice had seemed too much to bear. Cal's parents had done their best to comfort her and support her, but leaving Kentucky had been the right decision. Sophie set the bowl carefully on the counter. She loved the soft blue hue of the china and the tiny white flowers hand-painted around the edge. She also loved what the bowl represented–a new chapter in her life.

"Mommy, are you still sad?" Maggie tugged on the edge of Sophie's apron. "I'll give you a hug."

Sophie set the bowl on the counter and crouched down, wrapping her arms around Maggie. "Only a little, but your hug is already helping me to feel better."

"Good, 'cause you can't be sad on Christmas."

Sophie smiled. "You're right, and it's almost time to go to Grandma and Grandpa's house. Uncle Keith and Aunt Debbie and the kids will probably be there soon."

Maggie jumped up and down. "Can I bring my dolly to show them?"

"Of course." Sophie touched the soft blonde strands of Maggie's hair. "Let's tell Garth it's time to go."

While the kids gathered up their toys, Sophie removed her apron and changed into a dark red dress with a lace collar. She put on a pair of gold earrings shaped like bells. When she reached for the bag of pennies for poker she thought of Leland Halverson. Keith had reminded her that his friend would be coming. Sophie's stomach tightened with a thread of nervousness because Leland intrigued her. She glanced at her reflection in the mirror and saw a smile that was meant for Leland. There was a solidness about him, a depth to his eyes that made Sophie want to ask him a hundred questions. His quiet manner while he put together Maggie's bed left her wondering what the silence meant. It was silly, but when Sophie had looked into his hazel eyes, she'd felt that perhaps Leland knew something of what she struggled with, if only she was brave enough to talk to him.

After he left the other night, Sophie remembered when her mother had told her about the sudden heart attack that had taken Mrs. Halverson's life. It had been several years ago and although Leland was an adult at the time, it still seemed like a young age to be without the guidance of his father or mother. Perhaps that was the loss that she'd seen in Leland's eyes—she couldn't imagine losing her mother now. Sophie needed her mother and her father as she struggled each day to raise her children by herself.

Applying a coat of red lipstick, Sophie tucked a few curls back with pins and straightened the tie on her dress. What if Leland decided not to come? She shook her head. It was better not to dwell on the unknown. She grabbed the bag of pennies. "Come on kids. Let's make sure your coats are buttoned up. It'll be cold tonight."

Keith had offered to pick up her little family, but Sophie wanted to show the kids some of the Christmas trees in the windows of their neighbors' homes. When her parents and Keith chose this house, one of the points they emphasized was the proximity to Grandma and Grandpa—only three blocks away. The cheese ball and crackers Sophie had prepared were tucked in a box, along with a lemon Bundt cake. Sophie helped Garth and Maggie down the steps and then retrieved the box, carrying it in one arm while holding Maggie's hand with the other. They walked slowly, the winter chill nipping at their cheeks as they stared at the Christmas lights and icicles reflecting light on the front porch of their neighbor's house.

With each step, Sophie commanded herself not to think of Leland, but the carpenter would not be dismissed. "Let's walk a little faster so we don't turn into icicles."

"Can I run?" Garth asked, his cheeks pink with cold.

"Not until after we cross the street," Sophie replied. "And you must stop at Grandma's house."

"Okay. Hurry up, Maggie. You're so slow," Garth said.

"I'm hurrying. I'm not slow!" Maggie retorted.

"Garth, be kind to your sister." Sophie tapped his shoulder and gave him a stern look. She shifted the box to her other arm and switched places with Maggie so she could hold her other hand. "Almost there." They could have driven the old Ford, but Sophie still worried that they hadn't seen the last of the gas rations.

As soon as he was given permission, Garth sprinted and slid the rest of the way. Maggie giggled as she watched him go and she began walking faster. By the time they reached the front porch of Sophie's parents' home, her arms ached. At least the box would be mostly empty on the way home. Grandpa Wayne held the door open for her and Maggie as they approached. "How is my little Margaret?"

Maggie scrunched up her nose, the same way she did every time her grandpa called her by her given name. "Maggie is a good girl," she replied.

Sophie and her father laughed, the same way they always did. He took the box from her and pulled her into an embrace. "How are you tonight?"

"Glad to be here," Sophie said. "It's colder than I thought."

"Supposed to be below zero later tonight. Course, we'll all be cooking in here. C'mon, Keith is here with his friend. He said you've met?"

"Yes, I hope he can handle everyone tonight." Sophie gave her father a meaningful look and he chuckled.

"Leland can hold his own." Her father took the box to the kitchen, leaving Sophie momentarily with her thoughts. Of course her parents would also know Leland. Aspen Falls wasn't a big town, but the thought had escaped her until then. She heard his voice before she saw him, and her stomach flipped as he came into view. Leland was looking at Garth and listening intently as her son showed the stranger every detail of his World War II bomber.

"And the bombs are inside here." Garth pointed to the underbelly of the plane. "So you can bomb the Japs!" Garth lifted his plane higher and made shooting noises. "The Japs killed my daddy!"

Leland flinched, but quickly smoothed his expression. Sophie shook her head. "The boys at school have been filling his head full of stories."

"Garth, we're at peace with the Japanese now," Keith said. "We won't be bombing them anymore, okay?"

"But they killed Daddy," Garth replied, his voice rising.

Leland crouched in front of Garth. "The people who killed your father were men. They might have been from Japan or anywhere in the world, but they were still men, just like me and your uncle Keith. Sometimes men make mistakes, but not all men make the same mistakes. Do you understand?"

Garth frowned and then shrugged. "Mommy doesn't like me to say 'Japs'."

Keith put a hand on Garth's shoulder. "You should listen to your mommy."

A look passed between Keith and Leland. There was a story there that begged to be told, but Sophie straightened and tapped Garth's head. "Why don't you run along and show Amy your bomber?"

"She don't want to see it," Garth replied. "She's too busy playing babies with Maggie, but this guy likes my plane."

Leland chuckled. "I do. That is quite the model. I like how the American flag is painted right there."

"Do you want to hold it?" Garth held out the plane almost reverently.

Leland's cheek twitched and he glanced at Sophie before taking the plane. "She's a beaut." He handed the plane back to Garth and turned to Sophie. "I take it you had a nice Christmas?"

Sophie nodded, her mouth suddenly dry. "I did, and yourself?"

Leland shrugged. "It's nice to be around some family tonight. It was kind of you to invite me." He winked.

Sophie felt her cheeks flush, remembering how Keith had intervened. She smiled and leaned toward Leland. "I hope you're good at poker."

Leland patted his pocket, jingling the coins inside. "Me, too."

"Does this cheese ball need parsley?" Sophie's mother, Betty, called from the kitchen.

"Sure, Mama." Sophie approached her mother and put an arm around her shoulders. "I didn't have any."

"Well, I dried some from my victory garden. I think a pinch would look nice," Betty replied. "Taste good too."

"That will be the finishing touch," Sophie agreed. "Merry Christmas, Mama."

Betty paused and hugged her daughter. "Merry Christmas to you, too. How are you holdin' up?"

"I'm good. The kids have been so excited today. They're going to crash tonight."

"I made up a bed for them. We'll see who crashes first." Betty arranged more crackers on the cheese platter. "So, I see you've met Leland."

Sophie nodded, turning slightly to see Leland talking with Keith and her dad. "I have. He seems like a nice fellow. How does Keith know him?"

"Leland has lived in Aspen Falls his whole life, but he's a few years older than Keith so I don't think you ever knew him. They came to be friends when Keith needed to repair the old rocker Debbie inherited from her grandpa. Seems like Leland can fix anything." Betty patted Sophie's arm and lowered her voice. "You know his history?"

"No, but I can tell he's suffered some hardship too."

Betty frowned. "Too much for one man, yet here he stands. I'm glad he came."

Betty carried the cheese ball over to the table, leaving Sophie to consider how much of Leland's story she would learn that night.

The table overflowed with roasted turkey, potatoes, stuffing, green beans, and an assortment of Christmas goodies. Debbie's hand-dipped chocolates were hidden in a cupboard for later. Sophie's mouth watered when she remembered the smooth taste of her coconut truffles. Everyone exchanged greetings and soon the meal was under way. By clever maneuvering on Keith's part, Leland ended up next to Sophie for dinner. Conversations flowed easily around the table. Discussions of the aftermath of Germany's surrender and Stalin's movements from Russia dominated until Betty suggested a lighter subject. Like most conversations over the past few years, the next topic wasn't any lighter.

The hunger devastating Holland, Germany, and Poland made everyone pause when they reached for a second helping of the delicious feast.

"We have a lot to be grateful for, but it doesn't make everything easier." Leland dipped his head toward Sophie. "I'm sorry to hear about your husband. Keith told me about his passing."

The piece of roll Sophie had swallowed lodged in her throat and she had to drink half a glass of water before she could respond to Leland. "Sorry, I guess I've eaten too much. But you're right; we do have a lot to be grateful for. I appreciate your kindness. Today has been better than last year."

"Time does help. Although at first it doesn't seem like that's possible." Leland stirred more gravy into his potatoes. "Your children look like they're going to run until they keel over."

Most of the kids were already done eating and racing up and down the hall with their toys, squealing and laughing. Sophie was glad for the change in subject. "They've been going since before six this morning. I'll give Maggie another half hour before I put her to bed. Otherwise we might have a Christmas monster on our hands."

Leland chuckled. "Wish I had that kind of energy."

"According to Keith, you do," Sophie said. "He told me about how busy you've been building things. Do you only build certain furniture pieces like tables and chairs?"

Leland turned to her and she was struck by the flecks of gold in his hazel eyes. "I'll build whatever the customer orders, within reason. There's a lot of variety to what I do."

"I can tell you enjoy it. Have you always been a carpenter?"

He set his fork down and clasped his hands together. "More or less. There have definitely been some lean years, and my business went through a rough spell, but the past year has been good to me."

"I'm glad to hear it."

"What about you?" Leland asked. "It looks like those two keep you pretty busy, but what else do you enjoy?"

"I'm a seamstress. I'm working on custom drapes for the Alexanders right now."

Leland gave a low whistle. "You must be very good at what you do. That family only works with the best."

Sophie straightened under Leland's look of admiration. "I try."

Wayne clapped his hands together. "I'm full to bursting. Betty, it's about time we clear this table to make room for tradition."

Betty rolled her eyes, but rose from the table and within a few minutes everyone had carried off the food to the kitchen. Sophie carried a bowl of mashed potatoes and set them on the counter. Debbie brought the gravy boat and poured it into the leftovers. She glanced behind her and then turned to Sophie. "I saw you visiting with Leland. Are you glad that he came?"

Sophie ducked her head. "He's a nice man. I don't really know him well, but he seems . . . humble.

"You hit the mark directly there," Debbie said. "I think it has a lot to do with his past. How much has Keith told you?"

Sophie met Debbie's piercing blue eyes. Her sister-in-law was petite, barely over five foot, but she had enough spunk to make up for her slight stature. Sophie leaned toward Debbie and murmured, "Nothing. Well, he said something about me giving Leland a chance to tell me about himself."

Debbie stopped scraping the potatoes out of the bowl and tucked a strand of light blonde hair behind her ear. "Is that right? He didn't tell you anything?"

"Deb, you're worrying me." Sophie put down the dishrag. "What happened to him?"

"I've put my foot in it. I'm sorry, I thought Keith had talked to you." Debbie patted Sophie's arm. "You both have history. Leland doesn't really know all of your history, so I'm guessing Keith thought it best for you two to have a chance to get to know each other without a lot of baggage."

"Leland knows that Cal died in Pearl Harbor," Sophie said. "He gave his condolences during dinner."

"But he doesn't know the whole story."

Sophie opened her mouth to speak, but stopped when Debbie arched an eyebrow. Heat rose up her neck as Sophie considered all the things that no one knew about her marriage to Cal. How much had Debbie guessed? She swallowed and turned toward the dining room. Keith and Leland were shuffling cards while her dad stacked up a pile of pennies. Leland must have felt her gaze on him because he looked up, caught her eye and smiled. She spun toward the sink and scrubbed at a pot with quick strokes.

"Just enjoy tonight," Debbie whispered. "It's not meant to be a stressful time. It's a taste to see if you want to know more about each other."

Debbie meant well, but her words set Sophie's stomach to churning, and she wished she hadn't eaten so many mashed potatoes. She finished scrubbing the pot and dried it with a dish cloth. Wiping the moisture from the silver pot, Sophie resolved to swallow her fears and take Debbie's advice to get to know Leland Halverson tonight. She could worry about how her past kept creeping up on her future later.

Chapter 4 – Holding Truth

Poker wasn't one of Leland's favorite pastimes, but playing with the Harper family was definitely a different experience. Most of the children were tucked into their grandparent's bed at the other end of the house which was a good thing because Leland flinched every time Keith banged the table and whooped. The commotion of the poker game was a stark change to Leland's quiet house and wood shop, but he was enjoying himself. Every time Debbie tried to cheat, Wayne would call her out and Keith would start laughing and banging the table again. Sophie kept her cards close with a poker face that he wasn't able to read no matter how long he studied the rose curve of her mouth. At least that was the excuse he gave when Keith elbowed him for staring at his younger sister.

"I can't figure how she does it," Leland said. "She looks just as sweet with an ace in the hole as she does with a bunch of twos and threes."

Sophie laughed and ducked her head, a blush rising on her cheeks.

"Now there's a reaction," Keith said. He reached over and pinched Sophie's cheek and then expertly dodged when she tried to swat him.

"Betty, I think it's time for a celebratory round," Wayne called to his wife in the kitchen. Betty was content to putter in the kitchen while her husband and children played poker. He craned his neck, trying to see into the kitchen. "Did she hear me?"

"Yes," Keith said. "She's headed down to the root cellar. I'll deal this hand."

A few minutes later, Leland heard the clink of bottles and looked up as Betty entered the room with two bottles of homebrew. The familiar brown glass bottle caught his eye, even though Leland tried not to notice when Wayne pried off the top of his beer. Immediately, the noise in the room was muted as his heart pounded in his ears. The back of Leland's throat itched and he reached a finger under his collar. One year and three months ago he'd had his last drink. Not long enough to forget the thirst, but enough to put distance between Leland and the all-consuming alcohol that had ruled his life for two years. Pushing back his chair, Leland stood and cleared his throat. "I'll be right back."

Everyone stopped talking and laughing as he headed for the front door, but Leland didn't hesitate. He stumbled out into the cold, gripping the icy railing and gritting his teeth. One minute, and then two passed. Leland took in a deep breath of the chilly night air and closed his eyes. From the quiet hallways of his mind, he could almost hear the tune from the music box. He let the memory of the music free, the song washing away his desire for liquor, reminding him of the promise he'd made to Jessie, to Rhonda, to himself. He looked up at the sky, clear and cloudless. The stars glimmered like ice crystals hung from the windows of heaven. He could be strong for Jessie. He stepped back into the house and came face to face with Sophie. He closed the door and forced a smile. "It's too cold out for more than one breath of fresh air."

"Are you feeling okay?"

He could see a thousand questions in Sophie's eyes. Those big beautiful eyes, the color of aspen leaves in the spring. Her skin looked as soft and white as freshly sanded pine. "I am now." Leland pressed his lips together, hesitated for two counts and then said, "I used to have a drinking problem. I don't drink anymore, but it's still tricky to be around beer—and I know how talented your dad is at making homebrew."

"Oh," Sophie said. "I'm sorry. We shouldn't have—I thought Keith was more considerate than that."

"He is. Keith warned me that there would be alcohol tonight. He said it's one of the few times your dad drinks." Leland shifted from one foot to the other. "I told him that I'd be fine."

Sophie nodded. "Mother keeps a close eye on Dad so nothing gets out of hand."

Leland put his hands in his pockets and the coins jingled. He was about to ask Sophie if she was ready to be dealt another hand in poker, but she stepped closer to him.

"What happened? I mean, why did you have a drinking problem?"

It was bold of her to ask and the way her eyes tightened with worry, he knew she hadn't asked the question lightly. He took a slow breath. The clean slate was about to be broken, and yet, Leland didn't have to tell her everything, did he? "I had a three-year-old daughter, Jessie."

Sophie's hand flew to her mouth and she began shaking her head. "Oh no, I'm so sorry. I shouldn't have been so nosy."

Leland reached out and pulled her hand carefully toward him. "It's okay. Jessie was the light of my life. When she died in '42, I fell apart, and Rhonda—my wife—was patient, but finally it was too much for her. She left me. I let the thirst consume me, gave everything to get it, traded rations that left Rhonda having to ask for help with food to eat."

"Oh, Leland, I'm so sorry. I feel awful."

Leland gently squeezed her hand. "If I didn't tell you, someone else would have. The whole town knows my story—just like they know that you're the widow of a war hero." Aspen Falls knew the full story, with every gritty detail that had fed Leland's addiction to the bottle for years. How long would it be before someone spoke the worst truth Leland had ever known? How long before Sophie would find out what he hadn't told her?

Sophie shook her head and the pain in her eyes was familiar to Leland. She had her own dark secrets, memories etched with such agony that thinking of them brought a physical hurt. There were stories in the depths of those green eyes and Leland wanted to know them, to know Sophie. As he studied her face, the dimple in her right cheek twitched and Leland grinned. "Let's play another hand. I might have figured out one of your tics."

"Oh, really?" Sophie tilted her head, studying his face. "You think you know me so well already?"

He pulled out a handful of pennies. "I'm willing to bet on it."

Chapter 5 — Delivering Drapes

January 1946

Sophie thought about Leland every day after the Christmas party, but he didn't call or stop by. They had shared a connection that Christmas night and somehow Leland had even discovered a way to break through her poker face. He had seemed interested, but cautious, and Sophie held out hope that he might want to see her again. After a week had passed, she tucked away the hope that she would learn more about the quiet, mysterious carpenter. A door in her heart closed tight and Sophie imagined throwing away the key. It was probably better this way. Her heart was an island surrounded by the painful secret that kept her trapped and afraid of stepping out into the water where love and hurt surely awaited. Better to stay on her island, holding her two children close. Keeping everyone safe from harm was the only thing that mattered.

Sophie finally finished the drapes for the Alexander's home and on a brisk January morning, she started up the car and drove through the snowy streets to the edge of Aspen Falls. The neighboring town of Calloway Grove was just a few streets over and the stately homes along the avenue spoke of the wealth in that part of Colorado.

It would take several trips for Sophie to carry the heavy draperies into the house, so she'd put on her sturdy black shoes and wore long johns under her favorite green and white checked dress. Her mother always commented on how the fabric emphasized Sophie's green eyes. She smoothed down the skirt and stepped out into the snow, walking carefully to the trunk of the car. There were sixteen heavy panels of material, double-lined for the picture windows that dotted the front of the Alexander's home. It was a mystery how Mrs. Alexander had managed to come by the yards of fine material while everything was still rationed to the last inch, but Sophie guessed that for the wealthy, there were ways around the rations. She leaned over the trunk and tugged on the first set of drapes, her breath coming out in frosty clouds in front of her.

The sound of another car engine came up behind her and she turned as a man pulled in front of the house in a shiny black Oldsmobile. Sophie gripped the material and stepped over the snow onto the walkway.

"Hello there, you look like you could use a hand," the man called as he shut the door of his vehicle. "Can I help you carry those?"

Sophie nodded toward the trunk. "Would you? I have over a dozen of the heaviest drapes on earth in my trunk."

"I'd be happy to," he grinned, and Sophie immediately recognized that smile. David Alexander, the esteemed fighter pilot didn't hesitate to grab an armful of his mother's draperies. And for some reason, Sophie knew that Mrs. Alexander would find the action disagreeable. The woman was kind, but pretentious and Sophie was always keenly aware of how far beneath the Alexanders she was when she visited the home.

He grabbed an armful of draperies and nodded. "I'm David Alexander, by the way."

He didn't remember her. She was a few years younger than him in high school and back then, he'd been king of every sport and surrounded by friends. There was no reason for him to remember the skinny Harper girl from across town. "Yes, I recognize you from your pictures. Your mother is very proud of you." They walked toward the front door.

David grinned. "She's my mother, she has to be."

Sophie smiled. "I appreciate your service to our country as well."

David halted mid-stride, and his expression softened. "Thank you."

Sophie nodded and climbed the steps to the front porch carefully.

"And your name, Miss?"

"I'm Mrs. Sophie Wright. My husband was killed in Pearl Harbor."

Again, David stopped abruptly, shifting the draperies over his shoulder. "My condolences. I was about to comment on how that beautiful smile of yours brightens the day, but I will watch my tongue and my step."

Sophie furrowed her brow and he chuckled.

"Not only is God watching over you, but you have a guardian angel husband too, don't you?"

Sophie sucked in a breath. "No, I don't believe that."

It was David's turn to look confused. "Pardon me. Did you say you don't believe in God?"

"No, of course not. I mean, yes, I believe in God, but I don't believe my husband is anywhere near heaven." Sophie gasped and buried her face in the drapes with a groan. The words had come out of their own accord.

She felt a hand on her back. "Your secret's safe with me."

Sophie turned and met David's crystal blue eyes. "Thank you."

"Shall we?" David hefted the drapes and opened the front door, calling out, "Good morning mother. I have a very special delivery."

Clutching the drapes, Sophie stood behind David as Mrs. Alexander entered the room. She had silvery gray hair, ironed to the side and Sophie recognized the sapphire earrings Mrs. Alexander often wore. They matched the ice-blue color of her eyes, which were narrowed as she took in the scene before her. "What are you doing with those drapes, David?"

David stepped back so that he stood next to Sophie. He inclined his head and grinned. "Mother, you'll never believe it, but I finally met Mrs. Right. It would have been a lot easier if you'd introduced me yourself."

Mrs. Alexander's nostrils flared and she pursed her lips. "David, this isn't a time for jesting. This poor woman has lost her husband in that horrible war. She's a widow, left with two small children. There is nothing *right* about the situation."

The admonition was like a thunderclap. The message couldn't have come across clearer if it had been written in stone. Mrs. Alexander wanted David to know that Sophie was a single, widowed mother, unsuitable for her vibrant young son. But David didn't miss a beat. "Yes, she and I were just talking about the war. I have the notion that you've been bragging about me again Mother." David turned and winked at Sophie. "Let's get these drapes to the front room and I'll go fetch the others."

"David, Mr. Okado can do that."

"I know, but I can do it a lot quicker." David nodded at his mother and dashed out of the room.

Sophie set her drapes down and straightened the material. "These are ready for hanging. You were right, Mrs. Alexander, this color will transform the room." Sophie fingered the navy blue brocade and glanced at David's mother.

"Yes, well, I am glad the fabric held up during travel." Mrs. Alexander lifted the edge of a drape and ran her finger along the edge. "You'd do well to ignore the attentions of my son, Mrs. Wright."

The room seemed to go still, as if listening for Sophie's reply to the slightly veiled threat. "No need to worry. I have no interest in your son," Sophie replied. "Now you mentioned that you'd like to see some sketches for cushions to accent these drapes. I have a few ideas that would go nicely with your sofa."

"Here's the rest," David announced as he entered the room with another armful of the drapes.

"Thank you again for your help," Sophie said. "It was most considerate." She dropped her eyes and studied her notebook, but she could feel David's gaze upon her. The tips of her ears grew warm and Sophie was grateful that her hat covered the evidence of her pulse racing as she heard David's footsteps draw closer.

"David, if you'll excuse us," Mrs. Alexander interrupted. "I have business to attend to with Mrs. Wright. Shall we meet for tea later?"

Sophie busied herself with her notebook and pencil, ignoring David's magnetic pull. If she looked up now and met those jovial blue eyes of his, she could kiss the next order goodbye. Mrs. Alexander wasn't someone to be trifled with.

Chapter 6 – A New Friend

On January sixteenth, the freezing temperatures broke and the sun warmed the ice until the icicles began to drip steadily from the rooftops, decreasing rapidly in size. A few days later, the front sidewalk was clear enough that Sophie decided to venture out for a walk with Maggie and Garth. They walked in the opposite direction of her parent's home. Garth splashed in puddles and sloshed through the snow no matter how many times Sophie asked him not to get soaking wet. Maggie sang fragments of Christmas carols mixed in with a hymn she'd heard in church. Sophie smiled at the simple wonders her children discovered in each day of life.

They had walked a little over a half mile from their house when they saw another woman walking slowly with a young girl. Garth stopped in front of them and began chattering away. As Maggie and Sophie grew closer, Sophie recognized the Asian features in the woman and her daughter and prayed that Garth wouldn't say anything disrespectful about the Japanese.

"Mom, look at Emika!" Garth shouted. "She was in my class until she got sick. She has metal legs!"

The little Japanese girl stood next to her mother, her legs tightly bound in braces of metal and leather. Sophie's stomach clenched. This was the girl from Garth's first grade class who had fallen ill to polio and been sent away to a treatment center. Sophie's hand flew to her mouth as she made eye contact with the girl's mother. "Is she well?" Sophie whispered.

The woman smiled and motioned to her daughter. "Is a miracle. Emika learning to walk again and she so strong." Her words were clipped with the accent of her native language and Sophie leaned forward, listening carefully for understanding. Emika was looking down at the ground, and Sophie sensed that the words were meant to bolster the young girl.

"I'm so happy to hear that. I'm Sophie Wright. We live just around the corner near my parents, Wayne and Betty Harper. You might know them as well as my brother Keith and his wife, Debbie." Sophie held out her hand.

The woman took her hand with a gentle grasp. "My name is Serena Tanaka. I am pleased to meet you." She spoke carefully, enunciating each word, although her accent still dominated the sentences. "I have met your brother. He help Mr. Halverson deliver my desk before Christmas."

At the mention of Leland's name, Sophie stood up straighter. "Oh, I'm glad to hear that."

"Mom, why won't you look at Emika's legs?" Garth asked. "They're strong like metal."

"Yes, dear. They are, but have you asked Emika about her Christmas yet?" Sophie turned back to Serena. "I'm sorry about Garth," Sophie said. "He gets over-excited about everything these days."

Serena held out her hand and moved it up and down. "He is young. That is how it is supposed to be. I have baby boy. He sleeping now, but he be like your son someday, I think."

"And Maggie just loves to play dolls. She's four." Sophie inclined her head toward her daughter.

"Emika love dolls too," Serena said. "Hello, Maggie."

Maggie looked down at the ground and whispered, "Hi."

"Garth was so worried about Emika. We all were." Sophie reached a hand toward the girl and patted her shoulder. "I'm so happy to meet you, Emika. I've heard so much about you. You're a very brave little girl."

Emika lifted her eyes, the beginnings of a smile tugging at the corners of her mouth, but then she looked back down, shifting her leg. The brace jangled and Emika winced.

"It is difficult for Emika to walk. There is still much pain." Serena gripped her daughter's hand.

"Emika, let's play," Garth said. He ran in a tight circle. "We could slide on the ice or play with my new bomber."

Emika held tighter to her mother's hand. "I have a dolly and a music box that plays a magic song. Do you want to hear it?" Emika's face brightened. "Maggie could come too."

Serena watched the children and looked over at Sophie with a cautious smile on her face. "I'm glad to meet you today."

"Me too," Sophie said. "Could the children get together to play sometime?"

Serena hesitated. "You understand that I am Japanese, yes?"

Sophie wasn't sure how to answer. She placed her teeth on her bottom lip, searching for words.

"This town is small." Serena motioned to the neighborhood. "I hear of the woman who move in with her two children. The woman who lost her husband in Pearl Harbor. I am sorry for your loss." She bowed slightly.

Sophie took a step forward and grasped Serena's hand. "You are American, and my neighbor. Our children are friends. There is no reason that we cannot be also."

Serena smiled so wide that her eyes disappeared in the folds of skin. She gripped Sophie's hand and nodded. "American friends."

Chapter 7 – The First Date

The orders continued to pour in after Christmas, and Leland put in twelve hour days trying to keep up with the customers. He didn't have time to call Sophie or stop by and see how things were going for her in the New Year. It was probably safer that way, but he couldn't shake her from his mind. Keith had asked him a couple times if he needed help to ask Sophie out, but Leland had refused. He was attracted to Sophie and he'd like nothing more than to ask her out on a date, but the thought seemed impossible.

If Sophie did agree to go with him, how long could he really tempt fate before she discovered the truth? He should have let Keith tell her when he had the chance. He was so distracted by thoughts of Sophie that he had to measure the same board three times before cutting it. The saw whined and spit sawdust in the air. The particles danced through the beams of sunlight from the window. Leland was reminded of Emika, the little Japanese girl who had won her battle against polio. Before she'd taken ill, she used to dance like those particles of sawdust, as the music box churned out its melody. And then, when tragedy struck and Leland learned that Emika might die from the effects of polio, he'd given the music box to Emika. It was the right thing to do, but sometimes, he still thought about the tune and the tiny ballerina that danced to the music–the music that had helped heal his heart.

The Tanakas were special friends of his—even though friendships with the Japanese were often frowned upon. Pearl Harbor was still a day of infamy that had marked a clear enemy of the United States, and many people had trouble seeing the difference between the real enemy and their Japanese neighbors. The Tanakas were numbered among those in Colorado who were forced to the Granada relocation center in Amache. When they returned to their home, they found it stripped of most of the furniture, including Serena's prized desk.

Not long after Shunsaku had placed the order for the desk, Emika had been stricken with polio. The injustices against the family had motivated Leland to work even harder to build the special desk for Emika's mother. In late December, he'd worked for hours on end to finish the desk before they returned from the polio treatment center. Emika was six years old, the same age Jessie would have been. The same age as Sophie's son, Garth. The little boy with the bomber plane who'd lost his father to the war.

Leland blew the sawdust off the panel of wood thinking about the families around him and the love they shared. Sometimes he thought about the possibilities of his future—starting over, taking a second chance. Could someone as broken as Leland ever hope to be accepted into a new family? And yet, every time he put Sophie from his mind and told himself that he wouldn't burden her with his past or uncertain future, she appeared again. The laughing dimple in her cheek, her striking green eyes and ebony curls—it was enough to undo any man's resolve.

Leland set aside the cut planks for the hardwood dining table he was building. If he hurried, maybe he could get a few groceries and make himself a decent meal. And if he kept his head out of the clouds, he would realize that too many weeks had passed. Sophie would think that he didn't care for her because he hadn't asked her out after Christmas. It was better to concentrate on the work at hand.

The post office in Aspen Falls closed early on Fridays so Sophie had barely made it in time to mail a letter to Cal's parents. They were disappointed when Sophie decided to move to Colorado to be near her family. They would always be Garth and Maggie's grandparents, but Sophie was thankful for the distance. The scars she carried from her marriage to Cal would never disappear, but distance from everything related to him would help them fade.

"Well, if it isn't Mrs. Wright."

Sophie lifted her head to see David Alexander striding toward her. Her first impulse was to duck her head, but his mother wasn't with him, so she held eye contact and smiled. "How are you today?"

"Things could be worse, but I have a feeling they're about to get better," he replied.

Sophie fiddled with her purse strap, unsure of how to respond. David was one of the golden boys of Aspen Falls—handsome, wealthy, and confident. She was probably just a passing flirtation. "Thanks again for your help the other day, and I do hope your day gets better." She turned to go and David pivoted in front of her.

"I know that my mother demands it, but you shouldn't be so submissive to her."

Sophie felt like he'd thrown a bucket of ice water on her head. Her eyes widened as she grappled for a response. "She basically threatened me if I so much as spoke to you," Sophie replied. "I'm sorry if I appeared rude. That wasn't my intent. I don't have many options for employment with my young children."

"Where are those children of yours?" David asked.

"At Grandma's house. I live near my parents." Sophie took another step toward the door.

"I'm not afraid of my mother and you shouldn't be either," David spoke softly.

"I'm not," Sophie replied. "But I try to be wise when I'm able. Good day, David."

Sophie hurried out to her car, not looking back. The grocery store was her next stop and she hoped the lines wouldn't be too long today.

When Sophie reached the Safeway, her insides were tangled up in knots. She couldn't decide if David Alexander was truly interested in her, or if he was just making conversation. Either way, it didn't matter because he was out of her league. The little red brick home that Sophie loved could fit inside the first floor of the Alexander's home. They had old family money that started with the coal mining industry of Colorado and continued to grow. Mrs. Alexander loved to boast about her only son, so Sophie knew that David had taken over his late father's position as president of the mine when he'd returned from the war. David's mother had been raised in New York and she clung to that high society with hopes that David could benefit from her relations back east. Sophie shook her head and reminded herself again that none of it mattered. Carrots, celery, and potatoes—now those mattered because they would make a delicious soup for Garth and Maggie tonight.

Sophie smiled to herself and chose four long carrots and added them to her basket. She was reaching for a large potato when her hand brushed someone's fingers. Pulling back quickly, Sophie murmured, "Sorry about that."

"Sophie, you're welcome to that spud. I'll take this one." Leland Halverson picked up a potato and put it in his basket.

"Oh, hello Leland." Sophie took the knobby potato and added it to the other vegetables in her basket. "I'm going to make potato soup for the kids tonight and I'll tell them that you helped me pick out the perfect spud."

Leland chuckled. "I'm happy to help." He stared at her, gnawing on his bottom lip. "I've been meaning to call you, but things have been so hectic at my shop."

"I'm sure you've been busy. I keep hearing what great work you do," Sophie remarked. She was careful to keep her poker face in place even though she wanted to ask Leland why he wanted to call her.

"Well, they have, but that's not a good enough excuse," Leland said. "The truth is I'm scared spitless, but I want to take you on a date."

Sophie grinned. "You do?"

Leland picked up another potato and handed it to her. "I do. So would you?"

"Would I?" Sophie took the potato, staring at the bumpy surface with bits of dirt stuck to the skin.

"Go on a date with me? I heard The Bells of St. Mary's is still playing and I'd love to take you. Keith and Debbie already offered to watch the kids whenever I got the guts to ask you."

"So this is a joint effort?" Sophie ribbed Leland, enjoying the way his neck flushed, making the dark stubble on his jawline stand out. She studied him, reminded how decidedly handsome he was. The overhead lights of the market emphasized red highlights in his hair that lent a boyish quality to his looks.

Leland followed her gaze and reached up to pat his head, smoothing his hair, the flush in his neck creeping up to his cheeks. Sophie laughed and bumped his basket with hers. "Your hair is fine. I was just noticing that it's sort of reddish-brown. I like that." Cal had blond hair that he grew longer in the back so that he wouldn't have to fight rooster tails. Sophie remembered how she used to cut his hair and she never got it right. Her smile slipped, and she swallowed. With a quick shake of her head, she leaned toward Leland. "I would love to go on a date with you. I've been hoping to see that film with Bing Crosby, isn't it?

The look on Leland's face was one of surprise mixed with jubilation. "Yes, it's Crosby and Bergman. Would you like to go to the Saturday night show?"

"I think that would be great. I'll give Debbie a ring and make sure the kids can come over."

Leland nodded, patted his basket, and nodded again. "I'll pick you up at six o'clock for dinner before."

"That sounds marvelous." Sophie lifted her fingers in a wave. "I'll see you tomorrow."

Sophie couldn't stop smiling as she finished her grocery shopping. She saw Leland at the end of one of the aisles and then again when he was leaving the store. He walked with a determined gait, his broad shoulders filling out his brown work coat. Leland was a solid man, someone that the people of Aspen Falls loved. It wasn't until Sophie was on her way home that she considered the fact that the people of Aspen Falls loved David Alexander as well.

Chapter 8 — The Music Box

The next day, Sophie walked over to the Tanaka's house with her children at about ten in the morning. Garth was so excited he was about to burst. "Now, please remember that you can't be rough with Emika. She's been very sick."

"I know, Mommy," Garth replied. "I'll be careful."

"I brought my dolly to show her," Maggie said.

"And I'm sure she'll love it."

The sun shone brightly with only a few puffy clouds dotting the sky. It gave Sophie hope that spring would arrive soon. She was looking forward to the new beginnings the season brought and sensed that this chapter of her life held good things in store. She helped Maggie up the steps to the Tanaka's modest home. It was painted white with blue shutters and the windows held planter boxes with dark brown soil and bits of ice. Garth knocked on the door and leaned forward, waiting for it to open.

Serena opened the door. "Welcome to our home." She motioned for them to come inside. "It is a good day for Emika today."

"I'm so glad," Sophie said. "Garth would've turned inside out if he couldn't play with her. It's all that he's talked about."

Serena smiled and motioned to the chubby baby on the floor next to Emika. "This is my son, Shunsaku. He is named after his father, so we call him Shun."

"He's adorable." Sophie tugged Maggie's hand. "Isn't that the cutest baby?"

The baby looked over at them, babbled and grinned. Maggie bent down and handed him a block. "Hi, baby Shun. I came to play with you."

"C'mon Emika, let's play bombers. I'm the best pilot," Garth said.

Emika clutched her doll and stood, wobbling slightly before righting herself. She took a few steps and looked to her mother with a shy smile.

"Go on." Serena motioned toward the back of the house.

Emika turned, and then hesitated. "Can I show them my music box, Mama?"

"Yes. Do you want them to come to your room to see it?"

Emika nodded, and Garth ran down the hall. "Wow, your room is clean!"

Sophie and Serena chuckled as they followed Emika to her room. The little girl took halting steps and Sophie noticed her grimace with pain a few times, but she continued on as if she was used to the routine. When they entered the tiny bedroom, Sophie saw the music box sitting atop a chest of drawers. She stepped forward, drawn to the piece with a curious wonder. The music box was about the size of a shoebox, constructed of pressed paperboard, and covered with ivory parchment. A narrow line of embossed gold ran along the outer edge of the paper covering.

Emika reached around the back of the music box and turned a brass windup key. Then she pushed a button on the front of the box and lifted the middle compartment. A tiny ballerina on a dais near the back popped up and began dancing an elegant pirouette in front of a mirror attached to the inside of the lid. Imitation red velvet lined the box and the narrow chamber with padded ridges to hold rings and other pieces. There was one silver ring with a fake pearl in the box, but the ballerina commanded everyone's attention. As she danced to a melody that Sophie had never heard before, the room quieted. Maggie hugged Sophie's leg. Garth lowered his toy plane and stared intently at the music box.

The music climbed carefully up a melodic scale and the ballerina turned, then the tune scattered down with lilting notes, resonating with memories, love, sorrow, peace, and something Sophie couldn't name. The melody was ethereal and alluring and Sophie blinked back the moisture forming in her eyes. The ballerina kept spinning, rocking back and forth as she tilted toward the mirror and then away, and still the music played.

A chill breeze tickled the back of Sophie's neck as the music slowed and she turned toward the open window in Emika's bedroom. The wind from outside stole the heat from the room, but Sophie had the distinct feeling that it had taken a piece of the music with it.

Serena turned toward the window and shook her head. "Emika, you can't have this window open. It's much too cold."

"Sorry, Mama. I was hot."

Serena crossed the room and shut the window and the spell of the music was broken. Garth buzzed around the room with his bomber plane and baby Shun fussed on Serena's hip.

"That music," Sophie commented. "It's lovely. Where did you get that music box?"

"Leland gave it to me." Emika smiled brightly and twisted the brass key again. The music began and Sophie's heart thrummed along to the tune.

"Leland Halverson?" Sophie asked.

"Yes," Serena said. "It meant a great deal to him, but he gave it to Emika when she got the polio."

"Oh." Sophie put a hand to her cheek, struck with the intensity of the moment and what it said about Leland.

"Do you know Leland?" Serena asked.

"Yes, I—uh—I do," Sophie stammered.

"His heart was broken I think, but it's lined with gold. Come, I show you what he do for our family." Her accent was more distinct the faster she spoke. "He make our Christmas miracle."

Sophie followed Serena, leaving behind the music box with its mysterious tune. Serena led her to a corner of the front room where a beautiful secretary stood. The desk had three drawers and two paned glass doors. "Did Leland build this?"

Serena opened the secretary and withdrew a slip of paper from one of the compartments. There was a sketch of the desk on the paper. "I draw this after we return from the camp and find my mother's desk stolen."

Sophie took the paper and studied it. Serena had referred to the relocation camp that several Japanese-American citizens had been forced to move to after the bombing at Pearl Harbor. Camp Granada was a place of sadness and confusion. The back of Sophie's head ached whenever she thought about the hardships that families just like the Tanakas had been forced to endure because of their straight black hair and slanted eyes. The God she knew was no respecter of persons and when Sophie had said as much to Cal's mother, she'd been furious, cursing the Japanese for killing her son. It had always been different for Sophie; perhaps because of her marriage to Cal, she knew that a person's heritage or ancestry did not make them guilty, just as it also didn't guarantee goodness. "I'm sorry for what you suffered."

Serena shook her head. "We are blessed. Leland built this desk for us and would not accept payment. He shared his gift with us. I want you to know I speak truth when I say his heart is lined with gold."

"Thank you for sharing that." Sophie ran her finger along the edge of the desk, examining the fine craftsmanship. Leland was a skilled carpenter; the workmanship on the desk was unrivaled. Sophie felt a small thrill in her middle when she thought of her date with Leland that evening. She was looking forward to learning more about the man with a golden heart.

Chapter 9 – The Silver Lining

Sophie took Garth and Maggie over to Keith's house just before six. She'd asked Leland to pick her up there so she wouldn't have to trudge back through the cold. Debbie was fixing supper and ushered Sophie into the kitchen. "Are you excited?"

"Yes, but that's all I'm saying because you and Keith can't be trusted."

Debbie laughed. "I want all the details later."

Sophie arched an eyebrow. "I guess I owe you something for taking care of the kids."

"You know I don't mind," Debbie said. "It keeps my crew entertained. I hope you have a good time."

"Come on in Leland." Keith's booming voice carried to the kitchen.

"That's my cue," Sophie said, and she scurried out of the kitchen. She looped her arm through Leland's. "I'm ready."

Keith chuckled. "I can take a hint, Sis. I won't tease you in front of Leland."

"Seriously, I'm ready Leland." She looked up at him. "Can we go?"

The light in Leland's eyes made Sophie smile. "Sure thing. The pickup's still running, should be warm."

"Have a good night, you two," Debbie called from the kitchen. "Don't stay out too late."

Sophie tugged on Leland's arm and they stepped out into the cold before Keith could say anything. He helped her into his pickup and they drove toward the center of town. "I wanted to take you to The Silver Lining for dinner. Does that sound okay?"

"Anything I don't have to make sounds wonderful."

Leland smiled and tapped the steering wheel. "Thanks for coming with me tonight."

"Thank you." Sophie was grateful that Leland didn't seem to notice her nervousness. He didn't know that this was only her fifth date since Cal had died. Most men left her alone while Maggie was an infant, but once she reached about two years old, there were many unwelcome invites. Sophie had always found a way to kindly turn them down, save a few. Those men hadn't been terrible, they were gentleman, but Sophie couldn't explain the terror that gripped her during the date, not knowing who they really were. Cal's mother had even vouched for one of the men and given her blessing, but the moment he placed his hand on Sophie's leg, she had broken out in hives and the date had ended.

Sophie tried to shrug off those thoughts. She was determined to have a good evening with Leland. He was different. Keith's best friend would never hurt her—she kept repeating that to herself as they drove to the restaurant and Leland led her inside The Silver Lining. Despite her fears, she was attracted to Leland and intrigued by his quiet, gentle ways. Even though her marriage couldn't be called successful, Sophie had witnessed several happy couples within her own family. She wanted to date again because her children deserved to have a father, and eventually Sophie's heart might be ready to flutter with a love that would fill her from the inside out.

Leland noticed that Sophie seemed to be battling some sort of war in her mind, although she did a great job of hiding it. Most people probably wouldn't pick up on the way her eyes wandered for a moment while she was deep in thought, the way the soft flesh of her neck tightened with some remembered tensions. He guessed at some of her feelings because he was struggling with them himself. This was Leland's first date since Rhonda had divorced him. Keith had told Leland. "Listen, if you pick the right girl, you only need to have one first date, and I'm telling you, Sophie is the right girl."

Leland smiled at the memory, glancing at Sophie as he helped her from the pickup and into the restaurant. That night, there was a young man playing a guitar while another young lady sang familiar tunes. Leland had been to The Silver Lining a few times before and once since he'd stopped drinking all together. He remembered venturing out to hear the local favorite, Evelyn Patterson, sing her haunting melody. That song had sounded almost exactly like the tune from the music box that had changed his life. He half-expected to hear the notes floating through the air of the restaurant, but the melody was absent, replaced by guitar music. They placed their orders for the house special of chicken fried steak and fried onions with a side of coleslaw.

"Can I get you something to drink?" the waitress asked. She was a pretty blonde with the name LaRue printed on her name tag. "We have a nice red wine you might enjoy."

"Oh no, thank you. I'd like water," Sophie answered. She looked at Leland and smiled.

"I'll take a Coke with ice."

"I'll be right out with that."

"So how have you liked Aspen Falls?" Leland asked.

"I love being close to my family. I missed them so much."

"Keith mentioned that you were living near your in-laws before."

Sophie nodded. "Yes, but after Cal died, nothing was the same and everything was so difficult. This move was good for me and the kids. Keith and Debbie have helped me a lot."

"I'm glad to hear you like it. I've lived here most of my life and the people in this town feel like my family."

"I met some of my neighbors," Sophie said. "The Tanakas speak very highly of you."

"Oh, I'm glad to hear you know them." Leland smiled. "Shunsaku is a good friend of mine."

"I've met baby Shun, but not his father. Serena showed me the secretary you built. It's exquisite."

"Well, thank you." Leland sat up straighter under Sophie's praise. "The time spent building that desk was an important time in my life—felt like I was rebuilding."

"It looks like everything turned out fine," Sophie said.

"Thank you," Leland said again. He wanted her to know that he admired her as well, but he didn't want her to think that he'd been talking to Keith too much, even if he had. "Keith said that you can sew up just about anything."

"I do love to sew. I made this dress." Sophie lifted the collar of her navy blue dress. "I waited to get the fabric for six months. Won't it be nice when the rations are a distant memory?"

Leland leaned back in his chair. "Some people say they could go back to rationing gas, but I'm not sure what to believe. Everything keeps changing so fast."

"Are you worried at all that we might be heading into another war with Russia?"

"No, I don't think that will happen. There's too many empty bellies in Europe right now for much of an uprising. People are too busy trying to survive."

"I'm just relieved that it's all over," Sophie said. "I was so worried when Keith was drafted into the army. I never thought that a bullet would end up saving his life." She squeezed her napkin thinking about her brother's near-death. When Keith had been shot at Normandy, he had survived, but doctors couldn't remove the bullet. It was hidden inside his flesh and because of the risk, he was sent home, likely saving his life again.

"I felt the same way. I still remember seeing Keith when he returned. One of the best days."

"I hope you don't mind me asking, but how did you escape the draft?" Sophie wiped at the condensation on her glass of water.

"I don't mind." He stretched out his leg and wiggled his foot. "Feet flat as pancakes and a possibility of a heart murmur. I was rejected."

"What do you mean rejected?"

Leland looked down at his plate and when he lifted his head, he hoped that Sophie couldn't read the fear in his eyes. "I wasn't drafted, but after Jessie died, I was so torn up I tried to enlist."

Sophie patted her mouth with a napkin, watching Leland carefully. "You wanted to escape the pain by going to war."

"Something like that." Leland nodded. "I went down to the office, filled out the paperwork, and I was certain I'd pass. I mean, I knew my flat feet might be a problem, but then the Doc listened to my heart and stamped a big red 'Rejected' on my form." Leland tapped his heart with his right hand. "My heart was broken I guess because he thought he detected a heart murmur, but when I went back to my regular doctor for a checkup a year later, he couldn't detect any problems."

"That must have been scary," Sophie said.

"It's kind of a blur, and part of me wonders if the Doc put down heart murmur because he thought that sounded better than 'drunk'."

Sophie gasped and Leland reached out his hand to brush her fingertips. "I apologize. I shouldn't talk like that in front of a lady."

"No, it's just," Sophie licked her lips, "I keep forgetting that you used to have a problem. I couldn't imagine you ever behaving badly."

"I never really did behave badly," Leland murmured. "I didn't behave at all. I was an empty vessel, broken, and nothing could fill me up."

"But that's changed now?"

"It has and I know God is in everything," Leland said. "I was like that Psalm where David says "I am forgotten like a dead man out of mind: I am like a broken vessel." But my life is different now. I don't feel so broken anymore."

"That's beautiful, Leland."

"You are beautiful, Sophie. I just hope you don't hold it against me, you know, that I didn't serve my country."

"Why would I?"

"Because of your husband. He gave his life and I couldn't even enlist."

Sophie's fork clattered against her plate. "Of course, but that was different."

"How so?"

When she raised her head, there was anguish written in every feature and her striking green eyes were vibrant with hurt. Leland wanted to take back the turn in the conversation but he wasn't sure how it had become derailed. Thankfully, the waitress appeared.

"Would you two like to share a slice of chocolate pie this evening?" LaRue asked. "We have homemade ice cream as a special treat."

"However did you come by enough sugar to manage that?" Sophie asked, maybe with a bit of forced enthusiasm, but Leland couldn't be sure.

"Frank came by some extra coupons." LaRue winked. "Times are changing."

"Well then, we'd better not miss out," Leland said. "Bring us out a plate."

"I'll be right back with that."

"I think she likes you," Sophie said.

"Who? LaRue?" Leland looked after the pretty waitress. "She's married, and don't worry, she's not really my type anyway."

"What is your type?"

"Someone with a heart of gold," Leland said.

Sophie's mouth dropped open, but she quickly recovered. "Well that's how Serena described you."

"How's that?"

"She said that you have a heart lined with gold."

Leland smiled and reached across the table to take Sophie's hand. She squeezed his fingers gently in return.

Chapter 10 — A Night at the Movies

As soon as they walked into the movie theater, Sophie's nervousness returned like a jolt of electricity, shocking the good feelings she'd shared with Leland into a faded memory. She stumbled and Leland touched the small of her back, guiding her into the semi-darkened theater.

"How's this?" Leland indicated a row halfway up the theater.

"That should be fine." Sophie's hands shook and even though she told herself to settle down, her body wouldn't listen. Leland helped her out of her coat and they sat down next to each other.

He put his arm around her. "Are you cold? You're trembling."

Sophie bit her lip. What could she say that would explain the crazy terror spiking her blood pressure? She turned to Leland. He had leaned forward and was studying her face with a gentle expression. When her eyes met his, an authentic worry furrowed his brow. He really did care how she was feeling. Sophie swallowed and admitted her irrational fear. "I'm a little nervous because I haven't dated much."

"Would you rather I take you home?" Leland asked softly.

The way he asked undid her. The thumping terror in the background dissolved and suddenly the music playing reached her ears. Inch by inch she settled into the seat, letting the fear drain out. Leland wasn't Calvin. Cal was dead. Sophie lifted her hand and touched Leland's arm. "No, I'd like to stay. I haven't been to the movies with another man since my husband died and I don't know what came over me."

Leland studied her; slowly reaching toward her face he tucked an errant curl behind her ear. His touch sent heat across her shoulders and she leaned closer, inviting him to put his arm around her. "Whatever you need, Sophie, I'll do it for you. I haven't dated much either, and I want you to enjoy this night."

"Thank you, Leland." He relaxed back into his seat, draping his arm around Sophie. In the dim light of the theater, Sophie studied his profile. Leland exuded a quiet strength from his chiseled jawline to the cords of muscles in his neck. The way he held her gently, yet protectively, reminded Sophie again that Leland was not anything like her husband.

When the movie started, Leland pulled Sophie a little closer and she relaxed into the comfort of being near him. She concentrated on slowing her breathing from the panicked state and within a few minutes she felt better. The only problem was her heart had taken up a breakneck pace as Leland caressed her arm, his fingertips touching the bare skin just below her sleeve.

The movie was excellent. Both Sophie and Leland laughed, smiled, and enjoyed entering another dimension and escaping their own worries. Sophie's eyes welled with threatening tears a few times, and she appreciated how Leland squeezed her hand gently as if he too, noticed the feelings stirring within.

"I adore Bing Crosby," Sophie said. "His voice is wonderful."

"I enjoyed listening to those Christmas carols on the radio in December."

Sophie nodded and leaned closer to Leland. "Thank you for bringing me tonight."

"Definitely my pleasure," he murmured, his whisper close to her ear.

Too soon, it was time for them to exit the theater. Sophie liked the feel of her small hand against the rough calluses of Leland's large hands. He walked Sophie outside, guiding her around the puddles that seemed to grow larger every day. They were nearing the pickup when Leland halted abruptly. Sophie glanced over at him. His brow was furrowed, a troubled expression on his face.

"Leland, are you sick?"

"What?" he jerked his head closer. "No, I'm sorry. I'm fine."

Why was he apologizing? Sophie looked back, but only saw a few moviegoers, and then she heard it. A haunting melody rose up into the night from a house across the street. Someone was playing the piano softly and the music carried on the breeze. The music held a quality similar to the tune she'd heard from Emika's music box. Odd that a tune she'd only heard a few times would stay with her days later. Perhaps the memories surrounding that special music box were too painful and that's why Leland had given it to Emika. Sophie was about to ask Leland if the music was upsetting to him, but the music stopped and after a pause, the pianist continued on playing a different melody.

Leland cleared his throat. "Sorry about that. Let's get out of the cold." He helped her into the pickup and she slid a little closer to him, watching his face carefully for any sign of how he was feeling. Putting the pickup into gear, Leland backed out and headed toward Keith's house. "I'd like to drive you and the kids home so you don't have to walk in the cold."

"That's kind of you," Sophie said. "It might take a few minutes."

"I'll just wait here," Leland said as he pulled into Keith's driveway. "I'm not really in the mood for Keith's meddling right now."

"O-okay," Sophie whispered. "I'll be right back."

Had Leland changed his mind? Did he regret taking Sophie on a date? Her shoulders drooped as she walked up the front steps. It was her fault. With her nerves and panic, Leland probably decided that she was more trouble than she was worth. Cal's words snaked through her mind, "You're just like a puppy—cute as anything and nothing but trouble."

Sophie hesitated with her hand on the door knob, closed her eyes and offered a silent plea for help. She couldn't enter the house with all of these uncertainties circling her head. Focusing on the truths she knew, Sophie opened the door smiling brightly and called out for Garth and Maggie.

Leland softened somewhat when the kids climbed into the pickup. They were sleepy and Garth rested his head against Leland's side. Sophie held Maggie and didn't try to continue the stilted conversation. The driveway was clear in front of her house, so she hopped out and carried Maggie in the side door by the carport. When she turned, Leland was right behind her, carrying Garth. She nodded for him to follow her inside the house, and they carefully deposited the sleeping children on their beds.

"Thank you," Sophie murmured.

Leland nodded. "I'd best be going. We don't want to give your neighbors something to talk about."

Sophie forced a laugh. "Have a good night." She wanted to ask him again what was bothering him, but he tipped his head and was out the door before she had a chance. Sophie sank onto the couch, putting her head in her hands. Everything had been going so perfectly, or maybe like her marriage, it had just appeared so from the outside. She had no idea what might be simmering underneath the surface of Leland's careful demeanor.

Chapter 11 –
The Forbidden Invitation

February 1946

The Alexander home appeared more imposing than usual that clear, cold morning. It was the first week of February, and Sophie picked her way through the fresh snow, wishing with more fervor for spring to come. She was halfway up the walk when she noticed the shiny black car David had driven the last time she was there. It was parked on the side of the house and for a half second, Sophie considered getting back in her car and coming back later. But that was ridiculous. This was David's home as well, so if she ran into him, it shouldn't cause a problem. All the same, Sophie hoped he would be otherwise occupied.

A Japanese man wearing a carefully tailored dress jacket and slacks opened the door as she approached. Mr. Daisetsu Okado, an older gentleman probably in his fifties, worked for the Alexanders as their hired man. Sophie stood at least five inches taller than the slight man, but he towered above her in grace and presence.

"Good morning, Dai," Sophie called him by a shortened version of his name–one that he had asked his friends to use. Mrs. Alexander only ever addressed him formally, the same way she seemed to address everything in life.

"Hello, Sophie," Dai replied. "You look fine today. And the cushion is beautiful."

"Thank you." Sophie was grateful for his welcoming smile that morning, because the austere look Mrs. Alexander gave her a minute later could wither the hardiest spring flowers. Sophie held out the cushion she'd finished earlier that morning.

"I was able to include some decorative stitching around the edges here that I think gives it the quality you were looking for."

Mrs. Alexander took the cushion and a slight smile curved her upper lip as she examined the stitches. Sophie relaxed a tiny fraction, hoping that her employer would be generous today and provide a much needed gratuity.

"Mrs. Wright, this is very fine work as usual. Thank you for delivering it today. David has several items of clothing that need to be mended."

"Certainly. When do you need them returned?"

"Within three days would be best. David will be complaining as soon as he finds that his favorite pair of trousers are missing."

The lightness in Mrs. Alexander's tone was so unusual that Sophie nearly let her carefully controlled facial features slip. Instead, she employed one of her favorite tricks; she looked at the creases of skin directly between Mrs. Alexander's eyes. "I will do my best to get them completed. Would you like to point out anything specific with the clothing?"

Mrs. Alexander's eyes narrowed a tiny fraction. "That won't be necessary. You do such fine work that you'll likely find more to fix with David's clothing than he even noticed."

There it was again, and with a painful lurch of her heart, Sophie realized that Mrs. Alexander was testing her for a reaction. During the six months that Sophie had worked for her, there was often talk of David but today there was a distinct tone to Mrs. Alexander's speech. It was barely discernable but Sophie heard the underlying threat that dared Sophie to reveal her hidden thoughts about David. It was almost as if Mrs. Alexander knew that David had paid undue attention to her in public.

"That will be all," Mrs. Alexander said. "And Mrs. Wright?"

"Yes?" Sophie hated how she continued to call her Mrs. Wright, no matter that Sophie had asked her to please call her by her first name. She wasn't Mrs. Wright, and every time someone called her that, it was as if Cal's icy fingers were gripping her upper arm again, bruising the tender skin and claiming his wife for any of his base desires.

"Say hello to your children for me." She held out an envelope. "Here's your payment."

"Thank you very much." Sophie tucked the envelope in her pocket and turned to follow Dai who was weighed down with a larger than usual pile of clothing. Although it was a welcome blessing, Sophie noticed that nearly every article of clothing belonged to David. A sense of foreboding followed her out the door and to her car where Dai helped her arrange the pile of clothes.

"Thank you. Guess I'll be busy this week."

Dai rarely spoke in front of Mrs. Alexander, but always had a kind word for Sophie. He stepped closer and inclined his head. "Mrs. Alexander is throwing out several flower pots and a few house plants. Would you be interested in one?"

Sophie brightened. "Any sign of living in this dreary winter would be welcome."

"Follow me to the garden house."

Sophie nodded and walked up the driveway on the side of the house. The garden house was an old greenhouse that was mostly in disrepair. If Sophie had such an asset, she could grow fresh herbs and greens year-round for her little family. Dai pointed out an empty flower pot, a wilted fern, and an aloe vera plant that had nearly overgrown its pot. "Do you mind if I look around for a moment?" Sophie asked.

"Not at all. Please close the door on your way out."

Sophie pulled her coat tighter around her slight frame as she walked to the end of the greenhouse. She thought she'd caught a glimpse of green at the edge of the potting table. There was a broken pot on the ground and Sophie picked it up and breathed in with delight. A violet crocus bloomed, stretching toward the sunlight. She crouched down, studying the fragile petals.

"That's a sign that winter will end early." The man's voice behind her might as well have been a lightning bolt.

Sophie cried out as she stood and backed toward the table when she saw how close David was to her. "You scared me!"

His eyes softened. "I'm sorry. I didn't mean to sneak up on you."

Sophie tilted her head, pointing at the scant distance between them. "And yet, that's exactly what you did."

David grinned and lifted his hands. "Guilty as charged. I wanted to speak with you and when I saw you come in here with Okado, I might've leaped before I looked."

Sophie clutched the edges of her coat. This was exactly the kind of test that Mrs. Alexander might employ and she did not want to fail. "Well, I was just leaving. Mr. Okado offered a few castoff plants to me. I hope you have a good day."

"Sophie, wait." David touched her arm and she halted, looking at his hand on her arm and then at his face. He was handsome with his high-planed cheekbones and dark eyebrows that accented his clear blue eyes. They were nearly eye to eye with the heels of Sophie's shoes giving her a couple inches.

She guessed him to be just under six feet tall and her stomach roiled. Cal had been five-foot-ten inches and he often put his hand on top of Sophie's head and pushed her down. "I don't like it when a woman is taller than me," he'd said one day when she'd carefully curled and pinned her hair on top of her head. Sophie jerked her arm back.

"I really need to go."

"My mother doesn't know we're out here and I'll be damned if she can stop me from talking to you."

"She might not be able to stop you, but she can stop me." Sophie took a step forward and turned back. "David, I really need the money from this job. It might not seem like much to you, but my children need me."

"Please, wait," David took a step closer to her. "Just now, there was real fear in your eyes, but it wasn't because of me, was it?"

The self-assured smile he always wore was gone and Sophie saw a vulnerability that she wouldn't have guessed at before. She closed her eyes and took a deep breath, wondering why she felt compelled to speak to this man who belonged to a different world. "No, it wasn't you." She looked down at her feet, studying the paving stones that lined the floor of the greenhouse.

David touched her cheek with one finger. "Look at me," he said softly.

Lifting her eyes to his, Sophie struggled to slide her features into the mask of calm she usually wore in front of Mrs. Alexander. David shook his head slightly. "You can't fool me with that poker face of yours. Remind me never to go up against you in a game of pinochle."

Sophie's façade cracked and her face broke into a smile.

"Why are you afraid of me?" David asked as he took her hand, clasping it gently.

"I'm not afraid of you."

"But I must remind you of him, then?"

Sophie shook her head, and then she shrugged. How could she explain that almost every man reminded her of Cal because Sophie worried about the unknown? She didn't want to trust the possibility that a man was truly good and didn't carry secrets. "He was about your height and he had blonde hair."

David glanced out the window and then back at Sophie. "But I'm not like him, am I?"

"Honestly? I don't know. Cal—Calvin was a real sweetheart until he wasn't." Sophie gripped the potted plant tighter against her chest. What was it about David that made her tongue loose? Knowing she should be careful didn't seem to be enough to stop her from sharing her thoughts.

David's brows furrowed and he nodded. "Well, all I can do is give you a chance to know me."

"That's not a good idea either. I've already told you—"

"I saw you at the movies the other night," David interrupted.

"You did?"

"You seemed pretty cozy with the town drunk. You can do better than that."

Sophie straightened, pulling her hand from his. "That's unfair. Leland is not the town drunk. He's a good man."

"I take it you must not know about his daughter." David shook his head.

"Of course I know. Leland and my brother are best friends," Sophie retorted. "Don't think for a minute that Keith would let me go on a date with someone he didn't approve of."

"Well, we shouldn't have a problem then."

"I beg your pardon?"

"I know Keith. Known him for years. He's the same age as my older sister."

"So?"

"So, I'd like to take you on a date and I'm certain Keith would approve of me." He grinned and Sophie noticed his white, even teeth. He was clean cut and those blue eyes of his must have talked many a girl into whatever he wanted. She shook her head.

"I'm not someone to be trifled with. I have two young children."

"Garth and Margaret, right?"

"How did you—"

"Sophie, I'm interested in you. Can't you see that?"

Sophie hid her surprise that David had discovered who she was, and remembered her family. "I see a decorated soldier who is used to getting his way with sweet talk and flattery."

David groaned, putting a hand over his face. "The curse of the war. I'll never be free of it."

"What do you mean? You came home. You're alive and breathing," Sophie challenged him.

He let his fingers slip and peeked at her through his fingers. She couldn't help it. A giggle burst forth as she thought of how David looked just like Garth at the moment.

"Everyone thinks they know me because I came back alive," David said. "But just because all the uniforms look the same doesn't mean the men that wear them are."

The truth of his words warmed Sophie down to her toes. "All right, I'm listening."

"I'd like to get to know you, despite my mother's warning to stay away. She has very good taste and the fact that you're still working for her is a testament to you."

"So you want what you can't have." Sophie shifted the flower pot to her other hand. "That's not a compelling tale."

"Wait, don't take it the wrong way. I'm trying to say that I'd like a chance to get to know you better, to meet your children, to learn more about the woman who is quite certain that her husband didn't go to heaven."

Sophie sucked in a breath. The way David could so casually place her feelings for Cal was unnerving and yet, he didn't seem bothered in the least by her previous revelation. Hope flared in the hidden chamber of her heart. Was she standing before someone who might understand and accept her darkest secret?

Sophie checked outside and toward the house to see if anyone was coming. "You do realize that we've talked long enough now it's basically considered a date in Aspen Falls."

David smiled. "Well, Mr. Okado isn't going to tell anyone."

Another laugh bubbled up, even though Sophie tried to stop it. "I think you're a big tease."

"Maybe I jest to hide my insecurities."

Sophie arched an eyebrow. "Could be."

"You want to know what I think?"

"No, but I'm guessing you'll tell me anyway."

David placed a hand over his heart and winced. "She is ruthless, nevertheless, I will continue." He straightened and bowed slightly. As he rose, he grinned up at her. "Since we sort of have the first date over with, the second one won't be as awkward. What do you say? Will you come with me to the winter festival concert this Saturday?"

She wanted to resist. She wasn't certain how Leland felt about her or what he might think of her going with David Alexander, the town's golden boy. After the conversation she'd had with Leland about the war, it didn't sit right, but at the same time Leland hadn't said anything about another date. He'd been subdued, and almost defeated at the end of their date. She didn't understand what it meant and so she'd told herself to keep moving forward with faith that God would take care of her. The seconds were stretching to the point of awkward as David waited for her response. She pressed her lips together and breathed in. "Okay."

David grinned and put his hands on her arms. "Thank you. I promise to be a gentleman and I'll pick you up at five-thirty."

"At Keith's."

"Huh?"

"I'd like you to pick me up at Keith's because Debbie helps me with my kids. Unless you'd rather me send them to my parents and you can pick me up there?"

David blanched and Sophie bit the inside of her cheek. Wayne Harper could be quite formidable when he wanted to be, and David must have been familiar with that. "It'd be great to see Keith again. Does he still live out on Fourth Street?"

"That's the one."

"I'll be counting down the minutes."

Sophie rolled her eyes. "Do me a favor and don't use any more lines on me."

David snapped his fingers together and saluted. "Yes, ma'am. Anything for the pretty lady."

Sophie bit back a smile and pivoted on her heel, leaving the greenhouse. She glanced back and saw that David was still standing at attention. With a shake of her head, she laughed and hurried to her car.

Chapter 12 — The Note

Leland sat in his shop surrounded by planks of wood, sandpaper, and nails. He gripped the hammer tightly and rose, ready to pound more nails into the hardwood. It had been over a week and he was still sulking over his date with Sophie. He'd ruined an otherwise perfect evening with his self-doubt and worry. Everything had been fine until he'd heard the melody floating through the chill night air. The pianist had played something eerily similar to the tune of the music box. There had been a warning alongside the melody and it frightened him into a panic. In the darkened street, he'd distinctly heard the words, *Tell her.*

His gut twisted as he thought again of Sophie's face, her perfect smile falling when she had asked if he was well and he could barely answer—the fear stealing any words he might've spoken. The rest of the evening had been disastrous but, if anything, Leland wanted to date Sophie more than before. She had been kind and concerned and when he didn't want to talk, she hadn't pouted or brooded. Her behavior spoke volumes about the kind of woman she was, and yet, at the same time Leland worried. Did she take his mood swing in stride because she had experience with her first husband? The thought angered him because he should be better than that. Leland centered the nail and pounded with quick, decisive strokes. A knock on the door sounded between strikes. Leland dropped the hammer and strode to the door, swinging it wide.

"Hey, Keith." He welcomed his friend in, wondering if Sophie had spoken with her brother about their date. Most likely or Keith wouldn't have stopped by unannounced.

Keith walked in and leaned against the work table. "Sophie had a nice time on your date the other night."

"It was a good evening." Leland struggled to relax his jaw.

"Then why didn't you ask her out again?"

So she had talked to Keith, or maybe just Debbie. Either way the news was out—Leland was a coward who not only was rejected from the army, he couldn't even ask a beautiful, kind, and gracious woman on a second date.

"Did something else happen that I need to know about because Sophie seemed pretty disappointed when Debbie asked her about the next date. Then she pasted on one of her fake smiles and told Debbie everything was fine and you were a gentleman." Keith pounded his fist into his palm. "You said you wouldn't hurt my sister."

"Which is why I didn't ask her out again." Leland pressed his lips into a thin line. "I don't want to hurt her."

"How could you possibly hurt her by asking her on a date?"

"Keith, she doesn't know the truth about Jessie."

Keith pulled his bottom lip through his teeth. "I thought you said you told her that Jessie died?"

"I did. That's exactly what I said—that Jessie died and Rhonda left me after I couldn't stop drinking." Leland pushed another plank in place. "I didn't tell her *how* Jessie died."

"Then tell her," Keith said.

The words were like a bucket of ice water on Leland. He dropped the handful of nails to the ground. "I can't tell her. She'll think I'm a monster."

"Listen, I know my sister and she will not think any less of you." Keith stepped forward and put his hand on Leland's shoulder. "In fact, you might find her to be one of the most understanding creatures you've ever met."

Leland swallowed. "It's hard for me to say it out loud."

"If you can't say it out loud, put the words to paper." Keith dropped his hands and shoved them into his pockets.

"No, I can't do that either. I need to find the right time to tell her." Leland crouched and picked up the nails he had dropped.

"I don't know how you're going to do that if you don't ask her on another date."

"Do you think she'll go with me? Maybe I've scared her off." Leland straightened his hammer and square edge on his worktable. "What was her husband like?"

Keith frowned. "I didn't know Calvin very well. I know he had some trouble with drinking too much and that Sophie has been pretty torn up since his death. She practically yelled at me when I tried to bring him up. Said she didn't want to talk about him ever again."

"That's not a very good sign for me," Leland said. "I mean, she knows that I used to drink."

"You're right. It's probably going to be harder than it might be for some other guy." Keith picked up a stray nail from the floor. "So you gonna give up or give it a shot?"

Leland shoved Keith off balance. "I already gave it a shot. You sure are a pest."

Keith laughed. "Quit yer whining and just ask her on another date. Then we can both be happy 'cause Debbie will be off my case."

"What can I say? Things were so awkward when I dropped her off. I practically ran away from her."

"Like I said before, put the words to paper," Keith said.

"You mean write her a note?"

"Yes, women love that kind of thing."

"They do?"

"That's what Debbie keeps telling me. I think it's a hint, so maybe I should write one with you. We can share lines."

Leland hesitated. "What if they show each other the notes?"

Keith's lips twitched. "You're right—better not share lines. I'll give one to Debbie and you write one for Sophie."

"Now?"

"Why not? I'm here and I can deliver your note to Sophie on my way home."

Leland pulled out his work bench and handed Keith a slip of paper from the notebook he used to take order details. The two friends sat on either end of the bench, bent over their pieces of paper. At first, Leland just stared at the piles of sawdust built up along the edge of the table, but then he thought of something that might convince Sophie to give him another chance.

Chapter 13 — Tea Time

His words were written with force, the letters bold and thick, probably scripted with a bulky marking pencil from his carpentry shop. Sophie ran her fingers over the words as she read.

Sophie,

I'm sorry for how I acted the other night at the end of our date. Sometimes the past haunts me and I didn't know how to shake it. I want you to know that I think a lot of you and if you're willing, I'd like to take you out again. Are you busy Saturday morning?

Leland

Signed with only his name, Sophie was left to wonder how strong Leland's feelings were for her. Cal had been dead for over four years and she'd rarely gone out, and now she could have two dates in one day–if she agreed to Leland's invitation.

This was a problem that could only be solved with a little tea time talk. Sophie picked up the phone and dialed Keith's number.

"Debbie, I have a little problem and Maggie is down for her nap. Do you think you could run over?"

"I'll be right there." Debbie hung up before Sophie could even say goodbye. She understood their code for when Sophie wanted to talk about something that she didn't want the entire party line listening in on. Debbie had been the one to tell her about Patty Gillespie who spent the most part of every day listening on the party line. Sophie put the teapot on the stove and turned on the gas burner.

Debbie's cheeks were flushed when she arrived and Sophie laughed when she sat at the kitchen table and said, "I'm all ears."

Sophie told her about David Alexander's attentions that were basically forbidden by his mother and his invitation to the winter festival concert. And then she read Leland's note.

"Men," Debbie scoffed. "Keith and Leland must have written their notes together when Keith went to see him.

"Keith wrote you a note?"

"Yes, he did, but don't think I'm going to read it to you." Debbie shook her index finger. "So what do you want to do? It sounds like you already agreed to go with David—very daring, my girl."

"True. By the way, can you babysit because I asked David to pick me up at your house at five-thirty?"

"Of course. Lucky for you, Keith and I are just old married people."

Sophie laughed. "You're not old."

"Okay, maybe not old, but boring, definitely boring."

The tea kettle whistled and Sophie hopped up to prepare the peppermint tea that she and Debbie enjoyed during their visits. It was one of the few things she could indulge in without ration coupons, because her mother grew peppermint and prepared the leaves for tea.

"Maybe I should see if Mom wants to watch the kids and we could go on a double date."

Debbie nodded. "That would be fun, but first you need to have a chance to get to know Leland better—or wait, were you talking about David?"

Sophie rubbed a hand over her forehead. "I was thinking about Leland, but it would work with David as well."

"Do you like David?" Debbie asked. "I mean, what's not to like? He's handsome, richer than sin, and all that, but I don't really know how he treats a lady."

Her words held a double-meaning and again, Sophie was tempted for a moment to reveal more about Cal than she ever had before, but she resisted. Debbie was her sister-in-law and Sophie didn't want to give her any reasons to keep something from Keith. Sophie was definitely not prepared to tell Keith the hidden secrets about her marriage. Sophie took a sip of tea. "David *is* very handsome. His eyes are this striking blue color—I have to make myself look away from him so that I don't stare."

"But?"

Sophie smiled, stirring her tea slowly. "I didn't say 'but.' David is funny and lighthearted and I like that."

"But?"

"Oh, stop," Sophie swatted Debbie's hand. "Okay, David is a little cocky. I can tell that he's used to getting what he wants and he didn't give up when I gave him every reason to. Leland, on the other hand, is reticent. He's quiet and there's so much going on inside that he isn't telling me and then it felt like he gave up. I need someone who can be strong for me and it's too early to know what is best. So, I'd like to go out with both of them. Do you think that's wrong of me?"

"Of course not. David knows you went out with Leland and Leland knows that he sort of messed things up at the end of your last date. Neither of them has claim to you. This isn't the 1800s. You won't get in trouble for going on a date with two different men. . ."

"On the same day," Sophie finished.

"There's that." Debbie drank her tea. "One thing's for sure. You'd better come to dinner on Sunday so that we can analyze the results."

Sophie laughed. Thank goodness for her sister-in-law and for the beautiful little town of Aspen Falls. Her hometown made her feel safe to rediscover the woman she'd lost so many years ago.

"Aren't you going to call him?"

"Leland?"

"Goodness, it's confusing trying to keep up with all of your boyfriends," Debbie said.

Sophie rolled her eyes. "Now?"

"Sure, why not?" Debbie asked. "The poor man must be out of his mind worrying what you thought. Best to put him out of his misery."

Sophie stood and walked to the phone mounted on the wall. She dialed Leland's number with shaking fingers. The phone rang several times before Leland picked up.

"Halverson Carpentry," he answered in his deep voice.

Sophie could just picture him standing in his shop with a day-old beard edging his jawline. She shook herself back to the present. "Hi Leland, this is Sophie and I wanted to tell you I really appreciate your note. Thank you."

"Oh, that. Well I'm glad you read it." His voice tightened and Sophie remembered what Debbie had said about putting him out of his misery.

"I'd love to go with you Saturday morning. I think my parents can tend the kids if you'd like to pick me up there."

"Actually, I wondered if the kids would like to come along."

"Really?"

"Yes, just make sure they dress warm. It's supposed to be chilly and I have some outdoor activities that might be fun to do. I'll come by your house just before ten, if that's okay."

"That would be nice," Sophie responded. "And Leland?"

"Yeah?"

"I'm glad you're feeling better."

He cleared his throat. "Me too."

When Sophie hung up the phone, Debbie stood and hugged her. "I know it's not fair to choose sides, but Leland is my favorite. David doesn't stand a chance against him."

After Debbie left, Sophie tidied up the kitchen. She found herself humming a tune, but she couldn't remember the words. She thought about the two men taking her on a date. They were from opposite ends of town, one a blue collar worker and the other a wealthy business owner. Confidence oozed from David in such contrast to Leland that one might think he'd actually stolen a dose from the carpenter. The two men were vastly different and Sophie wondered how she could begin to make a choice between them. As she scrubbed at a stubborn spot on the enamel kitchen sink, Sophie realized that the tune she'd been humming didn't have words. It was the melody from Emika's music box—the tune that touched something deep within Leland's soul.

Chapter 14 – The Carpenter

The clock ticked closer to ten, and Leland should have felt excited but he couldn't shake his anxiety over the day he'd planned with Sophie and her kids. It didn't help that he'd awoken with words on his tongue—words of truth about Jessie that had nearly choked him when he'd tried to swallow them back down. The words were insistent, wanting Leland to share the story of his past. Today was only his second date with Sophie—not a good time to tell her about Jessie. Leland told himself that and ignored the warning flutters in his stomach that urged him to confide in Sophie before she heard the truth from someone else.

He managed to continue to ignore the urge to confide his secrets in Sophie as he picked her up and they settled the kids between them.

"Where we going?" Garth asked.

"I have a little surprise I'm taking you to see."

Sophie leaned forward. "How about a clue?"

Leland drove west across town. "I know the place like the back of my hand." Part of him still wondered if this was a good idea, but Keith had thought it was excellent and he'd been the one who urged Leland to invite the kids. He watched Sophie out of the corner of his eye as he neared his shop.

"Wait," Sophie said. "Are you taking us to your house or did you forget something?"

"Hmm, I've definitely forgotten a lot of things, but I haven't forgotten that the best hill for sledding in Aspen Falls is right behind my house."

"We're going sledding?" Garth cried.

"Yep, and if you're a good boy, we'll even have hot cocoa after."

"You have cocoa?" Maggie leaned forward and rested her little hand on his arm. "I love cocoa."

It was just a flicker, but for one instant, Leland thought about what it would be like to have a family again. Watching Sophie with that soft smile directed toward him made his heart beat faster. He wouldn't mess up today. They parked in front of the shop and Leland helped Maggie out before going around to the other side to help Sophie and Garth. Everyone was bundled up against the cold and the sun was shining—a perfect day for winter fun. Garth ran forward kicking up snow and Sophie hoisted Maggie onto her hip as they trudged toward the shop.

"Would you like me to show you around first?"

"I'd love that," Sophie said. "Garth, Leland wants to show us all of his tools in his shop."

Garth froze in place and spun around. "You have a shop for your tools?"

Sophie and Leland laughed. "I do. Come on in and I'll show you my lathe."

The wonder on Garth's face as they entered the shop only brightened when Leland showed him the pegboard with nails and hooks to keep his tools organized.

"You have everything!" Garth jumped up and down pointing at the tools, the wood planks, and a partially finished dresser. "Mom, he's like Jesus. He's a carpenter."

Sophie smiled. "Yes, Leland builds beautiful things and he is like Jesus because he helps people with his talents."

Leland lifted his head to meet Sophie's eyes. "Thank you," he said.

She nodded and pointed out a set of wooden spindles that Leland had cut and would later use for the back of a rocking chair.

"Can I build something with you?" Garth tugged on Leland's sleeve.

"We'd have to plan that with your mom, but right now I think it's time to go sledding before the snow melts. That sun is really shining today."

Garth's mouth had started to turn down, but at the mention of sledding he perked up and headed for the door. "Let's go."

Sophie tugged on Maggie's hand when the little girl lingered over a pile of wood shavings. "May I?" Leland asked as he held out his arms to Maggie. The girl studied him and then held her arms out. As Leland picked her up, his throat tightened as heat rose from his heart to prick the backs of his eyes. He blinked and held out his hand for Sophie. She took it and Leland led her out of the shop to his backyard which dropped off on a little hill that was perfect for sledding.

"I found the sled!" Garth tugged the smooth wooden toboggan to the top of the hill, its metal runners slicing through the snow.

"Ho there, boy," Leland called. "Let me give you a few pointers first. I've been sledding down this hill since I was younger than you."

"Younger than me?" Garth looked confused.

"Sure, I used to be a little boy too."

Garth shrugged. "Can I go now?"

Leland chuckled, and he heard Sophie giggling behind him. He set Maggie down and then helped Garth climb onto the sled. He showed him how to steer and gave him instructions about when to bail off the sled. A moment later, Garth was whooping as he sped down the hill, slowing at the bottom where the snow lay in a blanket of powder.

"Now, who's going to drag the sled back uphill?" Sophie asked. She watched Garth with a smile.

Leland walked over to the back wall of his shop and pulled a larger, rickety sled out. "We are. You ready to ride, Maggie?"

Maggie squealed and clapped her mittens together. Leland climbed onto the sled, tucking his knees almost up to his chin as Sophie set Maggie in front of him. With a gentle push, they were racing down the hill, the wind whipping at Maggie's scarf and freezing Leland's cheeks. Maggie and Garth cheered when they reached the bottom. Leland helped both kids on the sleds and he pulled them back up the hill. Thankfully it was more of a gentle incline than a hill, so even though Leland felt like a pack mule by the time they reached the top, he was still breathing.

"I think it's your mom's turn," Leland huffed. "Garth, why don't you ride with me this time?"

"Okay, let's go fast though."

Leland situated the sled for Sophie and helped her climb on with Maggie in her lap.

"Should we race?" Sophie asked.

"I don't know," Leland said. "What do you think Garth?"

"Yes! Yes! Yes!"

"One, two, three," Leland called as he pushed off and wrapped his arms around Garth. The kids cheered as they gained momentum down the hill. Leland and Garth beat Sophie and Maggie by a few inches and Garth tossed snow in the air as he whooped in celebration.

Leland and Sophie talked as they pulled the kids up the hill again. "Are you still sewing projects for Mrs. Alexander?"

Sophie glanced down at the ground and nodded. "Thank goodness there's a lot of mending to be done each week. In between she keeps coming up with new projects."

"Is she your only client?"

"There are a handful of others, but most people just get by. You know how it is."

Leland nodded. "I do a lot of trades and that has kept me busy."

"What kind of trades?"

"I get a quart of buttermilk and milk every week and a half pound of butter each month from the Crandell farms. I built his wife a new armoire for Christmas and they agreed to stock me with dairy products for the next year. Of course, they'll have a regular paying customer when the time's up because I won't be able to give up my buttermilk or the real butter."

"You lead the kind of life I've always hoped for," Sophie said. "It's one of the reasons I came back to Aspen Falls. The people in this town look out for one another. Not that they didn't in the other towns I lived, but it was different there. People here know my mom and dad. They knew my grandparents on both sides and my great-granddad. The roots run deep here."

"Sometimes it doesn't seem like my roots go as deep with the rest of my family gone, but I agree."

"I'm sorry about your parents. That must have been so hard when your mother died." Sophie adjusted her scarf. "I hope you don't mind me saying, but I still remember the shock I felt when Mother told me she'd suffered a heart attack."

"It was. I can't help but think how my life might've been different if my mother was still alive." His father had been gone for almost fifteen years already, but his mother had only passed away six years ago, right before his life turned on its way downhill. He looked over at Sophie. "I guess you probably wonder the same thing about your husband."

A dark shadow crossed Sophie's face and she pressed her lips together. "No, I don't dwell on his passing. My life is what I make it now and things are very good. You are good, Leland. I appreciate this."

"I'm grateful you think so." Leland noticed how deftly she'd changed the subject. She must have had a lot of practice. There was something she wasn't telling him about her marriage, and Leland worried that whatever she was holding back might rear its head when he was least prepared. It made him even more reluctant to share his past with her. How could you know how someone would react if you didn't know what sort of scars they already carried?

"I think this better be the last ride down the hill," Sophie said. "I know I'm worn out and my feet are numb."

"Agreed." Leland helped Garth onto the sled and winked at Sophie before pushing off. "Loser has to make the cocoa."

Everyone was soggy by the time they trudged into Leland's house. He worked quickly to stoke the fire, adding more wood and adjusting the damper. Sophie laid the wet clothes on the rug by the fireplace. Leland pulled out a set of blocks that he'd made for Jessie, and told Garth and Maggie to build him an ice castle.

"You have a very nice home," Sophie commented. She ran her fingers along the edge of the dining table and rested her hands on the back of a chair. "I can tell that a master craftsman lives here. This dining set is absolutely gorgeous."

"Thank you. I've been trying to decide if I should sell it since it's really too big for just one man and I've had several offers." He didn't mention how the table evoked certain memories that he'd rather not dwell on.

"Any woman with a family would probably break a few commandments just by looking at this dining set."

Leland laughed. "Keith said about the same. He'd like Debbie to have a set like this."

"She's been talking about a dining set for years. I'm sure the cost for something this large is high."

"It is pretty labor intensive," Leland agreed. "Chairs are a tricky thing. I like to think the reason I can build good chairs is because I tipped so many of them over when I was a kid. Never knocked enough sense into me, though."

With a laugh, Sophie stepped up to the kitchen counter and started filling the teapot. "How do you like to make your hot cocoa?"

"Well, I start with the secret ingredient."

"What's that?"

"Cocoa."

"Oh you." Sophie waved the dishcloth at him. "Where is it?" She opened a cupboard and Leland stepped up behind her as she reached for the cocoa tin on the top shelf.

"Here, I'll get it." He extended his arm alongside hers and grabbed the can. The air was fragrant with an aroma that made Leland's nostrils twitch. He leaned forward a centimeter and breathed in, his mind bursting with memories at the light scent of lavender on Sophie's neck. He handed her the cocoa and stepped back, taking note of the pink flush of her cheeks that wasn't all from the cold.

"Thank you. Now you were telling me something about buttermilk; you wouldn't happen to have a little cream?"

"As a matter of fact, I have a pint in the icebox." Leland retrieved the milk and cream and set it on the counter. "I have the other secret ingredient too." He opened a silver canister on the counter, revealing the crystal white granules of sugar that made cocoa into a real treat.

"I'll only use a little," Sophie said. "I know it's hard to come by. I'm trying to figure out how to get enough to make Maggie a unicorn birthday cake with *fluffy frosting*, as she requested." Sophie stirred the cocoa into the milk in a pot on the stove.

"Maybe I can help, it's just me here if you'd like to take some," Leland offered.

"Oh no, I don't want to take your sugar, and besides I need powdered sugar for that kind of frosting." Sophie waved the spoon at Leland with a grin. "My secret ingredient is a pinch of salt."

"Really?" He grabbed the salt shaker and handed it to Sophie. When she looked up to catch him staring, she smiled and refocused her efforts on the cocoa.

"I have some cold cuts in the ice box and a loaf of bread. I know it's not the greatest of lunches but when I was a kid, it was one of my favorites. Will your kids eat sandwiches?"

"They love sandwiches with a dab of mustard, just like their Mama."

"Well, that's the best news I've heard all day because I just opened a new jar of mustard." Leland chuckled and pulled the sandwich fixings out of the ice box. He and Sophie worked side by side to prepare the meal, with her keeping an eye on the cocoa. When it was just about to bubble, she pulled it off the heat and poured up the mugs, adding a generous helping of sweet cream to the top of each mug.

Leland was struck by how good Sophie looked in his kitchen, making cocoa and acting right at home. He felt warm all the way down to the tips of his toes and he tried to show Sophie how he felt by interacting with her and the kids with genuine smiles that didn't feel forced or contrived. After they finished the meal, Leland played jacks with the kids and he visited with Sophie about the coming week.

"Today was perfect," Sophie said. "This is something my kids have really missed out on."

"I'm sure it is 'cause last I checked southern Kentucky doesn't get that much snow."

"I meant having a man to look up to." Sophie squeezed his arm. "You were great today and I appreciate it."

Leland pulled her into a hug and sighed; he could almost taste the relief in his exhale. He had wanted so badly for today to be a good memory when Sophie and the kids looked back on it. He didn't anticipate how much he would long for the chance to make another memory with the little family, or his fear that it might not be possible. Shoving doubts aside, Leland held Sophie as the kids curled up in front of his fireplace. "Thank you," he whispered.

Chapter 15 – Words Like Honey

Sophie's hands trembled as she applied her lipstick and powder. She stopped and looked at her fingers, commanding them to be still. Why was she so nervous? David was a gentleman and he'd asked her to the winter festival concert before Leland had asked her on the most perfect date she'd ever been on. The kids were exhausted and Sophie hoped she could keep them awake on the way to Keith and Debbie's house.

The dress she chose for the evening was a dark green with a scoop neck and pleated skirt. The long satin ties went all the way around her slender waist and tied at the front in a graceful bow. When she sewed the dress, Sophie had worked to salvage every inch of material for her tall frame. There were three rows of satin that edged the skirt, brushing her knees. She pulled on a cream-colored shawl and then her heavy wool coat.

"Okay, kids. Let's go," Sophie called down the hallway. Maggie came out holding her blanket and Christmas doll.

"Mommy, you look booti-ful," she said.

"Thank you, sweetie."

"Are you going to a party?" Garth asked.

"I'm going to a concert tonight."

"With Leland?" Maggie yawned.

Sophie chose to sidestep the question. "Let's hurry because Amy, Michael, and Travis are waiting to play with you."

That helped them move faster and Sophie kept them chattering on the way over so that Maggie could keep her eyes open. She'd barely shooed them down the hallway when someone knocked on the door.

"Oh, he's early," Debbie murmured as Keith went to open the door.

"Hello, Keith. It's been ages," David said as he pumped Keith's hand. "How have you been?"

"Good. Always staying busy, you know the drill."

"I was glad to hear you made it back from the army in one piece," David said. "Is it true you're still carrying that piece with you?"

"Yep, that bullet is lodged somewhere in my gut. Debbie says that it's one of her favorite things about me."

"I'm sure it is. It's still a wonder you survived Normandy."

Sophie held her breath as David stepped right into one of Keith's most painful memories.

Keith frowned. "I lost most of my friends there. Terrible thing."

"I'm sorry about that. I hope you're well now."

"We all do the best we can."

David nodded and swept through the room with his piercing gaze, his eyes locking on hers and widening when he saw Sophie standing in the soft glow of the living room lamp. "Excuse me for complaining, Keith, but I don't understand why you've kept your sister in hiding. I've never seen a more beautiful woman." David stepped forward and held out his hand. "I hope you don't mind that I'm early. You are a vision."

Sophie wasn't used to being slathered with praise. She felt the familiar flush of uncertainty rising up her neck. David must have noticed because he grasped her hand and stepped closer. "I'm sorry. I forgot that you told me I wasn't supposed to use any of my lines on you." He tilted his head toward Debbie and stage-whispered. "Can you really blame me?"

Debbie laughed. "I think Keith could take a few lessons from you."

Keith stepped forward and put his arm around Debbie. "I can say things he can't. I don't need lessons."

"Like what?" Debbie asked.

He looked at his wife and smiled. "I love you."

"Oh, that's sweet Keith," Sophie said. "A little awkward right now," she motioned between her and David, "but sweet."

"I think that's our cue to leave," David said. He tugged on Sophie's hand and propelled her forward. He helped her into her coat and gave hurried goodbyes. As he tucked Sophie into his car, he asked, "Did we win round one?"

Sophie laughed as he hurried around to the driver's side. Once he'd climbed in and put the car into drive, she said, "You may have softened up Keith a bit, and you definitely won points with Debbie getting her husband to say he loves her in front of us."

David grinned. "I meant what I said, Sophie. I hope you don't mind if I hold your hand tonight. I want every man there to know that you're with me."

Sophie ducked her head, swallowed, and gathered her courage. "I meant to tell you thank you for your compliments. You're very kind." She studied his perfectly tailored suitcoat—the one that she had mended herself. "You look very handsome tonight."

"Yes, well I do appreciate the nice work you did on my trousers." He winked at Sophie. "What do you think my mother was trying to accomplish by sending you nearly half my clothes to mend?"

Sophie licked her lips. "I think she wanted me to be sure of my place."

David frowned. "I hoped that wasn't the case, but I had the same assumption." He reached over and took Sophie's hand, squeezing her fingers. "I'm sorry. I know my mother comes across as, well, unfriendly, but she is a good woman."

"I know, and don't worry," Sophie replied. "She's been very good to me, although after tonight, I imagine that will change. Did you tell her you were taking me to the concert?"

David withdrew his hand and rubbed the back of his neck. "About that...I was waiting for the right moment."

Sophie leaned back. "Who is she?"

David raised his eyebrows. "Who is who?"

"The girl your mother wants you to marry. What's her name?"

David groaned. "Do we have to have this conversation right now?"

"Would you rather I guess, because I think I have a pretty good idea." She rested her chin in her hands and stared at him, enjoying his moment of awkwardness.

His lips twitched. "Linda Marchant. She comes from the Marchant's in New York, and if my mother could she'd plan the engagement party right now."

"What's wrong with Linda?"

"Not especially so many things." David gripped the steering wheel. "It's just that I don't like to be told what to do."

Sophie straightened and arched an eyebrow. "So you don't like her because your mother does?"

"That makes me sound like a spoiled brat."

"Well, that's true, but you *are* an Alexander."

David laughed, and then instantly sobered. "That's the reason. Right there what you did is why I couldn't marry Linda."

"You mean how I just insulted you?" Sophie asked.

"You made me laugh. You turned the mirror and let me see myself. Linda would never do something like that."

His words struck a chord with Sophie and she wasn't sure how to respond.

"I'm sorry," David said. "I've made you uncomfortable."

"No, I was thinking about what you said is all." Sophie stared out the window at the snow-encrusted streets. "When I was younger I never would've spoken out the way I do now. I've been married. I have two children. My experiences have changed me. I've adapted. Some ways I like, and others I wish that I could go back in time to the innocent wide-eyed girl so in love with the world."

"That's eloquent, Sophie." David parked the car in front of the concert hall in Calloway Grove. He turned to her, and taking her hand, he lifted it gently to his lips. His kiss was feather light against the back of her hand, and her skin tingled all the way up her arm. He lifted his eyes to hers. "You have depth, a well of great beauty and I'm looking forward to discovering everything about you."

Sophie basked in the glow of David's words as they walked arm in arm to the restaurant in Calloway Grove. David spoke as if he wanted to see a lot more of her if he was planning to discover everything about her. She wasn't sure if she was ready for a relationship or not, but Sophie chose to let the worries she'd entertained earlier in the day to fade into the background. Debbie had advised her to enjoy the evening and not fret over the future. Sophie decided to take the advice. David treated her to a delicious dinner and they ended up talking about some of her favorite studies and how at one time she had hoped for a chance to attend the junior college. She had done well in school and even after her marriage to Cal, she'd often checked out books from the library to study topics like architecture and Renaissance period paintings.

"I wanted to take a community course, but Cal–well, he wouldn't allow it." Sophie hesitated. She despised the way Cal continued to taint her life with his ugly memories. Gripping her water glass, Sophie forced those thoughts from her mind and took a sip.

"Sophie?" David's voice sounded far away and she snapped back to the present.

"I'm sorry. I–uh..." Sophie scrambled for a reason for the lapse in attention.

"I lost you there for a moment." David reached across the table and took her hand. "He can't hurt you anymore, you know."

Sophie flinched and tried to pull her hand away, but David covered it with his other hand. "You are valuable. I don't know what he did to you, but you're safe now."

Her bottom lip trembled and Sophie blinked, her lashes growing dangerously damp.

"You are an incredible mystery and I want to uncover every facet of your beautiful soul," David said. "If you'll let me in. Will you give me a chance to know you—the you underneath your armor?"

She'd never heard words like his before. They caressed her with a truth that she couldn't deny and they shook the gate around her heart with such force that a tiny corner broke loose, and her heart pushed against the barrier, begging to be freed from its protective cage. Sophie looked at David's hands over hers and then at the kindness in his sapphire eyes. She nodded once. David patted her hand and his eyes brightened with a smile. He rubbed his thumb in a slow circle across her palm until the waitress returned with their check.

When they arrived at the concert hall, Sophie floated on the edges of David's words as they walked toward the opening. He was such a gentleman and even though a part of her knew that words probably dripped from his mouth like honey for every woman he spent time with, they felt authentic to her in that moment. But then, just as they were about to be seated, Sophie glanced around the hall and wondered if David had chosen the venue in Calloway Grove so that he wouldn't run into any of his mother's friendly spies.

The music was well-performed and the arrangements were delightful. Sophie found herself applauding enthusiastically after each one. Every time she turned to David to comment on the song, his eyes held hers with an intensity that burned into her soul. She forgot about her worry concerning his mother when he put his arm around her and pulled her close. He lowered his head to hers and whispered in her ear, "I can't stop thinking about you. Please say you'll see me again after tonight."

Sophie turned her head slightly. There was only a breath of space between them. "Only if you promise I won't get fired for doing so."

David grimaced, but then he chuckled. "I'll find a way because I'm not letting you go."

Chapter 16 — David

February 1946

Sunday dinner was at Sophie's parent's house and during cleanup in the kitchen, Sophie told her mother and Debbie some of what David had said. "He asked if I'd come to dinner with him at The Silver Lining this Friday, and he asked me before we had even left Calloway Grove."

"And what did you say?" Keith elbowed his way into the conversation with a pile of dirty napkins.

"I told him that sounded like a wonderful idea," Sophie replied.

"What about Leland?" Keith asked.

"If he wants to take Sophie out, he needs to ask her," Debbie answered. "Don't worry her right now. Can't you see she's had a nice evening?"

Keith furrowed his brow. "Just because a man is a sweet-talker, don't mean he'll be the man of your dreams."

"Keith, go check on Amy and Michael," Debbie interrupted. "I thought I heard her bawlin'."

Keith took the hint and left the kitchen, though not before shooting a parting glance at Sophie that indicated he was still her big brother. Sophie chuckled. "David said he wasn't going to let me go—that he wants to get to know me better."

"He did?" Debbie asked. "What else did he say?"

"Well, there *was* one sentence that I just keep hearing in my head," Sophie said. "He said, 'You are an incredible mystery and I want to uncover every facet of your beautiful soul.'"

"He sounds like one of those romance novels," Betty said.

"If Keith ever talked to me like that, I'd ask him if he'd been drinking." Debbie scrubbed at a pot and paused with the dishrag halfway out of the soapy water. "But Keith's compliments *are* sincere. He's a good man and I don't ever doubt him."

Sophie heard the words Debbie didn't say because they were the same ones that had been running through her mind. Wondering if David was just a sweet-talker was a scary prospect. Cal had been flattering when Sophie first caught his eye, but he'd manipulated her from the very beginning into thinking that she wasn't worthy of more than Cal offered her. The scraps of comfort and torn pieces that had once looked like love were all that he'd given her and as a result, Sophie had lived in her marriage always feeling naked, exposed to Cal's biting remarks and swift hand. Experience had forever altered her perspective and it was up to Sophie to decide how hard she would look for the dark clouds on the horizon, just beyond the rays of the sun.

Monday morning, the clouds returned and a freezing rain pelted the windows, but Sophie still smiled. For the first time in her life, the uncertainty that lay before her didn't frighten her. She had finished all of the alterations and mending on David's clothing. Garth was off to school and Maggie played with scraps of material, covering her baby doll with makeshift clothing. Sophie's back ached from leaning over her sewing machine, but she'd accomplished a lot. The pedal needed oil, and Sophie would need to get under the cabinet to wipe out the dust first. The squeaking had nearly driven her crazy when she had hemmed David's pants. She glanced at the scrap of paper she had pinned to the wall above her sewing machine. It was an advertisement for one of those fancy electric machines. No pushing the pedal up and down to keep the needle going. She could only imagine how that might be.

Grabbing a cleaning rag, Sophie ducked under the cabinet housing her sewing machine to begin cleaning. A light rap on the door made Sophie jerk and she nearly bumped her head on the underside of the cabinet. She scooted out. "Let Mommy get the door, Maggie." Her daughter halted in her approach to the door, clutching her dolly to her chest. Sophie glanced out the front window and recognized David's car. She swung the door open and gasped when she saw him standing there holding three red roses.

"May I come inside?" He held the roses out as he took a tentative step forward.

"Yes, of course." As she shut the door and turned, Sophie saw her home as if through David's eyes. It was clean, but cramped with a worn sofa and threadbare carpet. She opened her mouth to excuse the sewing mess but David stepped forward, handing her the roses.

"For the most beautiful woman I know. I'm a few days early for Valentine's, but I couldn't wait."

"Thank you." She took the roses and breathed in the heady scent. Cal used to bring her flowers after, but no—she wouldn't let him ruin this moment. Sophie touched David's cheek. "These are lovely."

He caught her hand before she could pull it away and kissed her open palm. A spark skittered across the surface of her skin. "I'll—uh, put these in water." She turned and then remembered Maggie. "David, I'd like you to meet my daughter, Maggie."

"Hi, David," Maggie said. "This is my dolly, Charlotte."

Sophie kept an eye on her little girl as she retrieved a vase and filled it with water.

David crouched in front of Maggie. "Well that's a beautiful name for a beautiful dolly."

"Yes, my mommy made this dress for her. It's pink 'cause I like pink and Mommy said that–"

David stood and patted her head. "You're cute." He walked into the kitchen leaving Maggie mid-sentence. The little girl looked at David and then back at her dolly. She held the doll close and whispered something that Sophie wished she could hear. She loved how Maggie made every moment magical with her sweet demeanor.

"She's my little piece of sunshine," Sophie said. "And Garth is my fireball. You'll like him."

"Oh, sure," David said. "Margaret's cute."

"It's Maggie. If you want to be on her good side, don't ever call her Margaret."

"That's her name though, isn't it?"

Sophie nodded. "But for some reason, she acts insulted if someone calls her that."

David chuckled. "Kids are funny." He surveyed the kitchen. "You have a nice little home here. I bet you like living so close to your family."

"I do. It's hard to imagine what I'd do without them, even though I've only been here for seven months."

"Interesting," David said.

"What?"

"I've only been back for six months. Sometimes it feels like years since I flew those planes, but then I wake the next morning, jumping out of bed ready to fly again."

"You miss it?"

David shrugged. "Sometimes I do."

"Did you ever consider going back to Peterson?" Sophie spoke of the Army Air Base in Colorado City where David had trained and learned to fly before fighting in the war.

"Briefly, but I knew my place was here with my father's business."

"And does that still feel like the right decision?" Sophie asked.

David opened his mouth and closed it. He stepped forward and put his hands on Sophie's arms. "How do you do that? You get under my skin—in a good way. You make me think."

"I could say the same for you," Sophie replied.

He dropped his hands and turned. "I probably should go before I kiss you."

Sophie's hand flew to her mouth. Her lips were already tingling. What would it be like to kiss David Alexander? She felt her cheeks warm with a blush and she dropped her hand to her side and breathed slowly. "Thank you for the roses. Oh, and David. I finished mending your clothes. Do you think—I mean, could I..."

"Of course, I'll take them with me and spare you the wrath of my mother for an extra day."

"Her wrath? Is she angry? I'm not late with the mending."

"Not angry about the mending..." David pursed his lips and his shoulders lifted as he inhaled.

Understanding landed on Sophie, making her feel the weight of impending doom. "She found out about our date?"

"Well, I wasn't hiding it. She's acting funny—won't come right out and ask, but keeps making little remarks that indicate trouble."

Sophie tensed. "Oh dear."

David put a hand on her arm. "Not for you. I think this is all on me. But it probably *is* a good idea to give her a wide berth for a few days."

Sophie nodded, unsure of the prospect of ever seeing Mrs. Alexander again. She walked over to the pile of clothing and lifted it carefully. "I hope these meet your expectations."

"They sure do." David pulled out his wallet and opened it up. "In fact, why don't I pay you right now? How much do I owe you?"

"No, I don't think you should. It wouldn't be right. I'd feel strange taking your money."

David laughed. "If it makes you feel better, this is my mother's money. She asked me to pay a few bills while I was in town."

Sophie flushed when she saw David pull out two dollars. The wages Mrs. Alexander owed her for hours of tedious stitching was pocket-change for David. Her face burned and even though she tried to talk herself out of the embarrassment, she couldn't change her body's reaction to the emotion. She looked down at her feet, the floor blurring so that she couldn't see where the worn pattern of the carpet inched towards a hole that needed patched.

"Ah, Sophie, I'm sorry. I've messed up again, haven't I?" David slipped his wallet back into his pocket. "I wasn't thinking about how that would make you feel. I really was trying to be helpful."

Sophie worried that if she raised her head, the moisture in her eyes would turn to traitorous tears and she refused to cry in front of another man. With a shuddering breath, she blinked and lifted her head.

"Darling? Are you okay?" David didn't wait for an answer, instead he pulled her into an embrace that nearly undid Sophie just as she was grasping for control of the situation. For a moment, she rested her head against his chest. Then she heard Maggie talking to her dolly about the man with 'fwowers for Mommy' and Sophie pulled back.

"I'm okay now." She stood straight and forced a smile.

"You don't have to pretend for me, Sophie. I apologize. I'd still like to take the clothes and we can work out the payment another time if you—"

"A dollar and sixty-five cents," Sophie blurted out. "She pays me about ten cents per alteration, sometimes more if the mending is more involved. Your mother is a kind and generous woman."

David pursed his lips. She knew he was looking for a facial tic that might reveal her true feelings, but he wouldn't see it. She *was* grateful for Mrs. Alexander even if "kind" was a white lie. He pulled out his wallet and counted out three dollars. He held them up. "Don't you dare argue with me. I can see that pile of clothes and I'd like them back. My favorite white shirt is in there. The one with the ripped buttonhole." David handed Sophie the money, his eyes holding hers.

Sophie hesitated for a second, but then she took the money, folded the bills in half and slipped them into the pocket of her housedress. "Thank you, David. If I were a betting woman, I'd guess that your mother has emptied the rest of your closet. Perhaps you could drop them by tomorrow." She waited two beats and then winked.

David burst out laughing. He ducked his head and kissed Sophie's cheek. "Tomorrow then," he murmured.

Sophie covered her cheek, savoring the soft brush of his lips on her skin. David scooped up the box of neatly folded clothing and opened the door. "Good-bye Margaret."

Sophie closed the door and Maggie folded her arms. "I don't like him. My name is Maggie, not Margaret."

Sophie laughed. "You're my Maggie." She hugged her daughter. "My little piece of sunshine."

Chapter 17 – Roses in Winter

It had taken Leland longer than he anticipated to glue a decorative piece of scrollwork on a china cabinet and then to scrub the glue from underneath a couple fingernails. He jogged out to the pickup, skipping over a large puddle, and climbed inside. He smiled as he put the key in the ignition. The plan was to use his ration card to purchase sugar for Sophie. Maggie's birthday was coming up and Sophie had mentioned that she wasn't sure how to fulfill her daughter's wish of a unicorn cake with pink fluffy frosting. He'd pick up the powdered sugar and deliver it to Sophie with an invitation for another date. It was only Monday so hopefully the store would still have some in stock by the time he got there.

He turned the key and the pickup jigged once and sputtered. Leland checked the gauges and popped the hood, stepping up on the fender to look at the engine. Everything appeared in order and his stomach clenched with worry. The pickup was fifteen years old and vital to his carpentry business. Hopefully Sterling Dennison would be able to fix it for him.

Leland called Sterling and asked him a couple questions. In the end, Sterling advised him to tow the pickup over to his shop. So Leland called one of his neighbors to help him get to Sterling's shop, and within an hour they had dropped him off and Leland was looking under the hood with Sterling.

"It does look like it's in good condition." Sterling hopped down and walked around the pickup, limping slightly from an injury he'd sustained in the war. He was only a year or two younger than Leland and he had served his country and returned with scars that would never heal. Even knowing that, Leland envied his ability to do what Leland had not. Sterling turned and smiled. "So how have you been?"

"As well as can be expected I guess. How about you?"

Sterling frowned. "I actually expected to be a lot better, but that's another story. Have you been seeing anyone?"

"I went on a couple dates and I was on my way to ask her on another date when my pickup wouldn't start." Leland didn't explain his roundabout way of asking Sophie on a date. He still needed to get to the Safeway to pick up the sugar. It was a lot easier to ask someone on a date when you had a reason for stopping by.

"Really? Who is she?"

"Keith Harper's little sister, Sophie Wright."

Sterling nodded. "I don't remember much of Sophie, but I've seen her since she moved back. She's beautiful."

"Well, don't get any ideas because as beautiful as she is I've probably already got too much competition."

"Can I give you a little advice?" Sterling wiped his hands on a greasy rag.

"Sure."

"Come with me." Sterling walked behind his house to an area off to the side of the back yard. There was a small building of tin, wood, and glass that Leland recognized as a hothouse. Sterling opened the door and motioned for Leland to follow. Inside were several rosebushes in bloom. The blood red hue against the white snow in the window was a beautiful contrast. Leland stepped inside and the aroma filled his nostrils.

"I didn't know you were a gardener too."

Sterling lifted one shoulder and let it drop. "Family tradition. This was my mother's legacy. I've made a lot of improvements to the building and now I sell some of these flowers. But you know, if I don't cut these the right way or handle them tenderly they will scarcely last three days. With the right preparation though and care afterward, they will bloom for a week and that's why people drive from Calloway Grove to buy one rose."

"These are lovely, but why are you showing me this?" Leland bent and inhaled the scent of a dark pink rose.

"Love is like these roses. I realized that too late." Sterling picked a petal off the ground and rubbed it between his fingers. "Don't hesitate. Don't wait to tell her that you love her. And if you think she's the one, put a ring on her finger before someone else does."

Leland took a step back, lifting his hands. "You talk as if it's easy for me. There's much better pickings around here than me."

Sterling shook his head. "You and I both know that's not true, Leland. I didn't get to see you as a father, but people talk and I know that you were a good one."

Leland shook his head. "Don't."

"No, you don't," Sterling said. "Don't let your fear keep you from grabbing the happiness that's right in front of you."

Leland swallowed. "I guess I'd better get moving then. I still need to walk to the grocery store."

By the time Leland had purchased the sugar and walked back home it was almost three o'clock. He'd expected to get a lot more work done that day, but all he had to show for it was the brown paper bag containing two pounds of powdered sugar. Maybe it would be better to wait until Sterling fixed his pickup. He had said it would probably be ready by tomorrow afternoon. The thought had barely entered Leland's mind when it was chased by Sterling's forceful words, "Don't hesitate."

Leland picked up the phone and dialed Keith's number even though he knew Keith wasn't home. Debbie answered and Leland told her briefly that his pickup had broken down but he needed to get something to Sophie.

"LaRue's husband, Billy, works not two blocks from your house and he gets off at four today. I'll get a message to him to come and pick you up. Keith can take you home later."

Leland replaced the receiver and looked out the window at the lowering sun. He'd work until Billy came to get him. He needed to stay busy to keep his nerves at bay. It took a few minutes to organize the orders that he wanted to finish up in the next two weeks, but soon Leland was cutting and shaping the wood for a hope chest. Mrs. Doris Marchant had ordered the hope chest to be made for her daughter, Linda. It was to be an engagement gift so Mrs. Marchant had asked that Leland keep everything confidential because David Alexander hadn't asked her to marry him yet. Leland pressed his lips together, a bitter taste in his mouth when he thought of David. The poor woman didn't know what she was in for if she was going to marry the fighter pilot who thought he walked on air.

"But if I wait until that happens, I can't rightly give her an engagement gift six weeks after the fact, can I?" Mrs. Marchant, of course, hadn't waited for a reply from Leland, "So I decided it's best to plan ahead and plan for the best. I've heard how very busy you're getting so I do so appreciate you agreeing to this. Linda has waited a terribly long time for this war to end so that she could marry David. I can't imagine that he'll keep her waiting much longer."

When she had left the shop, Leland had made a few notes, all the while wondering what someone did with an engagement gift if the engagement didn't occur. With a shake of his head, Leland refocused, marking more cut lines with a thick pencil. Since Mrs. Marchant had paid in advance, the worry had turned to a mere curiosity.

At ten after four, Billy pulled in and honked his horn, causing Leland's heart to jig and stall just like his pickup had earlier. Dusting off his hands, Leland put on his coat and grabbed the bag of sugar. By the time Billy dropped him off at Sophie's, the top of the brown paper sack was crumpled and Leland's hands were sweating. "Thanks again for the ride." He nodded to Billy.

"Good luck," Billy said. "I have a feeling you're going to need it." His smile was one of pity as he waved and drove off. Leland turned toward Sophie's front door, confused as to what Billy meant. Leland's shoulders dropped as realization brought everything into sharper focus. Billy was probably hinting at what someone else had likely said—that Leland didn't stand a chance with the beautiful Sophie Wright. Or maybe it was one of the hushed murmurs that he was unfit to be a parent. Doubts swirled through his mind. His history was a minefield of dangerous possibilities that any woman would be a fool to take a chance on. He stood rooted to the spot halfway up Sophie's walkway, indecision turning his insides into tight cords that reached up and bound his heart. Five minutes before, that same heart had been beating near out of his chest with expectation at seeing the joy in Sophie's smile when he gave her the sugar. But now, his lifeblood constricted and the pathetic gift of sugar seemed more than inconsequential, even laughable considering the person who held the gift.

Turning, Leland took one step back toward the road and was met by an icy gust of wind that flipped his coat open and made him take two steps back. Leland gasped as the chilling fingers of the wind seemed to go right through his clothing and jolt his heart awake. He had come today with a purpose in mind and as Leland's mind cleared, memories flashed through his head of his life before with Rhonda and Jessie—a life he had thrown away. He'd vowed to live again away from the shackles of guilt and grief and he would. With blood pumping in his ears, Leland pivoted and walked up to the front door before another thought could enter his mind. His knock was light, but the vibrations from the wood seemed to circle around his hand, emanating with a warmth that invited him inside as Sophie opened the door.

"Leland, what a nice surprise. Would you like to come in?"

"I'm sorry I didn't call first, I–uh, I just–well, I really wanted to bring you a little something," Leland stammered.

"Please come in," she repeated. "It's so cold out. I keep looking for spring to come, but she sure is taking her time."

Leland followed her inside, closing the door behind him with one hand and gripping the bag of sugar with the other. "I'm running low on maple and I've been holding off driving these roads to get another load in Colorado City, but I might have to brave the elements if we don't get a break from this winter soon."

"So instead of driving to the city, you decided to come here?"

Leland nodded. He shifted from one foot to the other, uncertain if Sophie would invite him to sit down or take his coat off. She must have picked up on his uneasiness because she reached out her hand. "Why don't you have a seat? Hang your coat on the peg right there."

Her smile was genuine, but there was a brief flicker of startled emotion in her eyes. Leland took in the room and was about to speak again when he saw the vase on the table with three red roses. Roses in winter were an expensive and extravagant gift. Leland would've said that they weren't even available in Aspen Falls had he not seen Sterling's rose garden himself. Pulling his eyes from the roses, Leland shed his coat and hung it on the peg. He swallowed and held out the bag of sugar before the last of his resolve drained away.

"I brought you something for Maggie's birthday."

Sophie looked at the bag and then at Leland. She reached forward tentatively, her fingers brushing his as he handed her the sack. "For her birthday?" She looked down the hall and as she did, Leland tuned into the sounds of Maggie and Garth playing. Sophie unrolled the bag and dipped her finger in the powdered sugar. She put her finger to her mouth and Leland could almost taste the sweetness. "How did you know?"

Leland shrugged. "You said she really wanted that cake with frosting."

Sophie's eyes softened and she stepped forward, embracing Leland while still holding the bag of sugar. He was so surprised that he wasn't sure what to do. He slowly hugged Sophie, resting his hands on the small of her back.

"Thank you," she whispered. "Thank you so much."

"I'm glad you like it." Leland's voice sounded small to his ears.

Stepping out of the embrace, Sophie set the bag of sugar on the kitchen table. "This is so kind. I can't believe you remembered such a small detail."

Leland remembered what Sterling had told him about grabbing the happiness in front of him and telling Sophie how he felt about her. He tasted the metallic tang of bitterness in the back of his mouth. Ironic that Sterling used roses as an example to move Leland toward expressing his feelings for Sophie and now those same roses stood guard making sure that Leland kept his words to himself. He cleared his throat. "Not a small detail. A little girl's birthday is the best day of the year."

"Oh, Leland." Sophie reached out and took his hand. "Thank you for saying that. One of my friends said I was making too big of a deal of a simple day and that plenty of cakes were made without frosting."

"What's a cake without frosting?" Leland squeezed Sophie's fingers gently. "Sophie, will you go out to dinner with me on Friday night?"

Her eyes widened and she turned toward the kitchen where the roses stood. "Um, I'd love to, but I can't on Friday and Maggie's birthday is Saturday. Would it be all right if we went a different day?"

Leland found himself nodding, unsure of how to respond. He followed Sophie's errant gaze to the roses and inclined his head. "I understand if you'd rather not. I see that another fellow is after your heart."

Sophie blushed and bit her bottom lip. Her reaction was like a punch to the gut and Leland sucked in a breath, trying to find words to fill the awkward silence. He put a hand on the back of his neck. "Well–I, uh..."

"Mommy, Garth is smackin' my dolly again and I won't stand for it!" Maggie ran down the hallway, crashing into Sophie's legs in tears.

"I wasn't!" Garth hollered, following Maggie. "All she ever wants to do is play with her dolly."

"Children, we have a guest," Sophie said. "Where are your manners?"

Maggie looked over to where Leland stood by the couch. "Hi, Leland."

"Hello, to you." Leland leaned closer to Maggie. "Did I hear that you might have a birthday coming up soon?"

"Oh yes! My birthday is tomorrow!" She bounced up and down.

"Not tomorrow," Sophie said. "You still have four days."

"Silly," Garth said. "She thinks every day is her birthday."

Maggie frowned at Garth, but turned back to Leland. "Are you coming to my birthday party?"

"Oh, no, I don't—"

"Actually, that would be perfect. Why don't you come?" Sophie's green eyes brightened. "We're only having a small family get-together—you already know all the guests."

Leland straightened and smiled at the little family. "Well, then, I guess I can't refuse, can I?"

"You might need to bring her a present," Garth whispered loud enough for everyone to hear.

Leland laughed as Sophie shushed Garth. He crouched down in front of Maggie. "You promise to be an extra good girl and help your mommy and I'll come to your party and maybe bring you a present."

"I will!" Maggie leaped into Leland's arms. "I love you," she said, and she wrapped her little hands around his neck, hugged him and then as quick as a breath she was running back down the hall with her dolly, chattering about her party. Garth ran after her, leaving Leland with a strange feeling in his chest and a lump in his throat. He rose slowly, forcing himself to make eye contact with Sophie.

"That was so sweet," she said. Her eyes glistened with moisture and the smile she directed at Leland helped him identify that strange feeling in his chest—it was his heart, beating steadily with a pattern he remembered from long ago.

It wasn't until Leland had said his goodbyes and was halfway to Keith's that he recognized the pattern his heart was beating. Those roses were a genuine problem because if Leland were being honest with himself, his heart was telling him that he was in love with Sophie Wright.

Chapter 18 — The Warning

It wasn't until Sophie's children were tucked into bed that she allowed herself to study out the confusing situation her heart was tangled up in. The bag of sugar rested on the table next to the vase of red roses. Leland had seen the roses and she was about to tell him that they were from David Alexander, but the children had come rushing in and there wasn't a good way to have the conversation in front of them. She'd had another chance there at the end before he left, but she'd chickened out and now she was left with the sugary sweet smell of roses and the vital ingredient to Maggie's frosting circling around her head.

How would Leland feel when he found out that she and David were dating? Because with a town as small as Aspen Falls, it wouldn't be long until Leland learned who his competition was. Sophie frowned. Is that how she viewed the two men? That wasn't it. They were so different and if she were being fully honest with herself, she hadn't told Leland because she didn't want to scare him off. His level of confidence couldn't hold a candle to David's. Leland had been practically sweating just giving her the bag of sugar which was a much more meaningful gift than the roses.

Thinking about how Leland interacted with her children, especially Maggie, made Sophie's throat thick with emotion. He was a completely different man than David, although they both seemed to be good men in their own right. After the mistakes she'd made in her past, she owed it to herself to study out the situation thoroughly. She would spend time with both men later this week and hopefully have a chance to sort out her feelings.

Tuesday morning, someone rapped on her door and Sophie paused to smooth her hair back. Had David returned with more clothing? Sophie licked her lips and opened the front door.

"Oh, Dai—Mr. Okado, uh—what are you—I mean, how are you?" she tripped all over her words.

Mrs. Alexander's favorite employee held out an armful of clothes. It only took one glance to note that none of David's clothing was in the pile. "Mrs. Alexander, she want you to mend these clothes and return Friday, please."

Sophie's stomach clenched with fear. There was some kind of veiled threat in the pile of clothing. Her mind whirred over the possibilities, trying to figure out what angle Mrs. Alexander was going for this time. Obviously her ploy to put Sophie in her place by mending all of David's clothing had backfired. Sophie reached out her arms for the clothing. Mr. Okado nodded and took a step down before Sophie blurted out, "Wait. Please."

The petite man turned. "Yes?"

Sophie had gazed into his eyes enough time to know that behind the meek innocence was a shrewdness that was often underestimated by others. She had the feeling that nothing got past Daisetsu Okado. She swallowed the ball of anxiety and clutched the clothing. "Dai, I have a question and if you could help me I promise I won't breathe a word to anyone."

Dai nodded once.

Sophie lowered her voice. "What is Mrs. Alexander trying to do by having you deliver these clothes to me?"

Dai's forehead crinkled. "She say to bring on Friday, but for you I tell. Bring the clothes Thursday, even if it means staying up through the night to finish." He held her gaze for a moment and then turned, walking briskly back to his car.

The foreboding tone to his words brought everything into sharper focus. Somehow Mrs. Alexander knew of David's plans to take her to dinner on Friday. But that wasn't until evening. What could she possibly plan during the day that would derail the date with her son?

The weather continued to make it difficult for the children to exert their extra energy. They ventured out into the snow for a few minutes, only to return, wet and miserable. Sophie ended up taking them with her to the market to grab a few things. The kids were walking down the aisles with their hands behind their backs like Sophie had instructed when Serena Tanaka walked around the end of an aisle. Sophie quickened her step. "Hello, Serena. How have you been?"

Serena looked up and her face lifted in a smile. "We are good, but tired of the cold."

"You and me both," Sophie said. "Hey, Garth has been asking about Emika. He said she doesn't come to school very often. Has she been ill?"

Serena shook her head. "No, but the doctors tell us to be very careful about school. She is still not strong enough to fight the germs."

Sophie nodded. "Do you think it would be okay if you came over to visit and let the kids play at our house?"

"I'm sure Emika would love that." Serena brightened.

"Maybe Thursday after school?"

Serena nodded. "I will come and bring my children." Serena touched Sophie's arm. "You are a good friend."

"Thank you," Sophie replied. "I'll see you in a few days." Sophie smiled as Serena made her way to the boxes of pasta. When she turned, she saw Mildred Chastain watching her with a horrified expression from the other end of the aisle. Sophie looked behind her to see what had caught Mildred's attention, but there was nothing but a stack of soup cans.

Mildred hurried toward her. She was in her mid-forties and she had lost her only son in the war. She still wore black, with her hair pulled back in a severe bun. "I can't believe you would be seen talking to a Jap in public."

Sophie sucked in a breath. "I was talking to my *friend*, Mrs. Tanaka."

"Your friend?" Mildred's expression was lined in deep shock.

"Yes, my friend. Garth is friends with her daughter, Emika. They nearly lost her last year to polio. She is a beautiful little girl."

"Well, it simply isn't right, you know. You're putting yourself at risk."

"How?"

"You think just because the war is over that everything is going to go back to normal?"

"No, it will never be the same," Sophie replied. "But it would be a shame to forget the lessons that Hitler taught us about hate and distrust."

"I see," Mildred sniffed. "Well, don't say I didn't warn you."

Sophie gave her a stiff smile and walked quickly down another aisle. The prejudice against the Japanese people from certain citizens of Aspen Falls was foreign to Sophie. First of all, because there hadn't been very many Japanese-Americans in her neighborhood when she was a child. And secondly, Sophie had been away from Aspen Falls for the entire war so she wasn't there to witness the subtle shift towards neighbors who were once trusted friends.

Sophie turned the aisle and flinched as she saw Mildred

approaching with her basket. There were so many words on her tongue that she could speak—of how Sophie understood that Mildred blamed the Japanese even though it had been the Germans who had killed her son. Sophie could speak of forgiveness, referring to the bombs at Pearl Harbor that took her husband's life—bombs that had been dropped by Japanese kamikaze pilots. But it wouldn't make any difference. She saw how Mildred wanted something to hate, something to blame, to make sense of her son's death. And Sophie didn't want to talk about something that would lead to a conversation about how she didn't blame the Japanese for Calvin's death. Sophie looked down and moved to a row of packaged cookies as Mildred passed her. A strange scent tickled her nostrils as the woman's steps receded. It was almost as if there was an acrid smell of smoke in the air, billowing like a cloud behind her.

Chapter 19 — Finding Hope

February 1946

On Wednesday night, Leland carried a paper bag full of supplies from the hardware store to his pickup, thankful that the old brute was up and running again. He dropped the sack into the bed of the pickup and had his hand on the door when he heard something that drew his attention. He stopped, listening in the darkness for the distinctive whining he'd heard. A couple seconds later, he was rewarded for his patient listening when he heard the cry of an animal.

There was an alleyway next to the hardware store that was often filled with junk and that's where the noise came from. Leland grabbed a flashlight from his pickup and walked across the muddy parking lot. The whimpering increased as he drew closer to a pile of boxes near the front of the alley. Leland flicked on his flashlight and lifted a wooden crate. The puppy was cold, its eyes shut tight as its chest barely moved. He didn't hear a cry and he wondered for a moment if the puppy was even alive, but the mournful whimper had been loud enough to draw his attention from across the street.

Leland shone the flashlight back toward the street and then to the pile of boxes. He nudged the boxes, but there was no sign of the mother dog. Tucking the flashlight in his pocket, Leland bent over and scooped up the puppy that was black as the night. The puppy couldn't have been more than two months old, definitely too young to be left out in the cold. Leland had always wanted a dog, but Rhonda didn't like them—had a deep-seated fear of them. He'd been on his own for nearly two years and though he'd thought of it occasionally, the right dog had never come along. But the little pup in his arms might be just the one for him. If Jessie were alive, the puppy would have been wrapped up in her doll blankets in no time. Leland immediately thought of Garth and Maggie and he prayed as he walked down the street that the helpless animal in his arms would live.

He drove home with the puppy whimpering softly in his lap. Flipping on the front room light, Leland wrapped the puppy in an old towel and put another log on the fire. Then he sat right next to the hearth and gently rubbed the pup's silky black fur. He stopped occasionally and pressed a finger on the puppy's chest, feeling for the weak heartbeat. After nearly twenty minutes, the heart rate grew stronger. Leland tucked the puppy next to the fire and went to the kitchen where he warmed milk in a pan. He returned with a saucer of milk, dipped his finger in the liquid and touched the puppy's lips. At first, there was no response, so Leland carefully touched the puppy's tongue with a milky finger. With a tiny squeak the puppy moved its tongue and Leland hurried to repeat the motion. When the puppy swallowed, Leland nearly cried out with joy. He helped the puppy swallow a few more drops of milk.

"You're going to make it, girl," Leland whispered. He held the puppy close and dripped milk, one drop at a time into the tiny animal's mouth. Gradually the puppy's breathing returned to normal but she didn't open her eyes.

Leland was awakened the next morning by someone rubbing the finest sandpaper against his cheek. How had he fallen asleep in his shop, and why would someone use sandpaper on his face? A tiny whimper jolted Leland from the last stage of sleep and his eyes popped open. The puppy licked his nose and Leland laughed. The puppy stood on his chest, tiny pink tongue hanging out and joy sparkling in her amber-colored eyes. Leland picked up the puppy as he sat up and looked to the side. The fire had burned down to coals and the dish of milk had been licked clean.

"Well, aren't you a good girl?" he rubbed the pup's belly and she licked his hand. Leland walked to the kitchen and rummaged around in the icebox until he found a piece of meatloaf from a few nights before. He set the meatloaf on a dish and laughed when the puppy growled and pounced on the meat. "I guess that means you're here to stay. I'd better come up with a name for you."

The wind blew outside, making the ice crystals on the trees shimmer in the early morning sunlight. Leland closed his eyes and listened to the wind. He remembered the time after Jessie died when the wind had howled with a haunting melody, and later when a lavender breeze had helped change the course of his life. The music box had played a significant part in changing the scenery of his life. The tune had compelled him to change and comforted him when it seemed he had no more strength. Through it all, he had developed a skill of listening to the world around him. He heard more than people said, and saw more in himself than he'd dared to hope because of the song of the wind.

Leland's breath was barely a whisper as he continued to listen to his surroundings. There was something humming on the current of wind that morning. It was a new sound that made Leland want to run outside and chase after the wind. There was a promise of new life on the breeze and Leland determined that he would hold onto that hope with everything he had in him.

"Hope," Leland whispered, stroking the pup's black coat. "I'm going to call you Hope."

Hope accompanied Leland to his woodshop later that afternoon where he found an excellent piece of wood from an old apple tree to make Maggie's birthday gift. A few hours later, he had almost finished a rocking chair that was the perfect size for her doll. Using a broken spindle from an earlier project, Leland fashioned the chair as a replica to the adult size rockers he built. Hope pulled on his pant leg with her teeth, whining, and Leland chuckled. "You're still a little mite, but you have some fire in you. I wonder what Garth and Maggie will think of you."

Leland smiled with the beginnings of a daydream where he gathered the courage to invite Sophie's little family to his house to meet Hope. Three red roses came to mind, dousing the excitement he'd just imagined when Sophie's kids held the little black pup. Hope licked his hand and Leland rubbed her head. Whoever had given the roses to Sophie must not be coming to Maggie's birthday party, right? Leland couldn't imagine that Sophie would invite him if there was an interested suitor on the invite list. He took comfort in that thought and promised himself that he would take what little courage he had and ask to see Sophie again.

First, he needed to finish Maggie's birthday rocker and then get on to the orders piling up after the impromptu gift. He didn't really have the time to build the chair that morning, but Leland prayed that God would make his hands more able to complete the work so that he could put a smile on Maggie's darling face when Saturday arrived.

Chapter 20 — The Alexanders

The fingers of Sophie's left hand had several prick marks from the needle she used to mend Mrs. Alexander's clothing. Her stitching had taken on a furious pace last night as she watched the hands of the clock move toward midnight. She had finished everything before one o'clock and slept fitfully the remainder of the night—a cloud of worry hovering above her in the shape of Mrs. Alexander. Thursday morning, the sun hid behind the clouds, but Sophie pasted on a bright smile as she bundled up Maggie and drove to the edge of town with Mrs. Alexander's clothes. The stately mansion appeared gloomy and ominous, but Sophie would not be deterred. Dai had offered her a lifeline and although she couldn't yet imagine the circumstances of Mrs. Alexander's scheme, she prayed that she would be able to avoid the worst of the woman's wrath.

She moved quickly up the walkway with Maggie in tow, and knocked on the door. Dai opened it immediately, as if he'd been waiting for her to arrive. He smiled and nodded, stepping aside for Sophie to bring in the clothing, with Maggie trailing behind her.

"I like this castle," Maggie said. Her bright voice echoed throughout the arched entryway.

"It will be just a moment," Dai said. He exited, almost marching to an invisible tune.

Sophie took the moment to compose herself, lifting her cheeks in a smile as she surveyed the room. She'd stood in this foyer on several occasions and each time, she'd been struck by the lack of warmth in the home. It was more like a museum covered with Mrs. Alexander's trophies of her wealthy existence. One shelf held five porcelain vases, hand painted in painstaking detail with different flowers. Sophie liked the one with a purple pansy, painted in lifelike colors and dainty strokes.

"These are pretty." Maggie crouched in front of a display of birds, all carved out of a dark wood.

"Don't touch anything. Just look at them with your eyes." Sophie pointed at a delicate hummingbird, its wings outstretched and long beak reaching toward a lily. The carving was exquisite. Sophie had never seen anything like it before. "Isn't that hummingbird wonderful?"

"Interesting you would notice the hummingbird," Mrs. Alexander spoke as she entered the foyer, startling Sophie. "That is one of David's favorites as well."

Sophie almost pressed her lips together before she remembered to smile and command complete control of her emotions so that none of them appeared in her eyes. "Good morning Mrs. Alexander. I've brought this clothing back to you. There are some beautiful pieces here."

Mrs. Alexander frowned. "I thought I sent a message for you to return them on Friday, and yet, here you are, on a Thursday interrupting my morning."

Sophie nodded. "Yes, I received the message, but I couldn't come tomorrow. I apologize for the inconvenience." She lifted the pile of clothes into Dai's waiting arms.

"You did a fine job on David's clothing. When he's married, I hope that I will be able to retain your services for he and his wife."

"Yes, of course." Sophie didn't hesitate, didn't even swallow, even though her throat burned like it was coated with ash. She reached for Maggie's hand, squeezing it gently, grounding herself in the moment.

Mrs. Alexander took one small step forward. "You do such fine work. Tedious patchwork like that would be quite beneath the future Mrs. Alexander."

The words were intended as a harsh slap across Sophie's cheeks. They were meant to leave red marks like handprints from being struck by her words, but Sophie merely straightened. Perfect control would be the only thing Nadine Alexander would see on the fine planes of Sophie's face. If there was one place Nadine had underestimated her, it was in the realm of control. Sophie hadn't shed real tears for five years. She knew how to survive under a dictator and Nadine was no match for Calvin Wright. "Do you have anything else you'd like me to work on in the coming week?"

Nadine's nostrils flared slightly. She was also a master of control and Sophie wondered where she'd learned the art and why her life had required her to practice it as studiously as a stage actress. That was a thought she needed to hold onto, because if Sophie had learned anything from being married to Cal, it was never to accept the reality people offered her without questioning it.

The woman reached inside her purse and extracted one dollar and a few coins. She extended her hand toward Sophie. "I've put in an order for more material, so if it arrives I'd like you to get started on a new dress for me."

"Oh, that would be lovely. What kind of dress?" Sophie took the money, grateful for the change in topic. She could talk sewing all day, but the veiled threats concerning David made her feel as if her smile were etched in stone.

"A summer dress with lace detail," Mrs. Alexander replied. "I'd like to wear it to David's wedding."

Another verbal slap stung Sophie's skin and she felt a bit of color seeping into her face. She took a quick breath, struggling for control. "Oh, I hadn't heard that David was engaged. A summer wedding would be wonderful." Sophie's mask clicked back into place, although she squeezed Maggie's hand a bit too tight.

"Mommy, can we go now?" Maggie slid her hand from Sophie's grasp and folded her arms. "I'm bored."

"David is not engaged yet," Mrs. Alexander said. "He's been a bit distracted, but you know how men are–such fickle creatures. None of them would get married without someone helping them along."

Sophie nodded. "Well, I hope you're able to get the material. It's wise of you to order it early. Life is so unpredictable these days."

"Yes, that *is* true. Good day, Mrs. Wright." Mrs. Alexander turned at the same moment that Sophie pivoted toward the door.

Dai hurried to open the door for her. On the way out, Sophie touched Dai's arm. "Thank you."

To an observer, Sophie was simply thanking him for opening the door, but both Dai and Sophie knew that she was thanking him for saving her from some unknown fate. Had she entered this same door tomorrow, Sophie could only guess at who might be waiting to receive her. Nadine Alexander was a dangerous woman, and Sophie felt like she'd barely escaped with her job intact today.

Maggie chattered about the pretty house as Sophie tucked her into the car, and Sophie answered but her mind was elsewhere. Maybe she should cancel her date with David tomorrow. Had his mother discovered his plans? How far would she go to keep her only son away from the poor seamstress who was only worthy to repair the holes in his trousers?

About thirty minutes after Garth returned home from school, Serena arrived with her children. Sophie barely had time to say hello to Emika before Garth was tugging her down the hall. Maggie lingered over the sleeping form of baby Shun for a few minutes before skipping away.

Once they were settled, Serena said, "Mr. Leland, he is a good man."

"Yes, you mentioned that," Sophie said. "I wonder, do you know him well?"

Serena leaned back in her chair. "My husband knows him better than I do."

"You see, I'm confused by him." Sophie tucked a curl behind her ear. At this time of day, her hair started letting itself down, the heavy locks unwilling to stay pinned back neatly. "He seems interested in me but at the same time he acts terrified."

Serena sat in silence, thoughts roaming over her features so quickly that Sophie couldn't grab onto any clues. "His past, it give him worries for the future, but I think you would understand him. You lost your husband."

Sophie's mouth went dry. "I—uh, everyone deals with their grief differently. Sometimes it feels like Cal was just here yesterday and other times, my life with him seems like a dream melting away into nothingness." She didn't add that most of it was like a nightmare that she was happy not to recall.

Serena nodded. "I guess, Mr. Leland—he maybe haunted by ghosts of his past. He think of failure, but it was a mistake."

"His marriage?"

Serena scrutinized her, the skin of her temples tightening. "I think we often have to forgive ourselves again and again for mistakes because we don't trust that God takes our mistakes and gives us forgiveness. Do you believe God has forgiven you?"

The words landed on Sophie's heart, piercing it so that she couldn't pretend that she hadn't heard them. Serena had spoken more clearly than Sophie had ever heard her speak, with barely a trace of her accent. Serena gazed at Sophie, her eyes soft, yet discerning.

"I do believe that he forgives me when I ask."

"And yet you do not ask."

"How do you–what do you mean?"

Serena reached out her fingers and touched the back of Sophie's hand. "It is written on your heart, hidden in your face, cool on your skin."

"What?"

"Sorrow. Pain. Suffering."

Sophie swallowed, withdrawing her hand. She covered her heart, looking down at her trembling fingers.

"Just like Leland," Serena whispered. "A heart lined with gold. You could heal each other's hearts."

Maggie returned to the table holding her doll, Charlotte. "Can I show baby Shun my baby when he wakes up?"

Serena smiled, touching Maggie's cheek. "Of course."

"I'm going to be a mommy someday and have real babies like Charlotte."

"You will be a wonderful mother just like your mother," Serena said.

The way that Serena spoke soothed the piercing ache in Sophie's heart and brought a light to Maggie's eyes. She held her doll close and twirled, humming a lullaby.

Sophie watched her daughter; her joy in the sweet innocence that Maggie lived with every day was revived each time Sophie let herself soak in the magic of these ordinary moments. She looked up to see Serena watching her. The woman who had endured the relocation camps, almost losing her daughter, and returning to her home to be snubbed by those who were once her friends had more strength than many. She had eyes of wisdom from experience. The choices that she and her family had made to live without regret, facing the future instead of the past were admirable. Serena smiled at Sophie and her eyes were nearly enfolded by her happy face. That small feature was enough to bring hate from the hearts of people who didn't understand forgiveness either.

It wasn't until much later that Sophie had time to consider the words that Serena had shared with her. Somehow she had read Sophie's soul—seen into that dark place where Sophie carried so much guilt over her marriage with Cal. For so many years she had wished that she could have been a better wife, that she could have been enough for him if she would've tried harder, known how to speak kinder. She knew now that it wouldn't have mattered what she did. Cal made his own choices in life without regard for others—especially without regard for his wife and family.

In quiet moments, Sophie had cursed God and screamed at him inside, asking why she had to suffer so much hurt and pain and the answer had always been there. But she didn't understand it until today. Serena was right. Sophie needed to ask forgiveness so that she could heal. She needed to let go of the pain, sorrow, and hate. If only it were as easy as filling up a bottle with her anguish and burying it with Cal. There was a constant war within herself. How could she be a good mother when she was grateful that her children's father had died?

Chapter 21 – Leland's House

Leland was making good progress on the dresser for the Montgomerys Friday morning when he discovered that his small planer was missing. He hunted around for a few minutes before remembering that Keith had borrowed it last week to fix one of the drawers on Amy's dresser. He'd also borrowed his favorite three-quarter inch chisel for the project. Leland frowned. He could use one of his larger planers, but he'd much rather be precise so that the drawers on the dresser would fit correctly. He needed both tools to finish the dresser with the quality he'd promised. Dusting off his hands, Leland called over to Keith's house and Debbie answered after only two rings.

"Debbie, have you seen my chisel or small planer around?"

"Yes, they're right here by the door. I told Keith to take them by your house this morning," Debbie said. "Looks like he forgot and now you're needin' one or the other, right?"

"Both, actually." Leland sighed. "I'll try to work on some other things first and maybe I can come over and get them later."

"No, don't bother. I'll get them over to you."

"I thought Keith had the car?"

"He does, but Sophie has her car. I know she had some errands to run today. I'll take these tools over and see if maybe she could bring them by."

Leland's heart tapped twice against his rib cage.

"Leland, you still there?"

"Uh—yes, that'll be just fine. If you can get them here one way or another, I'd be grateful."

"Sure thing."

After he hung up the phone, he moved back to his work bench. Would Sophie really come? And if she did, what would he say to her? She'd invited him to Maggie's birthday party on Saturday, but he hadn't asked her out on another date. He rubbed the day old whiskers on his chin and frowned. He hadn't taken the time to shave that morning. He peered at himself in the windowpane. His work overalls were patched in a few places and spotted from various shades of wood stain. It would have to do because he didn't have time to waste. The order for the Montgomerys had been on a tight schedule to begin with and he didn't want to set a precedent for being late on orders. Normally people might forgive something like that with hand-crafted furniture, but because Leland had been a drunk for two years, there wasn't much room for error in his business. Aspen Falls had been forgiving of his addiction and circumstances because everyone knew what had driven Leland to drink. That knowledge was a double-edged sword hanging over his head.

Sometimes he wished he could move away to a place where no one was watching for him to slip up. He shook his head because he didn't like that thinking. The community and their support kept Leland going once he was clean and ready to work wood again. His friend Shunsaku Tanaka spoke so highly of him that Leland had lost count of how many people had come in because of what Shun told them. Leland became lost in his thoughts as he worked with the saw, cutting pieces of walnut for a bed frame. When he checked his watch again, it had already been an hour. He stopped and dusted the sawdust from his hair and clothes and then jumped when someone knocked on the door to his shop.

Leland smiled when he opened the door and found Sophie and her two children standing there.

"We brought your tools!" Garth exclaimed, bursting with pride. "So you can finish building stuff."

"Why, thank you," Leland said. He smiled at Sophie. "I'm sorry you had to do Keith's dirty work. I would've come and got them later, but I do appreciate you saving me the time."

"You must be keeping very busy," Sophie said.

Hope chose that moment to let out a mournful howl. Leland stepped back and Maggie darted around to the box where Hope had been sleeping.

"Mommy, it's a puppy!" She crouched in front of the box and crooned, "Oh, you sweet baby. Can I hold you?" Maggie glanced at Leland for permission.

He nodded. "Hold her on your lap, and don't mind her licking you—it means she likes you."

"You have a puppy?" Garth asked. "Can I hold her too?"

Sophie took a step closer, smiling at the puppy. "As long as you don't frighten her, I'm sure Leland won't mind."

Garth approached cautiously. "When did you get her, Mr. Leland?"

"Just a few nights ago I found her in the alley next to the hardware store carrying on." Leland motioned for Sophie to come inside. "I couldn't find any sign of the mother dog so I don't know if someone abandoned her."

"That's sad," Sophie said. "She's a lucky pup that you found her. It's still been getting quite cold at night."

"What does bandoned mean?" Maggie asked.

"It means that maybe someone left this little pup all alone with no one to take care of her." Leland crouched next to Hope and rubbed her silky ears.

"So my daddy bandoned us?" Maggie sighed and pulled Hope closer to her chest.

Sophie gasped and crouched next to Maggie. "No dear, that's not what happened. Remember how I explained to you that Daddy died which means he can't be here with us anymore."

"Yeah, Dad is in heaven, Mag," Garth replied. "He's like an angel."

Sophie flinched, her eyes narrowed, but then she pressed her lips together and raised the edges into a smile that didn't reach her eyes. "That's right. We won't see Daddy anymore but that doesn't mean you've been abandoned. I'm taking care of you, right?"

If Leland hadn't been watching Sophie's face closely, he would've missed the maelstrom of emotions playing out on her beautiful features. He cleared his throat. "Your mother is doing a wonderful job of taking care of you. And we don't know what happened with this pup. Something could've happened to her mother or her owners. When I found her she was near frozen to death. I bundled her up in a towel and put warm milk on her tongue until she responded."

"So you brought her back to life?" Garth asked. "What's her name?"

"Hope. Do you like the sound of that?"

Sophie lifted her head and met his gaze. "That's sweet." Her eyes softened and there was something hovering behind them that made him want to draw her into an embrace. Sophie turned back and stroked the pup's head. Hope stopped licking Garth's hand and went for Sophie's. "She's a friendly little thing."

"That's for sure," Leland responded. "She's been following me everywhere today—cries if I get out of sight."

"I love her." Maggie rested her head against Hope's squirming body. "I'm going to hold her forever."

Leland arched an eyebrow when Sophie turned to him with a smile. "You're welcome to come visit her anytime you like."

"Okay," Maggie said as if she meant to do just that.

Sophie stood next to Leland, her eyes wandering around his shop. "I know you said you've been busy, but I had no idea how much work you do. There are so many different pieces."

Leland ducked his head, pride filling his chest. "Times have been good to me and I hate to say no because for so long that's all I could do.

I sat idle and now I have too much work to do. Went from one problem to the next."

"It says a lot about the quality of work you do that you're in such high demand."

"Nah, people are finally able to do something other than worry about the war. It's nice to see peace returning."

Sophie nodded. "I agree."

She looked up at Leland and he almost asked her out right then, but the time didn't feel right. He stroked his chin and looked at her two children playing with the black puppy.

"Well, I sure am looking forward to some little girl's birthday," he said.

Maggie looked up, turned the puppy over to Garth and jumped up. "It's tomorrow. Mommy said she's going to make me a cake and that I have to tell you thank you."

Leland chuckled.

"That was supposed to happen on her birthday," Sophie said. "But I wanted to say thank you again."

"My pleasure."

"Okay kids, tell Leland thank you for letting you hold Hope. We need to get back now so he can use those tools."

"Aw, Mom, I wish I could stay and help Leland with his chisel. He's a swell guy."

Sophie reached out and ruffled Garth's hair and he dodged out from under her hand. "Maybe another time. Let's go."

"Thank you for taking the time to bring that to me," Leland said. "I guess Keith will owe you now."

"No, I'll never make up for all he's done to help me and the kids get settled. It's the least I could do, for you too." Sophie smiled at Leland. "Have a good day."

The kids didn't want to leave the darling pup behind, but Sophie finally managed to get them back out the door. Leland stood in the doorway and waved once before letting the wind blow the door shut. He'd almost asked Sophie out on another date but he decided that maybe it was best if he waited until after Maggie's birthday party. She probably had plenty on her mind getting things ready for the get-together. With a glance at his watch, Leland reached for the small planer Sophie had returned to him and went to work.

He'd noticed something about her today that gave clues to her relationship with her husband. Those subtle facial tics described a marriage that might not have been as happy as everyone would consider. It was no surprise that Sophie was so skilled at poker. She must have learned how to hide her feelings years ago and kept practicing ever since. Leland tightened his grip on the planer. He wanted to help Sophie, but how could he when his own secrets were floating around his head begging to be told when they were together? Whenever his hands were idle, his thoughts went too much toward Sophie and the things he hoped his future might hold. As if she could read his thoughts, Hope yipped until Leland put her in the box of wood shavings, patting her head softly until her eyes drooped shut.

Chapter 22 – A Date with David

For the second time in the past month, Sophie entered The Silver Lining on the arm of a handsome man. Tonight, however, felt different than before because she was next to David Alexander. She would have to be blind not to notice the way the employees stood up straighter when David walked by. The waitress was especially complimentary, mentioning his service as a pilot and after they'd placed their orders, the owner of The Silver Lining made his way over to their table.

"I'm honored to have you dine with us tonight, Mr. Alexander." Frank turned to Sophie. "And this must be your valentine?"

Sophie blushed and David coughed, before responding. "Valentine's was yesterday, Frank, but it's my pleasure to be here. This is my lovely date, Sophie Wright, who *I'm* very honored to be here with." David winked as Frank shifted his gaze again to Sophie.

"Ah, yes. I know Sophie. You probably don't remember me, but I've been pals with your dad for as long as I can remember." Frank stood up straighter, his large belly pulling him slightly off-center. "How did you go and grow up so beautiful when just yesterday you were running around in pigtails?"

Sophie laughed and shrugged. "I'm still trying to figure that out myself. Now it's my daughter running around in pigtails being chased by her older brother. Like a page right out of my history."

Frank's face softened. "I was sorry to hear about your loss. Your husband was a hero. To think we have the Navy Cross right here in Aspen Falls."

Sophie stiffened, her spine a steel rod with cold, unforgiving shackles that kept her tense under the will of tainted memories. Thankfully, David intervened. "Sophie still has some difficulties with that tragedy, but thank you for your kindness."

Frank patted her shoulder. "I hope Aspen Falls is a place that will heal your heart. We're happy to have you back."

"Thank you," Sophie managed.

As he walked away, she clutched her napkin in her lap and took one, two breaths, and then pasted a smile on her face. David watched her carefully, mimicking her smile. "Do you ever dream about running away to a beautiful place where no one knows your name?"

Sophie chuckled. "With this endless winter, I think that's all I've dreamed about."

The shift in conversation was subtle, but Sophie was grateful for it. David helped ease her mind away from Cal and his medal of honor. She hated talking about the award for the most dishonorable man she knew.

"Sometimes I dream about the future I'm supposed to have, a wife and family and my father's business," David mused. "And then I dream for a moment about flying again, nothing between me and the earth but my plane and the sky."

"Maybe it's easier to think of flying because you were always in control of your plane." Sophie folded the corner of her napkin over, her fingers trembling slightly. "Life isn't quite like flying."

David leaned back against his chair. "I've never thought of it that way before." He gazed upwards at the ceiling with its decorative tin plates. Sophie followed his gaze, admiring the patina of the aged tin. The building that housed The Silver Lining was nearly sixty years old, and although most things had been updated, it still kept a touch of the nostalgia of ages past in tiny details. Like the brass door knobs on the front doors engraved with an aspen leaf.

David refocused on Sophie. "Do you think it's dangerous to dream?"

She furrowed her brow. "Of course not. Dreaming is what gets us through the hard times—at least it did for me."

David nodded. "My mother always discouraged daydreaming, new ideas, anything outside of her perfectly planned life."

"But surely her life hasn't always been perfectly planned?" Sophie thought of the brief flickers of warmth she'd seen in Mrs. Alexander. One time, she'd happened into a room where Nadine had been caressing a framed photo of her late husband. The woman put on a front that she was neither happy nor sad, but constant, and Sophie didn't believe it for a minute.

"I guess it hasn't, but Mother has always made it appear like her life is completely in control." David took a sip of water. "I know she still misses my father a great deal, which surprises me because they didn't seem like they were deeply in love. It was more like business partners."

"Oh dear," Sophie said. "Maybe that's what you could see, but hopefully there was more to their marriage than that."

David shrugged. "When you exist in the social circles they did, a partnership is vital. My wife will be expected to act a certain way simply because of my last name."

Sophie wrinkled her nose. "We're a long ways from New York and your mother's family. I think you're flattering yourself a tad much to think that this tiny town cares so much about your life."

"Well, tell it to me straight, why don't you?" David raised his eyebrows. "I'm not sure how to take you, Sophie. No woman has ever spoken to me like that before."

"I'm sorry." Sophie ducked her head, her face burning. What had come over her, to speak her mind in such a way to David? There was something about him that had her constantly putting her foot in it.

David reached across the table for her hand. "Please don't be sorry. You might just be more trouble than I bargained for, but I'm willing to find out more about you."

He brushed his thumb over her knuckles. "My question is, do you feel the same about me?"

Sophie lifted her eyes to his, studying his chiseled face and the perfect cut of his brows, almost a straight line across the top of his eyes. She thought of the verbal abuse she'd received from David's mother just yesterday. "I'm not sure how I feel about anything lately."

The waitress brought their food out and David released Sophie's hand quickly, adjusting his napkin on his lap. Sophie had a moment to collect her thoughts, to try to figure out how to answer David's question. There were several things he'd said tonight that tugged on her, made her wonder if trying to go down the path of the Alexanders was something she wanted to attempt.

When she took the first bite of the apricot glazed chicken and the sweetness burst in her mouth, she immediately thought of Leland and his humble bag of sugar. It was still too soon to know enough of either man to make a decision and she felt guilty for entertaining thoughts of both. The permission to take her time and discover who each man truly was came from years of experience living with a man who was nothing like he'd appeared. Although the thought of marrying again used to terrify her, Sophie had spent enough time alone to comprehend that she couldn't be a mother and a father to her children. She wanted them to have a father as much as she wanted to believe that her heart could find love again.

Sophie swallowed the bite of chicken and glanced at David. She'd opened up a tiny peephole into her life with Cal, and David seemed to understand and accept the kind of man she'd been married to. Leland had no idea because Sophie hadn't let him into that dark corner of her life. But David also seemed unaware of how seriously his mother was opposed to the idea of her son dating the seamstress.

Thank goodness David hadn't asked her out on Valentine's day. That would have been a declaration to the town of Aspen Falls that Mrs. Alexander couldn't ignore. Sophie wasn't ready for that anyway, but she did wish for the opportunity to get to know David, and her own heart, without his mother's threats hanging over her.

"This steak is delicious," David said. "How's your chicken?"

"Tender and sweet," Sophie responded, taking another bite.

"Just like you." David nodded. "Yes, I want to get to know you, Sophie, but you'll have to let me see inside that tender heart of yours.

Sophie smiled and took a sip of water. What would happen if she let David or Leland see the injured part of her soul? It might make the choice easier, but when Sophie thought of Leland again, she recalled her first impressions that he understood loss on a deeper level. She wondered if he would allow her to see the burdens that he carried. Yesterday when she'd taken the tools to him, he'd seemed so happy to see her and the kids, but he hadn't asked her out again. Sophie was almost certain at one point he had opened his mouth to do just that before chickening out. Something was holding Leland back; it was more than fear, something deep inside his heart that he kept secret. Sophie took another bite and caught David watching her with admiration. She wasn't sure how long she should keep waiting for Leland to get the courage to open his heart, especially with David Alexander sitting across the table from her.

Chapter 23 — The Rumor Mill

Leland whistled as he walked down the aisle and found the light oak stain that reminded him of Maggie's blonde curls. Every time he thought of giving Maggie the little rocking chair, his heart beat out a song of joy. He hoped that Sophie would see how much he cared for her and her family and happily agree to go out with him this week. There was a dance hall just past Calloway Grove that he was thinking of taking her to. He walked back to the front of the store, greeting the owner, Albert Gillespie. "How have you been?"

"Good. Good. You've been busy lately," Albert said. "Weren't you just in here a couple days ago?"

"Yes, I can't complain, but if things continue on as they have been I may need to hire someone to help me complete the orders."

"Is that so?" Albert leaned forward. "Do you have anyone in mind?"

"Well, my buddy, Keith, has offered to help me a few hours a week for now, so we'll see."

Albert nodded. "It's tough to find good help these days. I'm sure you and Keith Harper could make a go of just about anything though."

Leland set the can of stain on the counter. "I'm staining a miniature rocking chair this morning. I have to get it finished up before noon."

Albert nodded. "You're always hard at work. Who will get a delivery today?"

"Keith's niece. Maggie is turning five and she loves dolls."

"Oh, that's Sophie's daughter, then," Albert replied. "She is a lovely woman. It was nice to see a smile on her face last night."

Leland tilted his head. "Last night?"

"Yes, she was over to The Silver Lining with David Alexander. Looked for all the world like they were in love. My wife was on the phone talking with Mrs. Dymock all evening about how poor Linda Marchant will be crushed when she finds out."

Leland was having trouble catching a breath, but he rasped out. "Linda?"

"She's the daughter of that family that moved here from New York a few years ago. Mrs. Alexander has been planning the wedding ever since." Albert chuckled. "Of course, that's all according to my wife, and she knows these sorts of things."

Leland nodded numbly, he knew Linda Marchant. He also knew something that Albert didn't. Leland had delivered the hope chest he'd built to Mrs. Marchant last week. He'd finished the proposed engagement present for her daughter Linda—the woman who was supposed to be marrying David Alexander. He shook his head, remembering that Mrs. Gillespie was the town gossip. By tomorrow, the entire city of Aspen Falls would know that David Alexander had taken Sophie on a date to The Silver Lining. They'd probably know what they had for dinner too, but the rumors were often inaccurate.

"You okay? You're looking a little pale." Albert adjusted his glasses.

Leland's heart was a hammer, driving his blood pressure up, puncturing his lungs with tiny nails. "I haven't eaten breakfast yet, so I better get to it." Leland picked up the can of stain. "Just put it on my tab. Thanks."

He couldn't get out of the store fast enough; his legs felt like rubber and his head pounded with every word that Albert had uttered. Sophie and David Alexander? He climbed into his pickup and rested his hands on the steering wheel, thinking through the situation. It was probably just a first date. Maybe David had asked her out after Sophie invited Leland to Maggie's birthday party. Surely Mrs. Gillespie was exaggerating when she said they looked like they were in love, but Leland's stomach was busy tying itself in knots as he considered what that meant for him and Sophie. David wasn't blind. He'd want to see Sophie again—it wasn't possible that he could resist her beautiful face and sweet personality. Maybe he'd already asked her on another date. Had he kissed her?

Leland swallowed, trying to slow the beating of his heart. The back of his head throbbed with worry. He drove home and got to work on the rocking chair for Maggie. Sophie had invited him to the party, but maybe it was because she considered him a family friend. If David was also at the party, Leland would just drop the gift off and leave, knowing that his chance with Sophie had passed. He finished staining the chair and moved it away from the window where an errant breeze sometimes snuck through the cracks. Setting the chair to dry, Leland's ears perked at the sound of the wind whispering through the door. He hadn't shut it tight when he'd let Hope inside. He walked across the shop and reached out a hand to push it shut. The icy winter wind struck his cheeks with force as it whistled through the door. It was probably just his imagination, but he was almost certain he'd heard words on the wind again, *Tell her.*

Chapter 24 – Maggie's birthday party

Sophie had stayed up late the night before decorating Maggie's birthday cake and the sweet smell of sugar still hung in the air. Garth had practically been drooling while the cake was cooking, filling their little home with the tantalizing promise of a rare dessert.

The unicorn's horn was a rolled piece of paper, hand-drawn with ridges to look like the magical animal. Sophie adjusted the horn and piped more pink frosting on the unicorn's nose. To her eye, the head of the unicorn was amateur and she wished she had a few more supplies to make the cake like Maggie had envisioned.

"Oh, Mommy! My cake!" Maggie stood at the edge of the table, her cheeks spread wide with a grin. "The unicorn is so pretty, just like my dream!" She clapped her hands.

"Happy birthday, sweetheart." Sophie hugged her, careful to keep the frosting bag away from Maggie's blonde curls. "I'm glad you like it."

"It's the best birthday cake ever." Maggie held tight to Sophie, looking up at her with chocolate brown eyes. "I love you Mommy."

The back of Sophie's throat warmed with emotion as the impact of the moment hit her. Maggie was growing up. Her sweet little girl was speaking more clearly every day, losing the cute baby words that she'd learned that always made Sophie smile. She'd started asking for a drink instead of "ghink". There were still a few small vestiges from those early days that manifested, and Sophie was grateful for those. Like the other day when Maggie said she liked to wear her favorite pink dress now, not the "lellow" one.

Sophie straightened and put the finishing touches on the cake while Maggie and Garth watched with building excitement. Garth was deep in thought, studying the tips of the pink icing standing up on the cake.

"My friend Tommy doesn't have a dad either," Garth said. "He doesn't have a grandpa either. Who will teach him how to hunt?"

Sophie glanced at the Navy Cross, still sitting in a crumpled heap on the shelf in the front room. She couldn't imagine Cal ever having the patience to teach Garth to hunt. "Maybe when you're both a little older, Grandpa Harper could take you and Tommy hunting."

"Really?" Garth's eyes lit up. "I'm gonna tell him. Can I go across the street and tell him?"

"Just as soon as you clean up your room." Sophie pointed down the hall and Garth groaned, but ran to his room. Watching him go, Sophie was struck by the fact that Garth and Tommy didn't consider the possibility of a new dad coming into their lives. For Garth, Grandpa had taken that place and Keith too. How did a woman prepare her children for the ever-changing future? Sophie didn't want to be alone and now with both David and Leland paying attention to her, she had begun to think that maybe life could change for the better.

Garth returned in record time and Sophie shooed him out the door with strict instructions to return in one hour to help prepare for the party. She turned to Maggie and held out the frosting bag. "Would you like to help me frost a graham cracker with this extra icing?"

Maggie giggled. "This is the best birthday!"

Sophie plucked a wilted leaf from one of David's roses and refilled the vase with water. The roses still gave off a heavenly perfume and

Sophie had made a point of stopping and sniffing them several times a day. Each time, she thought of David and wondered if their relationship had the possibility to bloom like the roses.

Mrs. Alexander was like the thorn on the roses. In order to get to David, Sophie would have to be willing to be torn to shreds by the sharp words of his mother. Nadine didn't know anything of Sophie's past and so she couldn't possibly understand how skilled Sophie was at dealing with a manipulator. She had learned early on how to survive under Cal's temper, arrogance, and dictatorship. Sophie frowned. She'd also made a promise to herself after he died that she would never cower before another human being. Yet she had done just that in the face of Nadine's thinly veiled threats and scathing verbal wounds. Her hand clenched tightly against the crimson rose petal.

Uncurling her fingers, Sophie studied the lines where the delicate petal had been bruised, crushed, and nearly destroyed. She lifted it to her nose and inhaled the sweet scent that still clung to the damaged petal. Sophie closed her eyes, trying to block out the memories. She saw herself in the damaged and discarded rose petal and for some unexplained reason she saw Leland standing next to her with understanding on his face. Sophie opened her eyes and threw the rose petal in the garbage. With a shake of her head, she hurried to tidy up the kitchen before the first of the birthday guests arrived.

Mr. Gillespie's words kept repeating in Leland's mind as he drove to Sophie's house, but he pushed them out and forced himself to focus on a little five-year-old girl's birthday. When Maggie had asked about being abandoned, Leland's heart had hurt for her. It ached for the loss of his own child, and he knew that Jessie would want him to help Maggie find joy today. He forced a smile to his face as he walked toward Sophie's front door holding Maggie's birthday gift.

Garth opened the door before he could knock. "Leland's here!" he called, pulling the door open wide. His eyes went to the brown paper sack in Leland's hand. "And he brought Maggie a present!"

Maggie came running to the door, dodging her grandparents who stood just outside the kitchen. "Come and see my cake, Leland! It's the prettiest unicorn you ever saw." She tugged on his hand, leading him through her family.

"Afternoon Betty, Wayne." Leland inclined his head toward the family as Maggie pulled him toward her cake.

"It's good to see you too," Betty replied. Wayne smiled at him, a twinkle in his eye regarding his cute granddaughter.

Leland nodded to the Harpers as he entered the kitchen. Sophie stood just behind a pink cake. The unicorn was on a sheet pan and the frosting had been piped delicately to accent all the features of the magical creature. He leaned forward, smiling. "This is quite the work of art. Your mother is very talented."

"I know. She is the best Mommy."

"Thank you for coming," Sophie said. "I'm so glad you could see the cake."

Leland looked up at Sophie and she took a step forward, revealing the three red roses in a vase that stood on the counter behind her. He stiffened, sucking in a breath and taking a step back.

The roses stood tall and proud in their vase, mocking Leland's attempt to gain favor in Sophie's eyes. He realized now who the roses were from. His heart turned to lead in his chest and the heaviness made it hard to breathe. The roses indicated that last night wasn't the first time that David Alexander had practiced his charms on Sophie. Leland's shoulders curved inwards. He couldn't compete with the likes of David—the decorated war hero of Aspen Falls. Leland had misread the entire situation. Sophie had invited him as a family friend, which meant that at any moment, David Alexander could come walking through the door.

Leland panicked. "Uh—I really can't stay. I just wanted to bring this gift for Maggie and wish her a happy birthday." He held up his brown paper sack.

"Oh dear, are you sure? Keith and Debbie should be here any minute."

That jolted Leland into action. He couldn't stay here, with all of them walking around the roses knowing full well that they were from Sophie's admirer—her new love. He swallowed. "I'm sorry. I tried to catch up on my orders, but there's still so much work to do. Is it okay if she opens this now?"

Sophie's face fell and for a brief instant, Leland thought he saw hurt flash across her eyes. But that couldn't be right. Maybe he was reading her wrong. It didn't matter because he wasn't about to look the fool when David arrived.

Betty seemed to sense her daughter's discomfort and stepped forward, patting Maggie on the head. "Of course, she would love that, wouldn't she, Sophie?"

Sophie focused on Leland and nodded. "Yes, she's bouncing out of her shoes right now." He could tell that Sophie was doing her best to hide her disappointment and at the same time figure out if he was telling the truth. Leland held out the sack to Maggie and the little girl took it gently from his hands. She opened it and smiled as she pulled out the dainty rocking chair.

"It's a rocking chair for my dolly!" Maggie hugged Leland. "Oh thank you! I love you. Charlotte loves you too." She leaned down and picked up her doll and seated her in the rocker.

"That really is fine work, Leland," Wayne said.

"Thank you, but don't tell anyone. I'm already behind on my orders as it is," Leland joked.

Betty chuckled. "I'm afraid the word will be out on the street by tonight if Maggie has anything to do with it. Are you sure you can't stay, Leland? I know Keith wanted to speak with you."

"Yes, could you at least stay for a piece of cake?" Sophie asked.

He looked from Betty to Sophie and hesitated. There was something in Sophie's searching gaze that gave him pause. For half a second, he almost caved to the desire in his heart to bring her into his life. But one glance at the roses behind her reclaimed his good sense and he shook his head, turning for the door. "I'll catch up with Keith later." He hurried out before Sophie could tempt him with pink frosted cake or beguile him with the hurt in her vivid green eyes.

Chapter 25 — Finding Fault

Keith and Debbie arrived only five minutes after Leland left and Sophie felt the awkwardness all over again when she had to explain that he'd left. Keith had looked thoroughly confused and Debbie had deftly changed the subject with a false brightness that pushed everyone away from the taboo topic.

Maggie delighted in her gifts and ate too much cake, smearing the pink frosting across her right cheek as she ate. Sophie did her best to focus on her sweet little girl and push other worries from her mind. Once the kids were off playing in the other room and cleanup had commenced, she allowed herself to voice her concerns to Debbie.

"I still can't believe that Leland couldn't even take ten minutes to have a piece of cake with us," Sophie said.

"I can," Debbie said. "If you ask me, he's heard the rumor that you've stolen David Alexander's heart."

The plate Sophie held clattered into the sink. "What rumor?"

Debbie glanced over her shoulder where Betty sat talking with Wayne and Keith. "I didn't want to say anything until after the party, but I bet near half the town knows about your date to The Silver Lining last night."

Sophie gasped. "People are talking about me?"

"You and David, yes," Debbie replied. "Marla Checketts called me this morning, worried for you because she'd heard the rumor and knows that you work for Mrs. Alexander."

Sophie inhaled slowly and exhaled before responding. "Marla was kind enough not to say what everyone else is—that I'm not good enough for David."

"Oh no, quite the contrary," Debbie said. "Everyone loves you and they know that David would be fortunate to have a wife like you. The part where it gets tricky is that Mrs. Alexander has been quite vocal about his match made in heaven—Linda Marchant."

Sophie plunged her hands into the soapy water. "This is such a mess."

"That's right," Debbie said. "Do you trust David enough to go and talk to him about this latest development?"

"Go and talk to David?" Sophie shook her head. "He lives with his mother. You know, Mrs. Alexander."

Debbie lifted one shoulder and let it fall. "If you don't, I think you'll be out of a job by Monday. Once Mrs. Alexander has handed down her decree, she won't be swayed, but if David gets to her before, it might be enough to salvage your employment."

Sophie leaned forward, resting her head on her hand. "I should've left well-enough alone. I told David he was going to get me fired."

"And what did he say?"

"That was our first date. He told me he wanted the chance to get to know me better—that he wasn't going to let me go."

"That's all very romantic but it doesn't mean diddly to his mother." Debbie wiped crumbs from the counter and glanced at Sophie.

"I don't know if I should talk to David though," Sophie said. "Doesn't that imply that I'm feeling enough for him that I want him to stake his claim to his mother?"

Debbie looked thoughtfully from the dirty dish in her hand to the ceiling. "I guess you're right there. Do you even like David? I mean, sure he's charming, but he's kind of full of himself."

Sophie chuckled. "He's been very kind to me and it's hard to put my finger on it, but when I'm with him, it almost seems like he's opening up to me in a way he doesn't to others." She scrubbed at a chunk of frosting on a fork. "He is handsome, kind, and wealthy, but he also understands what I've been through."

Debbie arched an eyebrow. "Just because he's seen the war doesn't mean he knows what you've been through."

Sophie swallowed. Debbie had no idea the extent of her unhappiness with Cal and that was only Sophie's fault. But David, he had figured it out on the first day they had met. That was also partially Sophie's fault, but she felt a connection to him because of that understanding. "I know I haven't been on that many dates with him, but I can't see a reason to stop dating him—other than his mother and my employment."

"I know you've heard the saying, 'If it's too good to be true, it probably is,'" Debbie chided.

"I'm looking for his faults, I really am." Sophie twisted her hands in the soapy water. "I've also been asking myself if having too much confidence is always a bad thing. It sure would've helped me in the past."

Debbie finished scrubbing the stove. "I just wish Leland would get his act together. He's a great catch, but he won't put himself out there."

Sophie sighed. "What should I do? I've had a nice time on our dates and outings, and I thought he liked me, but then he gave up."

"Not many men would go toe to toe with David Alexander."

"So it's my fault?" Sophie ran her finger along the edge of a cup. "I guess if a man isn't willing to step outside his comfort zone for me, how could he possibly expect to take on a ready-made family?"

Debbie stood next to her and they both looked out the kitchen window. "Don't rule him out completely just yet, that's all I'm saying."

"Okay, but that still doesn't solve my problem with David's mother. Do you really think she'd fire me?"

"Don't you?"

Sophie let the water drain out of the sink wishing that her problems could drain away so easily. There were so many choices before her, but which was the right one?

Chapter 26 – The Good Samaritan

Sophie tried not to stare at the bench where the Alexanders always sat in church, but her eyes kept straying in that direction. Maggie sat in between Grandma Harper and Amy, while Keith and Garth sat between Grandpa Harper and Sophie. Sitting through sermons was Garth's least favorite activity. Sophie smiled to herself as she looked down the bench. The entire family was there to help and support her. When she turned forward, David and his mother were just sitting down. He turned his head slightly as he took his seat and caught Sophie's eye. His bright smile made her stomach flip, and Sophie smiled back. Mrs. Alexander chose that moment to turn, giving Sophie a cool stare. Sophie swallowed back the enthusiasm at seeing David and looked down at her hands.

It was difficult to pay attention to Father McCall with David sitting just a few rows in front of her, seemingly unaware of what his attentions might cost her. As a war widow, Sophie received a small pension which covered her rent. Her parents had been more than generous in stocking Sophie's pantry and helping her get settled in Aspen Falls. She was grateful for that, but she was also a capable woman and she didn't like depending on someone else for the well-being of her children. The job that Mrs. Alexander provided was not enough to subsist on, but it was enough to build up an emergency fund and purchase the few extras that Sophie's family needed.

With her skills, Garth and Maggie had beautiful, warm clothing but they grew quickly and it was hard to keep them in shoes. Garth's winter boots had been patched to the point that Sophie wondered if there was any of the original boot left.

Father McCall's voice pitched higher as he quoted a scripture from Luke and continued on to tell the story of the Good Samaritan. Sophie felt the meaning of the story keenly. What part did she play in the parable? There had been many times in her life when she'd felt like the beaten man, robbed of everything and left on the side of the road. It was uncharitable, but Mrs. Alexander most fit the role of the Levite—pious, above all, and unwilling to help her own people because they were beneath her. Sophie pursed her lips together. That wasn't really true. Mrs. Alexander had offered her a job as the seamstress for her household.

Sophie leaned back against the pew and listened to Father McCall. He spoke of the Good Samaritan, a man unconcerned with status or wealth, a man who chose to do the right thing. The Samaritans were despised of the Jews and yet he helped the Jew in need.

The back of Sophie's neck prickled as if someone were watching her. She turned her head slightly and caught the vibrant blue of Leland's eyes before he looked down at his feet. Sophie smiled when he ducked his head, his shyness evident in the way his neck flushed and his shoulders remained tense. She wanted him to look up and meet her eye, but he kept his head down. Sophie turned, facing forward again. She could picture Leland as the Good Samaritan, especially when she thought of his friendship and kindness toward the Tanaka family. A thought worried her as she looked at the back of David's thick hair and broad shoulders. How would David feel about Sophie's children playing with the Tanaka family?

Serena's children had been to Sophie's house to play and they got along well while the two mothers chatted over coffee. Garth couldn't wait to visit their house again this week. It bothered her that she didn't know for certain how David would react to her Japanese friends, but she knew Leland's heart. Sophie refocused on the sermon and tried not to think of things out of her control. She couldn't really afford to lose her employment anyway. Perhaps it was better not to see any more of David.

Sophie kept her head down as everyone filed out so that she wouldn't have to see Mrs. Alexander. She spoke earnestly with Marla Checketts as they gathered up their families to exit the church. They were almost to the car when Garth realized that he'd left his airplane under the bench. His eyes filled with tears.

"I lost my Christmas present."

"It's okay. Let's go find it," Sophie said. "I'm sure it's right where you left it."

"Do you need help?" Betty asked.

"No thanks, Mom. You go on ahead. We'll be over to the house shortly."

Sophie held Garth and Maggie's hands and walked back inside the church. They headed to the pew where they had sat, but Sophie stopped walking when she saw a dark-haired man rise from between the benches. David met her eye and held up a handkerchief, smiling. "My mother dropped her hankie."

Sophie nodded. "What a good son you are to go on the hunt for it."

David chuckled, aware that she was teasing him. He glanced at both of her children. "Hello, Garth." David extended his hand. "I'm David Alexander."

Garth took his hand and gave it as firm a shake as a six-year-old could. "Hello."

"Hi, Margaret." David held his hand toward her. "I heard that you had a birthday. I hope it was a happy one."

Maggie frowned and took his hand. "Thank you."

David chuckled and looked to Sophie. She wasn't sure if she

should remind him again about Maggie's name. "Maggie wants to get to her grandparent's home but we had to come back to look for Garth's airplane."

"An airplane, huh? Well, you don't want to lose that," David said. Garth ducked back under the seats, crawling along until with a whoop, he returned with the metal toy.

"Ah, a P-40 Warhawk. I used to fly one of these ladies." He took the airplane from Garth and examined it. "See, I'd sit right there in the cockpit."

Garth's face was wonderstruck. "Did you fight in the war?"

"I did." He handed the plane back to Garth. "I flew over Germany for several months, helping with the bombing effort." David's face lit up as he was swept back in time to his days in the war. "We flew so fast that nothing could touch us."

Garth gripped his airplane tighter, flying it through the air. "Did you bomb any Japs?"

"No, but I would have, if I'd been given the chance," David replied at the same time that Sophie took hold of Garth's arm.

"Garth, we don't speak that way about the Japanese. They are our friends, remember?"

Sophie straightened to find David studying her with a curious look. He shrugged and his face lifted with a debonair smile. "I wanted to talk to you for a minute. Is that okay?"

Sophie felt a moment of panic. Standing in the church talking to David Alexander was probably the worst thing she could do if she wanted to quiet rumors. She glanced around the room and relaxed. All but a couple parishioners had exited the building.

"Don't worry. I've already talked to my mother," David said.

Sophie's eyes snapped back to David's "What? What do you mean?"

"Okado is taking her home. I told her I needed some time to think...about you."

"David, I—have you—I don't want to cause trouble."

He took her hand and squeezed it gently. "You already have." He winked and took one step closer to her. "I knew exactly what I was doing when I took you to dinner at The Silver Lining. I also knew how my mother would react when she found out."

"So she knows?"

David chuckled. "Oh, she knows. I'm not certain, but I think she may have even known before."

"How would that be possible?"

"She's a very shrewd woman. When you came by on Thursday with the mending, she was practically in a frenzy by the time I arrived home. She wanted to know if I was interested in you. I told her that if I was she couldn't do a thing about it." David lowered his voice. "Imagine my surprise when my mother invited me to tea the next day and I showed up to find Linda Marchant and her mother."

Sophie stepped back, shaking her head. "Oh, no." The hint from Dai Okado made perfect sense if Mrs. Alexander had already scheduled the tea, hopeful that Sophie would show up with the mending during the visit with David's future fiancé.

"I didn't say anything to you on Friday because I didn't want to upset you."

"What do you mean?" Sophie ran her fingers along the edge of her sash.

"At the tea, my mother made a few pointed remarks about her excellent seamstress, Sophie Wright. She even went so far as to suggest that Mrs. Marchant hire you."

Sophie felt her face burn and she tugged at the hand David held, but he didn't let go. "She was hoping I would show up, you know. She even asked me to return the mending on Friday. I'm sure she wanted to put me in my place in front of the Marchants."

David stepped closer and touched her cheek with his other hand. "Sophie, I'm sorry. Maybe I shouldn't have told you."

"No, it's good that you did. Your mother was quite clear about my place in this town when I delivered the clothing." She lifted her face to his and blinked rapidly. One breath in and out reminded her of the game she needed to play. Life would always be a game, and if Sophie didn't play her hand of cards right, she'd lose everything. Her mask clicked into place and the corners of her mouth nudged upwards into the barest of smiles.

David frowned. "I'm sorry."

"My parents have been very good to me and I've tried my best to do some work to provide for my family. I realize what your mother thinks of me, and *I'm* sorry. I never should have crossed the line." Sophie pulled her hand from David's and turned to gather up Maggie and Garth from under the benches where they played.

"Sophie, wait." David put his hands on her arms and leaned forward. "I crossed the line and I'm only telling you this because I'm willing to cross all the lines, paint them over, whatever it takes to have you in my life."

Sophie sucked in a breath, shaking her head, but David touched her chin, swiveling her face toward his. "Do you really think I care what anyone in this town thinks?"

"Yes," Sophie answered. "You might think you know what you're doing, but you don't know the cost. David, your mother doesn't want me to even speak to you, let alone go on a date with you. In her eyes, the only contact I should have with you is with a needle and thread."

"Like I said. I've already spoken with my mother," David replied. "We've reached a compromise."

"And what's that?"

"I'm allowed to date who I want and she will neither threaten nor punish you because of me."

"And what about Linda?"

David closed his eyes and shook his head. "I do feel bad that I wasn't more firm with my mother in the beginning because I never should have led Linda to believe that I felt anything more than friendship towards her."

"Friends can get married," Sophie teased.

"You're right there," David said. "But there has to be a spark, and that's not something I'm willing to compromise on no matter what my mother says."

Sophie's heart raced. David wasn't just talking sweet to her. He'd gone against his mother and the rumor mill in town and was making his own way. "I have to say. I'm happily surprised."

David touched her face, his eyes intent on hers as if he were trying to read her soul. His fingers were warm on her cheek and he was so close, she felt like they were breathing the same air. He bent his head and gently brushed his lips over hers. Sophie hardly had time to respond, the shock was so deep. David had just kissed her in the church!

David smiled, his hand trailing down her arm to her fingertips where he grasped her hand. "Sophie, will you give us a chance?"

She looked down at his hand, smooth and strong. Slowly, she raised her head and met his gaze. "Since you don't have a ride home, would you like to come to dinner with my family?"

David beamed. "I'd love to."

"My whole family."

There was only a slight hesitation and then David laughed. "I never back down from a challenge."

"Good, because I've decided that I won't either." Sophie held his hand and her heart thrilled when David interlaced his fingers with hers. "Come on kids. Let's go to Grandma's." She held David's hand and walked with him out the front doors of the church.

Chapter 27 – Family Dinner

Thankfully, Wayne and Betty Harper were good poker players too. There was only the slightest hint of surprise when Sophie entered the house with her unexpected guest, David Alexander. They greeted him like old neighbors as the kids scattered throughout the house, unaware of the significance of the Sunday dinner guest.

Sophie saw Keith's pointed look where David held her hand, but Debbie only winked and helped Betty bring food to the table.

"The gravy will be ready in just a few," Betty called from the kitchen. "Have a seat."

Sophie led David into the living room and they sat on the loveseat next to each other. She didn't have a chance to say anything before Wayne plopped into an upholstered chair beside them.

"I hope you ain't aiming to get my girl in trouble," Wayne said. "She's had enough worry in her short life already."

"Daddy!" Sophie was back in high school all over again with Wayne doing his best to scare her dates with his veiled threats.

David straightened, his shoes clicked together and for a moment, Sophie thought he might stand at attention and salute. "I have no intention of dishonoring her, sir."

"Might not be your intentions that are the problem, but your own mother," Wayne grumbled.

Sophie put her face in her hands, but David only chuckled. "Like

I told Sophie. I've had a few words with my mother to make it clear that I'd like a chance to date Sophie and get to know her."

Wayne lifted his chin. "That may be, but some people can make other people's lives miserable in ways that you and I can only imagine."

"Daddy, please," Sophie interrupted.

David covered her hand with his. "He's right, of course." He turned to Sophie, his lips in a firm line. "You don't have to pretend that my mother hasn't been unkind to you."

Sophie looked down at her hands and squeezed David's fingers. She didn't want to have this conversation or think about Nadine Alexander anymore. "Let's just take it one day at a time." She reached over and patted her father's knee. "David has taken me on a couple dates and he's been a perfect gentleman. Did you know that he flew the Warhawk in Germany?"

"Is that right?" Wayne perked up.

"I'm going to help Mother dish up that gravy." Sophie stood and released David's hand. She walked to the kitchen, leaving the two men to discuss something other than David's mother and her cruelty.

Betty didn't even wait two beats before she cornered Sophie in the kitchen. "Why didn't you tell me you were planning to bring David to dinner today?"

"Because I wasn't," Sophie replied. "He asked to speak with me after church and, well, we had a good chat so I invited him over."

"That's pretty bold," Debbie said. "I don't see his fancy car out there. Does that mean you rode together over here?"

"Uh—yes, part of the reason David wanted to speak with me is because he told his mother that he didn't want her interfering with his dating and that he didn't want to marry Linda Marchant."

Betty and Debbie both gasped. "Well, I'll be," Betty said. She peeked into the living room. "I guess the war gave that boy a backbone. Never knew anyone who could stand up to Nadine Alexander."

"He's not a boy anymore," Sophie said.

"That's for sure," Debbie said. "He grew up just fine in the war."

Sophie swatted her arm and they both giggled. Betty shushed them and then called for everyone to come to the table. After Wayne offered a prayer, the conversation ebbed and flowed with the clinking of the dishes. The kids sat at a card table and gobbled through their food as quick as cats so they could get back to playing.

Sophie noticed that Keith was quieter than usual, but she ignored his moodiness. He would probably confront her later about Leland, but there was nothing she could do about the quiet carpenter who seemed uncomfortable any time he was away from his hammer and nails.

"How have you liked being back in Aspen Falls?" Betty asked David.

He straightened. "It's been an adjustment. When I left for the war, Dad was still alive and the business was running smoothly. There's been quite a bit of work to do. I never appreciated how hard my father worked until he was gone."

"We were all sorry when he passed," Wayne said.

"I imagine your mother must think of you as an answer to prayers, coming home to right things," Betty said.

David smiled. "Maybe you ought to have a chat with my mother."

Betty chuckled. "Well, we mothers do our best to keep our children in line no matter how big they grow. Isn't that right, Keith?"

Keith grunted, but must have realized Betty expected him to participate in the conversation. He set down his fork and leveled David with a cool stare. "What is it that you do now?"

"Besides trying to fill my father's bottomless shoes?" David met his stare, but his eyes softened. "When I came back, there was some instability with sections of the mine, but we have those fixed now. I've been able to hire thirty new workers. If the market for coal continues to rise, I may need to hire even more."

"That sounds wonderful," Sophie said. "Are a lot of those workers men from the war?"

David nodded. "As a matter of fact, they are. It's been a good experience for all of us to work together."

"Did you always plan to take over your father's business?" Wayne asked.

"I didn't really have much chance to think about it," David replied. "My parents were pretty thorough about making plans for me and I'd had some ideas of my own, but the war changed all of that."

"I've heard that many soldiers have had a hard time adjusting," Debbie said. "Having strange symptoms and mood swings and the like."

David pulled his bottom lip through his teeth. "I've seen some of that myself. Sometimes I still wake up waiting for someone to tell me what to do. My mother doesn't like it when I salute her and answer with 'sir'."

Everyone laughed because it was easy to picture Mrs. Alexander as a drill sergeant.

"Well, it's nice to have you back, David," Betty said.

"Thank you."

"Did Sophie tell you that she's been seeing Leland Halverson as well?" Keith said.

Betty shot him a dark look and by the shifting under the table, Sophie was fairly certain Debbie had kicked her husband.

David didn't seem to notice the scuffle. "Yes, she did. I didn't have a problem with it. Your sister is a beautiful and kind woman. I would be shocked if there weren't other men asking her out to the next picture show." David was smooth; by the look on Keith's face, he was too smooth.

"That's good you understand that you don't have sole claim to her," Keith said evenly.

"I understand that you're still friends with Leland, but even so I would think that your judgement wouldn't be so clouded as to think he'd be a suitable match for Sophie."

Debbie sucked in a breath and Betty's fork clattered to her plate. Keith made as if to stand, but Wayne put his hand on his son's arm. "That'll be quite enough chatter for now. Keith, if you have something to discuss with David, do so after the meal."

Sophie closed her eyes, taking in a slow breath. No one spoke and the awkwardness intensified. In the stillness, there was a loud pop almost like a gunshot. David dropped to the floor, rolling under the table. He cried out as he put his hands over his head and tucked himself into a tight ball.

"What was that?" Debbie asked.

Wayne shook his head. "Another bottle going off."

Sophie scrambled under the table, "David, it's okay." She touched his shoulder and he flinched. "It's just one of Daddy's bottles of homebrew blowing its top."

David moaned and pulled himself to a sitting position beside the table. "I don't know what came over me. It sounded like a gunshot." His eyes darted around the room and his breath came in short bursts. Sophie put her right hand over his and touched his cheek with her left hand. He lifted his eyes to hers and everything came into focus. Through his eyes, Sophie could see that he had suffered much more than anyone could guess.

"The war, it destroyed—it stole our future because none of us will live the life we would have," she whispered. "It changed everything."

David looked down at her hand, carefully interlacing his fingers with hers. "No, I can't give into that way of thinking. Our lives will be infinitely better because of the evil we stopped."

He was right, but it was hard to ignore the evidence of how war had stripped out the normalcy of life. Even now—months after the war had ended—it continued to wound innocent bystanders.

"Is that the same batch from Christmas?" Keith asked. "No wonder it's going off. We need to have another party and drink it up."

David chuckled and stood, pulling Sophie up beside him. "Now that sounds like fun. You can invite me as long as you've already opened all the bottles."

Betty laughed and Debbie smiled, but there was still tension in the room and most of it was radiating off of Keith.

Sophie tugged on David's hand, leading him away from the dining table. "I'm sorry about Keith. He's just a big brother."

David glanced back over his shoulder. "I guess I should be worried if he *wasn't* watching out for you. But maybe it's best if I head home."

"Would you like a ride?"

"That's nice, but I still need some time to think. It's only a couple miles, but I should have everything figured out by then. It's not too cold out today."

Sophie looked out the window at the melting snow. "If you say so."

"Hey, are you busy Tuesday night? I'd like to see you again."

"As long as my family can watch Garth and Maggie, I'll be free."

"Good. I'll give you a call." David leaned forward and brushed her cheek with a kiss. Then he walked into the kitchen and thanked everyone for the meal, shaking hands with Sophie's parents and lifting his hand in a wave toward Keith and Debbie. Sophie saw him to the door and stood at the window, watching him walk away. His purposeful strides halted after a minute and he looked up at the sky and shook his head. The actions made her want to read his mind and see what thoughts he was sorting out.

"Hey, sis." Keith came up beside her and put his arm around her. "I'm really sorry about being such an idiot."

Sophie turned to him, hoping the disappointment showed in her face. "I understand why you're doing it, but I want you to stop pushing Leland on me."

Keith looked down at the floor and sighed. "I wanted it to work between you two. What happened?"

Sophie shrugged. "I don't know if he heard about David and decided I wasn't worth the effort, or maybe he really is too busy."

"That could be part of it, but it's not the whole reason." Keith gazed out the window, but he wasn't seeing anything. "I hoped that he'd have a chance to tell you by now."

"Tell me what?" Sophie turned in front of Keith, blocking the view to the street. Keith's face pinched in a memory laced with pain. She folded her arms. "I think Leland is carrying something that keeps him from putting his heart at risk."

"You're right," Keith said. "And until he decides to let you in, I guess there's no point in me defending him."

The words struck Sophie's heart like a discordant melody. They were true on one level, Leland *was* keeping something from her, but it didn't make sense because he'd already shared his pain with her. Sophie was expecting things to play out like familiar music—the notes were supposed to follow a pattern, so when they went off course, it often sounded wrong to the listener. "He told me about his daughter dying, his divorce, and his problem with drinking."

"But he didn't tell you everything."

"What do you mean?" Sophie took a step back. "If he's done something horrible, then maybe it's better that we don't see each other.

Keith shook his head. "It's not what you think. Leland is one of the best men I know—better than Cal ever was."

Sophie inhaled sharply, but she gave Keith a curt nod. "I'm sure you're right about that."

Keith opened his mouth to reply but Garth ran in screaming.

"Maggie has my airplane and she won't give it back!"

"I think that's our cue to leave," Sophie said. "You kids are tired out." She patted Keith's shoulder. "Thanks for looking out for me."

It took almost a half an hour before Sophie could get the kids out the door. As she drove home, she replayed the moments she'd shared with David that day. Every time she imagined his smile and the way he'd kissed her—so feather light and brief, her heart sped up. But once she was home and the kids were playing quietly in their rooms, her thoughts returned to Leland. What secret in his life made him keep his heart locked away? And if she knew that secret, would it change the way she felt about him, or David?

Chapter 28 – Scraps of Wood

March 1946

With Keith's help to finish up some orders, Leland finally felt like he could breathe again in his shop. That was a feeling he hadn't experienced in a long time for a Monday morning facing down the week's work. Together, the two friends had worked out a system for Leland to take orders and plan out the hours he had each week to work on a new project so that he didn't get overwhelmed again. It meant that there were several customers having to wait longer than they wanted, but at least Leland could keep his word and his business strong.

Nearly a month had passed since Maggie's birthday and Leland had heard several people talking about Sophie Wright and David Alexander. They were now considered an item, much to Mrs. Alexander's disappointment. Leland had only caught sight of them together once when he drove by a park and saw David pushing Sophie on a swing. Her head had tipped back in laughter and it made Leland's insides squeeze tight, blood pooling around his heart in a stagnant pond of ache. He hadn't noticed the kids at the park and he wondered how they liked David.

"Hi Leland," Keith rapped on the door once as he entered the shop.

Leland was grateful for the interruption to his train of thought. "Thanks for coming by today. I think we're finally catching up."

"Good. Does that mean we can start on Debbie's table?"

Leland walked over to a pile of walnut planks and pointed. "Have at it."

Keith clapped his hands together and pulled off a length of wood. "Do you think I'll be able to finish it by June? I'd like to give it to her for her birthday."

"The chairs will be the hardest part, but I think we can manage it."

Keith pulled out another length of wood and Leland helped him arrange the planks on his table. They marked off cut lines and Leland gave Keith a few pointers about how to match up the edges so that the seams of the tabletop would appear perfect. They worked together for an hour and Leland caught a bit of Keith's contagious enthusiasm for the project. A full-sized dining room table had been on Debbie's wish list for as long as Leland had known the Harpers. It would be gratifying to see her dreams come to fruition through the hard work and love of her husband. Leland wanted to experience that same kind of love. He and Rhonda hadn't ever really had a chance. They'd only been married four years when Jessie died and her death tore a hole in their marriage—and a hole inside of Leland—that was beyond repair. Looking back now, Leland saw that he could have made different choices and maybe he and Rhonda would still be together, but he tried not to dwell on the past that he couldn't change.

"Seems like you have a lot on your mind lately," Keith murmured after driving in another nail.

Leland nodded. "There hasn't been much time to breathe and eat, let alone think the past few months, but now that I have a handle on this business my mind is dancing around the future."

"Oh?"

"I need to decide what I want."

Keith straightened and looked at Leland. "Can I be frank with you?"

Leland almost laughed—almost, because his friend was always full of blunt advice. "Go ahead. You'll say it either way."

Keith did laugh. "You're right. But I've been trying to bite my tongue and give you a chance to sort through things."

"I'm guessing that was Deb's idea."

"She knows me too well." Keith set down his hammer. "Look, you seem to have everything going for you, but you've been kind of down in the dumps. I'm pretty sure I know why, so I'd like you to say it."

Leland swallowed. What Keith thought he knew was only the beginning of his problems, but his friend would pry the information out of him one way or another. It was best to get it over with. "I know I can't live like this forever. I'd like to have a relationship like you and Deb have, but I don't know if that's possible for me. I already messed up once. What if I make another mistake?"

"First off, you see the good parts of my marriage. Deb and I have some fierce disagreements and there are lots of tough times, but we do love each other." Keith stuck his hands in his pockets. "We haven't had to go through what you did, Leland. Maybe we wouldn't have made it either. When are you going to forgive yourself?"

The back of Leland's neck prickled with the cool spring breeze sneaking in through his shop window. Keith's words struck deep to where memories of a music box melody and the turning point of his life began. When Rhonda left him, she'd written a note. "Forgive yourself—allow God to forgive." Leland had cleaned up his life and pasted the words in the music box that Rhonda had left behind. Together, the words and music had helped him put one foot in front of the other and overcome his battle with the bottle.

Leland looked at Keith and swallowed. "I thought I had forgiven myself, but then I realized that it's a continual process. I have asked forgiveness from God and I feel like a changed man, but every day I wake up and the facts of the past are still there. I have to forgive myself every day for destroying my family—ruining my life."

"But you've rebuilt." Keith picked up a chunk of cherry wood and handed it to Leland. "This is just a scrap, but I saw you use pieces just like this to build a rocking chair for Maggie's doll. If you can do that with a scrap of wood, why can't God do the same with you?"

The words reverberated in Leland's soul and his heartbeat quickened. "I believe he can, but I don't want to hurt someone else in the process."

"If you're talking about Sophie, you already did hurt her when you gave up," Keith said.

"I didn't give up," Leland said. "She chose David Alexander."

"She did no such thing, and she still hasn't if you ask me."

Leland shook his head. "I may not get out much, but I've seen them together. Sophie looks happy. David can provide a good home for her and those kids."

"So can you. Look at this place." Keith motioned to the piles of wood, tools, and pieces of furniture nearing completion. "You earn more than half the men in this town and no one would guess it."

"Money isn't everything," Leland muttered.

"Exactly." Keith pounded his fist on a board. "That's what I'm trying to tell you. David has money, but he's not a natural with Garth and Maggie the way you are. He seems like a good man, and he could probably take care of Sophie just fine, but I'm not sure he's the best man for her."

"What do you want me to do? I can't really ask her out now that she's dating David."

Keith frowned. "I wish you hadn't given up so easily."

"I didn't see it that way. I was trying to help Sophie. I didn't want to put her in an awkward position."

"Sometimes you have to put yourself out there, risk life to find love."

"I see that now." Leland pushed his boot through wood shavings under the table. "But it doesn't change anything."

"Just think about it okay?" Keith asked. "Make up some excuse to see her and the kids before she goes too far down this path with David."

Hope scratched at the door from outside and Leland let her in.

"See, there's your perfect reason. The kids love Hope. Maybe you should take her for a ride."

Leland chewed on his bottom lip "I don't know. I can't really just show up at her house with a puppy."

"Sure you can, deliver some furniture and stop on your way back to see how she and the kids are doing. Give her a reason to think about you. You don't have to ask her out on a date, but at least she'll know you're still interested in her."

"Do you really think that would work? Maybe we should ask Debbie."

Keith chuckled. "Don't say anything to Debbie or she'll be having Sophie deliver your tools to you again."

Leland smiled. "Glad to know I have good friends in my corner."

"Sure, just know that these friends are ready to kick you out of the corner and into the world. You're a fine man, Leland. It's time to admit that and let someone into that wooden heart of yours."

"Even though you're a pain, I hope you're right."

"Well, think on it. I'll be back Thursday and I expect something to have changed." Keith pointed at Leland and slapped him on the back.

Hope nipped at Keith's heels as they walked toward the door. Leland scooped her up and waved at Keith as he pulled away from the shop. His stomach growled, but he didn't stop to eat yet. He went back inside his shop and picked up the chunk of wood that Keith had handed him earlier. With a carving knife and a sharp chisel, he began peeling away layers of the wood, looking deep inside to where the grains of wood formed lines that pointed toward a hidden treasure that only he could uncover.

Chapter 29 – Spilled Milk

Sophie hurried around the house, tidying up before David arrived. It was the second Tuesday in March and Sophie had been dating David steadily for nearly five weeks. Although he'd kissed her briefly in the church three weeks ago, she hadn't encouraged any of his advances since then. David had been perceptive enough to offer only a few chaste kisses on her cheek in the past weeks. Cal had kissed her on the second date and she still blamed his ardent physical attraction for clouding her judgement. She didn't want to make the same mistake with David. But that didn't keep her from daydreaming about a kiss in their near future. Every time she did, her stomach flipped and she felt like a teenager falling in love for the first time again.

The vase of daffodils on the kitchen table provided the perfect decoration, announcing that spring had finally arrived. Sophie and her children had cheered when the last bits of snow had melted from the streets of Aspen Falls. The winter had been long, cold, and mournful. Sophie couldn't ignore the premonition that this spring would mark a new beginning in her life. It was still too soon to think about marriage, at least out loud, but Sophie found herself wondering if she and David might make a successful match. She had invited him over to dinner with her and the children tonight because he never had much of a chance to spend time with them. It was usually just the two of them, so tonight they would be dining together as a family. The thought caused little thrills to go up her spine. She hoped that David might consider introducing her formally to his mother so that the underlying tension might finally be resolved.

Although Mrs. Alexander had kept her word to her son and allowed him to date Sophie, she hadn't ordered any new sewing projects. The second set of drapes for the formal dining room that they had considered would have brought in enough to cover several upcoming expenses, but Mrs. Alexander hadn't continued with her plans. Sophie pushed down on the worry that gnawed at her stomach and instead focused on trying to find new clients who could help bridge the gap from the lost income. She cringed when she recalled her newest prospective client. Mrs. Doris Marchant had asked to meet with her Wednesday morning, and Sophie was fairly certain the meeting wouldn't be pleasant. A knock at the door brought her back from her worries and she scanned the living room once more before opening it with a smile. "Evening, David."

"You look lovely."

She had dressed carefully for the night in a green floral dress that brought out the color of her eyes. "Thank you." She stepped back and he came inside, shedding his jacket and placing it on a hook behind the door.

He turned to her and put his hands on her arms. "You really are a vision. I can't get enough of you." He leaned forward and Sophie tensed, worried that he would kiss her then, but Garth and Maggie bounded into the room.

"Hello, Mr. Alexander," Garth said formally, exactly as they had practiced.

Maggie gave a wobbly curtsy. "Welcome to dinner."

Sophie beamed and turned to David. His face didn't show the same enthusiasm as hers. "Thank you, children. I'm glad to be here."

Maybe he *had* been about to kiss her and didn't like that the children had interrupted his moment, but Sophie was glad. She wanted their first real kiss to be something special. The aroma of the chicken potpie wafted from the oven. "I think supper is almost ready. Why don't you chat with the kids for a moment?" She left David standing there in front of the kids while she walked into the kitchen. Grabbing a couple hot pads, she pulled open the oven and checked the pot pie. It looked perfect with a golden brown crust that was flaky near the edges. Sophie pulled it out, inhaling the savory dish. She set it carefully on the table and looked over to where David still stood, towering over her children. Maggie was chattering about something, but David wasn't paying attention—he was watching Sophie.

"Does that mean it's time to eat?" he asked.

"Yes, please come and have a seat." Sophie brought a knife and serving spoon to the table and sat down, helping Maggie scoot her chair forward. The table was small which worked well for her family, but only had space for one guest. Garth and Maggie sat on one side of the table and Sophie sat on the other.

David sat next to her. "This looks delicious." He picked up the knife.

"Wait, we gotta say the blessing first," Garth said.

"That's right. I was intoxicated by the delicious smell of this supper. Your mother is hard to resist." David winked at Sophie and set the knife down.

"Would you like to offer the blessing?" Sophie asked.

The tips of David's ears turned pink and he shifted in his chair. "Uh—sure, I can do that." He bowed his head and Sophie waited until the kids closed their eyes before sneaking a peek at David. He offered a prayer, blessing the food, and asked the Lord to watch over Sophie and her children. The words were thoughtful but David still seemed uncomfortable when he was finished with the prayer.

"Thank you." Sophie touched his arm, trying to convey her appreciation. David nodded and again picked up the knife. He served himself a large piece and then handed the spoon to Sophie. She dished up the food for Garth and Maggie who looked ravenous. "Make sure you chew your food politely."

"We will," Garth said as he shoveled in a giant forkful of crust. He immediately began stabbing pieces of chicken and crust, piling his fork with another huge bite.

David took a bite and Sophie held her breath, hoping he would like her cooking. He chewed and scooped up another bite. "This is delicious."

"Thank you. It's one of our favorites." Sophie relaxed and started eating, talking with David in between bites.

Maggie stood on her chair. "The peas are my favorite!"

"Maggie, please sit down," Sophie said. "I don't want you to spill your milk."

Maggie frowned, but she sat down and continued eating. Garth's plate held his full concentration, and Sophie only had to give him one stern look when he slurped his milk. The space in between her shoulders remained tight with tension even though the food was excellent and her children were being good. David seemed a little stiffer than usual. "Did you have a good day at work?"

"It was work. I suppose that I don't have much to complain about it. There are plenty of people with harder jobs than mine."

"That's true, but I think it's important to be happy too," Sophie said. "After all, you'll spend most of your life working that job."

David paused with his fork in mid-air. "I'm an Alexander. I don't have the luxury of questioning whether my job pleases me enough."

Sophie tasted his words in the back of her throat and she took a large swallow of milk, washing away the bitterness. She decided it was probably best to steer away from the topic of work, but she was at a loss for words.

"Oops, sorry Mr. David," Maggie said.

Sophie looked up in time to see milk dripping from the tablecloth onto David's lap. His brows knit together as he mopped up the milk.

"Oh dear, I'm sorry." Sophie jumped up and grabbed a dishcloth. "Maggie, sweetheart, you need to sit down and stay still."

"Can I have more milk?"

"No. Sit down and eat your dinner like your mother asked you to." David's answer offered no room for argument.

Maggie sat down, her chin trembling as a tear trailed down her cheek.

"Mommy, he made Maggie cry." Garth sat up taller in his chair and glared at David. "I don't like you."

"Garth! That was unkind. You need to apologize to David."

"I'm sorry you came to dinner," Garth said. He hopped down from his chair and stomped to his room.

Sophie looked up at the ceiling. "Well, this is a disaster."

"Not really, you could try it a different way," David said.

"What?" Sophie asked.

"Growing up, my sister and I always sat at our own table, while the adults sat at the dining table." He surveyed the room. "Although, I guess another table wouldn't really fit here."

The back of Sophie's neck tightened. Maggie sniffled. Sophie recognized the taste from earlier. It wasn't just bitterness, but the sharp taste of reality. David had been raised in a different world from Sophie even though he grew up only a few miles from her home. Suddenly everything about David came into focus. The way his mother despised Sophie simply because she couldn't afford the latest fashion and a housekeeper, and how David still didn't want to approach his mother with the idea that he and Sophie could have a relationship. Instead, he'd kept Sophie as far from Nadine as possible. Embarrassment creeped over Sophie's shoulders, making her hunch against her sniffling daughter.

She bowed her head and took a deep breath. "I think it's better if you just go now, David. I'm sorry that my children were out of sorts tonight." She scooped up her daughter.

"Wait, what just happened?" David stood. "We can finish eating. Just have the children go to their rooms."

Sophie narrowed her eyes. "Good night." She walked down the hall to her bedroom and sat on the edge of the bed with Maggie, rocking her slowly.

"I'm sorry Mommy. I'm a bad girl," Maggie cried.

"Hush Darlin', you are Mommy's sweetest girl and there's nothing you could do to change that. Even if you spilled all the milk in the world." Sophie kissed Maggie's cheek.

"All the milk would be a swimming pool and we could jump in!" Maggie giggled and Sophie joined her. She forced herself to laugh louder than she usually would in case David was listening. As their laughter died away, she heard the front door open and close. David had left without even trying to say goodbye.

Chapter 30 — The Rescue

Sophie awoke the next morning with a heavy heart. Her future was changing and it wasn't in the direction she'd anticipated. The mirror showed a young woman with dark circles under her eyes. Funny how yesterday when she'd looked in the mirror, she'd imagined what she might look like wearing the new hat she'd seen at the mercantile, on the arm of her husband, David Alexander. She'd fooled herself into thinking that David was interested in her, but she was nothing more than a curiosity. She was the forbidden toy and David had defied his mother to prove that he was a grownup who could make his own choices.

She pulled the long tresses of her dark hair into a bun, pinning it tightly against her skull. If David really cared about her, he would've made more of an effort to get to know her children. She couldn't be with a man who didn't love her children. She wouldn't sacrifice their happiness for her own. And she couldn't really be happy with someone who didn't adore her children the way she did. Hating the truth she'd uncovered because it meant more tough decisions, Sophie turned from the mirror.

Garth was out of sorts that morning, and Sophie did her best to cheer him up before sending him off to school and then she helped Maggie get dressed for the day. The telephone rang and Sophie knew it would be Debbie asking for details after last night.

"Hi Deb, I don't have long to talk. I have an interview with a new client today."

Debbie would know that she was talking about Doris Marchant and she could picture her cringing at the unmentioned name. For some reason, that made Sophie smile.

"You know you don't have to take on new clients just because they ask," Debbie said.

"Yes, but if I tell them that I'm too busy to take on new clients, the entire town will know before school's out."

"Hmm, you're right about that. She must have known you were smart enough to figure things out. See, I'm not quick enough on my feet. I hope that means that you'll be able to handle whatever she has planned for you."

"It's sewing and mending projects," Sophie replied. "She'll probably treat me the same way Mrs. Alexander always has—reminding me of my place and pointing out how insignificant my job is."

"And yet, they proudly wear all the clothing you sew and mend," Debbie grumbled.

"True. I'll let you know how it goes, okay?"

Sophie hung up the phone and picked up her sewing basket. She took Maggie's hand, surprised at how small her little girl's fingers were in her own. When she had turned five, Sophie had blinked back tears because her sweet baby was growing up, but she was still a child. She leaned down and kissed Maggie's chubby cheek. "I love you."

Maggie patted Sophie's cheek. "I love you Mommy. You're the prettiest Mommy in the world."

"Thank you." Sophie stared at Maggie's blonde curls and dark brown eyes. She wanted to capture this instant and frame it in her heart. For just this second, she wanted to stop time and never forget the sweetness of the moment. But the clock ticked forward and she needed to keep moving. Sophie shook off the melancholy that nipped at her heels after David's abrupt departure last night. She had reconciled herself to the truth that she couldn't hope to step into David's world. The only way she could do that is if David were willing to carry her across the invisible border that he couldn't see. That border loomed before her as Sophie entered the Marchant's neighborhood and pulled up in front of the stately home.

With false confidence and courage, Sophie took Maggie by the hand and carried her sewing basket to the front door. A stern middle-aged woman with a severe gray bun answered the door before Sophie could finish knocking.

"Right this way. Mrs. Marchant is expecting you," she said before Sophie had a chance to say a word.

Sophie nodded and tugged on Maggie's hand, helping her over the threshold. The pounding in her chest seemed to be counting down to an explosion that Sophie wanted to avoid. Maybe Debbie was right and she should have found a way to avoid the Marchants as long as possible. For the first time, she cursed the small, close-knit town of Aspen Falls. If the rumor mill hadn't put her in this predicament, Sophie would likely be at home working on another order for Mrs. Alexander.

"Ah, Mrs. Wright," a woman called in a tenor voice as Sophie entered the sitting room with Maggie in tow. Mrs. Doris Marchant was considerably younger than Nadine Alexander, or at least the amount of face creams and powders she used gave her the youthful appearance that could fool most people. She was a little on the plump side with her light brown hair pinned in curls. "Thank you for coming by on such short notice."

Another woman entered and stood beside Doris. "Oh, she's brought a child with her to work?"

Doris turned to the woman beside her. "This is my sister, Lavinia Stodhurst."

Sophie could immediately see the likeness in the woman who was obviously Doris's elder sister. Except Lavinia was overly thin and her hair was pulled back into a severe bun. "It's nice to meet you." She smiled and inclined her head toward Maggie. "This is my daughter, Maggie. She just turned five and she's a very well-behaved young lady."

Maggie smiled. "Hello."

Lavinia's nostrils flared. "See that she doesn't soil the cushions."

Sophie steeled herself against the introduction leading to the attack the two sisters must have planned. She could walk out the door; she didn't have to stay, especially now that she and David had found more uncommon ground between them.

Doris turned and sat down, not offering Sophie a seat. The foreboding tension in the air increased as Lavinia followed suit. Sophie pursed her lips and lowered herself onto a bench near the window. "What did you have in mind, something that needs repairs or a new project?"

"Ah, what did I have in mind, she asks," Doris turned to her sister and arched an eyebrow. The two shared a mirthless chuckle before turning icy gazes upon Sophie.

Sophie swallowed and sat up straighter. "I brought a few samples if you'd like to see some of my work." She reached toward her sewing basket.

"What I had in mind, Mrs. Wright, was a summer wedding for my daughter," Doris said. "But you probably already knew that."

"I wasn't aware that Linda was engaged." Sophie closed her sewing basket. She had walked into this trap, fully aware that Doris might be out for blood. But Doris couldn't hurt her. Sophie would stand her ground.

"Not officially, but she and David had quite the relationship until you came along," Doris replied.

"Pardon?" Sophie straightened, facing Doris without flinching.

"Nadine warned me about you, but I told her that it was laughable to think of David being distracted by a single woman with children from another man."

The way she phrased it made it sound as if Sophie had chosen to be single. The blow was lower than she'd ever encountered before and Sophie's mouth dropped open. "How dare you speak to me like that? My husband was killed in the war."

"Which is why you should leave David alone," Doris replied. "You aren't suitable to be an Alexander. I assume that is what you are after, but I can assure you that David would never marry someone like you—a servant who mends his clothing. If he's interested in you, it's because he hopes to secure you as a mistress."

Sophie put her hands over Maggie's ears and gently pulled her daughter closer. "If you were hoping that Linda would marry David, why would you ever speak of him in such a way?"

"Don't put on pretenses with me," Doris answered sharply. "I'm quite familiar with Mr. Brewster and I don't think he'll take lightly to certain information about his tenant."

Mr. Brewster owned the home that Sophie rented, but she'd never had any problem with him. Sophie stared straight ahead, trying to piece together the threat that hung in the air between them. Lavinia smiled, her beady eyes glinting. Sophie was reminded of a rat. There was a knock at the door and Sophie's heart jolted in her chest. She welcomed the respite from Doris's verbal execution, but she needed to leave before she lost control of her temper. She'd underestimated the witch.

"Who could that be?" Lavinia said, rising and walking toward the door.

Sophie heard voices as the stern woman greeted the newcomer. Her ears perked at the familiar cadence of one of the voices, but it couldn't be him, could it? Before Lavinia made it to the door, Leland entered the sitting room.

"I'm sorry to intrude but Sophie is needed at home straightaway." He turned to Sophie and there was a fierceness in his gaze that she didn't understand.

"What is it?" she asked.

Leland gave one shake of his head. "Not here. Mrs. Marchant, if you'll be so kind to send your order to Sophie later, I'm sure she'll be able to help you. Although, from what I hear, she is in high demand, so I wouldn't dawdle if I were you."

Mrs. Marchant sniffed. "I don't think I'll be needing her services."

"I apologize," Sophie said. "I'll–"

"That's probably best because Sophie's work is of much higher quality than you are used to." Leland took her arm and Sophie grabbed her sewing basket as he led her out of the room while Doris and Lavinia gasped in outrage. "Have a good day," he called over his shoulder.

Sophie quickened her step, towing Maggie behind her as Leland practically hauled her out of the house. He didn't slow once they had exited the house, if anything his pace increased.

"Leland, what are you doing?" Sophie hissed. "What is the matter?"

"Not here." He led her to her car and opened the door. "Please, hurry home and I'll meet you there. No one is hurt, but this is important."

"Okay," Sophie said because she couldn't think of another response. Leland tucked Maggie in the car, touching her cheek gently with his fingertips before closing the door. Sophie started the car and pulled away from the Marchant's house. What could Leland possibly need that was so important he would track her down and barge in on a meeting with the Marchant's? She was halfway home when she noticed that her hands were shaking. Her skin felt clammy and Maggie was unusually quiet in the back seat. "We're almost home, sweetheart."

"Mommy?"

"Yes?"

"I don't like those ladies. They were saying mean things to you." Maggie sniffed and Sophie turned, shocked to see tears coursing down her daughter's cheeks.

"Oh, dear. I'm so sorry that they made you sad. They were wicked, awful people. Let's not think of them any longer." A thought slammed into her with such force that Sophie gasped. Leland had rescued her from Doris Marchant and her horrible sister. Sophie pulled into her driveway as Leland parked his pickup. There was no one waiting at her house and nothing looked amiss. He jumped out and rushed toward the car, helping Maggie out as Sophie climbed out of the car. "Leland Halverson, what in the world is going on?"

"Why did you go there, Sophie? You had to know what Mrs. Marchant had planned. Why would you do that to yourself?"

Sophie felt her face go slack as the truth washed over her. He *had* come for her–Leland had saved her from those hateful women. Her chin trembled and Sophie closed her eyes, reaching deep inside for another stone to add to the dam she had built over the years to hide her emotions. It was crumbling and if she didn't do something, the walls would burst. She took a shuddering breath and opened her eyes, blinking rapidly. "I had to go," she whispered.

Leland grabbed Sophie and pulled her into his chest. "No," he said. "No, you don't ever have to do something like that again."

Sophie leaned into his chest, closing her eyes against the tears that wet her lashes. No! She couldn't let even a drop leak from the barrier. She wouldn't let him see her cry. Sophie turned her face into Leland's shirt, letting the flannel soak the few errant drops of misery oozing from her soul.

"Sophie. I'm so sorry. I've worked with the Marchants enough that I told them I'd never work with them again. No one should have to deal with their devil ways." He leaned back, looking her in the face. "Do you hear me? You don't have to put up with that kind of treatment."

Sophie took a shaky breath, swallowing against the jagged edge of humiliation and anger mixed together. "How did you know?"

"Thank goodness Mr. Gillespie is almost as big a gossip as his wife."

Sophie furrowed her brow. "But, I don't understand. How would they know anything about my schedule?"

"I was at the hardware store and I overheard Albert telling someone about how poor Sophie Wright was in hot water with the Marchants. I asked him about it and he said that he'd heard you had an appointment with Doris today and she had invited her sister from Denver to make sure you never thought of speaking to David again."

Sophie's skin turned ice cold. "How could I be so foolish?"

"Because you didn't know," Leland answered.

She shook her head. "I knew. I just tried to tell myself that it wouldn't be so bad and if I got another job from her, it might be worth the harassment."

"What did she say?"

"She threatened me–said something about giving Mr. Brewster information about me. Could she–I mean, he wouldn't believe something from her, would he?"

Leland's face darkened. "It wouldn't be so much what she would say, but what she might threaten him with. You may be in over your head, Sophie. I hate to say it, but the only way you're going to find peace is if David goes to bat for you."

A wash of heat blossomed over Sophie's cheeks. No one knew about what had happened last night. Sophie wasn't sure if she should expect to see David again or not. It was a simple misunderstanding, but in light of the day's events everything seemed bigger and more impossible than they had that morning. Leland stood before her, his face anxious as his eyes searched hers. She studied him, his dark brown eyes reminded her of Maggie. Sophie stepped out of Leland's arms, looking around wildly. "Maggie!"

"What Mommy?" Maggie stood right next to Leland, leaning into him, watching them carefully.

"Oh, you're right here." Sophie smiled and patted Maggie's head and then rested her hand on Leland's arm. "Thank you. I can't believe that you would barge into Doris's house to rescue me. I'm not sure what to do now, but, do you want to come in for a minute?"

Leland looked to the street and back to Sophie. His face held worry, but then he smiled. "I'd like that very much, but I'm afraid that I left things undone at my shop because I left in such a hurry."

"Oh, maybe another time then?"

He nodded. "Let me help you inside, though."

Sophie noticed how Leland scooped Maggie up in his arms and carried her into the house effortlessly. Maggie smiled and told Leland about how her doll, Charlotte loved her chair with all of her heart. Leland smiled. "I'm glad to hear that she likes it." He turned to Sophie and winked.

Sophie's heart warmed at Leland's ease with Maggie. He was the same way with Garth, and she couldn't ignore the quick comparison she drew between him and David's behavior last night. It wasn't fair to David—perhaps he'd been stressed and out of sorts. But Leland had been around her children several times and she'd never seen anything akin to David's annoyance in Leland's features.

"I'd best be going, but Sophie, will you give David a call and tell him what happened? I'm not sure what's going on between you two, but he needs to rein in his mother before she destroys this town with her manipulation and conniving."

"You're right," Sophie said. "I'm not sure what's happening either. David and I are dating, and I'm busy with my children and my job."

Leland held up his hand. "You don't have to explain to me. Let me know if there's anything else I can do." He turned to go, but Sophie grabbed his arm.

"Thank you for saving me," she murmured. "I don't know what would have happened if you hadn't come."

Leland covered her hand with his, pressing his fingers against hers. "You're a good woman, Sophie. You deserve the best life has to offer. Don't go looking for trouble, okay?"

Sophie nodded, swallowing words she wanted to say as Leland walked out her door.

Leland drove away from Sophie's house, wishing that he had the nerve to turn around and tell Sophie not to waste any more time or tears on David Alexander. He tightened his grip on the steering wheel and studied his surroundings, trying to keep his thoughts away from Sophie. The last of the snow had melted and icy puddles lined the edges of the road as spring's tentative fingers reached across the landscape. Soon, there would be leaves budding on the trees and new life would reach skyward. There was a lot of speculation on what the year of 1946 would bring for the world—times were still uncertain. Leland didn't like the uncertainty. He wanted this year to be better—one of the best years of his life—and so many things were going well for him.

His shop was profitable enough that he'd saved a nice nest egg and fixed up his house. He was in an excellent position to provide for a family. And there was Sophie again, dominating his thoughts with her two cute kids, putting ideas into his head. He'd acted rashly, going after her, but when he'd heard Albert carrying on as if Sophie's fate was already sealed, Leland had run to his pickup and sped across town. Well, there shouldn't be any doubt how he felt about Sophie, but then, women were curious creatures. How could he get Sophie to understand his feelings for her with David looming in the background?

Leland turned onto his street, anxious to return to his shop and work on the carving he'd started last week for Sophie. He greeted Hope with a pat to the head and pulled open the door of his shop. A gust of wind blew in behind him and swirled the sawdust on the table. Leland's shoulders tensed when he heard a faint melody. He walked forward and picked up the block of wood that no longer looked like a scrap of wood. Leland tried not to listen to the wind, but it tickled his ears with a hollow sound that echoed faintly with, *Tell her.*

He picked up his knife and began carving, shaping the wood and imagining Sophie's face when he finally told her the secret the wind kept whispering. For the thousandth time, he wished he didn't have to tell her the truth about Jessie's death and his part in the ending of his beautiful little girl's life. But he would tell her. The carving coming out of the wood was for Sophie and Leland knew that when he gave her the gift, he would have the courage to bare his soul to her.

Keith had said that Leland was worrying over something that Sophie would never hold against him. It was clear by what he'd said that Keith thought Sophie already knew. Leland swallowed. It was only a matter of time before something slipped. Leland notched another cut into the wood. Time was running out.

Chapter 31 – Stitches

Sophie spent the rest of the evening cleaning the house and organizing her sewing supplies–anything to keep her mind off the events of the day. She kept thinking about what Leland had said, urging her to seek help from David, but she didn't know how to approach him. Thoughts panned out in different scenarios–would David be her knight in shining armor and cast Doris Marchant from her throne? Or would he soothe Sophie, assuring her that things weren't as bad as they seemed and surely she'd read more into the situation than was really there. Cal would've flat-out ignored her, or worse mocked the situation, twisting it so that Sophie was left wondering if she were the one in the wrong. Her shoulders curled inward until Sophie's back ached with the pressure of what she needed to do.

She spent extra time rocking Maggie, singing lullabies and soothing her own heart along with her little girl's. Before she went to bed, she checked on Garth again. He slept heavily, his dark lashes resting against pale cheeks. Sophie pushed a shock of dark hair from his forehead. "Please, God, help him to grow up to be an honorable man," she whispered.

Sophie clung to her pillow and tried not to feel the loneliness that hung in the air around her. It had been a mistake to go to the Marchant's house, but Sophie had learned something from it that she wouldn't trade. Leland Halverson did have a heart lined with gold. If he would give her the opportunity, she would gladly get to know his heart, but every time he was close enough to open up, he ran the other direction. Despite the words that Serena had shared with her, Sophie didn't know if she had the courage to confront her past and let it go. Maybe they were both doomed to live lives alone.

The next morning passed by slowly with Sophie going to the phone several times, intent on calling David or Debbie, or even Keith, but each time she turned back to mundane household chores.

At two-thirty in the afternoon, there was a knock at the door, and David opened it and stepped inside before she could answer. He was carrying a heavy cardboard box. "I'm sorry to barge in, but this is heavy." He set the box down on the floor.

Sophie didn't know whether to invite him to sit down or not. There was so much that she wanted to say and they needed to address the incident from dinner a few nights before, but all she could do was hold a finger to her lips. "Maggie is taking one of her rare naps and Garth isn't home from school yet."

"My timing is impeccable," David replied lifting his brows and winking.

Sophie's heart fluttered when David looked at her that way, and it took all she had to keep her smile demure. "What do you have there?" Sophie motioned to the box.

David bent down and lifted the flap of the large box. "This is one of those new-fangled machines. It uses electricity and Mr. Cooper said you can stitch all night and the needle will stay true to the seamline. And he said something about this being the one with the new zigzag feature—whatever that means."

Sophie had seen advertisements for the Singer sewing machine and it cost more than four times what Mrs. Alexander had paid her for sewing the drapes. It had been a fanciful dream when she'd pinned the picture up on her wall next to her old sewing machine. She turned to the corner of her living room where her sewing station was set up. The advertisement was gone. "That's how you knew? You saw the paper?"

David grinned and shrugged. "I'm good at reconnaissance, what can I say?"

"I couldn't possibly accept a gift like this. I don't know how you even managed to come by one. It's too extravagant."

"Extravagant?" He motioned to the box. "It's heavy, but it's useful and needed. Now, if I were to buy you a diamond necklace, that might be extravagant, and definitely something I'd know a little more about." He stepped forward and cupped her chin with his hand. "I'm very sorry about how things ended the other night and I want to make it up to you. Sophie, I want to make you happy. Will you allow me to have this joy?"

Sophie glanced down at the box, most likely containing one of the first new sewing machines in Aspen Falls since the beginning of the war. She couldn't help it—the smile that spread across her face came from her heart and blossomed outwards. But she couldn't forget the things she'd learned in one short day. Or the way Leland had rescued her from Doris Marchant. "David, I'm afraid we're not suited for each other."

"I disagree," David said. "I was an idiot and I'm very sorry about how I acted, but I'm not going to give up on you because we had a little disagreement. Please don't tell me that you want to end any chance of what we have because I'm rough around the edges?"

Sophie opened her mouth and then closed it. She hadn't expected such a speech from David. If only she could be sure that his words were sincere. His blue eyes appeared earnest and he gave her a tentative smile. Sophie pursed her lips and gave a little shake of her head. "I don't know."

"Please." David leaned closer, and Sophie couldn't ignore the pounding of her heart at his nearness. She smelled the crisp scent of his aftershave and as she pulled her eyes from his, she noticed the fine lines of his suit over broad shoulders.

"I don't see how it could ever work between us," Sophie whispered.

"Let me show you," David said. "Don't let anyone else get in that pretty little head of yours. I'm right here and I know you can feel the connection we have." David put his hands on her arms and pulled her closer, his lips only a breath from hers.

Sophie looked up at him, studying his face for a telling sign of how she should proceed. Was it all just a misunderstanding? The attraction between them was real, but Sophie needed to concentrate on more than that. With David standing so close, touching her skin, it was hard to concentrate on anything but how his arms might feel around her.

She could turn her head and allow him to kiss her cheek as she had before, but David had no intention of a chaste kiss on the cheek. He closed the distance, claiming her lips, encircling her waist with his hands and pulling her towards him. Sophie parted her lips, kissing him softly, her hands resting on his chest. David pulled back and rested his forehead against hers. "You are so beautiful. I never want to hurt you. Please forgive me?"

She put her arms around his neck and leaned closer. "I guess I can give you another chance." She moved to step out of the embrace, but David held her still and kissed her once more. Heat rushed across her skin as David kissed her again and again. He unclipped her hair and the dark curls tumbled down her back. He groaned as he held her close. "You'll destroy me."

Sophie tipped her head back. "Why?"

"Because one kiss will never be enough now."

The hunger in his eyes reminded Sophie of Cal and the way he manipulated her, controlled her, and commanded her in the bedroom. And then Doris Marchant's words—hinting at her status as a mistress—stung her with ferocity. Fear rose up in the back of her throat and Sophie stumbled out of David's grasp. "No."

David reached for her and she stepped back. "No, David. I won't."

"Sweetheart," David held up his hands, "I would never ask you to."

The tension in the air hung heavy like a thick fog. Sophie studied him, her chest heaving with short breaths. She closed her eyes. Cal was gone. He couldn't hurt her anymore. After years of praying, God had answered her pleas and rescued her. Opening her eyes, she looked at David. "I know."

David knelt in front of her. "Sophie, I love you."

Sophie's lungs deflated. She thought of Mrs. Marchant and her sister, just two of many people who would wholeheartedly disapprove of a serious relationship between Sophie and David. A pain radiated up the back of her skull. "No, you can't love me, David." She reached down, grabbed his hands and pulled him upwards. "I'm not the right girl for you. The Alexander name wouldn't rest well on me and if this town ever found out about my past, it would destroy your mother. I won't do that to her or you."

David studied her for a moment with a furrowed brow. "So, I don't have any say in the matter at all?"

"No, I'm sorry," Sophie said. "I can't accept your gift. Please just go."

"I'm not leaving," David said. "This can't be just about the mishap at dinner. What happened?"

Sophie looked down, still tasting the remnant of David's kiss on her lips. "Mrs. Marchant asked me to come to her home for a sewing appointment."

"Oh, no," David murmured. "Please say you didn't go."

Sophie lifted her head. "I did. I knew it wasn't wise, but even her invitation was a threat. If I didn't go, she would try to ruin my business. And David, your mother hasn't asked for any more work from me."

David pushed his hand through his shock of black hair. "I'm sorry. I thought I had taken care of things, but I underestimated my mother...again." He sighed. "What happened?"

Sophie swallowed. Her stomach boiled as she recalled Doris's words. They were poison and she didn't want to speak them aloud.

"You can tell me. I want you to tell me what she did to you."

"She threatened me, said something about my landlord, my reputation, and that I was only fit to be your mistress."

David cursed and Sophie jumped back. He held out his hands. "I'm sorry." He hesitated, watching her carefully. His features softened and she saw pain flicker behind his eyes. "Are you afraid of me?"

"No—I mean, I don't know. I don't want to be hurt again."

Two beats of silence stretched between them. David stepped forward, pulling Sophie into his arms. "That kiss meant something to me. You mean something to me."

"It doesn't matter what I mean to you if your own mother and your neighbors are willing to crucify me."

David rested his chin on the top of her head. "I don't know what to do. If I confront my mother or Mrs. Marchant, things could get really nasty." His words reverberated through her. He kissed her forehead and leaned back to look in her eyes. "I think it's best if we weather the storm. Let me show them that I'm serious about you."

Sophie's heart sank as she realized that David wasn't going to do anything to protect her reputation or stop the attacks from his mother and other members of Aspen Falls' elite society. Her lips trembled and her eyes burned, but no, she couldn't break down in front of David—she wouldn't. Sophie shook her head, filling her lungs with breath and steadying her voice. "I've already weathered enough storms for a lifetime, David. I'm sorry, but I can't do this. I think it's best if you go now."

"Sophie, please don't do this." David reached for her hand, but Sophie turned and hurried down the hall. She closed the door to her room and slid down to the carpet, tears leaking out even as she shook her head, commanding herself not to cry. She wouldn't cry over a man! That had been the promise she'd made to herself after Cal died. No more useless tears. Except these tears didn't feel useless; each one felt like acid pouring down her cheeks, hot and unforgiving. Her heart hurt and the tighter she held her body the more tears leaked out.

The front door shut and Sophie crumpled into a heap on the floor, curling into the fetal position. She had been holding onto a shard of hope that David could make things right—that he could repair the awfulness his mother and Mrs. Marchant had inflicted, but he wasn't willing to stand up for her. She traced her lips, thinking of his kisses. They were pleasant and her body had responded to his affection, but her soul was still locked away, deep inside a prison that she'd carefully constructed over so many years. In a moment of weakness she had peeled back a layer of the prison wall and allowed herself to try to feel again—to venture out of the lockbox. It was a mistake. The hurt radiated like an electric shock against the cage of her heart. Sophie bowed her head and struggled to stop the tears. If she ever truly broke down, she might lose control of her heart for good.

Chapter 32 – The Music Box Discovery

David called three times that evening and each time, Sophie answered and told him that she was busy with the kids and couldn't talk. Maggie and Garth sensed that something was wrong and they went to bed without protest.

In the dim light of the living room, Sophie pushed the heavy box into her sewing corner. She sat next to it, examining the body of the sewing machine and reading over the instruction manual. The machine would be an incredible asset to her business and the basic necessities of her life, raising her two children who seemed to constantly need clothing mended. With a sigh, she dropped the manual back into the box. Her fingers brushed against another piece of paper and she pulled it out of the box. She unfolded the sheet of paper and her eyes flew to the bottom of the page where David had signed his name. Even though Sophie told herself not to read it, she couldn't help herself.

Sophie,

I'm so sorry for the pain that I've caused you. I never wanted to hurt you. I'm going to figure out a way to fix this. Will you give me a chance?

No matter what your answer is or what happens between us, this is your sewing machine. Please don't try to return it because I've already given Mr.

Cooper strict instructions to deny it. I want you to have this because you deserve to have something just for you to make your life easier.

Love,

David

Sophie held the note, her hands shaking and the words blurring before her. Did this mean that David was going to stand up for her and fix things, or did it mean that he would just try to help her ignore the mistreatments from others?

Leaning back, she rested her head against the wall, her hand resting on the sewing machine. He must have written the note before he left her house. Part of her wished that he had tried to say the words to her in person, but David was smart enough to know that Sophie wasn't in a good emotional state. In truth, she still didn't trust her emotions or David. She could stew over him all night, but that wouldn't help her or the kids tomorrow. Clutching the note, Sophie walked down the hall and climbed into bed. Hopefully morning would bring some clarity to the confusion pulsing through her heart.

When the telephone rang after breakfast, Sophie was tempted not to answer because she still didn't want to talk to David.

"Hello."

"Hello, Sophie." Serena Tanaka's voice with her light accent was unmistakable. "I am hoping this afternoon is still a good time for the children to play."

"Oh, yes, of course." Sophie had completely forgotten about visiting the Tanaka's, but she recovered quickly. "We'll be over and I have some applesauce muffins I'd like to bring."

"Those sound delicious. I'm glad you can come."

"Me, too. We'll see you later." Sophie hung up the phone and went to the cupboard and retrieved her mother's recipe for the muffins. The applesauce made with sweet yellow delicious apples took the place of sugar. The apples had ripened perfectly last fall and Sophie, Debbie, and Betty had canned as many bottles as they could. The naturally sweetened applesauce was a special treat that she'd used in many recipes to stretch her sugar ration as far as possible. Sophie looked up at the top shelf of the cupboard where the remains of Leland's sugar sat in a brown bag. Leland had brought sugar when David had brought roses. Leland had been certain that David would remedy the situation with the Marchant's, but David hadn't given her clear assurance on the matter. David had proclaimed his love for her, and Leland had quietly turned the other way keeping his feelings to himself.

It was easy to see what Debbie had told her before—in competition with David Alexander, not many men would want to waste their time. The odds were unevenly stacked against Leland from a bystander's point of view, but as Sophie took down the bag of sugar she couldn't help but see a distinct difference between the two men.

Garth ran as fast as he could to the Tanaka's house no matter how many times Sophie called for him to slow down. Maggie held tight to her dolly in one hand and Sophie's fingers with the other. Sophie carried a covered pie tin with the muffins, still warm from the oven. The last vestiges of winter had given way to spring and Sophie smiled at the yellow and white daffodils poking above yellowed grass. The Tanaka's flowerbeds showcased lovely daffodils and green shoots of tulips that Sophie was eager to see as the season progressed.

Serena met them at the door because Garth had already made his way inside.

"Thank you for coming. I put on some coffee just a few minutes ago."

"I brought the muffins." Sophie walked inside and set the pie tin on the table. The children giggled and squealed and Serena chuckled as they ran down the hall to Emika's bedroom.

"Do you think we've really seen the end of the rations?" Sophie asked. "My mother used to drink three cups of coffee a day. She'll think she's died and gone to heaven if things ever go back to how they used to be."

Serena looked thoughtful. "It has become a way of life for us now."

"I'm sorry. I didn't mean it that way. I'm sure that it was much worse for you when you were at the relocation camp."

Serena lifted one shoulder and let it drop. "It is in the past. We are blessed now, even if there is never enough coffee." She smiled.

The air pulsated with warmth from Serena's words and her sincere smile. Emika shrieked and Garth's high-pitched laugh floated down the hall. Laughter bubbled up inside of Sophie and she released it, adding to the good feelings in the home. "They get along so well."

"I'm glad that she has a good friend." Serena looked wistfully down the hall.

Sophie's throat tightened at the singular form of the word Serena had used. "Does Emika have some girlfriends too? Doesn't Mary Phelps live two doors down?"

Serena looked down at the table and sighed. "Not everyone is forgiving as you."

Sophie knew what Serena spoke of. All she had to do was think of Mildred Chastain at the Safeway and others who spoke negatively about the Japanese-American's in Aspen Falls to understand that it was probably difficult for the Tanakas. But fire burned inside her at the unjust situation. "I didn't have to forgive you for anything, Serena. Your family didn't do anything to me."

Serena pressed her lips together and her eyes shimmered with tears.

"Mrs. Phelps tell me that if it weren't for my people, we wouldn't have widows like Sophie Wright."

Sophie gasped, her hand covering her mouth. She shook her head. "How could she say something like that?"

"Shunsaku and I spoke of this–that you–the woman who lost her husband in Pearl Harbor have the most right to be angry at us. Instead you are our friend. Thank you."

Sophie stepped forward and hugged Serena. "You are *my* friend."

Serena hugged her and then stepped away, wiping her eyes. "Let me check that coffee."

"This town has changed since the war." Sophie pulled out a chair and sat at the table. "People weren't this way when I was a child. I pray each day that hearts will be softened so that we can all be neighbors again."

"We will be," Serena said, "because of people like you. Now, how about we try some of those muffins?"

Sophie chuckled and took the towel off her pie tin, revealing the fresh muffins. The sweet scent of apples made her mouth water. She put a pat of the yellowish oleo margarine on the muffin and watched it melt into the crevices of the muffin top. Serena brought over plates and they fixed a muffin for each of the children who seemed to have a sixth sense when it came to food. They all arrived in the kitchen, scrambling for a snack.

Serena and Sophie talked over the kid's laughter and chatter and then the kids raced back down the hall to continue playing. They had just a few moments of quiet before Baby Shun began fussing. Serena jiggled him on her hip, trying to calm his cries. She sniffed and wrinkled her nose. "Oh, I know why you're sad," she cooed. "I'll be right back."

Sophie nodded, content to sip her coffee. Emika limped down the hall a minute later. "Do you want to see our block tower?"

"I wouldn't miss it."

She matched strides with Emika's noticing how hard the little girl tried to keep her steps even.

"Look, Mommy!" Garth pointed at the tower that was leaning precariously as Maggie set another block on the top.

"Wonderful! You kids are quite the builders." Sophie clapped her hands and the tower fell, scattering blocks across the floor.

Maggie giggled and Garth scooped up a handful, immediately starting a new tower.

"Can I see your dancer again?" Maggie asked Emika.

Sophie noticed the simple music box sitting atop Emika's dresser on a lace doily. Emika walked over and pushed the brass button on her music box. The tiny ballerina sprang to life, twirling to the music in front of her personal mirror. Sophie felt drawn to the music, her heartbeat quickened. She'd heard the tune before and admired the miniature ballerina with her scrap of tulle forming a tutu. But as she listened, she felt compelled to touch the music box. She reached out and slid her finger along the smooth edge of the box. It was covered with an ivory paper that was edged in gold.

Emika leaned forward, grinning. "Would you like to see my March of Dimes pin? They are the ones who helped pay for my polio treatment when I was in Minnesota. Everyone gathered up dimes so that I could get better."

Sophie had heard about Roosevelt's campaign for the many children suffering from the horrible disease that had left Emika with braces and a limp. "Yes, I'd love to see it. Where is it?"

Emika lifted a side compartment that was lined in a red velvet paper and carefully removed the pin. It was a gray tin badge fashioned to look like a red and white ribbon was attached to a banner that read, "Fight Infantile Paralysis."

"This is very special," Sophie said. "I'm glad you have a safe place to keep it."

"Me too. There was a soldier at my treatment center. He loved my music box too. He helped me wind it, but now I can wind it myself." Emika reached for the brass handle and carefully turned it. "See?"

The music sped up and the ballerina continued her dance as the melody flowed through the room. Emika returned to the block tower, leaving Sophie to put the March of Dimes pin back in its compartment. She started to close the lid when she saw that the velvet paper on the compartment was loose. She pulled the edge so that she could tuck it back into place and most of the lining came away. Sophie worried that she'd inadvertently ripped the lining, but then she saw something on the cardboard backing. There were three scraps of paper glued onto the lid behind the red velvet-lined paper.

The first was a light blue piece of stationery that had been trimmed and glued into place with a message written in flowing script. "Don't die with me." The words held a power that touched her soul. What did it mean? Sophie whispered them aloud. "Don't die with me."

Next to the blue paper, there was a soft green piece of paper with an R embossed in the corner. In a feminine hand, the words, "Forgive yourself—allow God to forgive" seemed to resonate with the melody playing out.

Sophie leaned forward to examine the third piece of paper and her heart jolted in her chest. The paper read, "Live to dance again." The message was sweet and inspirational, but it wasn't the message that had her heart hammering in its cage. It was the handwriting. Sophie recognized Leland's bold pencil strokes on the piece of paper. The note he had written her had been in a similar style with paper ripped from his notebook. This piece of paper looked to have come from the same notebook, a scrap torn off, the jagged edge revealing a bit of amber-colored glue holding it in place.

"Emika, what are these papers?"

Emika was crouching over the blocks, but she looked up with a smile. "Oh, those are my secret messages. Leland wrote one for me." She stood and walked toward the music box. She pointed at the scrap with Leland's handwriting. "See, it says, 'Live to dance again', because Leland wants me to get better."

"And who wrote the other notes?"

"I don't know who wrote the blue one," Emika replied. "But my mom said that someone who used to love Leland wrote the green note."

Sophie struggled for a breath as she comprehended Emika's words. Someone who used to love Leland would have to be his ex-wife, Rhonda. It made sense that she would have stationery with an "R" but what did the words mean?

"I'm going to dance again someday," Emika said.

"Oh?" Sophie allowed the little girl to pull her from the mystery of the words before her. "I bet you will be a beautiful dancer."

Emika hugged Sophie. "You're so pretty."

Sophie put her arms around the little girl. "Thank you. So are you."

"Baby Shun is all clean now," Serena said. She entered the room and set the baby by the blocks. "Looks like everyone is having fun."

Sophie quickly removed any sign of worried concentration from her brow and smiled. "They are having a delightful time." Sophie opened her mouth to ask Serena about the papers in the music box, but then she hesitated. If she were to ask Serena about the words written on those slips of paper, Sophie felt certain that she would discover something about Leland that he had kept secret. Sophie turned and carefully pushed the paper back into place, covering the messages. She closed the compartment, briefly studying the ballerina frozen mid-twirl in front of the little mirror. Serena said that Leland was a good man, so if he was keeping something secret about his past, he had his reasons. The words, *Forgive yourself–allow God to forgive* kept running through Sophie's mind. What had Leland done that he hadn't forgiven himself for?

Chapter 33 – Just Down the Street

When Sophie left the Tanaka's house, she and her children were happy. The visit had been relaxing, and just what she needed to put her mind at ease about her life that seemed to be in constant upheaval. David loomed in the distance and Sophie knew that either they would resolve the troubles surrounding their relationship or it would have to end soon. She kept thinking about Leland and Emika's music box with its cryptic messages. Sophie didn't want to pry, but she couldn't ignore the burning curiosity she felt about the quiet carpenter.

They rounded the corner and Sophie saw a familiar red brick house. "Garth, do you know Mary Phelps?"

"Yep, she's in my class."

"Well, I'd like to stop by her house for a moment. Do you think you can be on your best behavior?"

Garth pushed his hands into his pockets. "I s'pose."

Sophie looked back at the Tanaka's house. Hopefully she wasn't about to cause more trouble for Serena. With a firm knock on the door, Sophie straightened her back.

Anita opened the door and Sophie was taken back a decade, with memories washing over her of the short, petite blonde from high school. They hadn't been fast friends, but she'd never had any disagreements with Anita. She hoped that Anita's memories of her were as pleasant. Anita had gained some weight and her hair had darkened to dishwater blonde but her blue eyes were still vibrant. "Why, hello Sophie. How are you doing? Come right in."

Sophie walked into the house, noticing the hardwood flooring with multi-colored braided rugs placed throughout the entry way and living room. "Your home is beautiful."

"Thank you. What brings you here today?"

"Well, I was just over for a visit with the Tanakas and I thought I should at least stop in and say hello since I was walking right by. I didn't realize that you lived this close to me."

A shadow passed over Anita's face and though she tried to keep her smile steady, it faltered. "Why were you at their house?"

Sophie paused. "Why don't I come to the point, instead of beating around the bush? I asked Serena if Mary and Emika were friends and she said that they weren't."

"Well, of course not," Anita replied. "I don't want my daughter keeping company with Japs, and I can't imagine that you would want to step foot in their house."

"They are our neighbors and they are a fine family. Garth and Emika get along wonderful. Serena is very talented, she has—"

"Her people killed your husband."

Sophie's sharp intake of breath echoed against the fine walls of Anita's house. She gripped the pie plate in her hand tightly and took a step toward Anita, lowering her voice. "My husband was killed in the war, and yes, there were Japanese kamikaze pilots involved in his death, but our neighbors were not responsible. The Tanakas are Americans and just because they have Japanese ancestry doesn't mean they are the enemy."

"How do you know that?"

"Because I've taken time to get to know them," Sophie replied. "I can see that you feel strongly about this, but I hope that you will refrain from talking about my late husband and especially casting blame for his death on any American citizen."

"I'm sorry, Sophie," Anita said. "I didn't mean to upset you. It's just the way things are now."

"No, it's not. Emika nearly died last year from polio and she might be crippled for the rest of her life. That little girl needs a friend. Don't let hate and fear keep Mary from missing out on someone who could be her best friend."

"Can you imagine what people would say if I let Mary play with her?" Anita looked down at the floor. "Fred would be furious."

Sophie shook her head. "I guess that's the difference between us. I've already lost so much that I don't care what people think. I have a freedom that has given me the opportunity to know a kind and gracious family. Will you please at least think about the sacrifices that the Tanakas have given in order to come back and rebuild their life?"

Anita clasped her hands together. "I'm not sure it would make much difference."

"You're a smart woman. You'll figure out a way to let that little girl have friends." Sophie turned to the door. "I'd better be going. I'm sorry if I upset you."

Anita put her hand on Sophie's arm. "No, I'm the one who should apologize. I'm sorry."

Sophie nodded and then took Maggie's hand and walked with Garth down the front steps. Anita was sorry, but would she do anything differently from this day forward?

David called later that afternoon. "Sophie, can I come by and see you after work? I need to talk to you about something."

"Okay."

He kept the phone call brief, but Sophie's neighbors would probably be looking for him after work if Mrs. Gillespie had been listening in on the party line. Sophie sighed. She had at least two hours to kill before she could find out what David wanted to talk to her about.

There were a few items that she needed to finish sewing. Sophie hadn't taken the new sewing machine out of the box yet, but she was sorely tempted to. Instead, she closed the flaps and pulled out her sewing basket. When Maggie wandered over with her dolly, Sophie handed her a scrap of material, a button, and a needle and thread. She helped Maggie get started and the little girl sewed five buttons on the scrap of fabric while Sophie worked. A neat stack of clothes waited for David to take home with him—these items he'd brought over himself. She'd already mended another torn buttonhole for David. She'd discovered the source of that problem. David loved to roll up his sleeves as soon as he left work and he'd often pop the buttons off in his haste to relax his clothing. Despite the state of things between the two of them, Sophie still worried about David's job at the mine. He didn't ever seem excited about it or want to talk about his work.

Garth ran through the room flying his toy plane and shouting about shooting down the enemy. Sophie smiled because it reminded her of the pure joy she saw on David's face when he talked about flying planes. There was a knock at the door and Garth hurried to open it.

"Hi, David. I'm flying my Warhawk!"

"That's good, kid," David responded. He looked up at Sophie and smiled. "You sure are a sight for sore eyes."

Sophie brushed off a few threads and fabric clippings from her skirt, strangely nervous to have David standing before her now. Was he thinking about their kiss as well? "It's good to see you too, David."

He walked past Garth and Maggie and pulled Sophie into his arms, brushing her cheek with a kiss. Sophie extracted herself quickly, aware that her children were watching intently. "What did you want to talk about?"

"Uh, I guess I didn't plan very well." He motioned to the kids. "Could we talk for a minute?"

Sophie nodded. "Garth, Maggie, could you go and tidy up your rooms so that you can show David how nice you've been keeping them?"

"Aw, Mom," Garth whined.

"I will, Mommy," Maggie said. She danced down the hall with her dolly.

"Don't come out until I come and check," Sophie called.

David took her hand and led her to the couch. He smiled, but it didn't reach his eyes.

"David, what's the matter? You're making me nervous."

"I could say the same I guess." He intertwined his fingers with hers. "Sophie, I told you that I loved you and I do. Have you thought about anything that we discussed?"

"Do you mean your mother and her awful neighbors?"

David closed his eyes and shook his head. He blew out a breath and then looked at Sophie. "I talked to Linda. I apologized and told her that I never had planned on marrying her."

"Oh, my." Sophie sat up straight, surprise and an emotion halfway between hope and sadness mingling in her throat. "How did that go?"

"She was heartbroken–said that it was all your fault. I don't think that you two will be friends. Is that okay?"

Sophie laughed. "You make fun, but it's not funny to have the Marchants and Alexanders against you."

"Now, wait a minute." David leaned closer, putting his arm around Sophie. "The Alexanders aren't against you."

Sophie arched an eyebrow.

"Okay, not all of them, and I'm working on it."

"Have you talked to your mother?"

"I told her that there was no chance I would marry Linda, and she went into a frenzy. Is it bad that sometimes I wish I was still in the war? It might be less dangerous."

"Where would you go, if you weren't here?" Sophie asked.

"I'd fly. Some of my friends are looking into flying commercial airlines."

"Have you ever considered that you might not be happy here in Aspen Falls?"

David jerked his head back as if he'd been jolted from a daydream. "What? No, like I told you before. This is my family business. It's a good life. I would be foolish to throw it all away."

"That sounds an awful lot like your mother talking."

"Well, then let's not talk about my mother." David put his arm back around Sophie and pulled her close. "Let's talk about us. We're here right now and I'm telling you that it's okay for me to love you."

Sophie shook her head. "But it's not, because I've told you that I can't be an Alexander. Life is hard enough without marrying into a family that doesn't want you."

"So we'll move to Calloway Grove. You'll only have to see my mother once a month."

The room grew quiet but Sophie could hear her heart beating in her head. Pounding with the words that David was speaking. "What about Garth and Maggie?"

"What about them?"

Sophie twisted her hands in her lap, until David covered them with his own. He leaned forward and put his hand on her cheek. "Tell me what's bothering you."

"It's just, you don't really seem interested in my children."

David scrunched his eyes. "I've hardly spent any time with them. I've never been a dad before. My dad was always at the office or away on business. I expect that I'll be much the same way, especially with the new tunnel we're opening up this spring."

He spoke the truth, and even though Sophie recognized that David didn't see any other way, she was unsure if he understood what she'd meant about not seeming interested in her children. Perhaps with time, she could ascertain his true feelings.

Sophie stood abruptly. "Let's go check on their rooms."

"Oh, you want me to come?"

"Yes." Sophie took his hand and led him down the hallway.

The bedrooms were tiny, but Sophie had done her best to make them a sanctuary for her children. They stopped by Maggie's room with her whitewashed bed set and the pink bedspread that Sophie had made. Maggie had her doll and the rocking chair from Leland in the middle of the floor.

"This looks very nice, Maggie," David said as he stepped into her bedroom.

"Don't you love my dolly? Her name is Charlotte."

"She is very nice. And what a special chair." David crouched down and touched the rocker.

Sophie watched them interacting. Maybe she needed to give David a chance to be around her children more. With the household he'd been raised in, she couldn't expect him to be a natural with kids.

David picked up the rocker, turning it around slowly. "Where did you get this?"

"Leland made it for me for my birthday."

"Oh." He set it down and put Charlotte back in the chair. "It's a nice chair."

"Yes, and Leland rescued Mommy from the two witches and brought us home. I love Leland."

"Is that so?"

The pitch of his voice changed and Sophie's heart dropped. David turned to her, his eyebrows raised in a question. Sophie lifted her right hand and let it fall to her side. How could she explain that Leland had heard other people talking about what Mrs. Marchant had planned for her and come to her rescue?

"Is there something that I should know about you and Leland?"

Sophie shook her head. "No, he only ever took me out on those two dates."

"But he obviously still cares for you. Is this why you're holding back?"

"No, I mean, I don't know." Sophie rubbed her forehead and tried to think of the right words to say. "Leland heard the Gillespies talking about me. Somehow they'd found out that I was headed over to the Marchant's house."

David looked up at the ceiling and groaned. "So the whole town knew what was going on and no one warned you?"

"Well, Debbie tried, and my friend, Marla Checketts warned me about your mother, but I guess I don't listen very well."

"Do you have feelings for Leland?" David stood next to her. Sophie looked into his crystal blue eyes and she couldn't lie. She bit her lip and swallowed. David's eyes narrowed. "How long have you felt this way about him?"

"Honestly? I don't know what I'm feeling," Sophie said. "I'm so confused. I like Leland, but he hasn't seemed all that interested in me and then he showed up at the Marchant's house just as she was threatening me. I didn't think about it until later when we talked."

"I guess I'm not a very good knight in shining armor, but Sophie, you can do better than Leland."

The words stung because they were the same kind of words that David's mother used. "And you can do better than me."

David rocked back on his heels. "I should just stop talking. I keep digging my hole deeper."

Sophie tilted her head. "Maybe."

David stepped toward her, gathered her in his arms and kissed her. His lips were warm, urgent, and Sophie kissed him back. He kissed her again, wrapping his arms around her waist and pulling her closer.

"Ew, Mom!" Garth cried out.

Sophie giggled against David's lips and he gently released her. "Is that better?"

She nodded. "But you know kissing doesn't solve everything."

"It doesn't?" David snapped his fingers. "I was sure we were onto something just now."

"Let's have a look at Garth's room."

"Um, it's not all the way finished," Garth said, "but I'm working on it."

Sophie opened the door and saw Garth's chest of drawers stuffed haphazardly with clothes, papers, and toys. "Garth." Her tone said it all and Garth stood up straight.

"I'll clean it."

"Good luck with that," David said. "You might start by keeping only clothes in these drawers." He pulled out a drawer and motioned to the rocks, cars, and twigs stuffed inside. "Quite a collection you have here."

"I know," Garth mumbled. "I'll put the rocks outside."

"So this is a regular occurrence?" David looked to Sophie and she gave him an exasperated nod.

"I'd love to see how clean you can get your drawers," David said. "You know, when I was flying planes, everything had to be clean and neat. Perfection is what we strove for to keep everything running smoothly."

"Really?"

David nodded.

"Okay, I'll get to work," Garth said.

David took Sophie's hand and walked with her toward the living room.

"Thank you for trying," she said.

He smiled. "You have really great kids. I can work on figuring them out better, but I need to know how you feel about me first."

"There's a lot to consider," Sophie said.

"You mean Leland?"

Sophie shrugged. "I don't know, David. All I know is that you haven't really reassured me when it comes to your mother. I don't think you understand the lengths she's willing to go to keep me away from you."

David sighed. "You're right. Tell you what, you take some time to think about us and I'll talk to my mother."

"Okay."

David leaned in and brushed a kiss over her lips. "You are so beautiful," he whispered in her ear and then kissed the side of her neck, sending chills down her back. He kissed her on the mouth again and then hurried out the door.

Sophie sank onto the couch, even more confused about her life than she'd been earlier that day. She traced her lips with her fingertips, reliving David's kiss. She tried to tell herself to stay sensible and remember that marriage wasn't all about kissing, but when David held her and whispered in her ear, it seemed like she could survive for quite some time on his affections.

Chapter 34 — Carving Hearts

It had taken him over a week with many late nights, but Leland had finally uncovered the hidden object in the chunk of cherry wood. He stared at the wood that he had sanded until his knuckles bled. He'd stained it and coated it with varnish until it shone. Every time he thought about taking it to Sophie, his heart nearly leapt out of his chest. He hadn't shown it to anyone yet, not even Keith. When the time was right, he'd take it to Sophie. He trusted that his heart would let him know the time. He traced the edge of the carving with his index finger.

The project had awakened something in Leland that had been dormant for too long. He loved creating, and he'd shut down one of the most creative sides of himself after Jessie died. Carving was a risk because he had to open up his heart to see what was hidden inside the grains of wood. If his hands weren't guided by that creative vision, he might notch out a portion of wood that was meant to be part of the final piece.

The block of wood contained his heart—he knew that now as he brushed fingertips over the rounded edges of the heart that he'd carved. But it wasn't a simple heart. Shaped like a heart, yes, but inside those curved edges was another story. The silhouette of a woman facing the horizon, her face half-turned toward him. The bottom hem of her skirt was a swirl of flowers that intertwined with the edge of the carving, winding back around the heart. The image evoked a feeling of longing.

Sometimes as he studied the image, he felt that if he looked at it long enough, the woman would turn her head and see him.

When he was carving, Leland was sure that it was Sophie's story, but as he studied the figure inside the carving, he recognized that it was the story he'd told himself about Sophie. That story was only true if Sophie could turn and see his heart. And as long as he kept his heart closed off to her, that story couldn't come to pass. Leland pressed his lips together, gripping the edge of the carving. He moved it to another table and put a drop cloth over it. The carving seemed to pulsate under the cloth with a heartbeat of its own, insisting that Leland deliver it to Sophie. The thought made his own heart shrink in fear. How could he present such a gift to Sophie if he wasn't willing to put himself on the line and ask her for more than friendship?

Perhaps he could stop by as Keith suggested and see if Sophie was open to seeing him again. Leland had gone against his nature and listened closely to the gossip, but he hadn't heard anything to indicate whether Sophie and David were still an item or not. He also hadn't heard anything about the incident with the Marchants. He should have asked Sophie out that day, but he had been a jumbled mess of nerves.

Leland kicked himself every time he thought of how he'd let the opportunity to date Sophie pass him by. He'd been weak and scared and had retreated into his work. At the time, it had seemed like the right thing to do, but as soon as David swooped in, Leland knew his mistake. Seeing her with another man had pounded the truth home that he hadn't wanted to admit: he cared for Sophie Wright a great deal. Leland also believed that he was better suited to Sophie than David. It was uncharitable of him, but he hoped that she would discover that for herself, sooner than later. That thought was chased with the notion that Leland would have to put himself out there so that Sophie could discover the truth of what he had to offer.

Another hour passed by with Leland finding things to do to keep himself busy and ignore the carving and its insistence to be delivered to Sophie. With a groan, Leland glanced at the clock. It was after three, so

Garth should be home from school. Hope's tail wagged as Leland approached her box under the work bench. He wasn't ready to take the carving to Sophie yet, but he had to see her today.

"C'mon, Hope." Leland scooped the puppy into his arms. She licked his cheek and nuzzled his neck. He laughed and set her in a box on the seat of his pickup. "Now, you mind your manners and make sure those kids fall right in love with you again, okay?"

Hope wagged her tail and panted, her pink tongue hanging to the side. She whined as Leland put the pickup into gear and pulled out onto the street. Leland rehearsed a few lines as he drove, trying to think of a way to smoothly cover the fact that he was showing up unexpected and uninvited. In the end, Garth answered the door and welcomed him in before Leland had a chance to explain himself or his puppy.

"Mom, Leland's here," Garth called down the hall as soon as the front door had closed.

Leland felt his face heat up, and he shifted his weight from one foot to the other.

"Can I hold her?" Garth asked.

"Sure." Leland handed over the excited puppy.

"I love her," Garth said. He held the pup close and nuzzled his head against hers. Hope licked his face and Garth giggled.

Sophie walked into the front room, a tentative smile on her face. "Hi, Leland. This is a surprise. I'm sorry about the wait. I was helping Maggie fix her hair."

"No problem. I'm sorry to drop by unannounced. I was in the neighborhood and I wanted to stop by and see how you and the kids are doing."

"That's kind of you," Sophie replied. "We're doing well. It's such a relief that the kids can go outside and play without worrying about frostbite."

Leland chuckled. "Now it's just the mud, right?"

Sophie sighed. "It is a mess, but I'd rather have the nicer weather."

Maggie bounced into the room then. "Hi, Leland. Oh, you brought Hope! I love her." She scrambled over to pet the puppy that squirmed in Garth's lap.

Leland breathed in deep, reminding himself that he had no reason to be a coward. "Sophie, I wanted to know. Are you busy tomorrow? I'd really like to take you out to dinner."

Sophie's cheeks turned a deep pink. "I—uh, well," she looked down, "I don't want to hurt you, Leland."

"But you're dating David." Leland struggled to keep his voice light.

"Yes, I just don't think it would be fair to him right now."

"Has David done anything about the situation with Mrs. Marchant?"

"Yes, he spoke with Linda and told her that he never intended on marrying her."

Leland nodded. "And what about his mother?"

Sophie chewed on her bottom lip. "That still remains to be seen."

"If David hasn't taken care of the problems with his own mother, can you really consider a serious relationship with him?"

Sophie raised one eyebrow. "It might not seem like it, but I'm putting a lot of thought into dating David. I care about you, but my heart is already confused. I'm not sure what I should do."

"Has he asked you to marry him?" Leland tasted bile in the back of his throat.

"Oh, no. Of course not." Sophie shook her head adamantly, but then she hesitated. "He has hinted at a future, but," she glanced at Garth and Maggie holding the puppy and giggling, "I have to think of more than myself."

Leland stepped forward and took Sophie's hand. "I'll never forgive myself for messing up my chance to know you better. I need to say this now." He swallowed and he detected a hint of fear behind Sophie's eyes. "Please, don't be afraid. I can't live with myself if I don't tell you how I feel."

"But, Leland, I told you I have to see this through with David."

He nodded. "I respect that and I respect you. Just please, will you let me tell you something that I was too cowardly to tell you when I had the chance?"

One side of Sophie's mouth quirked up in a smile. She nodded, looking down at his fingers covering hers and then back to his face.

Leland swallowed. "I care about you a great deal. And I know I don't have any right, but I love Garth and Maggie. You have a beautiful family and I wanted to date you, to get to know you, to see if we might get along well. But then I let fear take over. I have a past." He looked down at his feet, noticing the scuff mark on his left shoe. With the last crumbs of his courage, he took a breath and continued, "My past stole my confidence and I've struggled to feel I was worthy of goodness, of God's blessings, of a chance to know someone like you and your children. I stepped back when I should have stepped forward and taken your hand. It's a mistake that will haunt me, I suppose, but I wanted you to know how I feel."

Sophie pressed a hand over her mouth and blinked several times. Leland noticed how hard she worked to keep the tear on the edge of her lash from falling. She tipped her head back, continuing to blink and breathed in slowly through her nose. When she had regained her composure, she adjusted her head to look Leland in the eye. "Thank you for telling me."

Leland squeezed her fingers gently. "Before you make any big decisions, please consider that there is more than one option. You shouldn't settle for anything less than someone who loves you *and* your children and can provide for you."

Sophie's eyes widened and for a second, Leland felt like he'd read her mind. He had touched on the edge of her worry. She would never want for anything with a man like David Alexander, but her children would have a very different upbringing compared to what he could offer them. For a moment, he dared to hope that there might still be a chance for him to court Sophie properly, but then she withdrew her hand.

"I think it's probably best if you go now." Her face was impassive and Leland recognized the mask that she wore to hide her feelings was firmly in place.

He nodded. "If you need anything, please think of me?"

Sophie smiled, but it didn't reach her eyes. "Okay."

Despite Garth and Maggie's protests, Leland gathered up Hope and headed out into the chilly night. As he drove home, Leland patted Hope's head. He couldn't be sure, but he thought that he just might've taken a sliver of Sophie's heart with him.

Chapter 35 – David's Scars

Two days after Leland's visit, Sophie had just finished sewing a beautiful seam with her new machine when she heard a knock at the door. She jumped up, hurrying to answer the door before the pounding woke Maggie. She'd fallen asleep playing with Charlotte on top of her bed.

David stood on the front step, in his crisp black suit and a dark blue tie that brought out the color of his eyes. He was so handsome that Sophie sometimes wondered why he had chosen her—a poor widowed mother of two young children. He smiled. "Hi, Darling. Can I come in?"

"Yes, of course." Sophie stepped aside. "Is everything okay?" She closed the door behind him.

"Sure, I had a meeting over this way and I wanted to stop on my way back to the office. Is that okay?" He pushed a lock of his black hair back from his forehead.

"Yes, I've been trying out my new sewing machine and it's marvelous. Thank you so much, David." Sophie touched his arm.

He grinned and embraced her, brushing her lips with a kiss. "I'm glad you like it."

"I do. It means a lot to me."

David touched her cheek. "You mean a lot to me, and that's why I stopped by." He stepped away from her and loosened his tie. He tossed it to the ground and then began slowly unbuttoning his shirt.

Sophie eyes widened. "David, I don't think this is a good idea."

He shook his head. "It's not what you think. I need to tell you something."

"Okay?"

He continued to unbutton his shirt, and Sophie stood frozen to the spot, unsure of what she should do. He pulled his shirt off, letting it drop to the floor. The dark hair on David's chest was interrupted by a mottled pink scar that resembled a circle. The scar was just below his heart. David reached for Sophie's hand and put her fingers on the scar. Her heartbeat hammered and her fingers trembled as she felt the bumpy skin that had healed over a wound. "A bullet?"

David nodded.

"I didn't know that you'd been shot," Sophie whispered.

"No one does, except my mother. And now you."

"But how?"

"Friendly fire. It was an accident and it nearly cost me my life."

"Is your heart okay now?"

David nodded. "I wanted to show you this because I have scars too." He pulled her close to him and then guided her hand around to his back. He turned slowly and Sophie gasped when she saw the exit wound from the bullet. She touched the ridges of flesh that appeared pink and angry. David turned back around, slowly drawing Sophie in against his chest. "This was the scariest time of my life. I thought I had died. I looked down and there was blood coming out right where my heart should be. The bullet entered just below my heart, but the pain felt like someone had ripped my heart right out of my chest."

"Oh my goodness," Sophie cried. "I didn't know."

David gave one shake of his head and continued telling his story. "When I regained consciousness, there was so much pain, but my heart was still beating. I could have died. After that, things were different for me—they still are. I know I've been given a second chance and I want to make the most of that chance."

Sophie covered the scar with her hand. She knew what he was alluding to by second chances, but it seemed wrong to even speak of that in light of Cal's death and so many who died in the war. "I know what you're saying, David, but things are different for you than they will ever be for me."

"It doesn't have to be that way." David took her hand and moved it to her own heart, resting his hand on top of hers. "Your heart is still beating, too. Sophie, please give me a chance to show you how much I love you."

He bent his head toward hers and covered her mouth in a kiss that was different from the kisses they'd shared only a few days before. Soft, yet passionate, David commanded her mouth to respond to his and her body obeyed. She put her hands on his chest, feeling the strength of his muscles beneath her palms. The intent to push away was there, because she shouldn't be standing in her living room kissing David, feeling his bare chest under her fingertips. But she didn't stop kissing him. She wound her arms around his neck, standing on her tiptoes, her head angled as he deepened the kiss.

His hands moved down the small of her back, pulling her ever closer as he kissed her again and again. Their breaths grew shallow, and almost gasping. David picked her up, cradling her in his arms and turned. Her foot knocked against the sewing machine desk as he turned and he lifted her higher and then set her on the couch. He leaned over her, kissing her jawline and began to unbutton her dress. Sophie pushed his hand away and he moved it to her back, pulling her impossibly closer. They were experienced hands and as he kissed her neck, Sophie's chest flared with worry. How many women had he seduced in this same way during the war? Perhaps sharing this same story of his near-death to evoke emotions in his favor?

"David?"

"Hmm?" He mumbled as he kissed her mouth.

Sophie put her hand on his cheek. "David, we need to stop."

He smiled. "Are you sure?" He ducked his head and kissed her again.

Sophie swallowed and pushed him away. "Yes, I'm sure." She sat up as David gave her a confused look.

"Is something the matter?"

"Besides the fact that you're trying to seduce me when you told me you wouldn't?"

David groaned and put his fist to his mouth. "Sorry." He closed his eyes. "I thought... I don't know."

"David, I can't." Sophie bit her lip. "It's been a long time, but I was always faithful to my husband, no matter how awful he was to me."

"And he's dead now." David leaned forward and kissed her again.

Sophie shook her head. "Have you been with–uh, many women?"

David jerked back. "What?"

"You heard me," Sophie's voice sounded small. "Have you been with a lot of women? I know it was a problem during the war for many men, including my husband."

David's face turned a shade of pink that Sophie hadn't seen before. "Why do you want to know about that?"

"Because it's important. I think when a man sleeps with several women; it's harder for him to be pleased with his wife."

"But I'm not Cal," David said. "You told me he never treated you right once you were married."

"You're right and a lot of that had to do with him chasing skirts." Sophie frowned.

David looked out the window and then put his head in his hand. "I thought women didn't like to talk about these kinds of things."

Sophie arched an eyebrow. "That's a convenient idea."

"So you want me to tell you that I've made love to other women?"

"I need the truth. The things I didn't know are what got me in trouble during my marriage to Cal."

David's face turned a darker shade of pink. He stood and picked up his shirt, putting it on and carefully buttoning it up. "I think maybe it's time that I get going."

Sophie looked down at her hands clasped together that only moments before were touching David's bare skin. A part of her had wanted to give into the passion, the way David made her feel so desirable, but her fears had ruined any chance for that now.

David paused on the last button and sighed. "Sophie, I told you I love you. What more do you want?"

"I want a man who knows how to love one woman with his whole heart."

David shook his head. "And you don't think that I do?"

"I'm not sure. I don't trust my own heart enough to know what I'm feeling."

"Does this have something to do with Leland?"

Sophie flinched, remembering Leland's visit and words of caution. "I told you I needed time to figure things out."

David nodded. "That's fine, Sophie, but what you and I have seems pretty strong. How can you ignore the desire you have for me?"

"Lust is not love," Sophie replied. "I'm sorry. I let my guard down and I shouldn't have."

"No, I'm sorry. I thought you wanted a chance at a different life." David walked toward the door. "I could take care of you Sophie, and I'd never hurt you. We could be very happy together."

"As long as I don't mind that you have the freedom to sleep with as many women as you want?"

David's face hardened, his lips a tight line. "Men are different than women. We have different needs. My mother wasn't enough for my father, but he was discreet and made sure that she was always taken care of."

Sophie sucked in a breath. "Then maybe that's why your mother wants you to marry Linda. Everyone knows about the mistresses that Mr. Marchant kept. Linda would understand men's needs because she learned from her own father."

David blew out a breath and let out a harsh chuckle. "I'd better go. Let's take some time to cool off and see if we can work this out." He yanked the door open and left before Sophie could think of a response.

When he'd pulled his car out to the street, Sophie allowed herself to stand and look out the window. Her gut twisted as she thought of their parting words. The tears boiled under the surface, but Sophie clenched her fists, reinforcing the dam on her emotions. Now wasn't the time to cry. Nothing had been decided. David was just upset. She'd pushed him too far and he would have to come to terms with her demand for honesty and fidelity. No matter how much she cared for him, there was no future for them if David couldn't agree to complete fidelity. She didn't allow her thoughts to dwell on what she would do if he cast her aside now that she'd opened up her heart enough to feel his affection.

With shaking hands she made her way to the bathroom sink where she splashed her cheeks with water. Debbie had warned her that David Alexander had seemed too good to be true. Maybe she was right.

Chapter 36 – The Man with a Golden Heart

Leland tapped the finishing nails into place on a china cabinet Anita Phelps had ordered. He'd been distracted so he was a couple days past what he'd hoped–good thing he always gave himself a buffer of a few days on projects. By the end of the day, he'd have another happy customer. Leland turned and his eyes were immediately drawn to the cloth covering Sophie's carving. It was past time to give it to her, but the visit with his puppy hadn't turned out as well as he'd hoped. His mouth had run away from him and he worried that he'd pushed Sophie too far on the issue of David. A tapping sound on the window caught Leland's attention. He walked toward the front of the shop, looking for the source of the noise. He jumped back when a branch banged into the window. Covering his heart, he rolled his eyes at his jumpiness. The spring winds were whipping the trees into shape for summer. The oak tree outside his shop needed a good trimming, but he'd been so busy building that he hadn't spent the time he normally did on his yard.

Pushing the door open, Leland stepped out and tipped his head back to examine the tree and her mighty branches. The wind gusted again, blowing his hair back, reminding him that he was in need of a haircut. He tucked his hair behind his ear and the wind tickled his skin, whispering, *Tell her.*

Leland shook his head, rubbing his ear while trying to convince himself that he hadn't heard that same message before. But he had heard it and he knew what he was supposed to do. If he continued to ignore the prompting, he might lose any chance he ever had of getting close to Sophie. He stuffed his hands into his pockets and stared back up at the tree. "I'll tell her today," he whispered. He stepped back inside, the door banging shut behind him.

It took a moment for his eyes to adjust to the dimness of the shop after standing in the bright sunlight. Leland lifted the cover off of the carved heart. There was no point in waiting any longer. He replaced the covering with a new resolve. After delivering the china cabinet to the Phelps' home, he would stop by Sophie's for a visit. Leland walked over to the telephone and dialed Sophie's line.

"Hi, Sophie, I—uh, well," Leland stammered.

"Leland? Is that you?"

"Yes, well, I'd like to stop by and deliver a little something for you—maybe around four?"

"Sure, we'll be here. Are you bringing Hope again?"

Leland heard a smile in her voice and took that as a sign that all had been forgiven from his previous visit. And maybe there was still a corner of her heart that wasn't entirely devoted to David Alexander. "I could do that, if you'd like."

"I don't mind either way, but I think Garth and Maggie would insist."

Leland chuckled. "We'll both see you later then."

It took Leland a full thirty minutes to calm his nerves after talking with Sophie, but he finished the cabinet and was able to get started on another rocking chair before it was time to leave. With help from a neighbor, he loaded the china cabinet into the bed of his pickup and set off across town to make the delivery.

Anita and her husband were there to greet him and help unload the cabinet. They were thrilled with the finished product, and Leland tucked several bills into his pocket before driving over to Sophie's. His business was flourishing and he loved the work. It was time for him to prepare for the next stage of his life. There was a twinge in his heart that felt like regret and guilt intertwined, but Leland took a deep breath and remembered all he had learned over the past year.

He pulled into Sophie's driveway and scooped Hope into his arms. She was growing fast and soon would be too big for him to carry.

"She gets bigger every time I see her," Sophie said as she opened the front door.

Leland nodded. "I think she's put on about ten pounds since that night I found her." He stepped inside and set the pup down on the rug. Hope was immediately surrounded by Garth and Maggie.

"She loves me, huh, Leland," Maggie said. She put her head next to the puppy and Hope licked her cheek. Maggie giggled and rubbed Hope's silky ears.

"I brought something else. It's out in my pickup, if you don't mind." Leland thumbed behind him and then swiveled for the door. "I'll be right back."

"Okay, sure." Sophie's eyes held a dozen questions and Leland savored the look of anticipation as he retrieved the carving from his pickup. Outside the front door, he paused for one moment, whispering a silent prayer for courage and then went back inside. Garth and Maggie were busy with Hope, so Leland decided not to waste another minute. He held out the carving, wrapped in an old towel.

"I made you something."

"For me?" Sophie put a hand over her heart. "But I didn't—don't have anything for you."

Leland carefully removed the towel and placed the carving in Sophie's hands. "I want you to have this."

She sucked in a breath and her eyes filled with moisture as she studied the intricate detail of the heart. Her fingers traced the smooth finish of the surface and she brought the carving closer to study the woman inside the heart. "It's beautiful. Leland, you carved this?"

Leland felt his heart swell within his chest and he smiled. "I did."

"I don't know what to say. The details—they're so fine. I love it." She studied the carving and then lifted her eyes to his. "Thank you."

"I'm glad you like it."

"Kids, look at what Leland made for me." Sophie held out the carving for Garth and Maggie to examine.

"That lady is so pretty," Maggie said.

"That's 'cause it's Mama." Garth touched the edge of the heart, tracing his finger along the carving. "You're real good, Leland. I wish I could whittle like this."

"I'm sure I could get you started sometime," Leland said. "If it's all right with your Mama."

"Really?" Garth looked up with pure adoration in his eyes.

Leland nodded and Garth hugged him around the waist. Crouching down, Leland encircled the boy in his arms. Love welled up in his chest and overflowed for this little family, but how could he let them know his feelings? Garth pulled back with a grin and dashed over to where Maggie had released Hope momentarily. He scooped up the puppy and ran down the hall with Maggie whining after him. "Let me hold Hope. She likes me best!"

Leland and Sophie chuckled. She moved a potted plant to the kitchen and set the carving on a round end table in the living room. She turned to him. "I'm very touched by this gift. Thank you so much."

Before Leland could respond, she walked toward him and put her arms around him. He pulled Sophie against his chest and kissed the top of her head. He rubbed her back in a slow circle and hummed, the sound vibrating in his throat. She stilled, and Leland continued to hum fragments of the tune that were a familiar memory to him now. Leaning her head back, Sophie placed her hand on his cheek. "That tune, I've heard it before. Emika's music box."

Leland stopped humming. He wasn't sure how she knew about Emika's music box, but with those words, he knew that now was the time. He swallowed and looked at her intently. "Yes."

"Tell me Leland. Tell me everything."

Leland closed his eyes, wishing he could stop time and hold Sophie like this in a moment of peace before he shattered her reality of him. But the music swirled in the air around him, the vibrations moving from his chest–from his heart in an effort to tell the story. He opened his eyes. "You know that my daughter died and my wife divorced me, but you don't know why."

Sophie studied his face, slowly shaking her head. She didn't speak and Leland knew that the words were his to say. "It was the fall of '42 and Jessie was three. Rhonda and I had been talking about getting her a baby brother or sister, but it hadn't happened yet."

Leland cleared his throat, drawing courage from all that he'd overcome. "My business was growing and we were so happy. I went to get a load of wood and when I returned, I backed into the shop the same way I always did. I swear I checked before I put the pickup in reverse. I didn't see her and then I did and I stopped, but it was too late." His voice trembled with emotion and he struggled to keep talking. "I ran over Jessie. I killed my own daughter."

Sophie gasped and covered her mouth with her slender fingers. She shook her head and then put her hand on his. "Oh, Leland. I'm so sorry."

He shook his head. "It's a mistake that can never be fixed, and it destroyed my life. I couldn't breathe, let alone work, or be a husband to Rhonda. The guilt was acid eating my soul from the inside out."

Sophie's lip trembled and she bit it as one tear, followed by another slipped down her cheek. Leland continued on, forcing himself to say all the words he'd kept inside and hidden from her. He loved Sophie, but his hopes were slim that she would return the same feelings.

"I knew Rhonda hated me–that she could never forgive me. I

couldn't forgive myself. The joy was sucked out of my life and I could barely look at myself in the mirror. I took to drinking, sleeping, drinking, never wanting to wake up and live another day. I thought I knew how people felt, how God felt about what I'd done to Jessie." Leland paused when Sophie took his hand, the gesture encouraged him to share his secrets.

"But I was wrong. I was wrong about God, about everything. It took Rhonda leaving me for me to learn, but I *did* learn the truth. Rhonda is the one who brought the music box home from the church swap meet. She told me how a young war widow had brought the music box to trade because her husband had left her a note hidden inside."

"What did the note say?" Sophie asked.

"It's still there. '*Don't die with me.*' That widow had a little son who'd never met his father and she took his advice, trading the music box for a cradle—Jessie's cradle."

"I can't imagine—your poor heart," Sophie whispered.

Leland felt the smooth skin of Sophie's fingers next to his and took another breath. "Rhonda thought the music box was something special that might help us heal. When she left, there was a note explaining how she had forgiven me and she had pasted in the words, '*Forgive yourself, allow God to forgive*' in the music box. Something in me awoke then and I determined to change. I listened to the music box until I thought for sure it would wear out, but it didn't."

Sophie listened carefully, soaking in all of Leland's words. She licked her lips and swallowed. "Emika showed me her music box. She told me that you gave it to her, and I saw notes pasted in the lid. I don't know how, but I knew there was a story to the note about forgiveness."

Leland nodded. "Now you know the truth. I kept my heart in that music box while I struggled to heal. I don't know if I'll ever get my whole heart back, but I know that God has forgiven me."

"Of course he has," Sophie whispered. "Leland, it was an accident."

"It wasn't an accident that I turned into a worthless drunk and destroyed my marriage." He tasted the bitterness of his words and closed his eyes. "But I'm not that man anymore, and I never will be." He breathed deeply and opened his eyes to find Sophie studying him. "By the time I met Emika, I was confident that I would never drink again. There was something special about that music box. It wasn't meant for just one person, so I passed it on."

"I don't know if I could do that," Sophie said.

"The music stayed with me," Leland replied. "On my hardest days, the melody would ride the wind and remind me of where I'd come from and how I could stay the course."

"I'm sorry you felt you couldn't tell me about this before now."

Leland frowned. "I didn't know how you would react at first, and then when I knew you better, it was nice to be with someone who didn't know the horror of my past."

His words hung in the air. The confession from the darkest corner of his heart had been exposed and Sophie had the power to reject him based on the truth. Instead of recoiling, Sophie tucked herself closer to Leland, resting her cheek on his shoulder and smoothing the hair on the back of his head. "I'm so sorry that you had to go through that alone."

"It felt like it, but I know that I was never alone," Leland said. "God was with me, just like he is with you."

Sophie's shoulders tightened at his words. Leland had the sense that she carried guilt of her own, but he couldn't imagine why. He hugged her, praying for the right words to come to him.

"Sophie?"

She stepped out of his embrace. "Yes?"

"I want you to know that I care about you very much. I know you're dating David, but all I ask is that you give me a chance before you go much further down the path with him."

Sophie looked down at the floor and then to her children. She tightened her arms across her chest, her right fingers absently rubbing the sleeve of her dress. She looked at him. "Okay."

Leland's heart hesitated as his mind struggled to process her answer. "Okay, you'll give me a chance?"

Sophie smiled and nodded. "Yes."

Leland's face split into a wide grin and he took one of Sophie's hands. "Thank you. When can I see you again?"

Sophie licked her lips. "I need to sort through some things first, but maybe next week?"

"Okay, let me know if that changes and I can see you sooner." Leland didn't let his smile slip. He could hide his feelings too, if he was determined. He didn't know what Sophie's hesitation meant or what she needed to sort through, but she hadn't told him no. That was enough for him, for now.

Chapter 37 – The Hummingbird

Leland's visit was the best part of Sophie's week. She spent several minutes each day, staring at the carving, striving to discern the feelings that Leland had put into every line of the wood. She recognized the symbolism—the heart carved around a woman with her face turned away. The woman was her and at first she thought the heart might have been her own, but later she decided that the heart was Leland's. A realization that hurt was he had been the one to turn away from her. How ironic that after she was involved with David, Leland would decide to bare his soul to her.

She hadn't talked to or seen David for five days. By Thursday, when he still hadn't reached out, her heart felt like it had been blanketed in a heavy fog. Leland honored her wishes and hadn't called or stopped by either. And for some reason, Sophie was disappointed. The day ended leaving a bitter taste in her mouth.

And then on Friday, David called.

"Sophie, I've been thinking a lot and I'd really like the chance to talk to you. Can I take you out to dinner?"

Sophie's stomach somersaulted and she gripped the back of the kitchen chair. "When were you thinking of going?"

"I know it's late notice, but is there any way we could go tonight?"

Sophie looked out the window where the green ash tree swayed in the wind, tiny buds scattered across the branches. "Are you sure?"

"Sure?" David sounded confused. "Yes, I'm sure. I know things have been rough, but if you'll give me one last chance, I think I can explain."

"Okay."

"Thanks, Sophie. I'll pick you up at six. Wear something a little dressy."

Sophie scrambled to arrange for her mother to watch Garth and Maggie. She hadn't told anyone about her doubts concerning David. Part of her was sure that she'd blown everything out of proportion. Maybe it had sounded like David was excusing his behavior before, but she could have misunderstood. Sophie rubbed the ring finger of her left hand, thinking of how David had disregarded her feelings and concerns. He had acted like his past wasn't important, but Sophie didn't agree because the past could affect the future. Her own past had put her in this exact spot, and as she pinned up her hair preparing for her date, she wondered what it all meant.

Her skin looked creamy against her red lipstick. She smiled, making sure that her eyes sparkled with expectation. David had said to wear something dressy—that had caught her off guard because she always tried to dress nice. It took her a moment to realize that he meant something fancy and she almost laughed. David was so used to mingling with his mother's social circles that he probably thought every woman owned a sparkly, expensive dress for that special occasion.

In the back of the closet, Sophie pulled out a cloth bag with trembling hands. Underneath the light cotton fabric was a dress that grabbed onto every bit of light and sent it sparkling across the room. The rhinestones around the neckline had been a tedious chore to stitch, but Sophie had to admit they were beautiful. When she'd worn the gown to a special servicemen's ball, she'd felt beautiful and elegant up until Cal had ordered his third drink, but no—she didn't want to associate the dress with painful memories. She gave the garment a light shake, as if to unleash all the negative pieces of that night that still clung to the hemline. She was much stronger than she had been then and tonight she would wear the gown and feel beautiful again.

Carefully, she dressed in the gown, checking for any loose rhinestones. Although it had been years, the stitches held true and the dress still fit. The mirror caught her reflection and Sophie's heart froze as she examined the woman who appeared elegant and unaffected by the scars of the war. Maybe it was a mistake to go out with David again when there was a chance that Leland might be the one for her heart. But David had never treated her unkindly and he'd said he would work on figuring out how to be better with her children. Putting a hand over her heart, Sophie tried to read the message in between the steady beats, but there was nothing–only the silence between pulses. It was important to give herself a chance to make the right choice. She wouldn't throw everything away because of a little argument. David had given her a cooling off period and hopefully they could right things tonight.

When Sophie opened the door to let David inside, his mouth dropped open. "You're so beautiful it hurts." He stepped forward, pulling her into his arms.

Sophie scrunched her nose. "Thank you?"

David chuckled, releasing her slowly. "Your dress is stunning. Did you sew that as well?"

"Yes, but it's been in the back of my closet for years."

David touched one of the rhinestones near her neckline. "I'm glad that you felt I was worthy to see it."

His words were heavy on her heart and she rolled her shoulders back, trying to adjust to the unfamiliar tension. Did she really feel that David was worthy to see the dress, or had she simply been caught up in the moment with her longing to be beautiful and desired? "So, where are you taking me?"

"Over to Calloway Grove. I made reservations at The Hummingbird." He took her arm, guiding her down the front steps. "Does that sound okay with you?"

"Of course," Sophie answered. She wouldn't tell David that she'd never dreamed of setting foot in the high class restaurant that most people believed was too fancy to be in business during the after-effects of the war.

Debbie had mentioned it once, saying, "Well, rich people need a place to spend their money anyhow."

David helped Sophie into his car, tucking in the flowing silver material that trailed down from the fitted bodice of her gown. On the drive over to Calloway Grove, he held her hand, interlacing their fingers. "I missed you, Sophie. I hope you believe how sorry I am. I'm really going to try hard to be there for you."

Sophie turned to him, her heartbeat thumping with a familiar anxiety. Cal had been a master at apologies but they had always been empty words. Could she trust her heart to David, or any man after it had willingly betrayed her? She breathed in deeply, trying to feel for the truth in his words. "Thank you."

"Are you okay?" David asked. "You're kind of quiet tonight."

Sophie nodded. "I'm trying to sort through things to figure out what to do next."

"Hmm, will you give me some hints on my lines?" David smiled and his eyes sparkled. "I want to get this right."

Sophie laughed, shaking her head. "No cheating."

"On my honor," David said. He pulled to the side of The Hummingbird and hopped out of the car. As he helped Sophie out and they walked toward the front doors, she noticed a beautiful stained glass window, backlit with soft lighting. The window was fashioned to look like a hummingbird with purple, green, and blue feathers. Sophie paused to admire the window and noticed that the hummingbird was poised over a rose. The intricacies of color and glass reminded Sophie of Leland's skilled carving. Every time she looked at it, she would notice another detail and think about the depths of her own heart. There were hidden crevices filled with fear, pain, and sorrow, but there were also places of joy, beauty, and happiness. Sophie wanted to live in those good places and forget the bad. In order to do that, she needed to make the right decision—the one that would allow her heart to beat with joy.

"It's a beautiful window, isn't it?" David interrupted her thoughts. "Not too long until we might see a few hummingbirds here. It makes me excited for summertime."

"It will be nice to feel warm again." Sophie took his arm as he led her inside.

The restaurant was decorated with rich fabrics in deep burgundy and navy blue with elegant crystal catching the light from the glittering chandeliers above. The hostess took her jacket and as she turned, the light caught the rhinestones on her dress. It appeared that Sophie fit right in with the crowd of women dressed in their beautiful gowns and men in fine-cut suits, but a few well-placed glares from ladies at surrounding tables assured her that she wasn't welcome in their sphere. The few unfriendly looks from women dripping with style and sophistication added to the confusion surrounding her heart until she noticed several men glance her way. David must have noticed as well because he put his arm around her, tucking her to his side as they walked through the dinner room.

"I'm not the only one noticing how stunning you are," David murmured. He inclined his head toward a couple and the way he stood reminded Sophie of a showman and his horse.

Once they were seated, she was able to relax and for the most part, ignore the whispers around them. "Everyone knows who you are, don't they?"

David shrugged. "I suppose so. I take after my father, so it's easy to recognize that I'm an Alexander." He said it with a tone that reminded Sophie of his mother.

Throughout the meal, David told her all about the new tunnel in the mine, the workers they had to hire, the dangers of expanding the mine. He talked on and on about the demands of the job and Sophie listened, imagining that if she were David's wife, she would soothe him and thank him for working so hard for their family. "It must be difficult managing so many concerns, and such a large company," she said.

David reached across the table and caressed her fingers. "I'm working toward something. It'll all be worth it once my future is secure."

"As long as you're happy," Sophie said.

David furrowed his brow, breathed out, and then smoothed his forehead with his fingertips. "How has your week been? Have you done any sewing?" He winked and Sophie blushed, thinking of the way David had kissed her deeply, bumping into the sewing machine as he'd lifted her off the ground. Her stomach flipped and she knew he was thinking of the same moment.

"Garth finished up his animal report at school—he loved collecting facts on antelope. And Maggie—"

"I asked about your week, Sophie, not your children's week," David interrupted. "Tell me about you."

"Oh—well, I guess not too much," Sophie replied, feeling color rise to her cheeks at David's remark. She swallowed, struggling to keep up with the conversation. He had asked about the sewing. That was a safe topic. "The new machine is wonderful. I sewed up a patchwork quilt in an afternoon. It does use more thread, but I'm getting the hang of it."

"I'm glad you like it." David smiled. He sat back in his seat, rubbing his chin. "How late can you stay out tonight?"

Sophie laughed. "Well, my mother is watching the kids and she said she'd take them home and put them to bed, so..." she shrugged.

"That's good to hear." David waggled his eyebrows and squeezed her fingers. "I have a little surprise for dessert."

David walked with Sophie to his car and opened the driver's door. She slid into the middle of the bench seat and David sat next to her.

His broad shoulders bumped up against her as he pulled the door shut and Sophie thought of him with his shirt off in her living room. His strength, the bullet hole near his heart, and the way that he'd held her against his skin. She immediately blushed, ducking her head. David put the car into gear and they drove back to Aspen Falls. He put his hand on her thigh, moving slowly upwards until he found her hand and interlaced his fingers with hers.

Sophie's heartbeat quickened and she glanced at David, only to find him staring at her with a hunger in his eyes that twisted her stomach. "Where are we going?"

"I wanted to show you my office."

"Okay, that sounds interesting." Sophie infused lightness into her tone, curious as to why he wanted to show her his office. They chatted about the shift in the weather and the fields turning green with the spring rains. When David pulled up to his office, Sophie noticed the empty field across from the building. "I've never been near the mines."

"Maybe sometime I could take you out there, but the mine is a dirty place. I'm not sure you'd be impressed with a large hole in the ground." He helped her from the car.

"That's true," Sophie said.

David unlocked the door and led her through the darkened hallway to his office. He flipped on a light. "Here's where my secretary works." He tugged on her hand. "And this is my office."

Sophie noticed the fine oak desk, a wooden chair on casters, and an upholstered couch against a wall with a large painting of the mine. "This is very nice. Do you like working here?"

He shrugged. "Sometimes. A lot of the time I feel like I'm one of the men in the mine, buried under paperwork instead of earth." He touched the edge of the picture frame. "That sounds ungrateful. I have a good job and I'll be a solid provider for my family."

Sophie had witnessed his inner argument several times and bit her tongue, but the way David had shrugged gave her courage to speak her mind. "David, if you don't enjoy your job, you need to change it or find the job that you'll really love."

He turned, his brow furrowed. "You say that like I actually have a choice in the matter."

"We all have a choice."

David rubbed his chin. "That's true."

"Do you really believe that?" Sophie asked. "I know I've felt trapped and that I didn't have a choice, but I really did have one if I would've had the courage to make it."

"So, now I'm a coward?" David smiled, teasing her as he stepped closer. He helped her out of her jacket, laying it across the back of the chair. Then he took hold of both of her hands. "Do you care for me, Sophie?"

"Yes, you've been very kind to me, David. Thank you."

"I want to be more than kind to you. I want to show you how much I love you. Seeing you tonight, wearing this dress–you're gorgeous." He wrapped his arms around her and she rested her head against his chest. He put a finger to her chin and tilted her head upwards. She met his eyes and saw that same desire from earlier as he covered her mouth with his. The kiss shot thrills through her body as he pulled her closer. She put her arms around his neck, her fingers touching the back of his collar. She rubbed the edge of his short hair and tilted her head as David kissed her jawline. His hands moved lower on her back, pressing her body to his.

The lights flickered and Sophie remembered that they were in an inappropriate situation–alone in his office. She put one hand on his chest and the other on his cheek. "David, I'm attracted to you, but I can't do this."

David groaned. "Why not? I've told you I love you. I want us to be together."

"Yes, and yet, you haven't invited me to your home or talked to your mother about us."

David opened his mouth and closed it. "You're right. It's wrong of me. Would you like to go there now?"

"Now?" Sophie repeated.

"Yes, we can drive over and visit with my mother. I'll tell her that I intend to marry you. I'll tell her that we'll get started right away on producing grandchildren to carry on the Alexander name." He chuckled and stepped toward her, cupping her face in his hands. "I want to be with you, Sophie."

He covered her mouth with a kiss that left Sophie's knees weak. David kissed her neck and Sophie struggled to focus on the thought niggling in the back of her mind. The words left unsaid. There was something missing from David's declaration of love. He traced her collarbone with his fingertips, leaving a sensation like fire burning through her skin. Sophie stepped out of David's arms. He dropped his hands and sighed.

Everything clicked into place. It was Garth and Maggie—her children. Whenever David talked about love and marriage, he didn't talk about her children. And just now when he said they could get started on producing grandchildren, it was like her own children didn't exist. Sophie bit her lip. There was something else missing as well. She hadn't told him that she loved him. They were only words, but she couldn't say them.

"Sophie? Are you okay?"

Inhaling slowly, Sophie raised her chin with one brief nod. "Yes, but I'd like you to take me home."

"But I thought we were going to speak with my mother?"

"So that she can berate and belittle me in front of you? Are you really willing to stand up to your mother to defend me *and* my children?"

"Look, I know that Mother can seem harsh, but she's harmless."

Sophie laughed. "She's anything but harmless, but that's not the point. You haven't asked me to marry you, and I don't think you've asked my father for permission to do so." Sophie narrowed her eyes and pointed to the couch. "I wonder how many words you'd be willing to say to me tonight to have your way with me."

His eyes widened and then he frowned. "That's unfair. I'm not like your husband. You mean more to me than that." David put his hand over his face. "I know I've messed this up, but I can make it right. I got carried away thinking of what I'd tell my mother. It's too soon to talk of marriage, but couldn't we at least go over there so I can tell her that we're serious about one another?"

"Not tonight." Sophie turned to walk out of his office.

"Sophie, hold on." David grabbed her arm. "I'm sorry. I shouldn't have brought you here. I don't know what I was thinking. I just wanted to be with you and show you a part of my life. I spend so much time here at the mine. I don't want all this work to be for nothing. I'm ready to provide for a family."

Sophie couldn't meet his eye because if she looked she would see how he hungered for her. David thought he was in love, but Sophie wasn't sure if he understood how to truly love. She tugged her arm, releasing David's grip and grabbed her jacket as she walked toward the front door. She slipped it on and stepped outside, just out of the circle of light that a streetlamp cast on the ground. She waited in the semi-darkness for him to close up his office. Wrapping her arms around herself, she shivered against a chill that was bone-deep. Were there any men who were truly good and unselfish enough to love her and her children? A gust of wind pushed her toward David's car and she pulled her jacket tighter around her. The wind rattled a tin can, setting it to roll against the gravel and bump up against a metal flag pole. The discordant tones blended with the branches scratching against the side of a shed across the street and something about the noise reminded Sophie of a melody. She closed her eyes to listen, and Leland was there in her mind, answering the question she had just asked. With hands open, he was reaching for something, but Sophie had already closed that door.

"Sophie?" David's shoes crunched on the gravel as he approached. "Are you sure you want me to take you home?"

"Yes, thank you." He helped her into his car and they both noticed the distance between them that hadn't been there just an hour before.

"David, I'm not sure how to say this, so I'll do my best," Sophie said. "I don't think we should see each other anymore."

"You can't mean that. I made a mistake—kissing you like that. It won't happen again."

"It's not that, David. You don't love my children. And if you don't love them, there's no possible way that you could really love me because they are a part of me."

David tipped his head back. "So you're breaking up with me because I don't play with your kids enough?"

"No, because you don't care about them at all."

"I care about you—you're their mother. I want to take care of you *and* your children."

"And what are my children's names?"

He paused, arching an eyebrow. "Garth and Margaret. I know their names, Sophie."

Her heart sank. She hadn't wanted to believe it was true, but David had just given her proof. Certainly others would tell her she was foolish to worry over such things. It was ludicrous to give away an opportunity to be taken care of—secure in life with her children. She should be grateful that a man like David was willing to give her a chance at a new life. The thoughts were so clear that they gave Sophie pause. For a moment, she reconsidered her words, tasting them on her tongue, wondering if she should swallow them and forge ahead, grateful for the life David had offered her.

"She likes to be called Maggie, and she and I both told you that."

"So because I called her by her Christian name that means I don't care about her?"

Sophie sighed. "It means that you don't know her and that you haven't cared enough to get to know her. I realize that Maggie is only five, but she has a beautiful personality that I couldn't imagine my life without."

"Just like her mother," David said.

"It's not enough for me to have a man that loves me," Sophie said. "I need someone who loves my children equally."

"Sophie, please don't do this." David took her hand. "Let's slow things down. We haven't really dated that long. Let me show you that I'm worth taking a chance on."

Sophie let his words roll around her heart, testing them out for truth. She believed that David wanted to try, but she also doubted the level of his maturity and the ability to see the challenges of the future.

He caressed her hand. "You don't have to decide right now. Please just think about it."

Sophie's chest rose with a deep breath, she held it for two counts and then exhaled slowly. "Okay."

"I promise I'll do better," David said. "I'll show you that I do love you."

They didn't talk much on the way home, but Sophie kept questioning herself. How could she have confidence in her heart when it had betrayed her once before?

Chapter 38 – An Unwelcome Surprise

The following morning, Sophie helped Garth get ready to play at the neighbor's house, keeping her mind off the subject of David Alexander. The telephone rang and Sophie hesitated to pick it up, half hoping it was David.

"Hello."

"Hello, Mrs. Wright," Nadine Alexander's clipped tone was unmistakable. With only three words she could tie Sophie's nerves into a jumbled mess.

"What can I do for you?" Sophie said.

"If you would be so kind to return the mending that you have finished. I'm no longer in need of your services. Mr. Okado will have payment for you."

"But what about the drapes in the formal dining room?" Sophie asked.

"It's been so difficult to get the material. I've had to cancel many of the projects I wanted finished. Casualty of war I suppose."

"I'm sorry to hear that."

"Yes, well I thought it would be wise since you and David are no longer seeing each other."

"Wait–what?" Sophie's heart slammed into her chest. She stumbled against the kitchen table, struggling to find her footing.

"Oh, dear," Nadine said. "I suppose I let the cat out of the bag.

David told me that he was cutting ties with you last night. He assured me that he wouldn't see you again. It's bad for the family business, you see."

Sophie's throat tightened, and although she swallowed, no words would come.

Nadine cleared her throat. "I wish you all the best."

"I'm sure you do," Sophie finally found her voice.

"Excuse me?"

"I said I'm sure that you do wish me all the best, as long as I have nothing to do with your son. I hope you're happy."

Nadine gave a mirthless chuckle. "Of course, dear. Have a good day."

Sophie hung up the phone, clenching the receiver tightly as Nadine's words rolled over her. Just a few months ago the Alexanders had kept her busy enough that she didn't need any other clients to supplement her meager income. Because she had gone out with David and taken a chance on her heart, she didn't have any sewing jobs scheduled. Nadine Alexander had scared away most of her prospects and Sophie had been too wrapped up in her silly fantasies to prepare for the worst.

Her head pounded and Sophie dug through the cupboard to find her coffee tin. She wouldn't have any coffee if Clyde hadn't helped her out again by not marking her ration card last time she went to the Safeway. It couldn't be true. David wouldn't hurt her like that, and yet, last night she'd given him every reason to end the relationship. But Nadine had spoken as if her fate had been decided before the date last night. Had David kept that from her, or was his mother really that devious?

Sophie tidied up the kitchen and then sat at the table and sipped her coffee, staring out the window while Maggie played with her baby doll in the front room.

A light knock at the door made Sophie sit up straight, but she relaxed as Debbie walked in. "I hope you don't mind me stopping by, but I wanted to talk to you." She patted Maggie on the head. "Good morning, Maggie."

"Hi, Debbie. Charlotte says hello." Maggie held her dolly up and Debbie shook the doll's hand. She turned toward Sophie with a cautious expression.

Sophie closed her eyes. "Please don't tell me you've already heard."

"Oh, hon, I hoped it wasn't true," Debbie replied.

"I wonder how long it will take for David to hear the news." Sophie opened her eyes and focused on Debbie's worried features.

"What do you mean?"

"Last night when David dropped me off from our date, I agreed to give him more time to figure out how to love all of my family."

"That sounds like a breakup to me." Debbie shook her head. "This is all wrong. I thought things were going so well between the two of you. Tell me what really happened."

"Would you like some coffee?" Sophie stood and reached for another cup from the cupboard. "It's weak, but it's better than nothing."

"I shouldn't take your coffee, but yes, I'd love some."

"How did you hear? Mrs. Alexander only called me an hour ago."

Debbie's cheeks turned pink and she put her face in her hands. "I was trying to get a call through to mother and I overheard Mrs. Gillespie telling someone all about what she'd just heard."

"And what was that?"

"That you'd been fired because David broke up with you."

Sophie groaned. "I don't know what happened. Last night I talked to David about my concerns that he didn't care about my children."

"That was bold," Debbie said. "And what was his reply?"

"He asked for another chance to show that he cared about them *and* me." Sophie traced the edge of the floral placemat with her fingernail. "I guess he won't get a chance now."

"What are you going to do with that sewing machine?" Debbie asked.

"That's what you want to know?" Sophie lifted her hands in the air. "I tell you my broken love story and you ask about the sewing machine."

Debbie nodded with a sly smile.

Sophie turned to look at the new sewing machine set up in the corner. "I'll keep it like David insisted."

"Well, that's one good thing from all of this."

Sophie gasped. "Debbie!"

Debbie laughed. "Don't worry. I know you're not a gold digger. If you were, you'd still be with David."

"You make it sound like I had a choice in the matter."

"Of course you did and you still do. Sophie, I have no doubt that if you were truly in love with David, he would've felt that and fought for you. He may be a rich little Mama's boy, but he's also a man who lived through the war and came out on the other side looking pretty good."

"Maybe this is all just a mistake," Sophie said. "I wouldn't be surprised if David shows up at my door today explaining away his mother's bad behavior."

"And what if he does? Are you saying you'd want to carry on with him?"

Sophie twisted her hands, rubbing her bare ring finger. Everything was happening so fast. She needed more time to figure out what her heart wanted–what she wanted. An ache pressed between her shoulders, making her lean forward. The truth was there hanging in the air, and she couldn't deny it any longer. She wasn't in love with David. The wrestle with her heart and her head had been constant during their relationship and she finally accepted that the rhythm of her heart didn't match David's. Was she doomed to be alone forever?

"Sophie?"

"No, you're right. I don't love David. Maybe things could have changed over time, but nothing would change Nadine Alexander's mind."

"I'm sorry." Debbie patted Sophie's hand. "What can I do for you?"

"Help me find a job?"

Debbie shook her head. "You don't need a job. I know you want to be independent, but you'll just have to swallow your pride. No one in this family will let you give up your heart and soul."

"I've been working ever since I came to Aspen Falls and my soul is still intact."

"You know what I mean. Maggie needs you. Garth needs you. That's why sewing is where you need to keep working. Something will come up and in the meantime, we'll get you through."

"Thanks, Debbie."

"It's okay to cry. I think it would help you feel better."

Sophie stiffened and held her breath until the burn in the back of her throat subsided. "I will," she breathed. "I need time for it all to make sense."

"Would you like me to take Maggie for the day?"

"No, please. I promised to have a tea party with her and Charlotte today and we're making some butter cookies with the sugar Leland gave us."

Debbie leaned forward and whispered. "Think about what you just said and remember the sweet taste of sugar when David comes to visit."

"What do you–"

"I left the potatoes simmering on the stove, so I'd better go before they burn." Debbie hugged Sophie. "Call me if you need anything."

"I will."

After Debbie left, Sophie pulled the bag of sugar from the cupboard and carefully measured out a half cup. A little spilled on the counter, so Sophie wiped it off in her palm. She tasted a bit, her mouth bursting with the instant sweet flavor and she knew what Debbie meant. The roses David had given her had long since died, but the little packet of sugar from Leland remained. She'd rationed it out carefully, enjoying every bit of the sweet treats she and the children had made.

Sophie walked toward the end table and examined Leland's carving. The heart was full of beauty, the curves generous and smooth. The woman in the heart hadn't moved, of course. Her profile was still half-turned from view. The pose struck Sophie as she swallowed the last of the sweet flavor from the sugar. She hadn't really loved David because she hadn't allowed herself too. How long had she been rationing out her heart?

Chapter 39 – All Fool's Day

April 1, 1946

Keith got off work early Monday afternoon and arrived at Leland's eager to work on his dining set. "I have a new appreciation for how much you've been able to accomplish on your own, Leland. This is taking a lot longer than I thought."

"You're doing great with the few hours you're able to spend each week." Leland clapped Keith on the back. "Although, you aren't really helping me get out from under my workload."

"That's true," Keith replied. "I've been talking to Debbie about the possibility of me working a little later here in the evenings for a while. She said that'd she'd have to get Sophie to keep her company."

"I didn't see Sophie and the kids at church on Sunday," Leland said.

"I think Maggie wasn't feeling well, but I might as well tell you—walk lightly around Sophie if you see her in the next few days."

"Why's that?"

"News is that David's mother fired her Saturday over the telephone and laughed about David breaking up with her." Keith shook his head.

"Keith, don't fool with me," Leland said. "Sophie and David were still dating last I talked to her."

"It's no April fool's. But it probably seemed like a terrible joke to Sophie."

"Why's that?"

"Debbie went to see her and Sophie had gone out with David the night before. They were still an item when he dropped her off."

"So he had his mother break up for him?" Leland felt the back of his neck getting hot, almost as if he experienced the humiliation instead of Sophie.

Keith shrugged. "I'm not sure what's going on, but it's good news for you."

"I don't see how Sophie having a broken heart is good for me." Leland rubbed the back of his neck.

"She doesn't have a broken heart." Keith dusted off his pants. "Debbie went over there and talked to her, said Sophie didn't even shed a tear."

"Really?"

"Deb said she was just real thoughtful, and Sophie admitted that she wasn't in love with David."

The words shot a spark through Leland and he stood up straighter. A thousand thoughts sped through his mind of how the door might be open for him, but then his shoulders slumped. "She probably won't want anything to do with dating after getting burned."

Keith stopped sanding for a moment. "Maybe not dating, but I'm sure she wouldn't turn down a friendship with someone who understands loss and heartache."

Leland nodded. "I finally told Sophie about Jessie."

"I thought you'd told her already."

"I did, but I never got around to telling her the whole story—my part in it."

Keith tugged at his collar. "Oh."

Leland smiled at his friend. Keith was a rock, and Leland could always depend on his best friend, but Keith still had trouble talking about the accident that had taken Jessie's life.

Leland wiped the dust off his hammer. "Sophie was so kind. I'm glad that she knows." Leland didn't mention how liberating it had been to tell Sophie the truth about his past, the guilt he felt, and the struggles he still knocked up against. She had helped him see that the forgiveness God had extended him would never end. His heart had felt even lighter since he'd given Sophie the carving.

Keith nodded. "My sis has been through a lot, but she still has one of the biggest hearts."

"That's true," Leland replied. "You'll help me figure out how to approach her, right?"

"You'll know the right way. Same way you know how to build a chair to support a two-hundred-fifty pound man." Keith gripped the back of the chair that he'd been working on.

Leland chuckled. "You planning on having some heavy company over? You're not anywhere near two-fifty and neither is Wayne."

"I want these to last is all." Keith crouched and examined the spindles of the chair.

The two men worked until well past suppertime and after Keith left, Leland spent a few extra minutes sweeping up the shop. Something about what Keith had said didn't sit right with Leland. He claimed that Sophie didn't have a broken heart, and she probably put on a convincing face for others, but Leland knew about the heart's weaknesses. Even if Sophie wasn't sure about her feelings for David, the treatment she'd received and public humiliation from Mrs. Alexander was enough to bring any woman to tears. There was only one reason her heart wouldn't be broken by David's actions—if it was already in pieces before they began dating. Leland scooped up a pile of sawdust and took it outside. The air was still, with barely a breeze and Leland frowned. The oak tree was quiet, no whispers on the breeze, or pulsing melodies in his head. Everything seemed wrong and Leland knew why. He knew what it felt like to live with a broken heart—the pieces buried under layers of armor—shielding it from further hurt.

A thread of worry snaked down his spine as Leland recalled how far he'd fallen when his heart had seemed broken beyond repair. Sophie needed his help, but it would take a miracle to heal her heart. Fortunately, Leland knew a little about miracles. As he walked toward his home, he whispered a prayer, pleading for guidance to pull Sophie out from underneath her armor. If she could break free, she might see the love in his heart that could heal her own.

Chapter 40 – A Shadowed Heart

Tuesday morning, Sophie scrubbed at the eggs on Garth's plate, her focus on the breakfast dishes, the crumbs on the table, and the floor that needed mopped. David hadn't called. Debbie reported that he wasn't at church either, although his mother was and she'd visited for a long time after the service with several of the parishioners. Which was exactly why Sophie was focusing on scrubbing the sticky leftovers from the edge of the table. Every time she thought of David, she winced in pain, and that was unacceptable because there was so much to do. Picking up the list of spring cleaning to do, Sophie studied each line even though she had it memorized. She paused when she read, *Mend ivory skirt*. The hem on the skirt needed to be redone and Sophie had planned to use the new sewing machine to fix the skirt so that it would be ready for her next outing with David. Sophie drew a dark line through that item, pressing until the lead of the pencil broke.

Stepping back, Sophie covered her face and took a shuddering breath. It frightened her how close the dam inside her was to breaking. She had told Debbie she would cry over David later, but she didn't because crying would be admitting that he had hurt her–that she had let him in enough to do so was her own mistake. Sophie straightened and resumed scrubbing the table until she heard a knock at the door. She peeked out the front curtains, but didn't see a vehicle. Sophie opened the door and smiled at Serena Tanaka. "Good morning."

"I come to visit you and let the children say hello. Is okay?" Serena spoke with her clipped accent and a few missing words as usual. Sophie understood her friend much better now than the first time they'd spoken.

"Yes, of course. I'm glad to see you." Sophie motioned for her to come in. "I was just about to have a cup of coffee. Would you like some?"

Serena nodded. "Thank you." She set baby Shun next to Maggie on the floor, and Maggie immediately hugged the baby until he protested.

"Maggie, give the baby some space. He isn't a dolly," Sophie warned.

Maggie stood and put her hands on her hips. "I know that, but he loves me." She crouched and tickled Shun, who giggled.

Both Sophie and Serena joined the laughter. It felt good to laugh at something simple, to release some of the ache in her chest. Sophie poured the coffee and set a cup in front of Serena.

Serena took a sip, wrapping her delicate hands around the cup. "I hear about your job. Shunsaku and I would like to help you."

Sophie felt the color rise in her face. How fast had word traveled? For as many times as she'd tried to tell herself not to worry over what people thought, she hated gossip. "Oh, that's so kind of you, but really, we're doing fine," Sophie said.

"No, not fine. Your smile is not bright," Serena said. "We help you because we have friends in Calloway Grove and Newbold. They need a good seamstress."

Sophie looked down at her feet. Serena knew what she was up against in Aspen Falls. With the Alexanders and Marchants stirring the pot, it would be safer to find work outside of town. "That's actually a very good idea. I don't have many prospects right now."

"Shunsaku deliver package twice a week to the city. He help you to take the mending so you wouldn't need to use so much gas."

Sophie felt the heavy weight on her chest lift an inch. "He would do that?"

"He want to help." Serena smiled. "He hope you will look at Leland now."

Sophie smiled, shaking her head. "Things are complicated for Leland and I."

"Love is complicated. Always." Serena nodded emphatically.

Sophie hesitated, letting the words soak in. There was so much to think about, but she'd been so busy it was hard to take the time to sort through the thoughts in her heart and those in her mind. Garth and Maggie had needed a lot of extra attention, but Sophie was also avoiding time alone so that she wouldn't have to think about unpleasant things.

"Mrs. Phelps come to see me," Serena said.

Sophie sat up straight at the abrupt change in subject. "She did?"

"She invite Emika to play with Mary. I thank you." Serena reached out and pressed Sophie's fingers.

"Oh, that's wonderful, but you don't need to thank me."

"Yes, Anita tell me that you are her friend too."

Sophie chuckled. "This town can't keep any secrets."

"Secrets, not a good thing for the heart." Serena placed a hand over her heart. "The heart beat with truth."

"How did you get to be so wise?" Sophie tilted her head to the right. "I hope someday I can have half the sense you do."

Serena smiled and tapped the side of her head. "Not always wise. Hard to see for myself, but my friend—I can see better. I want you happy."

"Thank you."

By the time they'd finished their coffee, the two women had worked out the details of the plan to help Sophie continue her work as a seamstress. Sophie hugged Serena's slight frame. "Your kindness means so much to me."

Serena picked up Shun, lightly bouncing him on her hip. "And you to me. I hope your heart—it heal."

Sophie nodded, but didn't speak of healing hearts. As Serena walked down the sidewalk toward her home, Sophie wondered if the heart, once broken as badly as hers was from her marriage to Cal, remained in pieces. The most frightening thought of all was that Sophie had only played with a tiny sliver of her heart while dating David. The other pieces were swept carefully under a figurative rug, waiting in the gloom of shattered dreams. She swallowed against the rough lump in her throat and went back to her list. Her heart beat in shadow, and Sophie didn't try to climb into the light. With an old toothbrush, she began scrubbing around the faucet in the kitchen while Maggie dressed Charlotte for another tea party.

Chapter 41 – The Rocking Chair

April 1946

It had been almost two weeks since Sophie had taken the call from Mrs. Alexander to officially end her relationship with David. The house was spotless, and the list had been replaced with three others as Sophie immersed herself in working to complete all the unfinished tasks she'd let build up. She was also sewing again. The Tanakas had secured three clients for her between Calloway Grove and Newbold, and although it wasn't a lot of work, it felt good to sew again.

The April rains had come in full force and kept the children indoors for most of the week. Sophie peeked out the window at the wet grass. The clouds had parted, and if the weather turned, maybe Garth and Maggie could play outside. Garth had come home from school complaining about being wet and cold, so Sophie had helped him change into dry clothing. He and Maggie were playing in her room. At least the two of them had each other, no matter who else came and went in their lives.

Sophie heard a crash and a shriek that turned into a mournful wail coming from Maggie's room. She rushed down the hallway and found Garth holding a small cylindrical piece of wood and another curved piece that resembled– "Oh no, Garth, what have you done?"

"Mommy, he broke my chair! He broke Charlotte's chair," Maggie cried. The little girl held tight to the remains of the rocking chair.

"How on earth could you do something like this?" Sophie snatched the pieces of wood from Garth.

His eyes filled with tears. "I didn't mean to. Honest, I was helping Maggie build a throne for her dolly."

Sophie glanced at the pile of blocks, a red brick, a round stone, and Maggie's doll face-down on the floor. The trajectory of items indicated that the tower had tumbled and most likely, the brick had delivered the fatal blow to the rocking chair. Closing her eyes, Sophie took a deep breath, even as Maggie sobbed louder. It was moments like these that she needed to keep control because Cal never would have. Sophie opened her eyes, knelt down and pulled her children close. "Garth, it's not a good idea to bring bricks and rocks into the house. Those are for outside building and even then, you must be careful because you could get hurt."

Garth nodded against her blouse and his little body shook with cries.

"Can you apologize to your sister?"

"I'm sorry." Garth turned and hugged Maggie. She still clutched the chair, but she reached her other arm around him and patted his shoulder.

"It's okay, Leland will fix it," she said in between sniffles.

"Oh—uh, I don't know if that will work. Let me see the pieces," Sophie said.

Maggie handed over the chair. It was missing two spindles and the arm of the chair had broken off. The broken splinters of the spindle stuck up from the hole Leland had carefully hollowed out in the little chair. Sophie held the pieces up, tilting them from side to side. "I wonder if I could glue it."

"No, Mommy. That won't work. You have to get Leland to fix it," Maggie demanded.

"Can you call him?" Garth asked. "Maybe we could go over to his house and see Hope again?"

"I don't think so." Sophie clenched the broken spindle tight in her hand. She thought of the music box, the tinny song reaching into her heart and helping her understand the broken man who had tried so hard to rebuild himself. Leland had ventured across the path of her heart with the bit of courage he had left, trying in his own way to show her that he cared about her and wanted the chance to get to know her. He'd shared the most tender parts of his soul, and Sophie had closed the door on him. Regret hollowed out her chest where her heart once beat with excitement at the prospect of inviting a man into her life. A man who could fix things like the rocking chair, her broken heart, her broken hope.

That was before David had helped her see that no one could fix Sophie Wright except Sophie herself. If she were to invite a man into her life again, her heart needed to be whole first. Maybe Leland had recognized the same in himself. Was that the reason he wouldn't put himself out there for Sophie? As soon as he'd caught wind of David, he'd turned tail and run—away from any hope for a future. But then when he'd decided to try again, it was too late.

Sophie's heartbeat quickened as she thought of the mistakes that she'd made. The uncertainty of life had trapped her into a holding pattern where it often felt difficult to breathe.

"Mommy, don't be sad." Garth put his hand over hers. "Leland can fix it. He can fix anything."

A bird flew past the window, catching Sophie's eye and moving her gaze upwards to the bright blue sky. It always surprised her how quickly the weather could change. Spring had tiptoed into Aspen Falls with its flourishes of light green that would soon turn to a vibrant shade of new life. Garth's words repeated in the stillness, "He can fix anything." If that was true, then he could mend a broken heart, too. Her shoulders slumped even as the thought passed through her head. In Leland's mind, she had rejected him for the shiny new toy—the brass war hero who mocked Leland for not serving his country. Sophie choked on the bitter pill of her actions. There may not be any mending for her heart, but the least she could do was explain to Leland how she felt.

"It's a beautiful day today. Let's drive over to Leland's and see if he can fix this. Maybe we can walk over to the park afterwards."

"Really?" Garth jumped up, clapped his hands and scampered to his room.

"Thank you, Mommy," Maggie said. She hugged Sophie and picked up her dolly, carefully smoothing out her dress.

By the time they loaded into the car, Sophie wished that she hadn't agreed to go. There were a thousand reasons why Leland wouldn't want anything to do with her. She consoled herself by reasoning that they were only going to see if he could fix the rocking chair.

On the drive over, Sophie realized something that helped her to breathe easier. There was a slim chance that Leland hadn't heard all the details about the end of her relationship with David yet. She could be the one to tell him, and help him see that even though her heart still needed time, someday things would be different.

Sophie maneuvered around puddles and parked next to Leland's shop. Garth was already knocking on the door by the time she exited the car. Sophie clutched the broken pieces of Maggie's chair and stepped carefully over the muddy sections of the driveway.

"Hi, Garth, how are you doing today?" Leland said when he opened the door.

"We accidentally broke Maggie's chair and we need you to fix it because it's for her doll and we won't never be able to have tea parties again if you don't fix it."

Leland looked up, noticed the broken chair Sophie held, and his face softened. His hazel eyes were filled with empathy as he shifted his gaze to Maggie. "I'm sorry about that. I need to do a better job so that chair can hold up."

"Actually, the kids agreed that playing with bricks and rocks in the house is probably not the best idea," Sophie said.

Leland arched an eyebrow. "Good point. And how are you?" he reached for the broken chair and his fingers brushed Sophie's.

"I've been busy spring cleaning," Sophie infused brightness into her voice. "Don't worry; it's not as glamorous as it sounds."

Leland chuckled. "Come inside. We'll see about fixing this chair."

Garth and Maggie were already under a work table playing with Hope. The pup was another size larger and full of energy, barking and whining at the kids.

Leland set the broken pieces of the chair on a dresser he must have been working on. He turned to Sophie, that same empathy in his eyes. "I know about what happened."

"You mean David? I wondered if you knew."

"Small town." Leland shrugged. "Keith told me."

"I'm going to pound him," Sophie muttered.

Leland chuckled. "Don't. You're lucky to have a brother like him. He loves you so much and he wants you to be happy."

"So why did he tell you about David then?"

Leland opened his mouth and closed it, pursing his lips.

"Just say it," Sophie said.

"Keith worried that maybe David wasn't the best man for you, but I'll admit he is biased."

Sophie thought she might die right there on the spot. "How much did he tell you?"

"That you were dating David Alexander so his mother fired you *and* helped David break up with you over the telephone."

Sophie blinked several times and swallowed.

"You don't have to say anything. I wouldn't bring it up, but it was the best way for me to get on the topic to ask if you could help me around here a bit." Leland leaned against the dresser, one side of his mouth lifting in a crooked smile. "It's not very glamorous, but I got these three orders in for footstools and he wanted to know if I knew anyone who could do the upholstery work."

"Really? I mean, you think I could do a good enough job? Upholstering is different than sewing."

Leland chuckled. "You'd probably do better than anyone in three counties. I hear Mrs. Alexander hasn't found anyone to replace you yet and she's a might ornery about it."

"You're making that up." Sophie put her hands on her hips. "How would you ever hear something like that?"

"I have to go into the hardware store at least once a week and Mr. Gillespie likes to fill me in on all the tidbits his wife overhears."

Sophie covered her mouth, laughing quietly.

Leland took hold of her hand. "You have a beautiful laugh. Let it ring."

Surprised, she laughed again and then hugged Leland. "Thank you."

He put his arms around her and patted her back. "I'm glad to help." He released her and took one step back.

"When would you like me to start?"

"Well, first is the matter of picking out the right material. You wouldn't happen to know anything about that, would you?"

Sophie folded her arms. "I know you're teasing me, Leland Halverson, but what you don't know is that I have connections in three counties for acquiring material."

Leland leaned back against the work table. "You don't say? I guess I asked the right person then. See, I don't know a thing about fancy stuff like this. If you could pick out the right material, it would ensure that these footstools turn out."

"What color would your client like?"

"Well, he–uh, said something about green and blue."

"Okay, what shade? Darks or lights?"

"What would you suggest?" Leland pulled out his notebook and flipped through a couple pages. “My client asked me to find something that would look good with a walnut wood stain.”

“Good to know we’re working with someone flexible. Nadine Alexander was nearly impossible to please.” Sophie straightened. “There’s a little store in Newbold that might have some remnants we could use, depending on the size of the footstool.”

Leland grinned. “I knew you could do it. I’ll send you with some money to make the purchase, if that’s okay.”

Sophie nodded.

“Let’s get these details figured out. As soon as you can get the material, you can stop by and we’ll get to work.”

“Thanks, Leland. I think this will be an interesting project.”

Sophie was halfway home before she realized that she was smiling, and she felt...alive in a way that she hadn’t for weeks. Leland had kept everything strictly business, but he was still Leland: quiet, steady, strong, and caring. He’d reassured Maggie that the chair could be fixed, gently admonished Garth about bricks in the house, and then offered Sophie work. It started sprinkling again as they pulled onto their street, but the sun was still shining over Leland’s house. The soft hues of a rainbow stretched across the sky, fading into the clouds. Sophie smiled up at the sky. There was a promise there and she intended to grab hold of the possibility if she could.

Chapter 42 – Building

It took Leland until well past ten o'clock to finish building the framework for the two footstools that no one had ordered. It was a white lie that he meant to remedy as soon as possible. Tomorrow he'd contact a few of his best customers and tell them about the new pieces that would be ready within a week. He'd also have to work on the framework for the third footstool which he intended to keep. Leland wanted to be honest with Sophie but it was more important that he help her right now. His heart beat faster as he remembered how her eyes lit up at the possibility of working with him. He'd probably never hear the end of it from Keith, but it was worth it to be near Sophie.

She'd looked different today, like she was carrying too many worries and sorrows. It was a good thing that David Alexander hadn't been seen around town lately because Leland had a mind to find him and give him some choice words. But even that wouldn't satisfy Leland. He wanted to make Sophie happy. He wanted to take care of her children and make them his own. He'd noticed the way that Garth watched his mother for cues as to how she was feeling. Sophie thought that no one could read her stoic face, but her children could. Leland had taken to watching Garth to pick up on what was really going on inside Sophie's head. A little boy shouldn't have to worry over such things.

By Tuesday, Leland was worried because instead of finding a customer for the upcoming blue or green footstools, he now had an order for a matching pair of footstools upholstered in brown. He wondered if he could just call Sophie and tell her the customer had changed their mind about the color of the fabric. He thought about it all morning long and decided to give Sophie a ring after lunch. She didn't answer the call and ten minutes later, Leland discovered why when she stopped by with a plate of oatmeal and applesauce cookies and a roll of fabric under her arm.

"Sophie, I just tried to call you." Leland opened the door for her.

"Well then I have perfect timing." She handed him the plate of cookies. "What did you need?"

"Thank you for these." Leland set the plate aside, trying to think of a way out of the predicament he'd landed in. He cleared his throat. "Ladies first." Leland motioned to the material she held.

Sophie grinned. "I had to drive out to Newbold to take some measurements for a bridesmaid dress, so I stopped by the fabric store and found this." Sophie held out a dark green broadcloth with a hint of blue in the pattern forming squares across the material.

Leland took it, running his fingers over the stiff fabric. "This is perfect. You must have quite the luck to find something so quickly."

Sophie shrugged. "I don't know about luck, but I am pretty resourceful. Are you sure it'll be okay for the order? Who are these for anyway?"

"It'll be great. They really are going to turn out nice. What do you think of the size?" Leland carefully sidestepped her question and pointed out the two frames he'd made for the footstools.

Sophie tapped her chin and nodded. "Yes, I think if we use the right amount of stuffing, they'll be the right height for sitting in an easy chair and reading the paper."

"I'm really glad you could help me." Leland used a hand broom to sweep his medium-sized work table clean. "I thought this might be a good place to measure the fabric and start cutting."

"Oh, good. I hoped it would be okay if I came by to get started. Maggie is over playing at Debbie's with Amy and Michael." Sophie smiled at Leland and he noticed a light in her eyes that hadn't been there just a few days before.

"You look good today, Sophie," he said. "I mean—I really like your hair."

Sophie's cheeks turned pink and she put her hand up to her hair that was braided and twisted into a bun. "Thank you. I'll just grab my sewing bag from the car, now that I know I'm staying."

She returned, whistling a jaunty tune and carefully measured the material. "So, you didn't answer my question earlier. Who are these footstools for? Is it a secret? It helps me when I'm working to think of the person who will be enjoying it."

"Oh, that." Leland scratched the back of his head, trying to think of who he could give the footstools to because he knew for certain that working with Sophie was the right thing to do, even if the job did start out on false pretenses. "Well, it is a bit of a surprise. Clyde Jenkins is going to be delighted with your work."

"Clyde from the Safeway?" Sophie furrowed her brow. "I didn't know that man ever sat still—or went home."

Leland swallowed. He'd thought of Clyde because he was a good friend, and Leland had witnessed the many times when he'd looked the other way to help people stretch their rations during the war. The grocer was the first person who came to mind, but Leland realized that it was a little out of character for the man who hardly ever left the store. "I think they might be for gifts, but I can't remember. I'll have to give Clyde a call anyhow and have him come take a look. But you'll never believe it. The McCallisters just placed an order for a set of matching brown footstools. So you might need to take another trip to the store."

"Well, that *is* good news," Sophie replied. She turned and went back to work, cutting the material.

Over the next couple hours, Leland talked to Sophie like they were old friends. They talked about Garth and Maggie and how excited they were for summertime. Leland let Sophie have a peek at the dining table Keith was building for Debbie. And they talked about the end of the rations, joking about how it would feel to chew a piece of gum and purchase more without a ration ticket.

"Or sprinkle sugar over a piece of cinnamon toast without feeling like you broke the law." Sophie closed her eyes as if she were tasting the simple treat.

"How about sugar cookies with an inch of frosting?" Leland could almost taste the cookies his mother used to make him as a boy.

Sophie opened her eyes and they held a faraway look. She straightened and put her hand on his arm. "I still have some of the sugar you gave me for Maggie's birthday party. I want you to know that it was one of the most thoughtful gifts I've ever received."

Leland's heart thumped against his ribcage, his blood coursing to the spot where Sophie's slender fingers touched his skin. "I'm happy you liked it."

"Leland, can I ask you something?" Sophie's green eyes were luminous and Leland knew that he would gladly do anything for this beautiful woman standing before him.

"Of course."

"That day—Maggie's birthday—did you leave because you thought David was going to show up?"

Sawdust seemed to coat his throat as he struggled to reply. "I saw the roses. I didn't think I had a chance. I'm sorry."

Sophie clutched his arm. "I wish you would have stayed."

And Leland could hear the words she didn't say—that she wished he would have given them a chance to get to know each other before David broke her heart. "I'm really sorry, Sophie. I never wanted to hurt you."

"You didn't hurt me," she murmured.

"But I did. I didn't want to get hurt so I ran, but I want you to know that I'm through running."

Sophie nodded and removed her hand from his arm. "I'm glad to hear that. I guess I'd better finish up." She turned and smoothed out the fabric on the table.

"Can I ask you a question?" Leland's voice cut through the stillness. He stepped beside Sophie and laid his hand over hers.

She looked up at him with worry in her eyes. "Maybe."

Leland licked his lips. "I know you've been hurting. I just want you to know that I'm here. I'd still appreciate the chance to take you out on a date, but if that makes you uncomfortable, go on and pretend that I didn't say anything."

Sophie looked down and her other hand tightened around the edge of the fabric. "I don't know what to do," she whispered. "My heart is so confused."

"I respect that." Leland gave her hand a squeeze and smiled. "You've done great work today. We'd better not let word get out about how fast you work or we'll turn into a furniture store."

"Thank you." Sophie smiled and her posture relaxed. It wasn't what Leland hoped, but he was a patient man. In time, Sophie's heart would mend and he planned to be there when she was ready to try again for love.

Chapter 43 – The Seamstress and the Carpenter

May 1946

Over the next two weeks, Sophie helped Leland finish five footstools. It was tricky hammering in the fasteners to keep the heavy material in place. Leland had been a little mysterious about his customers, and especially when she picked out the brown material for the McCallisters set. He insisted that they finish that set before the one for Clyde since he wasn't in a hurry. Sophie went along with what Leland said because it didn't make any difference to her. She enjoyed watching Leland work, the way he sharpened a pencil with his pocketknife and had a lopsided smile when he was concentrating. He marked the wood and told her, "Measure twice, cut once." His hands were so capable and Sophie could see the way his mind worked as he put pieces of wood together like a puzzle–an intricate and beautiful puzzle.

On May first, Sophie returned to the shop to check over the footstools before the customers came to get them. "They really did turn out nicely."

"Only because of you." Leland ran his hand along the edge of a brown footstool. "How is it going with your other sewing work?"

"Well, this month I think I'll have three clients, which is a far sight better than last month. And I owe it all to the Tanakas."

Leland nodded. "They are a great family. I saw Shunsaku in town and he told me about how Serena had come up with the idea."

"Do you know one time I talked to Serena in the grocery store and a woman told me that I shouldn't be talking to her?"

Leland rubbed the back of his neck, the creases around his eyes deepening. "I've seen some of that myself. I guess it will take time for the animosity to fade. I'm glad that you found a friend in Serena and that Garth has been able to play with Emika. You're a wonderful example, Sophie."

"No, don't say it." Sophie stopped him because she knew what he was about to say—the same thing she'd heard too many times. That she was a pillar of forgiveness because she didn't take offense that her neighbors were of Japanese descent—belonging to the same race as the people responsible for her husband's death.

Leland appeared confused. "Okay, sorry about that. I was just going to say that you notice people and they can feel the way you care about them."

Sophie covered her mouth, the skin under her fingertips hot. She shook her head and dropped her hand. "I'm sorry. That was very rude of me. I thought you were going to say something about Pearl Harbor—everyone does."

"You're right, I would probably have said that, but I remembered you don't like to talk about your late husband." Leland put his hands in the pockets of his overalls. "I'm sorry you're still hurting. The pain fades, but it's always there isn't it?"

Sophie's stomach clenched and she tasted acid in the back of her throat. She wanted to run, but Leland was opening his heart to her so she stood strong. "I imagine that your pain was much more acute than mine. For me, Cal had already been gone for so long that he was merely a shadow in my life. I know that sounds harsh, but it's one of the ways that I dealt with the loss."

"I'm sorry to hear that. I wonder..." he pushed his boot against a pile of wood shavings. "What you just said about Cal—do you think you've allowed yourself to really mourn him?"

Sophie shook her head. Leland meant well, but his words were like knives in her heart. She couldn't speak, for if she did, her voice would betray her, spilling the secrets of her marriage to Cal, the secrets surrounding his death. She wasn't ready to give Leland access to those hidden memories. Even David didn't know the depth of her feelings related to Cal's death. The truth crept carefully up her spine and with a shudder, Sophie straightened, shaking off the chance to share the reality she'd lived through. The truth nudged her again with the idea that Leland, of all people, would understand her secret. Sophie lifted her head, meeting Leland's gaze. His hazel eyes held compassion, the flecks of amber more apparent as Sophie focused on the truth she saw there. She blinked and the moment passed as she denied the truth that had haunted her for so long.

The skin around Leland's eyes crinkled as he studied her. "You know, I've never been back to Jessie's grave."

"Leland, you don't have to—" Sophie reached forward, putting her hand on his arm.

"But I want to say the words out loud to someone. I'm afraid. I did wrong by Jessie after she died. I know she would've been disappointed in me." His shoulders turned inward.

"But you've changed," Sophie reassured him. "The Leland I know is nothing like the man that you've described to me. You're not him anymore."

"How can I be sure?" his voice cracked and the vulnerability in his face broke the last of Sophie's resolve to keep her distance. She took one step forward and put her arm around his waist. Leland stood a head taller than her and Sophie leaned her head against his chest.

"Because I'm sure that you're a better man than you allow yourself to believe."

Leland took a deep breath, his chest rising and falling under her cheek. He put his arms around her and kissed the top of her head. "Thank you."

Sophie didn't move because she knew if she turned her head, she would let Leland kiss her and she wasn't ready for that. Tightening her grip around his waist, she lowered her head toward his chest and murmured, "Thank you, Leland."

The shop door rattled with a staccato knocking and Sophie jumped back from Leland's embrace. They both smiled and quickly turned toward the door as it swung open.

"Well, good morning." Clyde Jenkins entered. "I hope I'm not too early. I'm anxious to get this furniture loaded up."

"No, not at all," Leland said. "Sophie just checked over every crease in the fabric to make sure it's perfect."

Clyde leaned over the footstools covered in the dark green material and ran a hand along the edge. "Excellent work, as to be expected from the two of you—the seamstress and the carpenter."

"That's kind of you, Clyde," Sophie replied, "but we both know that Leland is the master craftsman here."

"Well, Sophie, my dear, your stitches hold more of a reputation than you might think." Clyde chuckled. "Yep, I sure am glad you called me about these footstools. I was looking for something for the missus. I never would have thought of a special-made piece if you hadn't suggested it. She'll be tickled over this surprise."

Leland's neck flushed and he smiled, maybe a little too broadly. "Well, I'm glad you approve of them. Let me help you out with those."

"Good to see you again, Sophie," Clyde said. "Send those two munchkins over for a lollipop some time."

"I'll do that." Sophie smiled and waved as Clyde and Leland hauled the two footstools outside. Leland returned a few minutes later and

Sophie folded her arms, leaning back against the work table with a smile that she hoped seemed mysterious. "Clyde seemed happy about his order, but I found it interesting when he mentioned that you called him about the footstools."

Leland pulled on his ear and cleared his throat. "He was pretty happy about them, yes."

"You didn't have any orders for footstools, did you?"

Leland rubbed a hand over his mouth and smiled. "Well, that depends."

"Depends on what?"

"On when you asked the question."

Sophie stood up straight, her arms still folded with a no-mercy look. "You're being cryptic."

"I know." Leland lifted both hands up in surrender. "You know I'm no good at poker."

Sophie laughed. "Leland Halverson, did you make up work for me?"

Leland scuffed his boot through the sawdust on the floor. "Not exactly."

"Well, then tell me the not exact version of what happened."

"Promise you won't be upset?"

Sophie tilted her head to the right and arched an eyebrow.

Leland sighed. "I care about you a great deal, you know that. You were hurting so badly that day when you brought Maggie's rocking chair. I swear I didn't plan it. It's like the words just fell out of my mouth. I'm sorry I wasn't honest from the start, but as soon as I asked around, I got more orders."

"So you were hoping those would cancel out your little white lie."

Leland nodded. "My pa always told me that if you help someone, it will come back around to you. I think he was right. I'm sorry I wasn't honest with you, though."

His face had a boyish quality to it when he was worried. Sophie relaxed her arms and stepped forward. Before she could talk herself out of it, she embraced Leland again. "All's forgiven. Thank you for looking out for me."

Leland stiffened and then his arms went around her and pulled her close. It was only a few seconds but the air around them shifted and Sophie felt the connection to Leland that she'd been denying for so long. Earlier she had embraced him in a show of comfort for the tough topics they'd discussed, but this felt different. Leland cleared his throat and she had a feeling that if she didn't move soon, he would ask her out again. Sophie stepped back and immediately her heart burned with a desire to be held in his arms again. She ignored the pulsing rhythm and smiled up at him. "I guess it's time for me to get going. Garth will be home from school soon looking for his snack."

Leland only took a second to recover from the change in subject. "Can you come by Monday to help me finish up the last footstool? I'm not taking any new orders for a time, but you'll let me know if you need more work, right?"

"Sure. Thanks again."

Sophie kept smiling on the drive home as she thought about what Leland had done for her, creating more work for himself when he was already overscheduled. She thought back and couldn't think of a single time when Cal or David had acted so unselfishly. Perhaps with time, Sophie would have the courage to give some of her heart to Leland.

Chapter 44 – The Last Order

At church on Sunday, Leland arrived early, hoping that there might be room for him to sit next to Sophie and her children. He scanned the room, but the chapel was already half-filled and when he caught sight of Sophie sitting in the middle of her family with Garth and Maggie on either side of her, he changed direction and sat near the back. The meeting was about to start when David Alexander walked in, his arm looped through his mother's. The two made their way to the front of the chapel where they sat a couple rows in front of Sophie. Whispers bounced around the congregation and Leland saw several heads nodding together, as people discussed Sophie and David's breakup.

Even from across the room, Leland saw Sophie's shoulders stiffen. According to the gossip, it had been over a month and David hadn't spoken to Sophie. Leland knew more than the gossip because Sophie had told him that David hadn't even called or sent a note. Leland's blood boiled whenever he thought about the poor treatment that had been exacted on Sophie by a cruel woman. He did his best not to think evil thoughts in the house of the Lord, but watching David sitting there without even a backward glance toward Sophie nearly undid him.

David kept his attention forward, although he'd surely seen Sophie and her family. The opening hymn began and Leland saw Sophie turn back, her face flushed and eyes tight focusing on the door, as if she were searching for a way out of the church. As she pulled her gaze across the room, she made eye contact with Leland. He held still and then nodded once, trying to convey to Sophie that he knew she was strong enough to survive this. Sophie returned his gaze and dipped her head, facing the front again.

Leland's mind was so focused on Sophie and the hurt she must be experiencing, he didn't hear a single thing the pastor said. He wished there was something he could do to help her because as the meeting wore on, she seemed to shrink in the very spot where she sat. When the organist began playing the closing hymn, Leland searched for the most direct route to Sophie. There had to be a way to stop the ensuing confrontation between her and David. But on the second verse, Sophie stood and carefully led Maggie out of the pew, toward the back of the church. She smiled as she walked with her daughter as if nothing pressed on her mind, but when she walked past Leland, he saw the dimple in her right cheek twitch. He could read her tell, but he had no idea how deep the hurt went beyond that flicker of emotion.

He almost got up and followed her out the back doors, but that would only add fuel to the gossip's fires. Instead, he stared holes through the back of David Alexander's head so that when the man finally stood to exit the pew with his mother, he turned and met Leland's gaze. His eyes widened a fraction and Leland guessed that David must have recognized something of the venom in his stare. Leland didn't shift his gaze as David walked around the chapel with his mother, greeting neighbors and friends.

He was so intent on watching David that he jumped when someone sat next to him on the pew. Shunsaku Tanaka clapped a hand on his shoulder. "Hello, my friend."

"Morning, Shunsaku. How's your family?"

"They are well. Emika, she try to dance to the song of the music box." Shunsaku smiled. "She is a wobbly ballerina, but happy."

Leland grinned. "I'm happy to hear that. I'm sorry I haven't been over to visit for some time. I'm afraid that I've let myself get too busy."

Shunsaku looked toward the front of the chapel where David stood next to his mother, talking to the Marchant's. "Perhaps too busy hating that man?"

Leland shook his head. Shunsaku had a way of getting right to the point, the accent on his English pronouncing that point in a way that Leland couldn't ignore. "I don't want him to hurt Sophie anymore."

"He will," Shunsaku said in a flat tone. He watched David for a moment and then turned to Leland. "Why you wait to give Sophie your love? You could protect her heart."

Leland looked up at the ceiling and shook his head. "It's not that easy."

"Easier to look at the man who hold her heart and cast it away?" Shunsaku's dark eyes flicked from Leland to David and back again.

"She's hurting and not ready for another relationship. I know I messed up, but now isn't the best time."

Shunsaku shook his head slowly. "Live to dance again. That is what you tell my Emika, and she do it. She live and laugh. She cry and dance. She love. And you could do the same."

Despite Shunsaku's broken English, each word he spoke hung in the air on an unseen melody of truth. Leland looked down at his hands clasped tightly together. He had given Emika the music box at a turning point in his life. In her fight against polio, Leland had worried himself sick. If she died, it would've killed a part of him because Emika was born the same year as Jessie. The tiny Japanese girl represented the part of his life he'd lost after the accident, and he'd clung to hope until it fueled his every thought. When Emika came home from the hospital, a long recovery ahead of her, but a smile on her face and the music box playing in her room, Leland knew that his life would never go back to how it had been before.

Shunsaku somehow sensed the same things. In quiet ways, the man had been a friend to Leland and his friendship helped Leland accept the words he'd spoken. Leland turned and smiled at Shunsaku. "You're right. Sophie's coming by the shop tomorrow to work with me again and I'm going to tell her how I feel."

Shunsaku smiled. "You will find her heart where it is hidden like you carve the melody from the trees."

Leland nodded because he wasn't sure he understood what Shunsaku meant about carving a melody. He did know one thing. He wanted to find Sophie's heart.

Monday morning on the sixth of May, Sophie knocked softly on the door of his shop and pushed it open. "Good morning, Leland."

He picked up immediately on the cadence of her voice–the weariness in her tone. "Hi, Sophie. Are you feeling okay today?"

She nodded. "I'll be fine. I didn't sleep well last night is all."

"This isn't a rush." Leland motioned to the last footstool. "We can work on this another day."

"No, I'm excited to get it finished up." She set her sewing bag on the work table and bent over the last footstool. "You never told me who this one was for."

"About that..." Leland grinned as she lifted her head and narrowed her eyes. "It's not what you think. I had people who wanted it, but I decided to keep it for myself. I hope you don't mind."

Sophie's face softened and she smiled. "I think that's a great idea."

He held her gaze for a moment before she returned her attention to the material, carefully tucking it around the footstool. Over the next hour, Sophie worked and chatted with Leland about her plans to go camping with Keith's family over the summer. Leland told her about an idea that had been brewing to hire an apprentice and Sophie encouraged him to follow his heart. He showed her how to work the planer on a new piece of walnut and explained the importance of using high quality tools like his favorite three-quarter inch chisel.

"There is so much about carpentry that I didn't know," Sophie said. "Leland, you really are talented. No wonder people are willing to wait months for their order."

"Thank you. I'm happy that I can do something I enjoy. You have a gift yourself. The way you think about the person receiving your work and put extra care into each stitch."

Sophie looked thoughtful. "I do enjoy it. I love being with my children the most, but if I have to work, I can't think of anything else I'd rather do."

"I can't thank you enough for seeing this project through." Leland bent to examine the last footstool. "I'm really going to enjoy this."

"Well, if you don't, you only have yourself to blame—hiring a seamstress to upholster furniture."

"I take full responsibility." Leland laughed and Sophie joined him. When he stood he was closer to her than he'd intended, but he didn't step back. "I have half a mind to make up some more orders so I can see more of you."

Sophie tapped her cheek. "I think my prices just went up."

Leland chuckled and put his arm around her, pulling her next to him. "I can adjust my prices to cover it."

She shook her head. "Don't tempt me."

Leland turned until he was standing in front of her. The shop was quiet and the stillness between them pulled at his heart. The remnants of their laughter hung in the air and Sophie's eyes were bright with a happiness that hadn't been there when she'd arrived that morning. Leland touched her chin, tipping it up slightly as he brought his mouth toward hers, brushing her lips with a kiss that awakened his senses. She put her hands on his chest, clutching the fabric of his shirt as he kissed her again. Her mouth against his shot fire through his veins and he held her close, kissing her deeper. He paused, breathless. "Sophie, I—"

"I told you not to tempt me," she said at the same time. She rose up on her tiptoes and kissed his cheek.

Leland smiled and held her close, his mouth a breath away from hers. "Well there must be something I could do to keep you around." He kissed her gently. "I know, I have some trousers that need mending. Maybe you could give me lessons?"

Instead of laughing and returning his kiss, Sophie pulled away from him. "I don't know what I was thinking. I can't do this."

"Sophie, please. What did I say? I'm sorry I was making light of things." He could see that she was on the verge of running. Like a skittish deer, she'd bolt if he made the wrong move. "Please, don't run away."

Sophie's perfect lips turned upwards in a demure smile that didn't reach her eyes. "I'm not running. I just can't do this right now."

"Because of David?"

Sophie sucked in a breath. "No–I mean, I don't know. This year has been so different than what I imagined it would be." Sophie picked up her sewing bag. "I thought I'd survived the hardest things, but life is so cruel and unexpected."

"I saw him at church, and I nearly burned holes in the back of his head I was so angry at him for walking in like he didn't have a care in the world. He isn't worth your time." Leland wanted to walk toward her, take her in his arms, and comfort her, but he knew she wouldn't allow it. "I know it hasn't been very long since things went south with David, but will you look at me?"

Sophie raised her head and those green eyes set his heart to pounding.

"I've been here all along. I haven't changed. My feelings haven't changed. I know I messed up by not acting sooner. If only I would have asked you to be mine before David could. But I also know you had to make up your own mind."

"That's true, but David is the one who ended things between us. I didn't really have a chance to make up my mind."

"Keith says that you haven't even tried to contact David. That says to me that you don't love him." Leland's heart beat in his throat as he searched for the words that would keep Sophie from running. "You know what you want, what your heart wants, don't you?"

"That's just it." Sophie put a hand to her forehead. "I feel my heart beating, and that's a miracle because it's been blown to pieces. There's nothing left to give, to trust, to love..."

"You can't mean that," Leland tried not to sound desperate. "You're scared. I understand that. You scare me to death but it doesn't stop me from wanting to be with you."

Sophie dropped her hand, shaking her head. "I'm sorry. I appreciate the work you gave me, but the Tanakas found me another client so I'll be busy for the next few weeks. I have to go."

"Sophie, please don't go." Leland started after her, but she quickened her step and practically ran out of the shop to her car.

The wind slammed the door shut behind her, stealing Leland's breath; cooling his heart and making him wonder why he thought he ever had a chance with Sophie Wright.

Chapter 45 – Sandwiches and Secrets

Sophie rolled down her window as she drove and let the wind take every thought, every feeling about Leland like a kite string pulling upwards away from her heart. If she could let go of those feelings, the tears threatening to spill over might recede. She still tasted his kiss on her lips, felt the sandpaper scruff of his cheek against hers. For a moment, she'd forgotten all the hurt that David had caused, the humiliation of seeing him and hearing the whispers in church on Sunday. Sophie sucked in a lungful of air and pushed it back out through her nose, trying to steady her nerves before she stopped by Debbie's to pick up Maggie. Debbie would want to know what the trouble behind her eyes meant. Sophie clenched the steering wheel tight, angry at herself for letting her guard down and letting Leland kiss her. It was unfair, the way he'd melted the ground right beneath her feet with his kiss. The tender way he held her made her wish that she was still standing in that dusty shop in his arms.

The house came into view and Sophie noticed that the flowerbeds needed tending. Shoots of various weeds were coming up between the remains of the tulips. She'd promised Maggie that they could plant marigolds this year. Maybe they could get started this afternoon. It was important to stay busy and keep her mind off Leland. She drove past her home toward Debbie's, letting the wind cool her cheeks and wishing it could whisk away the hurt from her heart.

Tuesday morning, Debbie stopped by unannounced at lunch with roast beef sandwiches. "Sorry to barge in, but I needed a reason to finish off the roast from Sunday, and lucky you—here's your lunch." She nodded toward Maggie. "I brought enough for you and some for Garth when he gets home."

"Thanks, Aunt Debbie," Maggie said. "Garth likes his with extra mustard." She wrinkled her nose.

"He gets that from me I suppose," Sophie said.

They arranged the lunch at the kitchen table and chatted for a few minutes, but Sophie sensed that Debbie had come by for more reasons than roast beef.

Once they'd finished their sandwiches and Maggie was busy coloring, Debbie leaned forward and lowered her voice. "I'm really here to check up on you. Keith told me that you finished up the projects with Leland and told him you didn't want to work with him anymore."

Sophie put a hand to her forehead and groaned. "I think I'm going to move to Alaska."

"Why? You're already frozen here."

Sophie gasped and Debbie laughed. "Sorry, it was just too perfect to pass up. I thought you and Leland were getting along great. Are you going to tell me what's really bothering you?"

"I don't really want to get into it," Sophie said. "I'm a mess."

"Listen, I won't play matchmaker, but we need to talk about this. Something must have happened. This isn't just from seeing David at church on Sunday."

Sophie stood and cleared the dishes from the table. "That's because we've already talked about how horrible that was—you know all the details."

Debbie grabbed a rag and wiped off the table. "I don't think anyone ever knows all the details with Sophie Wright."

"What's that supposed to mean?" Sophie put a hand on her hip.

"Exactly what it sounds like," Debbie replied. "Do you really think I can't tell when you have your mask in place? Sophie, you've always hidden your feelings and I'm worried because I'm just realizing now that maybe the person you've been hiding them from the most is yourself."

Debbie's words struck a chord and the notes reverberated in Sophie's mind. She hadn't been aware that her family knew she kept her feelings hidden. But Debbie had just confessed that all this time they had known what a private person she was and given her space to deal with her emotions. "That's silly. I'm not hiding from myself. How is that even possible?"

"When you never allow yourself to feel, I think your heart forgets how to truly love. You can't expect to have a relationship with a corner of your heart."

Sophie leaned against the sink, watching the water swirl down the drain. "I don't know what to do. I love Garth and Maggie and all of you with my whole heart—at least it feels like it."

Debbie nodded. "I agree, but that's a different kind of love. The love I'm talking about is risky, terrifying, and all-consuming. It's a love you can't hide from."

Sophie didn't know how to respond because what Debbie said sounded like the truth, and it scared her. She filled a glass with water and took her time drinking it as she thought about Leland's kiss and how she had run from his love.

Debbie walked out of the kitchen and straightened a few books on the shelf next to the couch. "I haven't seen this piece before." Debbie leaned toward Leland's carving. "It's beautiful. Where did you get it?"

Sophie's heart jumped to life and she hurried over to the end table that held the carving. "Leland carved it for me."

Debbie raised her eyebrows. "He did?"

Sophie nodded. "I didn't know that he had a talent for carving, but it makes sense."

"Look at the flowers on the edge of her skirt." Debbie traced the fine lines of wood. "What does it represent?"

"Me." Sophie peered at the woman, again half-expecting her to turn and give Sophie the answers she needed to keep moving forward. The woman in the carving wasn't really moving forward or backward—she was caught in a moment, struggling to make the decision to face the future or dwell on the past. Or it could be something completely different. It seemed that every time Sophie studied the carving, it held a new message for her.

"He must really love you," Debbie said. "Leland stopped carving years ago. He said it wasn't practical. I suppose it wasn't during the war, but he has a rare gift."

"I agree." Sophie tugged at her apron. "He gave that carving to me weeks ago, while I was still seeing David."

Debbie straightened. "So you've known for that long that Leland loves you? Why have you kept the poor man waiting so long?"

"Waiting for what?"

"For him to hear how much you love him."

Sophie rolled her eyes. "You said you wouldn't be a matchmaker—that you'd let me have my peace."

"Well, that was before you conveniently introduced me to this manifestation of Leland's love for you." Debbie touched Sophie's arm. "I can give you all the peace you want but it won't make a difference if you're not at peace with yourself and the love you won't let yourself feel for a good man."

Sophie's throat tightened. Debbie was skirting close to the borders of Sophie's heart and she didn't like how near she was to seeing the truth. "Can we not talk about this right now?"

Debbie's face softened and she nodded. "Sure. I love you. Keith loves you. We all love you and want you to be happy. It just kills me to see two people who are so right for each other…" she shrugged. "When you're ready to talk, I'll be here." She hugged Sophie, and even though there was so much more to be said, Sophie was grateful that it could wait until another day.

Chapter 46 – A Heart to Beat Again

The sun shone brightly on Thursday, warming the earth so that Sophie was eager to get outside and plant the garden. The first week of May was still too early because of the frosts that often occurred, but soon enough they'd be out of the danger zone. Garth would be home from school in a couple hours, maybe they could start planning out the garden together. Maggie would definitely want to plant only flowers, and Garth would want cantaloupes and watermelons. Sophie smiled up at the sun and breathed in deeply. She'd thought a lot about what Debbie had said to her the day before. There was much work to be done in the matter of her heart and even though Sophie didn't want to admit it, she worried that maybe Debbie was right. She'd become so accomplished at keeping all of her emotions locked up that she might have forgotten what it felt like to live.

Maggie was out back playing with her doll, so Sophie took a few minutes to tidy up. A fine layer of dust had collected everywhere and even though it would quickly return, Sophie grabbed a cloth and began dusting the furniture. When she reached Leland's carving, she hesitated before carefully picking it up and setting it on the kitchen counter. She shook out the doily and shined the end table where the carving sat, all the while trying not to think about Leland and the power he had over her heart. How might her life be different if she were willing to let her emotions run free?

A heavy knock on the door surprised her and Sophie turned, dropping the dust cloth next to the carving. She pulled open the front door and the wind stole the breath from her lungs. She stepped back, struggling to pull in the oxygen that wouldn't help her wildly beating heart. "David?"

It was really him. His dark hair combed back carefully, his piercing blue eyes searching out hers. "Sophie, I need to talk to you. Please let me in."

He took a step inside before she could answer, and Sophie moved to the side as he let himself in and closed the front door.

"I know you're angry, and you have a right to be, but I need to explain something to you."

"You didn't even call." Sophie stepped back from him, folding her arms. "You let your mother give me the news over the phone! You might as well have taken an ad out in the paper."

"I was wrong!" He fisted his hands and put them on his forehead with a guttural moan. "I was weak. My mother gave me an ultimatum—the family business or you."

Sophie gasped. "I knew your mother didn't like me, but that is cruel."

"I know, and faced with the choice, I didn't know what to do." David's face was a picture of misery. "Without my job running the mine, who am I? I wouldn't be able to support a family. It wasn't a war I wanted to fight." He took a shuddering breath. "I gave in to my mother, when I should have stood my ground."

"I'm sorry how things ended, but sorry won't change how you mistreated me." Sophie clasped her hands tightly together so that David wouldn't see how bad they were shaking.

"But it can. When I saw you at church on Sunday, everything changed. I realized how wrong I had been and that I needed to do something about it." David put his hands on her arms. "I turned the tables on Mother. I told her that if she ever tried to interfere in my life, I would leave and not come back." He stood up straighter. "Two can play at her game. It just took me a while to realize that I had a piece to play."

Sophie felt his hands on her arms, and remembered how David had held her and kissed her. She shook off the memories of how he'd tricked her heart into thinking she was in love. "I don't see how that changes anything."

"But it does. I'm a free man, and I can pursue what I think is best—you. Sophie, can you ever forgive me?"

Sophie looked down, collecting her thoughts before lifting her gaze to meet David's clear blue eyes. "I forgive you, David. But it's been over a month. You could have at least written me a note explaining what happened instead of leaving me here wondering what went wrong and how I could be so foolish to fall for you."

David touched her cheek. "You weren't foolish. I was the foolish one. Sophie, I love you. I've never been in love before. I made so many mistakes and I can't undo them, but I can change the future. You said you had feelings for me. We could be happy."

Words raced through Sophie's mind alongside memories of the good times she'd shared with David, but nothing eased the broken beat of her heart. The pain she'd suffered alone and the public humiliation as the entire town of Aspen Falls learned of the end to their relationship was too great. "You say you love me, but you didn't even have the decency to speak to me. You might be feeling brave right now, but what happens when your mother changes her mind again? I'm not willing to risk it."

"Love is always a risk." David leaned closer to her as if he would kiss her, but Sophie stepped back.

"David, I think you're confused about love, because a man who loves a woman doesn't do the things you did to me."

"So you won't forgive me?"

"Forgiving you doesn't mean I have to let you hurt me again," Sophie said. "I don't know what you're looking for, but it isn't me."

David furrowed his brow as if trying to understand the words she'd spoken.

"Thank you for telling me," Sophie spoke softly. "That took courage and I'm glad to know what really happened, but I'm sorry, David. I don't love you."

David dropped his hands to his sides, clenching his fists. "You're broken, just like him," he spat. "There's nothing anyone can do to fix that."

The abrupt change in mood startled Sophie. It took her a second to understand what he meant. David was aware of Leland's attentions toward her. Sophie felt her spine stiffen. "Don't hurt me because you're hurting."

Her words caught him off guard and he stumbled back. "I could've made you happy. I would've taken good care of you and your children. We could've had a good life together. Are you sure you want to throw all that away?"

"I can't risk making the same mistake twice," Sophie replied. "I hope that you'll find the courage to follow your heart. I have forgiven you. Please don't do anything else because I'm not sure I have the strength to forgive you again."

David's eyes filled with moisture. "Please. I love you, Sophie."

"Goodbye, David." Sophie put her hand on the door, waiting for him to retreat before she closed it firmly.

Her entire body shook, nerves buzzing with anguish. She closed her eyes, but David's agonized plea filled her mind so she opened her eyes again searching for something to take her mind off the pain. Leland's carving was on the kitchen counter where she'd left it. The dust cloth next to it reminded her of how mundane her day had been up until then. Sophie walked over and picked up the carving, feeling the life force of the wood that had long ago been separated from the earth. She moved slowly toward the carving, tracing her finger around the smooth edge of the heart and struggling to breathe normally. She glanced out the window and saw Maggie sitting in the shade with her doll, Charlotte. The little girl was singing and the lilting notes traveled through the open window above the kitchen table. Sophie stepped closer, hearing a familiar melody interspersed with Maggie's childlike verse. Her heart felt like a stone in her chest, but as she listened, Sophie recognized the simple tune from Emika's music box—Leland's music box—and the stone in her chest shifted.

If only Sophie could tell her heart to beat again—if she could let Leland in, maybe things would feel right. The carving sat on the table calling out to her and Sophie saw something that she had never noticed before. A tiny trail of music notes were hidden in between the flowers on the skirt of the woman's dress. They couldn't have been there before—she'd spent hours gazing at the carving, running her fingertips along the details and thinking of Leland. His strong hands had carved the beautiful image out of a block of wood because he could see something in her that no one else could.

A breath of wind pushed through the kitchen window and caressed Sophie's neck whispering the remnants of a melody in her ear. Her strength and composure gripped the edge of the wind and drained out of Sophie's body. In that instant, she saw Leland in her mind's eye, his careful and gentle ways, his heart steadily beating through all the horrors he'd faced. Leland had lived a nightmare and awoken with a smile and determination to change his life. But she had not—she had kept herself in the realm of dreams, suffering through a nightmare, never allowing herself to wake up and face the pain of what had happened.

The shadows of the past crowded in on her happiness, smothering the joy she'd felt, making her question everything that ever was or could be. Sophie ran down the hall, her chest convulsing with sobs that could no longer be held back. Sliding to the floor, she covered her face with her hands, as her chest seemed to break wide open. Every breath was etched in pain as years of emotions collided, exploding the dam that she'd so carefully constructed with bricks of fear and regret. Sophie rocked back and forth slowly, trying to breathe past the hurt. Her lungs felt like they were filled with shards of glass, the sharp edges causing agony with every inhale, killing her from the inside out with every exhale.

It had been years, but once the dam burst, a flood of tears ensued. They trickled down her cheeks, and plopped onto the blanket. The tears escaped between her fingers, running down her forearms, and glistening along her jawline. Sobs shook her body and she gave into every feeling she'd fought for so long. Memories of Cal oozed out like black tar, burning her skin, but with every tear she cried, more came. She cried for Cal, for the promise of what should have been and the broken life she'd endured with him.

And then she cried for David, with his strength, wealth, and superficial love for her. The signs in their relationship that she'd ignored were so clear now—David didn't like her children and he would never be the kind of father that Leland Halverson would have been. Sophie's heart lurched and she cried harder as she thought of Leland—his offer of love, his kindness, his forgiveness—it all washed over her. The tears fell and Sophie's heart shifted in her chest, pulling fragments together to heal the jagged crevice so her heart could beat once more.

Chapter 47 – Sophie's Secret

Leland sang along with the chorus of "Oh! What it Seemed to Be" on his way over to Sophie's. When Marjorie Hughes sang about a wedding in June, Leland's heart skipped a beat. The kiss that he'd shared with Sophie had infused him with a desire to make her his bride. Ever since she'd left him Monday, he'd tried to come up with a reason to see her. Bringing Hope along for the kids to see wasn't a good enough reason anymore. The pup was getting big enough that she could cause some trouble in Sophie's front room. This morning when he'd landed on some good news for the seamstress-turned-upholsterer, he'd jumped into his pickup and headed across town.

A few people had seen Clyde's footstools and contacted Leland about new orders that he'd had to refuse, but that had turned into a conversation about Sophie and her many talents. Leland knew that her first love was sewing and alterations, so he was thrilled when two of his clients expressed interest in working with Sophie. He wanted to be the first to tell her about Mrs. Phillips who needed new kitchen curtains, and Billy's wife LaRue who wanted to special order a maternity dress.

Leland knocked on Sophie's door and waited for a couple minutes with no answer. With a frown, he turned to walk back down the steps but he paused when he heard the door open behind him.

"Hi, Leland," Maggie said.

"Hello to you. Is your mommy home?"

Maggie nodded, her expression somber. "Mommy's sad."

Leland hurried up the steps and walked inside behind Maggie, but Sophie wasn't in the kitchen or the front room. "Where is she?"

"She's hiding 'cause she's sad. Mr. David made her sad again."

Leland's chest pulsed with fear. "Did David come to the house today?"

Maggie nodded, her brown eyes filled with worry.

Had something happened to Sophie? Leland looked down the hall toward the closed bedroom door that led to Sophie's room. "Do you think she'll mind if I check on her?" he whispered to Maggie.

Maggie looked at her dolly and shrugged. "She said she was tired, but I heard her crying. Mommy's sad."

Sophie was crying? Leland had seen women cry many times in his life and according to Keith, it was one of those things you could just depend on with women, but Leland knew Sophie, and she didn't cry. Ever. There had been plenty of opportunities in the short time that he'd known her for tears to be shed, but strangely enough, Sophie had always held the tears back. The only time she'd allowed a few to escape was when he'd told her about Jessie's death.

Leland had noticed, perhaps when others hadn't. If Sophie was crying now, then the great dam that she must have built to hide her emotions would have exploded. He wanted to go to her and comfort her, but she also needed to feel the emotions she'd trapped inside. Leland knew this from his own experience—from the times when he'd drowned his emotions in a bottle.

He checked the clock. It was almost three-thirty. Any minute now, Garth would probably come bounding through the door. Leland patted Maggie's head. "Sing a song to your dolly and I'll be right back." With tentative steps, he walked down the hallway and stood outside Sophie's door. He knocked softly. "Sophie, it's Leland. I just need to know that you're okay."

He heard a muffled sob and movement in the room, and then a weight against the door. "Leland?"

"Sophie, are you hurt?" Leland's heart pounded with fear.

"No," came the muffled response. "I'm fine."

Leland chewed on his bottom lip, trying to decide what he should do. He turned and startled when he saw Maggie right behind him. "I have an idea. Can you get your shoes on? I'm going to take you and Garth over to play at Keith and Debbie's, does that sound okay?"

Maggie nodded, and scampered toward the front door. Leland turned back to Sophie's bedroom door. "I'm taking the kids over to Debbie's and then I'm coming right back here, okay?"

"Okay." Something about the resigned tone in her voice scared Leland. He hurried outside to intercept Garth before he entered the house. Maggie held tight to one hand as they waved down Garth on the sidewalk. The little boy whooped and took off for Debbie's when he heard the plan. Leland chuckled at Garth's energy and hurried Maggie along so they could catch up.

When Debbie opened the front door which Garth dashed through, Leland helped Maggie up the steps. "Sophie needs a little help with the kids while she finishes up a project for me. Will that be all right?"

Debbie arched an eyebrow. "A project huh?"

Leland shook his head. "Just trust me. This is important."

"Okay, then." Debbie wagged a finger at him. "I'll expect to hear the details and secondhand through Keith doesn't count."

"You got it." Leland hurried off before Debbie could ask any more questions.

If it wouldn't have drawn so much attention, Leland would've sprinted back to Sophie's house. Instead, he forced himself to walk as quickly as he could, pulling the worry from his face and holding it near his heart.

The house was eerily quiet when Leland returned. He'd hoped that maybe Sophie would have come out of her bedroom, but when he glanced down the hall, the door was still shut. Rolling his shoulders back, Leland approached her door and tapped lightly. "I'm back. The kids were happy to go play at Debbie's house."

He didn't hear a reply. Leland tried the door and the handle turned easily. He hesitated before opening the door. "Sophie, I'm coming in." He eased open the door and his eyes adjusted to the dim lighting. Sophie lay on her side on the bed, facing the wall. She didn't move as he approached. "Sophie, you're scaring me." He sat next to her on the bed and touched her arm. She shuddered under his touch and began crying anew.

"Maggie said that David came by. Can you talk to me about it?" Leland whispered, stroking Sophie's arm that was wrapped across her waist.

"He apologized, said his mother gave him an ultimatum: Me or the mine," Sophie's voice cracked. "He came back to tell me he'd convinced his mother to let him choose me and keep his job, but I told him I didn't want him."

"Thank goodness." Leland breathed out a sigh of relief. "I'm sorry you had to see him again. But what happened? You're crying, and you never cry."

Sophie turned her head slightly. "I do now. I shouldn't have kept it in so long."

"From when Cal died?"

She nodded her head and Leland watched as another tear trickled down the side of her nose. "A part of me died then, but I never knew it until now."

Leland leaned closer to her, brushing the hair from her face with his fingertips. "The past is there, but you aren't. You don't live there anymore in those memories. You're right here. Look at me," Leland said. "I know what I'm saying is true. Can you feel it?"

Sophie shook her head. She sat up slowly, another sob shudde-ring through her slight frame. "You don't understand."

"Maybe I do," Leland said. "My daughter died and I thought that I died with her, but I'm here now."

"I hated him!" Sophie screamed. "I'm so glad he's dead. Do you hear me? I'm happy that Calvin is dead! He was a monster and I hate him! I'm not sorry he's gone. I don't want to talk about him. I don't want to think about him, to think about what he did to me."

Leland grabbed Sophie and pulled her to him as the rage and tears poured out of her. He didn't say anything, didn't even shush her, he just held her as she cried. Sophie fought him, crying out, but then she fell back against him, crying harder. Leland shifted on the bed, cradling her in his arms and waited for the wave of her emotions to pass. He stroked her hair, and felt her tears soaking through his shirt. He remembered his own breaking point, when every emotion had broken through and he'd faced his fear—to live again without Jessie or Rhonda. Sophie's words hung in the air like dark stars. He'd sensed that something was amiss in her marriage, but he didn't understand the extent of what Sophie had suffered. He held her closer.

"Do your parents know? Does Keith know?"

Sophie shook her head. "I think Debbie suspects, but we lived in Kentucky. I didn't see my parents for a year or more at a time." The frayed edge of her sweater was soft against her skin as Sophie pulled it back to reveal a jagged scar on her left arm. "I almost bled to death from this one."

Leland sucked in a breath. "Sophie, I'm so sorry."

"Cal was a mean drunk with a huge ego. All he cared about was himself. When he enlisted, I began making plans to leave him and then I found out I was pregnant with Maggie. I almost gave up, but I couldn't give up on my baby. She was born and Cal still didn't come home. He was too busy chasing skirts in Hawaii. And then the bombing happened. For days, I waited, praying for all that I was worth that Cal would be found dead at Pearl Harbor. Everyone around me was praying that he would be spared, that they would find him unharmed. It was all I could do not to go crazy when my pastor came and prayed for my good husband to be returned to me."

Leland held her as she spoke, her voice cracking and shaking. "I hated him and now I'm being punished for it."

"That isn't true and don't you dare believe it for one more second." Leland lifted Sophie to face him. "I understand now. You don't have to push me away because I won't push you anymore. It's not fair of me to ask you to trust me. One marriage to an alcoholic is enough for any woman."

Sophie wiped her face with her sleeve. "But you're not—you don't drink anymore."

"You're right, but what if I slip? Every time I think I'm doing fine, my throat burns with that old thirst and I have to start the fight all over again."

"But you don't give in, do you?"

Leland shook his head. "No, but it makes me angry because you don't understand how badly I want to."

"Were you mean to your wife?"

Leland's eyes widened. "I would never hurt a woman. I never physically hurt Rhonda, but I hurt her in other ways."

"Weren't you just telling me something about the past? That you don't live in those memories?" Sophie asked. "Then why do you want me to hold you back in your past? If you've changed, I believe you."

Leland's face softened. "Because it's tearing my heart out right now, seeing you this way. I don't want to hurt you."

Sophie took in another halting breath and then wrapped her arms around him. She had exposed herself completely to him and he still loved her. Leland swallowed, struggling to figure out a way to speak the words from his heart.

"I guess we both kept secrets," Sophie murmured.

"Sophie, I don't want to let you go, but I will if that's what you want. I could never stand in the way of your happiness."

Sophie sat up and there was fear in her eyes. "What do you mean?"

"I mean, if you change your mind about David."

She shook her head, eyes narrowing. "I'm not changing my mind. David might have thought he loved me, but he didn't love my children. How can a man say he loves a woman if he doesn't love her children?"

Leland smiled because Sophie had just thrown him a lifeline that he meant to grab onto. It was obvious how much he loved Garth and Maggie. "Are you saying that maybe I have a chance?"

Sophie smiled. "From the very first time you met Garth and Maggie, I could see that you cared about them. I was foolish to ignore the signs when David spent time with my kids."

"Keith has spent a lot of time reminding me of what a coward I've been," Leland said. "And I mean to stop his abuse."

Sophie rested her head on his chest. "Keith still likes to boss me around, too."

"Well, I guess it's something I'll have to figure out because when your best friend is the older brother of the woman you love, you need to keep that friendship strong."

"Keith is always looking out for me," Sophie replied. "Wait, what did you say?"

"I said," Leland swallowed and his heart forged ahead. "I said my best friend is the older brother of the woman I love."

Sophie smiled and her dimple appeared.

Leland leaned in and kissed the dimple on her cheek. "I said I love you."

Turning her head slightly, Sophie pressed her lips to his, kissing him softly. "I love you too."

Chapter 48 – Carve Me a Melody

June 1946

Two weeks later, Sophie heard that David had re-enlisted and returned to Peterson Air Field. She felt genuinely happy for him. It had been painful to go through what they did, but if it had helped David to find the true course of happiness in his life, maybe it was worth it.

She walked lighter now, the great weight of the dam she'd built had been released and she'd made a promise to herself and Leland that she wouldn't be afraid to show her real face. It would take a great deal of practice and patience with herself, but Sophie knew under the care of Leland's love, her heart would heal completely. She would no longer be afraid to feel.

At Leland's insistence, Sophie dropped Garth and Maggie off to play with Hope so that she could sit down with her parents and Keith and Debbie. It wasn't pleasant to explain to them how she felt about Cal and the way he'd treated her during their marriage, but her family had enveloped her with so much love and support. Sophie regretted not telling them earlier, but it only added to her resolve to live her life differently from then on.

She smiled, reliving the joy she felt every time Leland held her, his strong arms around her, protecting her from pain, wrapping her in warmth and comfort. Sophie drove to Leland's house, admiring the wrap-around porch he'd been repairing. It was a beautiful home for a family and Sophie had a feeling that she and Leland wouldn't have to be apart much longer. As soon as she parked the car, the kids jumped out, racing each other to the porch where they hugged Leland and patted Hope on the head. Sophie stepped from her car and laughter bubbled up inside when her eyes met Leland's and he winked.

The trees were in full bloom, soaking up the last of the spring rains, turning a vibrant green that reminded Leland of Sophie's eyes. He stopped just inside the gates of the cemetery, clutching Sophie's hand. With one more step he would go farther than he had in the past four years. Sophie waited next to him, allowing him to take the first step. He breathed in deeply and pulled his foot across the threshold of the cemetery. Sophie matched his step and propelled him forward.

Leland carried a jug of purple irises that Sophie had helped him cut from her garden. He kept glancing at Sophie out of the corner of his eye as they moved closer to Jessie's grave. Garth and Maggie trailed behind them, in a reverence that must have been impressed upon them by their beautiful mother. "This means a lot to me," Leland whispered.

Sophie squeezed his hand. "You mean a lot to me, too."

When he faced forward again they had reached the headstone. Leland blinked rapidly as he leaned over and traced the letters of Jessie's name carved in stone. He knelt down and carefully arranged the flowers. "I love you, Jessie. I know you're not here, that you're in a better place, but I want you to know that I love you. I'm working hard to be the father you loved." He kissed his fingers and brushed them across the stone. Tears rolled down his cheek, and Leland let them come. Sophie knelt next to him and Leland put his arm around her shoulder. When he looked at her, he noticed that she was crying as well, but smiling at the same time.

"Garth and Maggie, this is where my daughter Jessie is buried. She would have been about your age, Garth." Leland put his hand on the headstone and stood, pulling Sophie up next to him. "And I think she would have loved you as much as I do."

Garth nodded and Maggie tiptoed across the grass to hug Leland's leg. "I love you, too."

"I'm sorry that I'll never get to know Jessie," Sophie said, "but I'm grateful to know her father."

Leland hugged her and then he crouched next to the headstone. "I'll try not to make it so long between visits. Thanks for being patient with me." Then he stood and took Sophie's hand. They walked out of the cemetery with Garth and Maggie racing each other to the car. The fears that Leland had carried for so long vanished, and he wondered why he'd ever been afraid to visit Jessie. He had been forgiven, and as he looked at Sophie with the soft smile on her face, he knew that she had accepted forgiveness as well as given it to Cal. They were both in a better place, and even though they walked the streets of Aspen Falls, it seemed like a different place.

They drove the few blocks back to his home and Leland patted the swing he'd fixed on the front porch. Sophie sat down and Leland hesitated for one moment before he knelt in front of her. "Sophie, I know this might seem sudden but I've wanted to ask you this question for too long. Will you marry me?"

Sophie grinned, her eyes shining like brilliant gems. "I will on one condition."

"Anything for you? Name your demand."

Sophie took his hand and pulled him up beside her. "Carve me a melody, Leland. One that I can see every day and hear in my heart. One that will never let me forget how much I love you."

Epilogue – One year later

June 1947

Leland placed his hand on Sophie's rounded belly and whispered, "We're all waiting for you." He leaned forward and kissed Sophie gently. "I love you."

"And I love you." She put her arms around his neck, loving the feeling of their baby kicking inside.

Leland kissed her cheek. "Do you think that Debbie could be right?"

Sophie shook her head. "Don't you be taking stock of her predictions. I'm not carrying twins. This is just one big baby."

"Well, if you are or you aren't, I'm the happiest man in the world either way."

"Thank you, Leland."

"For what?"

"For sharing your heart with me."

"What heart? You took it the first time I laid eyes on you," Leland said. "Remember Maggie's bed? I was a goner."

"Sure took you long enough to do something about it."

"Measure twice, cut once." Leland rubbed her belly. "Being careful is the only way I could take a step in your direction. I was terrified of making another mistake."

Sophie put her hand on his cheek and looked him in the eye. "We'll both make mistakes Honey, and we'll work through them together. We're not perfect, but I think we can have a perfect love."

Leland pulled Sophie closer to him. He hummed softly and as Sophie rested her head against his chest, she recognized the tune he was humming. "Isn't that the song from Emika's music box?"

Leland nodded and continued humming, and then he paused. "It's our song too."

"Oh? How so?"

"It brought you back to me and gave me the chance to never let you go."

Sophie smiled and when he started humming again, she joined in with him, placing her hand on top of his. His fingers rested on her belly, caressing the new life they had made together. The wind brushed her skin, cooling Leland's kiss and picking up fragments of the melody. Sophie looked heavenward, smiling as she listened to the song of the wind.

The End

Book Club Questions For Carve Me a Melody

1) The characters in this book lived through the rationing efforts of WWII. How do you think your life would change if everything were rationed? How would you feel if you couldn't buy a pair of shoes that you really needed because you didn't have the ration coupon to do so?

2) Sophie carries a secret about her heart that makes it difficult for her to trust herself and find a new love. How might she have handled her feelings about Cal differently once he was killed?

3) Discuss how you would feel about your Japanese-American friends being sent to a relocation camp? If the government declared that your neighbor was an enemy of the nation, how would that change your relationship?

4) During WWII, it seemed that everyone took part in the war effort. Do you think it was difficult for men who were rejected from service to carry on while their friends were in the war?

5) What role did the music box and its melody play in this story? How did it affect certain characters?

6) If you were Keith, what would you have told Leland or Sophie to save them heartache?

7) How would your conversations with friends be different if you knew that someone (like Mrs. Gillespie) might be listening?

8) Sophie and Leland both had to deal with strong emotions and grief that were buried deep within their hearts. Have you ever bottled up emotions about something? Why do you think the act of letting go of emotions is so important?

9) What is one of your favorite lines or passages from Carve Me a Melody?

Acknowledgements

I have a deep appreciation and gratitude for every man and woman involved in World War II. As I have continued the research I started with *The Soldier's Bride*, my eyes have been opened to the extensive sacrifices that everyone gave during that time of war. There are so many tiny details that I fear will be lost and I hope that this important part of history can live on.

I'm grateful to the many readers who asked for more of Leland's story after reading *The Soldier's Bride*. I thought of you on the days when I didn't think I could get the story right, and I kept on working, creating this story one word at a time so that you could read Leland's happy ending.

I'm thankful to my dear friend Frankie who at the writing of this novel is nearly 99 years old. She answered many questions about the WWII era and told me stories and details that I could never have found through researching online. Her ever-cheerful demeanor has been a great example to me.

Thank you to my friends and neighbors who answered questions in person, via Facebook, email, and helped me get my facts straight. I'm grateful for the many talented people I'm able to work with in my writing. Kelli Ann Morgan created the perfect cover for this story—I love it! Heidi Brockbank and Sabine Berlin with Eschler Editing, once again helped me polish this story and answered all kinds of tough questions during the editing process.

A huge thanks to my wonderfully talented and supportive beta readers: Patrick and Necia Jolley, Tim Jolley, Christina Dymock, Cathy Jeppsen, Nina Johns, and Phyllis Helton. I'm grateful to my review team who reads and supports my novels, encouraging me to continue writing.

Thank you to the Kindle Scout program and to Kindle Press. Because of a publishing contest where *The Soldier's Bride* was awarded a publishing contract, this series came into existence. I'm grateful for all the different avenues of publishing available so that this story could be told.

Being a writer is often called a solitary and lonely occupation, but I couldn't disagree more. I have an incredible husband and family who are my biggest support system. I have dozens of writing buddies who I interact with online, at retreats, and conferences and each time I come away inspired and ready to buckle down and write the next book! My family is incredible, from my patient husband, Steve, to each of my five children, I owe you a million thanks for your support and love.

I'm most grateful to my loving Father in Heaven. He has blessed me with many talents and I'm thankful for the opportunities I have to continue polishing those talents. I write because the melody in my heart insists on singing and I know it comes from Him.

Sneak Peek of The Kiss Thief: An Echo Ridge Romance

Chapter One

The maple leaves skittered across the sidewalk and crunched under Britta Klein's black low-heeled shoes as she walked toward the Echo Ridge Library. She paused for a moment to watch a dark red leaf twirl in the slight wind coming from Parley's Canyon. She narrowed her eyes—that leaf was carefree, no expectations, nothing to do but dance with the wind. She huffed. If only her life could be that simple.

It was never wise to give in to dramatics, but Britta had just gotten off the phone after talking to hepr mother for forty-five minutes and the message was loud and clear: *Find a German man and marry him so I can have some enkelkinder.* Her mother wanted grandchildren so she could spoil them with strudels and kuchen.

Britta put her hand on the cool metal handle of the door to the library, grounding herself before she headed inside to greet the staff of her library. She reminded herself, again, how good it felt to be in charge of the Echo Ridge Library. At the young age of thirty-one, Britta had achieved her dream of becoming head librarian, but the dream carried more stress than she'd ever imagined.

Tomorrow was the kickoff to the huge library fundraiser that Britta had been working on for the past three months. The children's section was in desperate need of capital, and she worried if this venue was not a success, they'd lose patrons. The library board meeting started in fifteen minutes and Britta hoped that all of the key players for the Harvest Hurrah would show up.

The familiar, dry smell of books greeted Britta when she stepped inside. She never tired of that smell—the tart aroma of new books, freshly marked for distribution in Echo Ridge, mixed with the musty scent of books over a hundred years old that patrons could still check out. The library was once a large stone church house built in the mid-1800s. When Britta first moved to Echo Ridge for her entry-level job at the library, she'd fallen in love with the romantic building. A single staircase curved up to a loft that overlooked the open building with its stacks of books. The old choir room adjacent to the loft was now an office and an open room with a couch and table. That's where the board meeting would be held, but when they didn't have meetings, people could sit on the comfortable couch and read with thousands of volumes below them, seemingly waiting for their turn to be picked next.

The rickety lift that lowered into the basement had always captured her imagination. Whispering of stolen kisses, shadowed mysteries, and a hideaway to read dime-store novels. Or maybe Britta infused her daydreams onto the ancient elevator. But either way, the lift needed an update so they could move the children's section to the basement. That was of utmost importance according to Marian Montgomery, the assistant librarian and grandmother, protector, and overlord of all books. The woman was obsessed with order and decimal systems, but in a different way than Britta.

"Shh," Marian shushed a child who jumped up and down with a picture book in front of his frazzled mother.

"Good morning." Britta forced a smile, hoping to soften the tension humming around Marian. Her flat brown hair interlaced with gray was punctuated by the dark glasses hiding the wrinkles around her eyes. Her shoulders turned slightly inward, probably from carrying stacks of bestsellers around the library for the past seventeen years.

"Noisy ones today. No one can seem to keep their children quiet," Marian grumbled.

"By the end of the month, we'll be able to order the white noise transmitters to cover some of the sound," Britta replied. The state-of-the-art speakers would sit atop each stack of books and transmit a frequency to eliminate some of the noise in the library. The high ceilings of the old church were beautiful with stained-glass windows set in the arches and over the front door, but that feature didn't transfer well when the church became the new library. The extra space contributed to the noise problem. The echoes of children's laughter and whispers carried upwards and echoed right back down. Britta loved the sound, but it drove Marian crazy.

"Well, I'm worried we won't have enough funds for everything we need to do with this old building, so I've come up with an idea to help with the book drive," Marian replied.

Britta brought her view back to ground level. "Oh? What do you have in mind?"

"Oh, no." Marian wagged her finger. "You'll have to wait just like everyone else for the unveiling." She hugged her clipboard closer to her chest.

Hopefully her plans wouldn't involve boxing up patrons under the age of ten and shipping them to Timbuktu.

"I'm heading upstairs to prep for the meeting. I'll talk to you later." Britta waved at Marian and meandered through the stacks to the back of the library.

Britta let her hand trail along the dark walnut railing as she climbed the staircase. The tops of the stacks looked a bit dusty. She made a mental note to have Trish clean them before the weekend. Britta's stomach clenched with nerves when she thought of the prestigious Armand D. Beaumont flying in from France to do a special author reading for Echo Ridge. He had written over fifteen books and was a New York Times bestselling author with quite a following of readers eager to devour his next novel.

When Shennedy Layton had come to her with the idea of bringing in a famous author to kick off the library fundraiser, Britta had immediately thought of Armand because he was related—sort of. Her uncle's sister-in-law had pulled the family strings to get Armand to come to the States.

Britta paused at the oak door which opened into the offices off the old choir loft and turned back to view her beloved library. The framed portrait of the wealthy Vannakin family hung over the circulation desk, reminding everyone of the incredible generosity that had made the Echo Ridge Library possible.

She turned and entered the meeting room, letting the door shut behind her. Britta had only a few moments to prepare before she heard the door creak open.

A blond-haired beauty in her mid-forties popped inside. "I can't believe he's really coming. Britta, it's happening for Echo Ridge!" Shennedy always arrived early and her enthusiasm was catching as she flitted about the room.

"I just hope that Armand will be enough to get this fundraiser into motion. We have a lot of work to do." Britta found herself smiling despite her worries. With Shennedy there to help her, the Harvest Hurrah would surely be a success. She had done wonders with the Big Barn Boutique, partnering with Kenworth's to create a unique offering of antiques and handmade items. The young woman had plenty of fire and grit, and Britta reminded herself that she could relax and allow her and other board members to relieve some of the stress from her shoulders.

Britta nodded at Kirke Staples, who entered the room inconspicuously and sat down. He was a playwright, but didn't like to talk about it much—at least the one time Britta had tried to get him to come out of his shell. He kept his head down and scrawled out notes on a pad of paper. Hopefully he would contribute to the meeting today.

The owner of Fay's Café, Fay Griffith, came in at the same time as a husband and wife team. They sat near the front, eager to help their beloved library. When the lovely white-haired Mrs. Tumnus arrived, Britta felt reassured once again that the fundraising events were in good hands. The older woman was tiny, maybe only five-foot-three, but she carried a presence that inspired others to do their best.

At five past ten there were seven board members present, and Chayton Liechty slipped in right before Britta called the meeting to order. As a high school teacher and lacrosse coach at Echo Ridge High, his insight had proved valuable to integrate students' needs into the library.

"Thank you all for coming today. We have several things to go over, so I printed these agendas." Britta passed the papers around the table. "First, the book drive kicks off tomorrow. Our goal is to bring in five thousand books. Many of those books will be sold to our patrons through our revolving bookstore so that we can purchase new releases."

"Do you have the manpower to sort through five thousand books?" Fay asked.

"We have all year to get through them," Britta answered. "We store the extra boxes in the basement and put new ones out each month. I've made a request from the city for another part-time librarian who might help with that, but they're waiting to see how the fundraiser goes because the lift project is not optional."

Kirke nodded. "That thing is way past due for an update."

"We also have the white noise speakers, moving the children's section downstairs, purchasing new stacks to fill the space that creates ..." Britta held up her fingers as she ticked off each item. "... a new computer table, and furniture for the children's section."

"Wow, this will be like a whole new library once you're finished," Shennedy said.

Britta beamed. "That's the plan."

"How much do we need to earn from the fundraiser to cover all of these projects?" Chayton asked.

Britta knew the amount, $23,583.07, to the penny. But she was hesitant to voice the total. It sounded outrageous. She swallowed, looking at the expectant faces of the library board; then she smiled. "This year we have a lot more going for us than the community has seen. My goal is to reach $25,000 with all projects combined."

Shennedy clapped her hands, but Kirke's mouth dropped open. Shennedy patted him on the arm. "Don't worry. With Armand coming, it'll blow our celebration through the roof. People are going to be driving in from all over New York to see him."

The board members continued to discuss how they could meet their goals and several of them seemed worried about the amount needed. Ideas were shared about cutting back in order to get the most vital things the library needed. A healthy debate ensued with each person noting how valid all of the items on Britta's list were and the dilemma they faced.

Britta didn't let the scary amount of money derail the meeting. She continued on in the next breath. "In the meantime, if you could take ten posters each and place them around town, I'd appreciate it. These have all the dates and info about our fundraiser, Armand's visit, and the Harvest Hurrah." She passed out a sheaf of glossy posters to each board member.

"Good work, Britta," Chayton said. "I'll post some of these at the high school."

"Thank you for your help. The city of Echo Ridge is depending on us to meet our goals, so no pressure." She smiled. "I'll see you next week."

Chapter Two

Britta waited until the last board member had left before she chanced coming down the stairs—she didn't want to answer one more question about the huge amount they needed to earn for the library. She hefted the remaining posters, probably fifty of them, and mentally strolled through Echo Ridge, thinking of where she might hang them. A tension headache was building behind her eyes, and she didn't think she could handle one more request for the Harvest Hurrah. Britta clutched her posters and stopped just short of tripping over Emma Turner's darling girls. "Hello, Emma."

"Hi," Emma greeted her.

"How are these cute girls today?"

Maryn tilted her head to the side. "We're still cute."

Britta laughed.

"Thank you, Miss Britta," Addison said properly. "I love your hair."

"Well, thank you back, Miss Addison." Britta smiled back at Emma. "You're so lucky to have these girls to brighten your day."

"Yes, I am." Emma put her arms around her girls and led them to the front of the library.

Britta watched them go, a tendril of longing reaching out toward the little family. Dropping the posters in her office, she straightened and walked along the laminate flooring in the children's section toward the drinking fountain, not really noticing her surroundings. The water was cool and the fountain kicked on as she drank, making a low hum that added to the murmur of patrons.

"Good morning, Britta."

She recognized the voice and took one last sip in an attempt to compose herself. Britta raised her head and licked her lips. Milo Geissler stood next to the community bulletin board, clasping a sheaf of papers and business cards. He smiled and the dimple in his left cheek deepened. Britta caught herself staring at the dimple and focused on his eyes, commanding herself not to get lost in the crystal-blue color.

"Milo, how are you today?" Britta stepped away from the water fountain and eyed the bulletin board, where a new page was tacked. "That's a new flyer. I like the colors."

"My sister designed it for me," he replied. "You don't think it's too bright?"

"No, the orange and red catch the eye and remind me of autumn," Britta said. "It's my favorite season." *Why did I just say that?*

Milo took a step forward and handed her a business card, also sporting the new design for "Perfect Pitch Piano Tuning by Milo."

The very first time Britta's mother had traveled from Buffalo, New York, to the tiny town of Echo Ridge, she'd canvassed the town for a suitable German husband. As luck would have it, Mother saw one of Milo's flyers and called him up to tell him all about her beautiful German daughter. Remembering the conversation still brought a flush to her cheeks. Britta ducked her head and pretended to cough.

"I hear you've been busy prepping for the big fundraiser," Milo said. "Everything looks so well organized this year. I think the turnout will be great."

Britta met those sapphire eyes again. He was several inches taller than her five-foot-four- inch frame, but not too tall—maybe close to six feet. His blond hair brushed the top of his collar and edged over his ears. Every time Britta saw him she had the strange desire to tuck his hair behind his ears; the man needed a good haircut. But he was still far too good-looking.

"We have a lot of new events planned. I just hope it will be enough to cover all the costs of updating the library," Britta said.

"You do wonderful things for this library," Milo said. He had the faintest German accent rounding out his words. If Britta hadn't grown up listening to the beautiful language, she probably wouldn't have noticed it. "It reminds me of my grandmother. Oma loved books, and I loved visiting her bookshelves. It always feels nice in here."

"Danke," she answered.

Milo's smile deepened. "Gern geschehen."

It took a moment for Britta to realize that she'd slipped into German to thank him and he had responded. She hadn't done that for years, ever since her early teen years, when she'd stopped speaking German at home. She had explained to her parents that she wanted to work on her English, and since her mother needed practice, they consented. But just then, listening for the accent on the ends of Milo's words and the way he spoke of his Oma, Britta became lost in memories of the Klein home. She could almost feel the bear hugs from her own Oma, and that had her slipping into old ways. "Well, I'd better go."

"Wait, are you busy next Friday night?"

Britta's heart did a little flip. Milo's dimple trembled as if he was biting the inside of his cheek. He'd asked her out once before, right after her mother's meddling, and she'd turned him down flat, embarrassed because of her mom's matchmaking attempt. But today he tempted her with his low voice and kind eyes.

Milo didn't look dangerous, but for Britta, he was the catalyst that stirred up painful memories from her past. "No, I can't. I'll be prepping for Armand to come into town. We have to pick him up from the airport and get him settled."

The dimple disappeared as the edges of Milo's mouth turned down. "Maybe another time?"

Britta glanced at her watch. "Oh dear, I didn't realize it was so late. Have a good day, Milo."

"Tschüss."

Milo's casual German equivalent of goodbye tickled her ears as she turned and scurried to the front of the library. Her mother would throw a fit if she found out how Britta had just treated Milo, but it could never be. All her life, Britta had worked hard to fit in. She grew up in a boisterous German home bursting with tradition, the melodic language and songs, the delicious breads and meats. Britta was proud of her German heritage, until she moved to a new school in the seventh grade. That was a turning point in her life.

Several of her classmates made fun of Britta's German accent. Her English was good, but the remnants of the Slavic language appeared on certain words. At first the teasing was innocent, but then it turned nasty when an eighth-grade boy spread a rumor that she was related to Hitler. At the same time, her history teacher had them complete a project about WWII and the heinous crimes of the Germans.

Britta kept her head down and worked hard all through graduation, spoke little, and tried not to call attention to herself. She did everything she could to erase any touches of her German heritage from her outward life to avoid being hurt and degraded. In public, she kept working with her mother to speak English, her gut twisting with anxiety every time she slipped into her native tongue. Britta wanted to protect her family from the pain she'd suffered. She even dyed her light blond hair a dark brown, something that her father didn't understand or condone.

That was so long ago now—nearly twenty years had passed—but the pain felt raw and angry in her memory. She'd tired of dyeing her hair and let it grow back in blond before she moved to Echo Ridge. She didn't like pretending to be someone she wasn't. The hardest part was that Britta still loved her German heritage. She knew the history of WWII that wasn't taught in the American schools, how her relatives suffered from the evils of a crazed man of power. The devastation left in Europe years after the war changed the German people. Her family survived, coming out of the ashes stronger, but some didn't.

She wouldn't allow herself to be in that position again, where someone cursed her because of her ancestry. Britta sighed. All of the old memories and feelings stirred up emotions that she'd rather not dwell on. She pushed those thoughts out of her mind and concentrated on making the Echo Ridge Library fundraiser a success. Milo was off limits.

Learn more about *The Kiss Thief* and all of the Echo Ridge Anthologies at www.echoridgebooks.com.

About the Author

Rachelle is a mother of five who writes mystery/suspense, nonfiction, and women's fiction. She solves the case of the missing shoe on a daily basis. She enjoys raising chickens and laughing with her husband. She graduated cum laude from Utah State University with a degree in psychology and a minor in music.

Photo by Erin Summerill

Rachelle is the award-winning author of over a dozen books, including *The Soldier's Bride (a Kindle Scout Selection & Whitney Award Finalist), Diamond Rings Are Deadly Things, Veils and Vengeance, Proposals and Poison, Hawaiian Masquerade*, and *Christmas Kisses: An Echo Ridge Anthology*. Her novella, "Silver Cascade Secrets," was included in the Rone Award-winning *Timeless Romance Anthology, Fall Collection.*

Join Rachelle's VIP mailing list to learn more about upcoming books & get your free book at www.rachellechristensen.com

www.ingramcontent.com/pod-product-compliance
Lightning Source LLC
Chambersburg PA
CBHW030552310726
48979CB00011B/2125/J

* 9 7 8 0 9 9 6 8 9 7 6 4 8 *